THE
TAWNY
SASH

THE TAWNY SASH

War Without An Enemy

BOOK TWO

A.J. LYNDON

TRETOWER PUBLISHING

First published in Australia in 2023 by Tretower Publishing

PO Box 6003, Brown Hill, Victoria 3350

A cataloguing–in–publication entry is available from the National Library of Australia: http://catalogue.nla.gov.au

ISBN: 978-0-9876261-2-7

Cover layout and design by adamhaystudio.com
Cover photography by NJ Turton
Typeset by Karl Hunt

CONTENTS

Cast of characters   vii
Prologue   xi

PART 1   RETRIBUTION   1

PART 2   THE TAWNY SASH   141

PART 3   THE FLOODED MARSH   263

PART 4   HOMECOMING   291

Epilogue   336
Historical notes (and Oliver Cromwell)   339

CAST OF CHARACTERS

** = historical figure*

ROYALISTS (CAVALIERS) – LOYAL TO CHARLES I, KING OF ENGLAND AND SCOTLAND

Oxford

Sir Henry Lucie, baronet, Assistant Secretary to King Charles's Council of War
Sir Edward Walker, Secretary to King Charles's Council of War*
Lieutenant Brown, castle prison
Parsons, a guard
Mary, Sir Henry's servant
Sergeant Jones, a spy

At Basing House

Colonel Marmaduke Rawdon, military governor*
Captain Gabriel Vaughan
Captain Robert Amery*
Lieutenant Francis Cuffaud*

Father Allen, Jesuit priest
Lieutenant Colonel Robert Peake*
Lieutenant Colonel Thomas Johnson*
Captain William Payne
Colonel Henry Gage* (head of volunteer relief force from Oxford)
John Paulet, Marquess of Winchester and owner of Basing House*
Lord Edward Paulet (his younger brother)

At The Allt

Sir Thomas Vaughan, baronet (Gabriel's father)
Lady Alice Vaughan (Gabriel's mother)
Bess Vaughan (Gabriel's wife)
Cedwyn, page
Lewis Griffith, steward
Ieuan, man servant and bodyguard to Gabriel
Merfyn, porter
Goodwife Isobel, housekeeper
Gwyneth, Bess's maid
Betsy, Lady Vaughan's maid
Twm, head groom
Dafydd, groom
Elspeth Henderson and her parents (friends of the Vaughan family)
Richard Morrison

Northampton's Regiment of Horse

Captain Will Lucie (Bess's brother)
Lieutenant Hayes

Sir George Vaughan's Regiment of Horse

David Pengelly Sayer (captain lieutenant, commanding Gabriel's own
   troop)
Captain Huw Gwyn
Captain Edward Greenman
Lieutenant Sykes
Lieutenant Hooper
Corporal James Foal
Alexander Foal
Charles, Alexander's friend
Trooper Cary

Wilmot's Brigade

Lord Henry Wilmot*, Lieutenant General of Horse
Aymes Pollard*, Wilmot's second in command
Ralph, Sir Henry's bodyguard.

Boconnoc House

Lady Mohun*

PARLIAMENTARIANS (ROUNDHEADS) –
REBELS AGAINST KING CHARLES I

Colonel Hugh Lucie, Sir Henry's younger brother
Robert Devereux*, 3rd Earl of Essex, Lord General of the Army of
   Parliament

Sir Robert Pye's Regiment of Horse*

Captain Seymour Pyle *
Captain Robin Lawrence
Major Hamilton
Quartermaster William Ardington
Lieutenant John Trenchard *
Cornet Will Kent*
Trooper Moor
Trooper Archer
Trooper Baxter
Trooper White
Hephzibah, camp follower

Skippon's Regiment of Foot

Captain Gale*

At Lanhydrock

Lord John Robartes *
Lady Lucy Robartes *
Robert, Hender, Anne Robartes (their children)*
Nan, servant

*At Chadshunt Hall (home of the Lucie family,
confiscated by Parliament)*

Ben, groom

PROLOGUE

September 1644

His boots were the last to go. Wrapping them in his cloak with hat, gloves and doublet, Gabriel concealed the bundle under a thorn bush. Would he find them again? That depended on staying alive. He must deliver the message.

Mud oozed between his toes and the stench of the marshes, rotting vegetation and sulphur, filled his nostrils. He thrust his way through waist-deep water and tangled reeds while the mire sucked at his legs and the rolling wall of fog receded before him inch by inch.

Lurching, splashing, Gabriel struggled across the flooded marsh. Lapwing wading through the water rose into the air alarmed, with a cry of 'peewit, peewit'. Onwards towards his goal, the farm and beyond it the curtain wall. With heart-stopping suddenness, the ground dropped away. Legs flailing and scabbard banging against his leg, he plunged into deeper water. It was the river. Forced from its course by earthworks it had spilled across the ancient marshland among the reeds and half-submerged bushes. Water filled the hollows of the remaining alder trees, those few not cut down for fuel, gun platforms or the hafts of weapons.

He struck out in what he hoped was a straight line for the invisible bank not far away. This was no great stretch of water like the Severn. In summer it ran clear, and children picked the wild watercress, but not since damming the river had muddied its crystal waters, not since the war began.

His scrabbling feet found a firmer bottom beneath them. There was chalk, gravel, flints to spark the powder in musket or pistol. It was the other side of the river. A sharp stone lanced through the sole of his foot like a knife, the flowing water washing away the blood.

'*His angels will bear you up, lest you strike your foot against a stone.*'

'Michael,' he prayed.

Reaching for another foothold, he stumbled and fell, his mouth filling with noisome, gritty sludge. Now there was only the riverbank to negotiate, a further stretch of marsh, the wall. Would the garrison believe the news he carried, or would they hang him? Step by step, shirt and breeches plastered to his shivering body, Gabriel floundered on.

PART 1

RETRIBUTION

CHAPTER 1

December 1643

'Gone?' Sir Henry Lucie glowered at the man before him. 'Do you mean that Gabriel Vaughan is dead? If so, he has escaped the hangman, but spared us the necessity of a trial.'

The blue-coated army sergeant shuffled his feet. A drop of moisture fell from his bulbous, red-veined nose and he wiped it away with his sleeve, sniffing. 'No, Sir,' he mumbled. 'The officer at the castle prison, Lieutenant Brown, said that Captain Vaughan was released.'

'By whose orders?' The baronet's voice was hushed, but the colour had risen in his cheeks. An explosion was imminent. Sir Henry Lucie was a powerful man in Oxford, King Charles's capital since civil war had broken out with Parliament. By all accounts, he was not one to be crossed. As the sergeant glanced longingly towards the door, a clerk's black-gowned form appeared in the doorway.

'Sir Henry, I have papers for you to sign for His Majesty's Council of War.'

'Later,' Sir Henry snapped. 'I am going to Oxford Castle's prison.' He reached for his cloak. 'You will accompany me, sergeant.' But when he turned around, the officer was gone.

On reaching the foot of the prison's St George's Tower, Sir Henry found Lieutenant Caleb Brown gnawing a chicken leg in his lair, the picture of contentment. At the sight of the haughty gentleman in late middle age, the fur-lined cloak, feathered hat and velvet doublet, the stout lieutenant gaped, revealing blackened teeth in a mouth stuffed with chicken.

'Where is he?' Sir Henry unfastened the clasp of his cloak and shook off the melting snow into the glowing brazier. The coals hissed.

Lieutenant Brown lumbered to his feet, the half-eaten fowl clutched tightly in one fleshy hand while the other rubbed ineffectually at greasy streaks on his dirty coat. 'Who?'

The baronet took two steps toward him and kicked the stool away. 'Who? Who? I have had more wit from a barn owl. Vaughan, you imbecile. Captain Gabriel Vaughan! Your prisoner! On whose orders was he released?'

'I was not here that day, Sir,' Brown answered, his face sullen. 'You should question the guards who let him out.'

'Fetch them. Tell them that I, the Assistant Secretary to His Majesty's Council of War, demand answers. At once.'

Brown was evidently loathe to leave his warm nook but laying down the chicken leg on a wooden platter he ambled away like a bad-tempered bear.

Sir Henry remained in the same posture, legs planted wide and arms folded until Brown returned, accompanied by a lanky guard. The flustered man removed the woollen cap from his bald head, his hand shaking.

'Your name, fellow?'

'Parsons, Yer Honour, Corporal in the garrison, Captain Smith's company.'

Parsons proffered a thick sheet of parchment adorned with a plump, ornate wax seal. 'The release order for Captain Vaughan, signed by Sir 'enry Lucie.'

'What?' Sir Henry snatched the parchment. 'I am Sir Henry Lucie!' he thundered.

'Is that not your seal, Yer Honour?' the guard gulped.

'My seal but not my writing. What did he look like, the man who gave you this?'

'A King's officer,' the hapless guard said, 'Tall as Yer Lordship.'

'Dark hair? Resembled me?' His younger son, Harry Lucie, was the obvious culprit.

Parsons peered at the ceiling as if seeking the answer in its soot-blackened beams. Impatient with the guard, Sir Henry turned to the surly lieutenant, whose face bore an expression of horror. No doubt Harry had bribed Brown with Lucie family wealth to release Vaughan – a felon, and a Catholic traitor. Brown would pay for it.

'No, Sir,' came the belated response from Parsons.

'No, Sir? What?' the baronet growled.

'Tall 'e was, but flaxen 'aired like corn, not dark. Gave 'is name as Lieutenant William Lucie, not 'arry.'

Sir Henry's face blanched. 'Will?'

'Yessir.'

Audit House, Christchurch College, Oxford

It could not be true, Sir Henry fumed. His elder son, his heir, Will Lucie, using the family seal and forging his own father's signature so that the whoremonger who had destroyed the family honour might go free?

Gabriel Vaughan was a captain of cavalry in the royalist army. He had wormed his way into the Lucie household when he and Harry Lucie, fellow prisoners of war, were released by the roundhead rebels holding them at Warwick Castle. He had repaid the family's hospitality by stealing the affections of Bess Lucie, raping and abducting her, forcing her to marry him to cover her shame.

The Lucie family had suffered enough since the civil war began the previous year when King Charles raised the royal standard at Nottingham and declared war on his troublesome Parliament. Harry's capture by the rebels during the battle at Edgehill, his own wife's death while Harry was held prisoner, the parliament sequestering their home, Chadshunt Hall and the family estates for its loyalty to the King.

The Lucies had fled to Oxford, leaving everything behind. Vaughan had taken their honour too. Sir Henry had made a solemn vow that Vaughan would die. Now the man had escaped him and, of all things, through the interference of Sir Henry's son, Will.

Brushing aside beggars, pie sellers and others who dared approach him, Sir Henry stormed through the filthy streets to the Audit House in Christ Church College where King Charles resided and the Council of War sat.

Oxford heaved with soldiers and their families, courtiers, thieves, spies and royalist refugees. King Charles had moved his court and his parliament, those members loyal to him, to Oxford on the outbreak of the civil war. London was controlled by the rebels, who continued to meet in the Palace of Westminster, proclaiming that they were the lawful parliament.

Both sides claimed to want peace, but while the King refused to make any concessions over taxes, religion or his own divine right of kingship, the war flourished.

Every square inch of Oxford and its colleges had been transformed into part of the King's inefficient war machine, with quadrangles and gardens filled with cattle and artillery while scholars had been displaced by officers and ammunition stores. Seamstresses were sewing uniform coats and breeches out of whatever colour cloth was available. Soldiers protected the city gates and earthworks circled the crumbling medieval walls.

Back in his modest office, Sir Henry scrutinised the forged release order by the meagre light filtering through the small window. The signature was a reasonable facsimile of his own. It could, perhaps, have been counterfeited by those who had seen it on official documents. But the Lucie family seal was locked in a chest in his rooms in High Street. None but himself and his sons knew its whereabouts. He might have believed it of Harry, but not of level-headed Will.

Filled with cold fury, he was about to rip the release order apart, but then he stopped. Rolling it into a neat scroll, he locked it away in a writing desk and rang the bell for his clerk.

The man bustled in, clutching his bundle of papers for signature, and bowed. Sir Henry dismissed the papers once more with a wave of his hand. 'Later. I require you to draw up two arrest orders. Firstly, Captain Gabriel Vaughan to be rearrested and court martialled, the charges as before.'

'Under which of the army's Articles of War, Sir, is he to be charged?' the clerk squeaked. 'They mention neither rape nor abduction.'

'God's teeth, man, they are not so precise. The Article which proscribes mistreatment of the inhabitants of the country and commands that men act in a soldierly manner will surely suffice.'

'And the other, Sir?'

There was a long pause. Sir Henry was grappling with fury and the grief which he knew would surely follow his decision.

'The second order, Sir?' The clerk repeated.

'The second is a new order. The charges are theft and forgery. I care not which Article, for the arrest and court martial of Lieutenant William Charles Lucie. Now, get out!'

* * *

Sir Henry stared at the pile of unsigned documents before him. Lying on the top was the arrest warrant for Will, along with the one for Vaughan.

'This ink is too thick. Am I to write with sludge?' He knew he was playing for time. Forgery was a felony under civil law. If Will were caught, a military court martial would almost certainly take an equally harsh view and sentence him to death. For a moment, he hoped that Will would escape. That was mere foolishness, for the honour of the family was at stake.

How Will's eyes had shone when he presented him with his first rapier on his thirteenth birthday. *I will wear it with honour, Father,'* the boy had promised, folding his fingers lovingly around the hilt with its ornate curved guard.

Younger son Harry was often boisterous, and daughter Bess headstrong, but Will never forgot he was the heir to Chadshunt Hall. Now he was lost.

A strong waft of vinegar heralded the return of the clerk and the inkpot. Sir Henry felt the fellow's intrusive eyes upon him. He signed his name with a flourish, the clerk sanded and folded it and Sir Henry pressed his signet ring firmly into the hot sealing wax.

'Take it away,' he ordered, fighting the stinging sensation from unshed tears.

'And the other, Sir?' the clerk prompted.

Sir Henry rubbed his hand across his eyes. Lying before him was the other warrant he had almost forgotten in his anguish. He stabbed at the paper hard, blunting the nib and hurled the quill to the floor. The clerk, accustomed to the Assistant Secretary's moods, proffered another without comment.

With greater restraint, Sir Henry took the pen, dipped it in the ink and signed the paper. He devoutly hoped he was signing Vaughan's death warrant. This time he would not have him await trial at the Oxford Assizes. The delay had been his mistake, giving Vaughan the opportunity to escape.

* * *

'Worse than usual today?'

'Prisoner escaped from the castle. I thought he would have an apoplexy.'

Sir Henry's clerk, thin shoulders hunched, drank deeply from his mug of beer and wiped his mouth. He glanced behind him. The alehouse in Magpie Lane was crowded with soldiers and townsmen intent on their own pursuits. A noisy card game was in progress. One man close by was engrossed in the latest edition of *Mercurius Aulicus*, the royalist newsbook.

'Prisoners escape,' his companion said, leaning forward. 'What sent Master Assistant Secretary into a rage?'

When the clerk finished his tale, the other man chuckled. 'So this Lieutenant William Lucie he wants court-martialled is his own son! I would not be in his shoes for ten sovereigns.'

'If he keeps away from Oxford, him and this escaped prisoner, the warrant will not be executed. The army has to find them first and with a war on . . .' The pair turned their attention to a game of backgammon.

The man reading the newsbook returned it to his pocket and paid his reckoning. It had been worth his while lingering there. Sir Henry Lucie was a man with a grudge. No doubt he would pay well to find the fugitives.

CHAPTER 2

Basing House, Hampshire

January 1644

'So little again in the way of provisions. With everything in the barns, every sack of grain, bacon, cheese, every barrel of ale burned to ashes, we will have much ado to survive until spring, even with no more attacks by roundhead rebels.' Colonel Marmaduke Rawdon, the elderly military governor of Basing House, sat in his quarters in Basing's Old House scanning the inventory a clerk was showing him. The lines on his stern face deepened.

Basing's owner, the Catholic Marquess of Winchester, had made him responsible for the safety of the house. It was no light responsibility. The royalist stronghold had become a refuge for Catholics who had lost their lands during the war. It was the largest private house in England, a crumbling and sprawling complex of buildings, some built in the time of Good Queen Bess, some far older.

Basing House had been under siege from the Parliamentary army of Sir William Waller two months earlier. With the coming of spring, conditions on the roads would improve, and fresh forces might attack Basing.

There was a light knock and the door flew open. On the threshold stood his 26-year-old cavalry captain, Welshman Gabriel Vaughan. As usual he was attired in his long-sleeved leather buff coat, which was the closest that most cavalry got to armour. He wore his thigh-length leather riding boots as if ready to leave on patrol, but his long dark hair, as he doffed his hat, was rumpled and his sword belt was twisted.

Rawdon had the impression that the meticulous officer had thrown on his clothes in a hurry. Gabriel pushed an unruly lock of hair from his brow, revealing piercing green eyes full of joy.

'Well, Captain Vaughan? Is it something urgent?'

'Yes, Sir.'

'Leave these with me,' Rawdon said to the clerk. The man bowed, glancing curiously at the excited captain of Horse.

'Now, Gabriel.'

'Colonel, I am here to ask leave to resign my post so that I may return to my home in Wales. Bess will be safer there.' The melodic Welsh lilt in Gabriel's voice intensified. 'She is with child.'

Rawdon's heart sank. Another blow to the garrison, and its two cavalry troops. 'I am happy for you and your lady. We must hope that your son will be born into a more settled world. I will send an armed escort with you. Will four troopers suffice?'

'Basing cannot spare four men. We lost too many repelling Waller. The roads are quiet in January; and I have my sword and pistols.'

After Gabriel had gone, Rawdon sat staring at the wall. If it had not been for the captain and his young bride, Bess Lucie, Basing House might well have fallen to the enemy. They would be sorely missed.

* * *

Crickhowell, South Wales

'Not far to go now, Bess.' The long journey from Hampshire, over roads treacherous with slush and ice or sticky quagmires, had been blessedly uneventful. They had little with them to steal, nothing but a sumpter horse carrying their modest belongings and fodder for their own horses. Nevertheless, Gabriel was relieved to reach the safety of his own valley where they were beyond the reach of Bess's father Sir Henry for the present.

Bess reined in. Clambering from her mare Faerie's chestnut back, she stumbled towards the muddy bank in the shadow of the Black

Mountains and vomited. Gabriel dismounted to help. Despite wearing the old woollen breeches he favoured for winter travelling, even he was somewhat saddle-sore. He pushed back his fur-lined cloak and extracted a kerchief from the pocket of the breeches. 'I am so sorry, *cariad*.' Gabriel gently dried her face. Bess's skin had turned unnaturally pale, and beads of sweat stood out on her brow.

The wave of morning sickness subsided as quickly as it had risen. 'For what?' she mumbled between folds of linen, breathing in the chill, moisture-laden air. 'When I married you, I expected children to follow.'

'But not so quickly,' Gabriel said. 'Maybe you should have agreed to travel in a horse-drawn litter.'

Bess shuddered, the thought of a jolting litter making her queasy again. 'I am better on horseback.' She was unwilling to confide that the thought of entering into her new life under the Vaughan family's roof with its Welsh-speaking servants and his formidable mother was contributing to her nausea.

It was foolish, she knew, for had she not taken an active part in the defence of the fortress of Basing House, dropping bricks from the towers on the heads of enemy soldiers? Now she was cowed at the sight of the peaceful Breconshire valley.

The wind buffeted their faces as they descended towards Allt yr Esgair, commonly known as The Allt. Peering through stinging drops of sleet, Bess glimpsed the stone ramparts of the fortified manor house. Behind, crouching protectively like a lion over her cubs, was the ancient castle.

Hunched figures were scurrying from the house to the brewhouse, bakehouse and wash house, or across the courtyard towards the two-storey gatehouse. A horse with a blanket covering its back was being led down the lane separating house from stables. The groom turned his face towards them. Moments later a smaller figure hurtled across the lane towards the gatehouse.

Bess squirmed in the saddle. Her bladder felt overfull for the third time in as many hours. She was sick of squatting beside dripping hedgerows and craved rest. Gabriel's eye fell on her. Sensing her renewed discomfort, he urged his horse into a trot with a slight touch of his legs.

'You will soon be resting on a clean bed with plenty of victuals at your elbow.'

Bess forced a smile. She craved rest, but the thought of eating held small appeal. Pregnancy had all but removed her normal hearty appetite and she knew that Gabriel hoped their arrival at what was to become her home would strengthen her. She must begin to put a little flesh onto her flat stomach if she was to bear him a healthy child at harvest time.

CHAPTER 3

The Allt

Lady Alice Vaughan stood in the centre of the tapestry-hung Great
Hall surrounded by a circle of servants. Dignified as ever, her figure
was attired in a rose silk gown with a pale green jacket embroidered
with intricate blackwork. Around her slim waist was tied an apron. She
was directing a string of crisp instructions chiefly at the stout, grey-
haired housekeeper. The latter bobbed her head at the end of every
sentence.

Two more servants were setting the high table with the finest linen,
silver and Venetian glass.

'This cannot be in honour of our arrival,' Gabriel murmured. 'They
have not known of it a quarter of an hour.'

Bess sank into a wobbly curtsey and Gabriel bowed as Lady Alice
swept towards them.

'My dear Bess, welcome. Gabriel, why did you send us no word of
your coming?' She embraced them both. Gabriel kissed her hand and
she reverted to a rapid torrent of Welsh. From the look on her face, Bess
guessed that their arrival was as ill-timed as it was unexpected. Gabriel
had shown momentary surprise but, after a quick glance at Bess, his
expression had changed to one of professional detachment, the mask
he wore when wrestling with complex issues.

'You must be weary and in need of refreshment,' Lady Alice continued. 'Gwyneth will see to your needs, Bess.' She beckoned to a pretty,
red-haired maidservant. Bess followed Gwyneth to Gabriel's chamber,

shivering as a cold blast swept through one of the apertures in the open-sided long gallery. Through the door she could see a fire already crackling in the grate.

When Gabriel arrived some minutes later, Bess was sitting on a stool while Gwyneth combed the dark silky mass of her hair. Gabriel spoke to the maid and she left the room carrying an empty ewer.

Gabriel rubbed his unshaven chin. 'I have asked her to bring warm water and towels. Are you very tired *cariad*? Our friends the Hendersons are arriving in time for dinner. They will make a stay of one or two nights. That is why everything is in a bustle.'

'Do the family have a long way to travel that they are staying some nights?'

'Not so far, eight or nine miles, but it will be a pleasure to spend a day or two in their company. I have seen them only once since Catherine's death.'

Reminded of that unwelcome milestone in Gabriel's past, his first wife Catherine's death, Bess coloured. Seeing her discomfort, Gabriel took both her hands in his. 'I have told my mother of the baby. Would you prefer to rest and have Gwyneth bring you meat and drink?'

'No, I am not an invalid.' They joined the waiting household in the Great Hall. Delicious smells of roasting meat mixed with garlic and nutmeg wafted down the service passage. When the clock struck twelve, uneasy glances passed between her parents-in-law. Bess's belly gurgled audibly.

'You should eat, Bess, as should we all, or the dinner will spoil,' Lady Alice said. There is a dish of mutton and veal with minced capon I hope our guests will enjoy. And the cook has prepared pears from our orchards poached in honey and wine. I found it most wholesome when I was with child.'

'Too little snow has fallen for the roads to become impassable. Perhaps a lame carriage horse has delayed them – I will send one of the men to keep a look out,' said Sir Thomas, flicking a grey-streaked strand of hair over his shoulder. His reassuring words were at variance with the nervous gesture.

The afternoon was well advanced when a servant announced the guests' arrival. '*Diolch i Dduw*,' muttered Sir Thomas thankfully. Seated at the window, Bess laid down her needle and frowned at her imperfect first attempt at embroidering the Vaughan badge on a baby cap.

The Henderson family were full of apologies. Bess found herself at eye level with Master Henderson and his son Robert, while she towered over Mistress Henderson and her pretty, blonde daughter Elspeth. 'Gabe,' cried Elspeth. Bess repressed a twinge of jealousy at the familiarity as Gabriel kissed her hand.

'I am sorry we have put you to so much trouble.' The last member of the party was a man of about thirty, attired in a mud-splattered coat over equally muddy breeches and riding boots. He swept a low bow, removing his beaver hat. 'I had promised my cousin I would arrive last night but was delayed.'

'Our kinsman, Richard Morrison,' Master Henderson interjected. 'You are prepared to receive him?'

'An honour,' Sir Thomas mumbled.

They had a pleasant evening. Bess liked Elspeth immediately. Her seventeen-year-old brother Robert said little, playing with the dogs, toying with some dice and glaring at Bess. He had not spoken to her directly, but the word for heretic appeared to be the same in Welsh as English. Robert disliked her for what she had once been.

Richard Morrison was more entertaining company. He had evidently spent quite some time in France. When Gabriel mentioned the plans he had once had to join a French monastery before the death of his older brother in a riding accident made him his father's heir, Richard Morrison switched effortlessly from English to French.

Bess followed their conversation as best she could, but outside the court French was no longer spoken widely and she was bone-tired. Supper over, she was relieved when Gabriel made his bow and apologised for their withdrawing. Behind her a burst of excited chatter suggested that Lady Alice had announced the happy news.

* * *

Gabriel padded across the darkened bedchamber and there was a glow as he stirred the banked fire into life and used a piece of kindling to light candles.

'Wake up, Bess. We are going to Mass.'

'Where?' It must be no more than a few hours since she had fallen into an exhausted sleep.

'Here.' There was a hint of laughter in his voice.

Puzzled, Bess pulled on slippers and Gabriel laced her stays. She was aware that priests came secretly to The Allt. Often, they were Jesuits from their Welsh headquarters at Cwm. One had called the previous year when Harry and Bess had been staying there. Their early return from a ride had caused consternation that it was the sheriff's men come to arrest the priest.

Gabriel took up the candle stick. Treading carefully in case snow had blown in, they made their way down the open-sided long gallery, the moon shining through the apertures, and across the upper floor of the house into the servants' quarters. In a corner of the house was a storeroom filled with disused furniture. A tall cupboard had been pulled away from the wall. Behind it was the glow of candlelight. On either side of a narrow doorway door, armed with pistols, stood Lewis Griffith the middle-aged steward, and Ieuan, Gabriel's sandy-haired manservant.

Gabriel and Bess squeezed past them into a cramped and window-less space, packed with shadowy, kneeling figures. This was no chapel like that at Basing House, adorned with stained glass and devotional pictures. There was neither statue nor painting, nothing but a small table adorned with a silken cloth embroidered with grape vines and ears of wheat. On the cloth, between four tall candlesticks, stood a small silver crucifix, the precious metal gleaming in the candlelight. Two or three lanterns further illuminated the gloom. Gabriel dipped his fingers in a bowl of water and crossed himself.

No one spoke, yet the air hummed with anticipation. 'Do not kneel on the bare floor,' Gabriel whispered, guiding her towards a stool with a thick cushion beside it. He placed a missal in her hand, knelt beside her and bowed his head. She closed her eyes to pray, but curiosity and excitement intruded. Brought up with the humdrum routine of compulsory weekly Church of England services in the parish church, Bess had thought little about how those who prayed illegally as Catholics might behave.

Father Allen, the Jesuit priest at Basing House who had instructed her in the Catholic faith, had said Mass daily. The safety of that fortress had furnished an unrealistic introduction to the hidden world of the Catholic recusants of England and Wales, of which Bess was now one. She peered behind her at the vigilant shapes of Lewis and Ieuan. Where was the priest?

A floorboard creaked and there was a breath of air as the door opened. With a faint sigh, the congregation rose to its feet and stood motionless, silent, facing the altar. The door closed and Bess heard the grating sound of bolts being slid. Heart beating fast, she craned her neck for an early glimpse of the unknown man. First came Sir Thomas's young page Cedwyn, carrying a bulky bible. Then the flickering flames caught the shimmer of silken vestments.

The priest's face was in shadow. She could see nothing but his hands, long slim hands bearing a chalice and wearing a ring that looked familiar. He passed into the light and to her amazement she saw that the priest was their guest, Richard Morrison.

As he walked the short distance from door to altar, his posture was somehow more erect and his expression more intent than their entertaining companion of the evening. But when he spoke, his voice was the same. 'In nomine Patris et Filii et Spiritús Sancti.'

'Amen,' the congregation chorused. Bess opened the missal self-consciously. By flickering candlelight, she traced the newly learned Latin prayers with a finger. She heard the passionate fervour in Gabriel's voice as he responded, reciting the words from memory. Bess was the only person holding a prayer book. Missals, she supposed, were yet one more forbidden object to obtain by stealth from Catholic France and conceal from the curious.

Gabriel hummed a few notes under his breath and broke into the haunting opening bars of William Byrd's *Kyrie,* the prayer for mercy.

Familiar though she was with her husband's sweet tenor voice, Bess caught her breath. She felt uplifted. Music and candlelight blended, filling her with warmth. Those kneeling around her too, seemed transported somehow. They were, Bess knew, none but Gabriel's parents, the Hendersons, the servants of the house and neighbours, but for an hour they were all part of something separate.

The sonorous beauty of the Latin liturgy and the plaintive Elizabethan music of William Byrd flowed about them. Whether it was the night-time setting and the semi-darkness, or something greater, she was enthralled, wrapped in a cocoon of community, faith and mystery.

When they reached the communion, the priest eased his way between them with the chalice. They knelt before him one at a time. As he prayed aloud that the peace of God would descend upon them, Bess sensed that peace. For a few precious minutes it stilled her fears about war and uncertainty about the future. The prayers drifted to a close. She opened her eyes. There was no one remaining but Gabriel, holding out his hand to help her rise, and Cedwyn snuffing out the candles. She dawdled, unwilling to leave behind the serenity remaining in her soul.

'That was special, I feel different.' It was a struggle to find the right words.

She had said something similar to him on the day when, amidst the dangers of a siege, she had been confirmed as a Catholic at Basing. It was the only way to wed Gabriel; and she had told Father Allen she expected no sudden revelations, merely practical acceptance. And yet, despite her innate cynicism, something had altered. Now it had happened again.

'Why did you not tell me Father Morrison was a priest?' Bess asked as they returned to their chamber hand in hand.

'We try to keep the identity of a visiting priest secret until the last moment. Today he poses as a kinsman of the Hendersons, tomorrow as a friend or a fellow merchant at the house of another family.'

'Is it even so dangerous during the war?'

'If anyone betrays him, he could suffer public execution as a traitor, for his allegiance to Rome. Even during the war.' The remaining traces of warmth, the lingering calm, vanished. She shuddered as if icy water was trickling down her back.

'What would happen to us if a priest was captured here?'

'The Vaughan family would have a penalty to pay.'

'More fines?'

Betrayed by an informer, Gabriel and his father had been arrested and convicted of recusancy, refusing to attend the services of the English Church. The magistrates had levied heavy fines, fines which remained uncollected many months later due to the war.

'No. Harbouring a priest and attending Mass are greater crimes than simple recusancy. It would mean imprisonment. And the thought of that for you, public arrest, the shaming, the dragging through the streets before a jeering, cat-calling mob.' He folded his arms around her, his face taut with the pain of memory. 'I could not bear it.'

CHAPTER 4

'I know you are a man of peace, Sir. Yet do you not remember my advice to you last September?' Gabriel cupped a goblet of mulled wine. 'If the rebels attack us, the old castle is the only defensible part of The Allt. You agreed to make a few repairs.'

The lines on Sir Thomas Vaughan's good-humoured face deepened. He stretched his feet reflectively towards the coal fire in the study. 'We might use the stones from the hill pastures, I suppose. Lewis and I plan to carry out some works when spring comes, employing stones from the ground to build walls. If we enclose parts of the high ground on our hill farms, we could run more sheep. What do you think?'

'Removing the stones should improve the pasture quality besides. Our animals will gain weight with better quality feed; and fetch more at market. But don't change the subject Father. We need stone to hold the castle, or we will have no pastures to enclose.'

'But is it truly necessary?' Sir Thomas spread his hands. 'From what we hear, His Majesty is winning the war.'

'The summer campaign finished well,' Gabriel acknowledged, 'But there is much more to do before the war is won. England and Wales are split down the middle. Wales and the west remain loyal to the King, as does much of the north. But the rebel forces of Parliament have a strong hold on London and the eastern counties of England, much of the midlands too.

'The cities are the worst. Bristol, Manchester, Portsmouth, full of Puritan merchants who hate having the English Church ruled by the King and his bishops almost as much as they hate Catholics. And who have sufficient money to resent the King's taxes and to finance arming apprentices and sending them to war.'

'Raglan Castle is held for the King,' Sir Thomas argued, 'Abergavenny Castle too. They are our closest garrisons, so why should we worry?'

'You must not think yourself safe because there is no hostile garrison on the threshold. Garrisons patrol far and wide. At Basing House, we had plenty of trouble from the Farnham garrison, though Farnham was a full fifteen miles ride. Cavalry move rapidly.'

Sir Thomas met his son's unrelenting eyes in the countenance so like his own and sighed. 'Have it as you wish. May we at least wait for spring? If there is a frost, the mortar will crack.'

'If you will give the word, as soon as a thaw sets in, we may at least begin the work of digging the stones from the earth. This valley has a mild climate. We need not wait for spring.'

'Very well, we will prepare The Allt for war, and Bess will be safe with us.'

'Thankyou.' Gabriel finished his cooling wine and stood up. 'And now that the Hendersons and Father Morrison have left us, I must pay my respects to Catherine and Michael. It is three days since we arrived here.'

'Gabriel,' his father called to his departing back, 'Don't neglect your own safety when you leave here. You escaped Lucie once. I fear he will not rest until he has you under lock and key again.'

* * *

Pushing open the wooden gate in the low stone wall surrounding the church yard, Gabriel experienced the familiar pangs of sorrow. He paused, his hand on the latch. The sexton was there, hacking at the half-frozen ground as he carved out a fresh grave. Seeing Gabriel he turned his back and continued digging with every appearance of concentration on his task.

'Gabriel!' It was Bess, standing in the road. 'Why are you here? I did not think you would cross the threshold of the parish church with its Protestant services.'

'I might ask you the same question, but come with me and I will show you.' Gabriel trudged past the handful of stone memorials until he reached a spot near the far wall where there was nothing but a grassy sward, dull with the muted greens of midwinter. The rushing sound of the River Usk, swollen with winter rains, came from beyond the moss-covered stones.

'Is this where your wife and son are buried?'

Gabriel nodded. 'I come sometimes to pray. Catherine lies there.' He pointed at a featureless patch of grass. 'Michael is beside her. I laid them no more than a hand's breadth apart. They had no coffins.'

'Because of the pestilence which killed them? The smallpox?'

'Because when digging graves at night, in secret, it is far quicker to make them shallow,' Gabriel replied. There was a tightness in his chest. He had never had to explain this before.

Removing his hat, he knelt on the damp grass and bowed his head remembering. Standing in the darkened churchyard. Lanterns shining on the woollen winding sheets containing the mortal remains of his wife and child. Digging until there were blisters on his palms and his shirt plastered with sweat to his body despite the cool night air.

There had been no priest, no funeral service, no procession. Nothing but three of the men servants shovelling earth beside him and his parents standing as if turned to stone. It had been spring, and the scent of blossom had mingled with the odours of damp earth and herbs, rosemary and lavender sprinkled among the folds of cloth.

Gabriel felt a comforting hand on his arm. There was a rustle as Bess knelt beside him. 'I had forgotten what Father Allen said. That Catholics have neither headstone nor footstone. That it is forbidden to bury Catholics in consecrated ground. And yet you did so.'

'Could I have done otherwise?' Gabriel asked simply.

* * *

For better or worse, visiting the churchyard had brought Catherine and Michael closer to Bess. When they retired to their chamber that night, her eyes fell on the miniature of Gabriel's dead twin brother, another Michael, hanging on the wall.

'What did your son look like?' she enquired tentatively.

Gabriel shot a surprised glance at her. She held his gaze. Little by little the tension left his brow, his jaw, his shoulders, as they unclenched around another precious memory. He turned to his desk and unlocked a drawer. Within was a small roll of paper, neatly tied with a scrap of blue ribbon. Gabriel passed it to her with as much reverence as if it had been the sacrament. With the greatest of care, she plucked the ribbon free and smoothed the paper flat. The sleeping face of Gabriel's son lay before her. The ink had smudged at one corner as if a solitary tear had fallen upon it.

Michael's face had the roundness of babyhood, but the closed eyelids had the same upward slant as his father's. Dark hair covered his head, and across his brow tumbled the beginnings of a lock of hair like Gabriel's.

'He is with God,' she muttered, though the conventional words rang hollow in her ears.

'He is,' Gabriel said with certainty. 'He was baptised and I know that my son is safe. Michael Gabriel Thomas Vaughan. I hoped that as he grew, he would make his own path to Heaven.'

* * *

The Allt lay under a thin covering of snow. Sheltered as the valley was, it rarely saw the wintry weather Bess's old home, Chadshunt Hall in Warwickshire, experienced. The tip of Gwyneth's nose was red as she entered the shadowy chamber in the bright light of the snow-tinged dawn.

Behind the closed bed curtains, Bess wriggled her naked body closer to Gabriel's. The banked fire in the hearth had died down to its sullen overnight glimmer, but Gabriel's body glowed like a furnace. Fire irons clanked as the maidservant stirred the coals into life. Bess smothered a squeak and stuffed a handful of the sheet in her mouth. Gabriel had fastened his lips on a swollen nipple.

Once Gwyneth had left the room, a noisy tussle ensued, leaving bed sheets in a tangle and the heavy, embroidered covers on the floor. Gabriel lay back panting, smacked Bess on the bottom and then rubbed his chin.

'I am selfish, Bess, sinful, using you so when you are with child, but the temptation is too great when you are beside me.' He took her hand and ran his fingers lightly across her palm. 'My mother proposes fitting up the adjoining chamber for you. The chimney smokes less, she says. There is a good bed and if we rehang the tapestry with the scenes from Agincourt, it will keep out the draughts.'

'Do you not want to share a bed with me?'

'Yes of course I do, but I was afraid I would disturb your rest.'

'I would rather spend my nights surrounded by reminders of you while you are away fighting. And our child should enter the world in our bed, where the warmth of our bodies, our love, lingers on.'

Gabriel's passionate response suggested that he had instantly forgotten Bess's need for rest. Nothing more was said of separate rooms.

CHAPTER 5

Oxford

February

Sir Henry was finishing a solitary supper in his hired rooms in the High Street when the maidservant tapped at his door. He pushed aside the dish of congealing mutton chops. His victuals had little attraction for him these days. Revenge was the only thing that would whet his appetite.

'What is it, Mary?'

'A person asking to see you, Sir.'

'What manner of person?'

'Not a gennle'man, Sir, might be a soldier. Said you'd want to see 'im when you 'ear what 'e 'as to say.'

Sir Henry's first instinct was to deny entry to the unknown man. There were many spies in Oxford, striving to make their fortune by bringing intelligence of the enemy. Yet it was rare that they approached him by name; and a man approaching him by night at his private lodgings might have more than commonplace intelligence.

'Very well, I will see him.' As a precaution he tucked a dagger into his belt, concealing it beneath his coat.

The door creaked open; and a man stood upon the threshold in cloak and hat, his face shadowed.

'Well, fellow, why are you so intent on seeing me? And remove your hat in my presence.' Sir Henry scowled at the silhouetted figure.

'I thought you might wish to see a letter from your daughter

Elisabeth to your son Will.' The voice carried a faint upward inflection which told Sir Henry that the stranger, like Vaughan, was Welsh.

'Show me this letter. How did you procure it?'

The man closed the door and leant against it. He made no attempt to uncover his head as a gesture of respect.

'What is your name?'

'I must be known by a name? Then let it be Jones, Sergeant Jones if you will. I am an old soldier, returned to England in these troubled times to be of service. I make it my business to hear of gentlemen such as your honour. As to how I procured the letter, that is my affair.'

Sir Henry was not accustomed to insolence and familiarity from the common sort, but something prevented him hurling the man from his threshold. He gnawed hungrily at his thumb. Beneath the broad brim of the shadowing hat, he detected fleshy lips curving into a smile.

The stranger, apparently tiring of the game, delved suddenly beneath his cloak. Sir Henry fingered the hilt of his dagger, but the man produced nothing more deadly than the letter. He tossed it to Sir Henry, who took it and examined the broken seal. It was a man's head with some sort of neck covering, the Vaughan seal. He had last seen it when Gabriel Vaughan wrote to him seeking a meeting of reconciliation and revealing that he was in Oxford. It had been swiftly followed by Vaughan's arrest.

Eagerly he unfolded the paper. Dated some days previously from Allt yr Esgair in South Wales, it was Bess's hand. He recognised the ornate flourishes she added to the letters j and y. He traced the loop of a j with his finger until he noticed the man smirking.

'My dearest Will,

I write to say that Gabriel and I are arrived safely at The Allt. Gabriel has brought me home for, dear brother, I am with child and he wishes to keep me safe. I am well and his family are all kindness. As you may imagine, the whole household hopes that an heir may be born. I must play my part in this it seems whether I wish it or not.

My husband hopes to re-join Lord Byron's forces in Chester. I would accompany him if I could, for inaction irks me.
Be as cautious in battle as you are in other ways.
Your loving sister
Elisabeth Vaughan.'

The letter was addressed to Lieutenant William Lucie, Earl of Northampton's Horse, Banbury Castle.

'Is that not worth money?'

It was indeed. At a stroke, Sir Henry knew the whereabouts both of his fugitive son and of Vaughan himself. As to Bess, so she was to whelp. The child might be born an orphan, his father already dead, if he had his way.

'Have you seen my – William Lucie?'

'Do you wish me to? Describe him.'

Sir Henry thought for a moment. 'Will you carry a letter for me?'

The man inclined his head. 'If you make it worth my while.' Sir Henry compressed his lips. The fellow made no secret of his greed. He unlocked a drawer and pulled out a heavy purse.

'Return tomorrow for the letter and this will be yours.' The man eyed the purse and nodded, satisfied. Sir Henry reached once more into the drawer and retrieved a velvet-covered box. He handed the miniature portrait inside to the spy, his fingers reluctant to break their contact with it.

'This is William Lucie?'

'It is,' Sir Henry barked, curiously averse to parting with his only likeness of his firstborn. The spy returned the miniature with a mocking bow.

'How will I know that you have delivered my letter?'

'Is it not said that he who pays the piper call the tune? Pay me well and I will do your bidding. I will return before noon.'

Sir Henry returned letter and portrait to the open drawer.

'And yet, you might wish me to keep the letter now you are satisfied it is genuine? It has a curious seal. If I make an impression of it . . .'

'Very well.' Sir Henry returned Bess's letter to Jones. Neither then, nor later, did it occur to him that he was condoning the self-same crime for which he had condemned his son.

* * *

The Allt

'Must you do that?' Bess snapped. Gabriel was praying before a silver crucifix in the hidden room. The portable altar stone had departed with the visiting priest, along with vestments and a small gold chalice. Yet the remaining ritual objects, and praying in what was sometimes a sacred space, brought solace to her husband.

It was a Wednesday, one of his regular fast days. On those days, he ate nothing but bread, spending the hours of dinner and supper in private prayer. Bess found his twice-weekly fasts more of a trial than he did. The Sacrament of Penance had been unknown to her in her former life as a Protestant. And in recent days she had found herself resenting anything which kept them apart, for Gabriel was awaiting orders to return to the army.

He tucked away the rosary in his breeches pocket and rose to his feet, looking puzzled.

'You know I must fast and pray, Bess. It is my penance for murdering women and children when we took Birmingham last year.'

'So you have said,' Bess niggled.

Gabriel frowned. 'I see you are out of sorts, love. The baby is being troublesome, I think.'

'It is not the baby, but dining with only the company of Lady Alice and the servants.'

'Has my mother offended you?'

'She was the soul of courtesy, as always.'

'Then what is wrong? Rest yourself in our chamber, Bess and your spirits will improve.' He pressed his lips to her hand and strode from the room without a backward glance.

Her eyes fell on the silver crucifix. It was proof that she had upset Gabriel. In his haste to leave, he had forgotten to replace the forbidden object in its hiding place. Sighing, she picked it up, wondering if it was she who should be praying for forgiveness.

Later that afternoon, the arrival of a letter for Gabriel gave Bess the excuse she needed to seek him out at the old castle and make peace.

A thaw had set in. With the aid of a mason from Abergavenny, work had commenced on repairing gaps in the walls. Running towards the castle, Bess passed another wagon full of stones from the hill farms drawn by plodding draft horses. Servants, builders and farm labourers, leather mittens on their hands, waited with handcarts to unload.

Striding around happily in no more than shirt and breeches, Gabriel was supervising a small work party. Bess waved the letter. 'From Lord Byron.'

Gabriel broke the seal. 'At last – a response to my letter informing him that I am no longer with Basing's garrison. He has summoned me to Chester, where he is governor. There have been losses since I was with the regiment last year.' His eyes shone with excitement. 'I believe he will offer me a fresh commission as captain of Horse.'

Bess forced a smile. 'You are longing for action.'

Gabriel looked from Bess's face to the letter and back again. He reached for Bess's hand, but she noticed that his other hand retained its careful grasp on the precious sheet of parchment. 'My own love, does not leaving you with child when I might remain here with you make me an inconsiderate husband?'

'Gabriel, I watch you writing music in the evening. You are restless and drop the pen. Then you walk up and down, up and down. Go with God, and with my blessing.'

Sir Thomas looked resigned when Gabriel expressed his renewed resolve. Lady Alice's feelings were expressed in Welsh. Bess's understanding of the language was scanty, but the first word, 'Pam?' she knew meant 'Why?' So much was her meaning, the rest was commentary.

The remainder of the day passed in a flurry of activity as Gabriel readied himself to leave for Chester, accompanied by Ieuan. The grooms checked every piece of tack for the horses and took them to the farrier for new shoes.

Fearing that her husband might ride away with nothing but soldier's rations of dried meat, biscuit and hard cheese if it were left to him, Bess went to the kitchens. A venison pastie, a jar of honey, a flagon of mead and half a wheel of cheese wrapped in dock leaves were added to his supplies.

Dawn flecked the eastern sky with pink as Gabriel, followed by Ieuan leading a spare horse, trotted up the lane and headed for the road northward toward Chester. Bess watched from an upper window until the hoofbeats had faded into silence.

* * *

Chester Castle

'Enter, Captain Vaughan. Tom, bring meat and drink for the captain.'

John, Lord Byron, Field Marshal General of North Wales resumed his former posture, leaning on the windowsill. The spartan quarters at the top of the gatehouse, known as Agricola's Tower, commanded an excellent view of the ancient castle's outer and inner bailey; and Byron appeared engrossed in watching the comings and goings below him.

When the servant brought the food, Byron gestured to Gabriel that he might be seated to eat. Between bites of cold beef, Gabriel glanced at his former commander, now occupied in kicking a booted foot against the uneven stone flags. After some minutes, Byron cleared his throat.

'Gabriel, you know I have valued your service as one of my captains. And I understand both you and your lady were of use at Basing House during General Waller's failed attempt to capture the place. I wish you had been at Nantwich with us in recent days. With more officers like you we might have prevailed against Fairfax's forces.' His voice tailed off.

Gabriel sensed the conversation was about to take a turn for the worse. Puzzled, he laid down his knife. 'My Lord, if you will forgive me, for what purpose have you summoned me? Is it not to re-join your forces defending Chester and north Wales from the rebels?'

Byron grunted. His eyes swivelled towards Gabriel. They were filled with regret. 'That is not why I sent for you. You understand the necessity of holding together His Majesty's forces. The King cannot afford the seeds of discord to spread among his commanders.' He paused, 'Nor between his advisers and his commanders.'

Gabriel's heart sank. He guessed the direction to which Byron's remarks were tending.

'The Assistant Secretary to the King's Council of War.' Byron cleared his throat noisily.

'My Lord.' Gabriel rose to his feet. 'Has Sir Henry Lucie made some complaint against me?'

Byron scowled. 'I wish it were otherwise; but I cannot be seen to condone certain actions, even those which might be considered a private matter.'

'No, My Lord.' Gabriel was angry with himself that he had seen only what he wanted to see in the summons to Chester.

Byron rang a bell. A pimply ensign entered the room, twitching at the red officer's sash he wore across his shoulder.

'Wait there.' Byron turned back to Gabriel and addressed him in the hardened tones of the battlefield. 'Captain Gabriel Vaughan, I am placing you under arrest. You are charged with raping and abducting Elisabeth Lucie, daughter of Sir Henry Lucie. I must ask you to surrender your sword.'

Gabriel's face blanched. He slid his blade from the scabbard, handing it to Byron with a low bow. The commander accepted it, biting his lip, and placed it on a table. 'You will face a court martial as soon as one may be arranged. A day or two, no more unless the enemy attack in force.'

'I welcome the chance to defend myself.' Gabriel picked up his gloves and wiped his sweating palms. Byron would see through his words as mere bravado. They both knew that swift or not, there was likely to be only one outcome of the court martial. Gabriel's mouth was dry. Too late now to drink the goblet of wine he had barely touched.

'Might I write to my wife? She is with child. My servant is waiting below with the horses and could carry a letter to her.'

'God damn it, man,' Byron exploded, the battle scar standing out lividly on his cheek as his colour rose. 'Of all men, why did you have to pick Sir Henry Lucie as your mortal enemy?

'Ensign!'

'My Lord?'

'Captain Vaughan is to be confined within Agricola's Tower. Fetch two guards from the guard room in the Flag Tower. Make haste as I, myself have urgent business elsewhere.'

The ensign bowed and rummaged in the leather purse at his belt.

'I said urgent business, Ensign, yet here you stand.'

'My Lord, I was looking for a piece of cord, to bind the prisoner,' he apologised, dropping two coins and a comb in his haste.

'That will not be necessary. I expect that Captain Vaughan, as an officer and a gentleman, will remain here until you return for him.'

The ensign looked uncertain, but an icy glance from Byron sent him scurrying down the spiral stairs in the direction of the Inner Bailey and the distant Flag Tower.

Gabriel remained silent. There was no point in saying more. Byron himself, despite his words, appeared in no hurry to leave. When the ensign's footsteps on the stairs could no longer be heard, Byron moved towards the window overlooking the Inner Bailey and stood staring out. A minute or so later he nodded, snatched up his cloak and made for the door. After glancing up and down the empty stairs, he clicked his tongue impatiently at Gabriel before stalking through the open doorway. The message was unmistakeable.

* * *

Fleeing south, away from Chester, Ieuan at his side, Gabriel at first thought only of retaining that precarious freedom Byron had granted him. But as mile after mile of cold and snowy roads lay behind them, pursuit became ever less likely. The hard-pressed King, short of both men and money, could not hunt every renegade soldier on the run. They turned westwards into Wales and Gabriel slackened the pace. Climbing into the hills, the ways were narrower, less traversed and more likely to be blocked by snowdrifts. In the valleys it was slush and mud. Sleet was falling, stinging their cheeks and making the horses shake their heads when they came upon an inn as night fell.

Despite his weariness, Gabriel was wakeful as he lay in the low-roofed attic above the taproom. His sword and dagger were beside him, but it was questions rather than danger which drove sleep away.

Why had Byron summoned him only to encourage him to escape, Gabriel wondered. Had he planned it, or had it been Gabriel's disclosure about Bess that had prompted his commander to open the jaws of the trap he had sprung?

Byron was no fool, and the young ensign could bear witness to Gabriel's arrest. His escape would appear momentary carelessness on Byron's part, further dishonour on Gabriel's. Noone would suspect Byron, upright and honourable to a fault, of aiding a prisoner's flight.

Ieuan yawned as Gabriel turned over yet again on the narrow straw mattress they were sharing. 'Shall I light a candle, Master?'

'No, I did not mean to wake you. I have brought you on this journey, but where it will end, I do not know.'

'Back home?'

'No. Somehow, Sir Henry discovered my plans to join My Lord Byron. Once he hears that his device has failed, he may expect I will take refuge at my home. And if I do so, it might endanger The Allt.'

He fell silent, picturing a party arriving from the royalist garrison at Abergavenny Castle to take him, his father closing the gates, the servants arming themselves against the King's soldiers.

'What of returning to Basing House?'

'I would be welcome as a Catholic officer; and it would place me beyond Sir Henry's reach. But it would be taking refuge of another kind.' Gabriel rolled onto his back and put his hands behind his head. 'When I joined the army I did so hoping to die in battle. My wife and son were dead, and I no longer wished to live.

'But in doing so, I made a vow to fight for the King, our Protestant sovereign. He does not protect the liberties of Catholics, but while he loves his Catholic Queen, our faith is able to survive for those who cling to it. If he loses this struggle, the rebel Parliament, the Puritans within it, will suppress the Catholic faith in England, Wales and Scotland for all time. Our children will be forced to obey the rules of the Church of England, and our grandchildren will forget the faith of their ancestors. For me there is no choice.' That recognition calmed him. Finally, Gabriel slept.

Ieuan woke him with bread, ale and a bowl of water. 'No hot water, Master but the towel is clean.'

'*Diolch*,' Gabriel thanked him. 'The horses?'

'Saddled. Where are we riding to?'

'I will ride on to Pembrey west of Swansea in search of my kinsman, Sir George Vaughan. He may have need of an officer for his regiment. If not, I will offer my services as a volunteer, for I must honour my vow. But you may return to The Allt if you wish. You have not taken any vow.'

'Then I will do so now.' To Gabriel's astonishment, Ieuan dropped to one knee and said, 'I swear to be faithful to you, Gabriel Vaughan, to fight beside you and to follow you as long as you need me.' He pulled a crucifix from beneath his shirt and kissed it. 'Now may we leave? It is past dawn.' Grinning, Ieuan rose to his feet.

CHAPTER 6

March

It was a wet and windy day, and the house stifled her. Bess was splashing towards the gardens where the yellow daffodils were in bloom when the sound of a cantering horse broke the silence of the moisture-laden air. The rider's woollen cloak was dark with rain and mud. A gust of wind blew it open. The man wore a nondescript grey jacket and brown breeches, but a leather satchel hung from one shoulder, a sword belt from the other. An army messenger, travelling incognito for fear of enemy patrols seizing his messages.

Impatient for news, Bess hurried back towards the house. She tore off her shoes, pattens still attached and ran in search of Sir Thomas. He handed her a letter. Sealed with the emblem of the Vaughans of Allt Yr Esgair, a man's head encircled by a serpent, it must be from Gabriel. He had written from Salisbury, not Chester, and it was dated no more than a few days earlier.

'My dearest wife,

I fear this will be but a short letter for I am much pressed with business. I wish I could have enclosed a song for you as I have done in the past. When I imagine you singing one of my scribbled melodies, it brings you closer to me.

You will wonder at this not coming from Chester but your father's arm had reached there before me, and so, like a wise general, I retreated into Wales, to my kinsman Sir George Vaughan. He has offered me a commission as lieutenant colonel in his Regiment of Horse. He was wounded last year at Lansdown Fight and is happy to share the burden of command with a younger man.

The regiment is summoned to Winchester. I wish I could send for you, my love but we are going on campaign, and it would be dangerous for a woman who carries a child. Be not alarmed that I am likely to fall foul of your father. He spends his days at Oxford, and I am many miles from that city.

I remain your loving husband'

He had signed it as usual not with his name but with a drawing of a linnet. Seeing the pen strokes of the miniature bird, its expression faintly humorous, Bess was torn between the desire to laugh and cry.

* * *

Winchester

The curfew bell was tolling from St Peter's church, and the city's west gate was about to close, when a blast from a trumpet signalled the approach of yet more royalist cavalry.

'Sir George Vaughan's Regiment of Horse,' was the shouted response to the challenge from the gate. The men in charge of lowering the portcullis raised it again to allow the regiment entry into Winchester, a city loyal to the King.

Followed by a handful of carts and wagons, three troops clattered through the gate, each following a blue and white silk colour fixed to a pointed stave like a lance. Bedraggled crimson sashes worn by the officers and some of the men were the only indication that the regiment's allegiance was to the King. Their hats, blue cloaks and leather buff coats were dark with rain, as were the crossed leather belts each man wore across his chest, from which hung a sword on one hip and a carbine on the other.

Breathing a sigh of relief, Gabriel gave the order to dismount. He winced as he put his right foot to the ground and his weak ankle, broken at the battle of Edgehill, shook. Handing Blackbird to Ieuan he went to report their arrival, leaving behind the bustle of steaming, mud-splattered horses and tired riders. The final day's march had been a long one, but he had pushed on, not wanting to spend another night seeking billets, demanding scarce provisions for his men and their horses, from the overtaxed countryside of northeast Hampshire.

He was directed, not to the many-towered castle looming above, but to a half-timbered house hard by the Buttercross in the King's Road. A boy carrying a lantern led the way towards the pale stone cross with its delicate sculptures of the Virgin Mary and the saints, ghostly in the gloom. Rotten fruit, eggshells, cabbage leaves and onion skins were scattered across the steps of its plinth, evidence that they had been used that day for trade. The continuing war had not stopped country people braving the roads and Parliament patrols to bring a smoked ham or a cheese or two to sell.

Inside the house, standing by the fireplace while he pored over a sheet of paper, was an officer, hat pushed to the back of his head. Behind a desk groaning under the weight of muster rolls and inventories, a clerk scratched frantically with a quill.

'Oh, leave it, girl. If you cannot mend the fire, get out,' the officer barked at a serving girl struggling with a smoking chimney. He glared at the newcomer. 'And you are, Sir?'

'Lieutenant Colonel Gabriel Vaughan, officer commanding Colonel George Vaughan's Horse.'

The other officer sighed. 'You are welcome, Colonel Vaughan. My Lord Forth will be glad to have another regiment join him. Your strength?'

The clerk hastily reached for a fresh sheet of paper.

'Three troops, Sir. 207 men. My quartermaster and clerk will provide you with names and other necessary information. As to our needs,'

'My clerk here will make what arrangements are possible, Colonel.' The officer tugged at his moustache. 'We may find your officers lodging within the town, but your men will have to quarter wherever we can find shelter for them and their horses. The numbers of Horse and Foot have doubled these last few days. There will be disorder if the armies do not march soon to fight the rebels.'

Gabriel dropped his hat on the bare floorboards, set down his candlestick and collapsed across the truckle bed fully clothed. The small, chilly chamber at the top of a house next to the church of St Lawrence, had evidently been used as a storeroom. Ieuan glared at the stool and pile of empty sacks which were its only other contents.

'Now let me pull off your boots and take your cloak and coat, Master. Then I can find you a bite to eat.' Gabriel reluctantly sat up while Ieuan removed his riding boots, unfastened the clasp on the thick blue woollen cloak, splattered with mud from the roads, and unhooked Gabriel's buff coat.

Gabriel yawned. 'I only need rest and some ale. My throat is dry as dust.'

The sandy-haired manservant shook his head. 'Now you know you wouldn't let the men go to sleep hungry, nor the horses. No more should you.'

Gabriel snorted. Ieuan took this for consent and scurried down the narrow stairs to find the kitchen. But when he returned with a tray bearing a generous slice of rabbit pie, a loaf of coarse cheat bread, cheese and a pot of beer, he found his master asleep, his long hair spread in disarray on the rough pillow. His doublet and breeches were neatly folded over the stool. A faint gleam caught Ieuan's eye. Moving the candlestick closer, he saw Gabriel's rosary lying on the floor.

Ieuan replaced the amber and silver beads with the small crucifix out of sight in the pocket of his breeches, then dragged a blanket over Gabriel's sleeping form. He tiptoed from the room carrying boots, cloak, doublet and breeches. The silk covering of one of the buttons on Gabriel's doublet had frayed, exposing the wood beneath, and a hook intended to fasten the doublet to the breeches was bent out of shape. While his master slept, Ieuan would repair their garments as best he could. His own rest could wait.

* * *

Gabriel was squeezing through the early morning crowds of soldiers and civilians on his way to meet the captains of his three troops, when a hand snatched at his sleeve.

'Gabriel! Did you think to skewer me? Does every stranger now meet with this courtesy?' It was Bess's brother Will Lucie. Gabriel removed his hand from the hilt of his sword.

'Move on, can't yer,' a fat merchant complained at the obstruction caused by the conversation.

'This way,' Gabriel edged between a man pushing a laden hand cart and two blue-coated soldiers into an adjourning alley. Only God knew when he might find himself with his brother-in-law Will again.

'Gabriel, we must talk,' Will said.

'Not here.' The alley was already occupied by a soldier and a whore.

'Fivepence each for you 'andsome gennelmen,' she called, winking at Gabriel.

'The tavern,' Gabriel said, pointing ahead at a tall modern building, adjoining the King's Road. Finding the parlour filled with officers, Gabriel led the way down the stairs into a cellar. Half a dozen soldiers were engaged in a noisy game of shove groat around a smooth slate board. The two officers found stools in a corner of the low-roofed room. Harried servants squeezed past with jugs of ale and platters of bread, cheese and cold bacon.

'I did not know Northampton's Horse was here in Winchester,' Gabriel said as soon as he could make himself heard over the cheering of winning shots and the groans at unsuccessful ones. 'Is Harry here?'

'Only my troop. The rest have remained at Banbury Castle,' Will said. 'Harry has gone to Ireland with the new lifeguard for the Marquis of Ormond. But why are you here? I understood Byron's regiment to be in the north. Is Bess here too?'

Gabriel stopped with a hunk of hard cheese halfway to his mouth. 'I am no longer with Byron's. But Bess told you this in her letter. Did you not receive it? She wrote to you at Banbury Castle. She is with child and under my parents' protection.'

Will embraced him. 'Excellent news. I wish there was time to talk of it, but I must acquaint you with Father's latest move.'

'I already know. My Lord Byron placed me under arrest, on your father's instructions that I was to be court martialled.'

Will turned pale. 'Then how are you here?'

'It is a long story.' Gabriel got to his feet. 'But Sir George Vaughan offered me a commission as lieutenant colonel in his regiment. God be with you, Will.'

'Wait,' Will said. 'I received a letter from a friend in Oxford, warning me. Father has charged me with theft of the Lucie seal and forging his name on the order releasing you from Oxford Castle.'

'He did what?' Hearing the sharp cry, the soldiers paused in their game. Gabriel dropped back onto the stool and the soldiers, losing interest, resumed play.

'It cannot be true. Forgery is a felony. Your father seeking your death? This is my doing. Your goodness to me has brought you to this.'

'It is not your doing, Gabriel,' Will argued. 'It was I who revealed to Father how things stood between you and Bess when I found you together that night. If I had not done so you would not have been arrested by him. Stealing the family seal and forging his name was the only way to make amends for what I had done to you.'

Numb with shock though Gabriel was, he noticed the resignation in Will's voice. He could not begin to comprehend how Will must have felt when he received the news. Now he had the calm resignation Gabriel had sometimes seen in condemned men facing the gallows.

'Things are not so bad yet,' Gabriel said. 'The King remains at Oxford and so, too, your father. If we die in the coming days, it will be at the hands of our declared enemies, the rebel armies.'

It was cold comfort, he knew, but there was nothing to be done, no way out of the predicament, at least not today. The rebel army was on the march.

CHAPTER 7

Cheriton, Hampshire

28-29 March

Huddled in his fur-lined cloak against the sharp wind, Will clapped his gloved hands together. His bay gelding, a blanket thrown across the saddle, was being walked up and down by a horse boy. The royalist armies' forced march from Winchester to Cheriton had succeeded in heading off General Waller's rebel forces. But now there was nothing to do but keep troops in order and excited horses quiet while waiting for the enemy to stand and fight.

Will filled the vacuum with brooding on his father. He had faced death in battles and skirmishes a dozen times or more. Why this creeping dread of his father's vengeance? 'Have a care,' he snapped at two straying Foot soldiers barging their way between the lines of cavalry horses.

'Miller, Williams! Stand straight in your files.' An exasperated corporal shepherded the two men back towards the infantry lines.

'Baaaa,' mocked one of Will's men. The corporals of the Foot were hard pressed, keeping their hungry, half-frozen men from wandering off to forage for food or find shelter from the cold. It would be dark in an hour or so and the chill was increasing.

There was a rumble of drums from the high command followed by a sequence of trumpet. Will groaned. No battle today. 'Stand down!'

There was no shortage of kindling in Cheriton Wood; and soon cook fires dotted the camp. Lines of dots across the ridge showed where the enemy lay.

'Did you bring me a change of linen, John?' he enquired through bites of cold pie the servant had bought at an Alresford cook shop. It was Will's habit to don a fresh shirt before battle. He feared that if he were wounded by bullet or sword, unclean cloth might be trapped within his body, causing inflammation.

'Aye Sir, your night shirt too.'

'Thank you, but no night shirt tonight. The enemy may disturb our slumbers.'

Lying on the ground wrapped in cloak and blanket, Will slept by his hobbled beast. He dreamed that he was standing in his shirt, his shoulders pressed against a cold stone wall. Facing him was a line of musketeers; and the officer commanding the firing squad was his father. He woke with a cry, opening his eyes on a raw and misty dawn. Nearby men and horses were wraith-like in the growing light. Chilled and stiff, he rose to his feet.

The command to saddle up came as a relief. He inspected the ranks of mounted, armour-clad troopers. 'Why is Foster not wearing his back and breast plates?'

'Lost them, Sir. Dicing in Winchester,' the corporal said.

'Then he must ride without them.' He raised his voice. 'Remember men, the word of the Day, the password is 'God with us', and the colour of the day is white. Forget the password, or lose the field sign in your helmet, and you may be mistaken for the enemy. If a man is not wearing a coloured sash, and most foot soldiers do not, look for the white token in his hat, or the ribbon on his shoulder.'

After addressing his troop, Will loaded his pair of pistols and wound the locks with the spanner. He ran his thumb lovingly over the polished maple, inlaid with the Lucie arms in silver. Then he pushed the white piece of paper into its place behind the visor of the steel helmet hanging from his saddle, the chosen sign that day to other royalists that he was a friend.

* * *

Will strained his eyes, peering between clouds of smoke belching from cannon and musket at the scene below the ridge where the cavalry waited. Tall blocks of pikes wavered like trees in a forest, as if Burnham Wood were come to Dunsinane. The battle had begun. Lone horsemen – messengers and officers, were cantering between companies.

Hours later the ground below was dotted with fallen bodies, blue, grey and red coats. There were blue, grey and red coats on both sides but he knew that most would be royalist corpses, for the great blocks of royalist pike were being pushed back.

'Orders, Sir?' Will's cornet had unfurled the troop standard hours earlier. He lifted it once again from its holster and rammed it down as if by doing so he could conjure up the order to engage.

'Nothing yet and past three o'clock. Ah!' A messenger was cantering towards his troop.

Within minutes blankets had been removed from the horses and girths tightened. The troop funnelled into narrow Bramdean Lane, already churned to mud by hooves. Crouching musketeers lined the high hedges at either side, resting the butts of their heavy muskets on the ground.

'Lieutenant!' Will's second in command, Lieutenant Hayes reined in beside him. 'Form two files, close order. Keep the troop to a good round trot.' Lowering his voice he said, 'This lane is too confined. The enemy will pick us off as we file into the open two by two like the animals into Noah's ark.'

'Should we question the major, Sir?'

'No, Hayes. It is not for us to question our orders.' But Will was filled with foreboding. It was not only the thought of death or capture but the fear of being buried naked in a mass grave, stripped of dignity and every possession until no one knew who he was.

Shuddering, Will gathered up the reins, taking his place at the head of the troop. He must say something to inspire them. It was expected, but it was his first battle as captain. Taking a deep breath he prepared to speak, but a cloud of smoke made him cough. He tried again. A few words would do.

'Northampton's Horse! The time is come to show our mettle. Let us leave our names in the tale of this day or leave our bodies on the ground. And remember your cry is 'God With Us'.'

'Blow the advance,' he ordered the trumpeter as the troop gave a dutiful cheer. Relieved that his voice had remained steady, Will drew his sword. Behind him a bay mare was cantering sideways while her rider, legs clamped to her sides, attempted to restrain her. Ahead were confused sounds of fighting, the clash of sword play, gunfire, screams of man and beast mingling with the urgent throb of drums. The ground shook and clouds of smoke drifted lazily skywards above the treetops. Will's blood pounded in his ears; and sweat dripped down his face. 'Draw swords,' he bellowed, inhaling a lungful of smoke. Coughing, eyes streaming, he rounded a bend in the lane.

There before him lay the battlefield. Red flashes unveiled glimpses of dim, ghostly outlines, men and beasts trapped in a black wall of fog. Square taffeta standards swirled in a myriad of hands, massed blocks of 16-foot sharp tipped ash pikes, pikemen stamping their feet as they thrust at the enemy, musketeers firing by rank and retreating to reload.

Will knew they were there, but his eyes could not disentangle those images any more than his ears could make sense of the banging, blaring, thudding, crashing torrent of sounds. The stink of fear, gun powder, sweating men, horses and wet clay mingled with the familiar, sweet smell of blood. Gagging, he reined in.

Then came the drumming of hooves. Emerging from the murk was an advancing line of Horse, swords and pistols raised. They wore the tawny orange sashes of the rebels. Will screamed the words 'Cornet, to me!' The trumpeter blew the charge.

CHAPTER 8

'Is there nothing we can do, Sir?' Captain Lieutenant David Pengelly Sayer begged Gabriel. 'This is slaughter.'

'Not without orders. We are a small regiment, and we are being held in reserve.' It was afternoon and Gabriel was as desperate as Sayer to act. Below them, the scattered figures running up the slopes of East Down were becoming more numerous by the minute. Now a pursuing troop of roundhead Horse had got in among them, wolves among sheep. Gabriel fidgeted.

'Let me see those straps, Master.' Ieuan dismounted from his sturdy Welsh cob and reached up to check the straps holding Gabriel's back and breast plates in place. 'Now leave them be.' He glared at Gabriel, whose restless hands were in danger of displacing his careful adjustments. 'Your helmet.'

Ieuan took the heavy lobster pot helmet which hung from Gabriel's saddle and handed it to him. The manservant wore a sleeveless buff coat of thick hide and carried both sword and dagger.

'And your own head?'

'I have my cap.' Ieuan tugged the blue woollen cap over his sandy hair. 'Better than wearing a scold's bridle.'

'As always, you refuse to look after yourself,' Gabriel sighed.

He knew that the day was irrevocably lost, but he had no idea why. The King's men were falling back in disorder. For the rest he could see little but clouds of smoke. Firing the fields in front of Hinton Ampner had worsened matters. Cannon fire resumed and was drawing nearer. Could it be that Waller had dragged his guns forward to fire on the fleeing royalist Foot?

Unable to continue the pretence of calm, Gabriel dismounted, stomping back and for, spurs jangling to relieve his feelings.

'Colonel!' The galloping messenger lay flat against his horse's neck. He reined in sharply. 'You are commanded to cover the retreat of the Foot.'

* * *

'To Basing House? But Winchester is closer by far, Sir.' Gabriel objected to the staff officer who was giving him his orders.

'The town is not strong enough to shelter the remnants of our forces,' the officer snapped. 'Our main body of Horse will march to Alresford and then to Basing while you follow with the Foot.'

'What of the wounded?'

But the man had cantered away. How was Gabriel to protect the army's broken remnants with only two hundred men at his disposal?

* * *

Will's eyes were red rimmed with smoke and fatigue. Cold sweat beaded his brow, trickling down his neck. His hands trembled, the hand clenching the reins, the right holding his naked sword ready to react to another attack. It felt as if he had always been like this, as if he would ride the blood-drenched battlefield until the world ended.

Another roundhead closed on him, a blue coat, shouting the new rebel battle cry, 'Jesus with us.' He swiped wildly at the man. The blade sliced into the horse's neck. The panicked beast reared, tossing the screaming rider under its hooves.

'Jesus was not with you,' he thought. He must get his remaining men to safety.

'Fall back,' he bellowed, signalling to the one surviving trumpeter. 'Now.' A blast on the trumpet, plunging horses turning, backing, wild-eyed riders fighting to control them. 'Thank God,' he muttered, seeing Lieutenant Hayes emerge from the melee.

'Hayes,' he shouted, 'We must retreat. Take the men. I will join you. Keep them with the colours.' At least they had not lost their rallying point. The cornet had been killed in the first charge, but one of the corporals had grabbed the green and white fringed silk as it fell from the dying standard bearer's hand. So many of his troop were missing. Will felt compelled to search for any who might be lying wounded.

It was a scene of butchery. Many of the infantry lay face down, shoulders and heads covered with sword cuts from pursuing cavalry. The odour of opened bowels and spilled entrails was powerful enough for Will to detect even in the midst of the all-pervasive clouds of black powder which clung to his face, filled his mouth and clogged his nostrils.

An unseen dip in the ground concealed a musketeer sprawled on his back, a hole in his chest and a bloody rag clenched against it in his stiffening fingers. Beside him crouched a ragged woman and child. Even in the midst of his terror, Will felt a pang of pity.

He reined in, fumbling at the purse on his belt for a coin or two. It would not ease her grief but could at least buy bread. Her child wore nothing but a scrap of what resembled a woman's shift knotted about his thin body. At the sound of hooves, the crouching figures leapt to their feet.

'I will not harm you,' he called, hurling the small coins in their direction. The boy snatched them up and took to his heels, the woman following. In her hand she carried a cloth sack. A small bundle tumbled out as she ran.

'Wait,' he cried, but the woman did not pause. Shortening the reins, Will urged his horse into a trot. He must find his troop. Passing the spot where the woman had been, he glanced downwards. The modest bundle had burst open, spilling its contents, a bloodstained knife, a greasy stub of candle and a small unidentifiable object with a gleam of gold at its centre. Will put spurs to his horse and his tired mount responded gallantly. Moments later, Will's horrified brain interpreted what he had seen, and he vomited the meagre contents of his stomach. It was a gold ring, wedged tight about a severed finger.

* * *

Will called a brief halt so that the men might reload pistols and carbines with the last of their powder and shot. Seventeen-year-old Lieutenant Hayes was pale with shock beneath the streaks of powder and blood stains. Tom Draper, one of Will's troopers, slumped in the saddle, the side of his buff coat dark with blood. He was from Banbury and Will had known him since he was a lad.

He had retreated too late, for he had found no other troops of Horse. If only he could rest for a few minutes, stretching out his limbs on the bruised hillside. He imagined closing his eyes and clasping his hands over his breast. If he could transform himself into a stone effigy, how peaceful that might be, to suffer no more and to inflict no more suffering.

A swarm of running infantry crested the hill. Faces blackened by powder, coats and breeches streaked with blood and filth, they bore little resemblance to the seasoned troops who had started the day. Their muskets and pikes were long gone, an obstacle to swifter flight. Pushing and jostling, the rabble of men were like hares before the hounds, scarcely aware of the battered and bloodstained cavalry troop. The enemy must be close upon them, Will realised.

'Face them, for God's sake, face them.' The hoarse cry came from a terrified pikeman. He fell to his knees, almost under the hooves of Will's horse, clutching at the horse's bridle.

Will cocked a pistol and pointed it at the soldier's head. 'Take your hands off my horse.' Cowed, the pikeman dropped his hand.

'Face them!' It was the same words again, but from another throat. A murmur of assent, then one after another was screaming, 'Face them, face about.' A knot of hopeless, anguished faces. He must remove his mounted men before they shared the fate of the slower foot soldiers.

'Time to march, Lieutenant,' he growled, holstering the pistol.

'Sweet Jesus. For the love of Christ, Sir, don't leave us to them scum.'

Will forced himself to look the pikeman in the face. He had lost his helmet and the bare head was the more vulnerable for the missing earlobe, dripping blood. Did he know he had lost half an ear? Did it matter? He would be dead in minutes.

Will turned back to his waiting troop, some almost catatonic, others in urgent need of the surgeon's care. Beyond them, two miles away, lay the town of Alresford and the prospect of safety. He swore under his breath. Dashing the sweat from his eyes, he pulled savagely on one rein, dragging his horse in so tight a circle that the beast stumbled and nearly fell. He held up his hand and the trumpeter was at his side. Will attempted to speak but no coherent sound emerged.

'Captain?' the trumpeter queried. Heart pounding, Will tried again.

'Blow regroup. Then the charge. We face them.'

CHAPTER 9

'Colonel, there is fighting ahead.'

Gabriel swore. Despite the efforts of his men, they were not yet at Alresford, less than two miles travelled from the battlefield.

'Horse or Foot? How many?'

'Skirmishers, Sir. A few troops of Horse attacking men fleeing on foot.'

'Who are undoubtedly ours. But you said fighting? They are resisting?' Gabriel's first thought was that the fleeing infantry must take their chances. His duty was to escort those who had retained enough sense and discipline to remain with their colours, not to chase down strays.

'A single troop of Horse attempting to hold the enemy off. Our Horse, I think.'

'Colours?'

'A green cornet with white stars, red coats.'

'Tell Captain Gwyn I need his entire troop. At once.' Gabriel raced past plodding lines of dispirited pikemen and musketeers towards the front of the column and the growing din of combat.

Protecting other cavalry from skirmishers was no part of his duty. Yet Gabriel had recognised the green and white colours as those of Northampton's Horse. Will's troop. He could not abandon Bess's brother.

'Load your pistols,' Gabriel ordered. 'The red coats are Northampton's men, the others the enemy.'

The din from the fighting ahead was covering the sounds of their approach, but the attacking roundheads would see them as soon as they emerged from the shelter of the hedge. He hoped that he would be in time to save Will. But first he must find him in the cavalry melee of red, blue and grey coats at the bottom of a hill.

Drawing a pistol, Gabriel transferred it to his left hand and drew his sword. The shrill notes of the charge sounded across the wooded hillside.

The enemy had abandoned their attack on the helpless infantry, now scrambling for the safety of the woods, turning their savage attentions to the outnumbered single cavalry troop who had denied them easier prey. Gabriel urged Blackbird onward with body, legs, voice. Fifty paces. A knot of men menacing the green and white troop cornet.

Was that Will swinging his sword in a wide arc as he fought off the men threatening him and his troop's standard bearer? Twenty paces. Blackbird barged through into the opening next to the cornet and Gabriel reached for the bridle of its desperate defender, ducking beneath the flailing sword.

'Damn all rebels,' the officer snarled and Gabriel realised he was mistaken. It was not Will's voice.

'God with us, God with us,' Gabriel yelled. 'We're Vaughan's Horse. Where is Captain Lucie?'

Staring at the face smeared with blood and blackened with grit, Gabriel recognised Will's young lieutenant, Hayes. Astonishment crossed Hayes' haggard face and a flicker of humanity surfaced beneath the hunted wild beast.

'Vaughan's Horse?'

The arrival of Gabriel's troops had turned the balance. Within a minute or so, the enemy skirmishers were cantering away, while Gabriel ordered a trumpeter to sound recall. 'Captain Lucie?' he repeated to Hayes. The surviving members of Will's troop were regrouping. There was no sign of Will Lucie.

'Wounded? Captured? I saw him fall from his horse but when I went back he was no longer there. Believe me, Sir, I did not abandon him,'

Hayes said. Tears oozed from his eyes, carving clear streaks through the grey ash.

'If Captain Lucie fell, it was your clear duty to take command Lieutenant, not to search for him.' Despite the reassuring words, Gabriel longed to question Hayes further, or to ride back himself and search every inch of the ground before he gave Will up. If Will had disappeared then, wounded or not, he had probably been captured. The victorious rebels would not have left a captain to die on the ground when they could boast of how many officers they had taken.

'Orders Sir?'

Sayer's words reminded Gabriel of his task. He forced Will from his mind. 'We march on.'

The first houses of New Alresford came into view, sheltering below the old church of St John the Baptist, its square Norman tower visible in the twilight. The sound of marching feet and drums sent figures scurrying indoors. A solitary boy pursued a stringy brown and white mottled dog, which was barking at the trotting cavalry. Grabbing the animal by the scruff of the neck, the boy vanished around a corner of the deserted street.

Gabriel glanced at the darkening sky. Once beyond the new town, they must cross the ancient Sewers Bridge over the River Itchen and pass through the old town, before they were within reach of safety. Yet many of the men were kneeling at the shallow, chalky streams flowing beside the road, gulping the fresh water, spitting out the powdery grit clogging their throats. Some had torn off their shoes and stockings and plunged their feet into the icy water. He called a brief halt. It would allow stragglers to rejoin them.

He shook the leather bottle at his saddle. No more than drops remained. Ieuan snatched it away. Gabriel undid the chin strap on his helmet. It was a relief to remove the weight from his sweating head after so many hours and feel the chill evening air blowing through his hair. A breathless man from the troop left in the rear cantered up.

'Sir, a body of the enemy in sight, both Foot and Horse. Less than a mile behind us.'

'In what strength?'

'We counted eighteen or nineteen colours of Foot. A few hundred Horse, I think.'

Gabriel was overcome with hopelessness. If the companies were at full strength, that could be as many as eighteen or nineteen hundred men, without counting the Horse.

His small regiment could do no more than hold the enemy at bay for a few minutes, even if he sacrificed every last man. But perhaps if he acted quickly, and Lieutenant Hayes pulled Will's remaining men together, some of the Foot they were escorting might make their escape. Gabriel beckoned Trooper Foal, a recent recruit who was acting as a messenger.

'Find the lieutenant commanding the troop of Northampton's Horse and tell him to march on with the Foot. Vaughan's must form a shield and hold off the enemy.'

'Should he use drums, Sir?'

'No drums.' Foal cantered away, his face glowing with excitement.

'Drums,' Gabriel muttered. Foal's words had given him the kernel of an idea. With the twilight fading, it might just work. He scanned the crowd of infantry, searching for the one surviving senior officer he had noted among the grizzled sergeants and youthful lieutenants shepherding the defeated soldiers. The man was standing beside his horse while the beast drank from the stream.

'I need your help, Sir. Colonel?'

'Cooke, Sir. Francis Cooke, Lieutenant Colonel.'

Quickly Gabriel explained his sketchy plan. While Cooke mounted his horse and cantered off, Gabriel paced up and down, drinking from the refilled bottle while the plan took shape.

Sergeants and corporals were herding soldiers back into their ragged files, using threats, oaths, kicks. A few paces away, a big, sandy-haired fellow in a torn blue coat shook his head defiantly and continued sitting, bare feet dripping grime, water and trickles of blood from welts and scratches. His corporal spat in disgust and moved on to the next man 'On your feet!'

A trumpet sounded the command to march. The uneven tramp of dragging feet and the clatter of hooves receded towards the Old Town. Gabriel began fumbling with his armour. There was a growl behind him. 'The back and breast plates will impede me,' Gabriel told his glowering servant.

To his left lay the wide square with its market hall, shops and a sprinkling of inns. The broad street sloped downhill towards the bridge and Old Alresford. Straight ahead was a street lined with houses.

Cooke was riding towards him, followed by a purposeful group of a hundred musketeers marching in step. Gabriel counted eighteen drummers with them. Cooke grinned. 'I have them.'

'With so many drummers the plan may work.' Gabriel watched as Cooke returned to the musketeers methodically cleaning the barrels of their matchlocks with scouring sticks, loading them with powder and shot and priming the pans so that they were ready to fire once the lighted match was touched to them.

Gabriel turned his attention to his three captains. 'Gwyn and Greenman, block the road with your troops. All trumpeters to the fore. We must persuade the enemy they face a sizeable force. The more clamour and commotion, the better. Vaughan's must delay the rebels while the Foot march clear.

'Sayer, your own troop will fire the town. The smoke will provide a screen.'

'What about the townspeople?' Sayer asked.

'Their only crime is being in the path of our retreat. I do not want them put to the sword.'

'And if they resist?'

'Then defend yourselves,' Gabriel snapped, 'I will bear the responsibility.' Alresford was nothing but a peaceful market town. After killing civilians at Birmingham he had sworn he would never do so again. And yet his duty to the King meant protecting his soldiers. 'God forgive me,' he muttered.

Captains Gwyn and Greenman's troops positioned their horses across the road. Cooke's musketeers were taking cover behind walls and hedges. Only glowing tips of match betrayed their presence. Gabriel dismounted and pressed his hand against the ground, feeling the vibrations. It had begun. The enemy were coming.

A rumble of many wheels was carts filled with ammunition. Hoof beats and the regular tramp of marching feet grew louder. Cooke barked a command and on either side of the road, the drums started up in unison, beating the steady rhythm of the march. Gabriel's four cavalry trumpeters added the shriller notes of their bugles.

At the top of East Street, Sayer and his troop were drawn up, a menacing mass of shadows, faces illuminated by the flaming torches they held. Gabriel joined them. 'Proceed. Fire the town.'

Another town burning. Terrified women and children, barricading doors with stools and tables against the leather-and-steel-clad men who swooped down on their war horses, flailing hooves trampling underfoot everything in their path.

It was a bitter struggle, hand to hand, fist to fist, body to body. Women struggling to hold their doors shut against the invading troops. They threw pails of water, slops or pig swill, until driven back by searing heat as flames licked at dry thatch and timbers. Cursing men burst through doorways wielding cudgels or pitch forks, jabbing and thrusting at the circling horses.

Diabolical faces loomed, lit up by the flames. Some wore coifs, loosened in the struggle, their mouths gaping holes in blackened faces. They hollered abuse and wielded brooms, or kettles snatched hot, glowing from kitchen hearths. Others wielded swords in one hand and fire in the other – death by the one means or the other to any who would not forsake their homes or threatened defiance to the King's defeated but all-conquering cavaliers. Their snarling faces were blackened by smoke, some streaming blood, cut by knives or scratched by women's nails. Sounds of barking dogs, screaming women and cursing men mingled with the whinnies of horses, fearful of the smoke and flames.

'I will bear the responsibility.' Here and there a body, stretched out on the ground, marked the awful passage of Vaughan's Horse. As if the four horsemen of the apocalypse had multiplied, man and beast spread destruction, pervading the town with choking smoke and burn-ing embers.

There was fresh blood on Gabriel's blade and hairs caught in the bars of the guard. A daring townsman had seized his silk sash, intend-ing to pull the commanding officer from his horse. Ieuan was there in moments, but Gabriel's sword was faster, cleaving air, cloth, flesh. As the man released his grasp on the sash, a flaring brand fell from a roof and the frightened Blackbird reared, trampling the wounded man beneath his hooves.

'To the market square,' Gabriel wheezed, his lungs full of smoke. The troop wheeled and cantered back up the slope towards the cross-roads. Their goal was the timber-framed Market House, standing proud at its centre, an island of darkness amidst the glowing, crackling flames. A crowd of townsfolk chanted defiance beneath its arches. Wisps of chaff from the previous Thursday's market drifted lazily in the smoke while sparks from the torches shot into the air.

There was a bang from above. Peering upwards through blackness and swirling smoke, Gabriel saw the menacing outlines of long barrels on the town hall's balcony.

'Musketeers above us! Back, back, withdraw!' Followed by jeers from the townsfolk and billowing smoke from the dwellings in East Street the cavalry retreated. Then came a rush of feet close at hand, men shouting the password 'Charles, King of England'. It was Cooke and his musketeers.

'We have spent all our powder, but the enemy advance has halted outside the town. I believe the ruse has succeeded.'

'Then we will hope they do not find it out until morning. Mount your men behind mine,' Gabriel said, 'We will ride for Basing House.'

* * *

The array of towers and gatehouses that was Basing House emerged piecemeal from the ever-present mists rising from the Loddon's marshes. Gabriel shivered in the chill of pre-dawn. The crumbling edifice, part fortress, part palace, appeared deserted, an empty shell. His exhausted mind was playing tricks on him.

It had been a hard night march, men dropping beside the path, in the woods and lanes. There was not an inch of space to be had on the carts, crammed with wounded, packed like ballast around the ammunition boxes, barrels of match for their pillows. Now the drums, silent for much of the night, started up again so that the rag, tag and bobtail crowd might march through Basing's Garrison Gate like soldiers.

A group of riders appeared from the House, phantom-like, the damp air muffling hoofbeats and jingling harness. Halting they waited until the standards of the approaching soldiers exchanged shades of slate and stone for the red crosses on white ground of Sir Henry Bard, the blue and gold of Sir Charles Gerrard, the blue and white of Sir George Vaughan's Horse.

Accompanied by a trumpeter, Gabriel rode forward and removed his hat, the better to be recognised. 'Charles, King of England,' he called.

'Gabriel Vaughan, if I am not much mistaken.' The leader of the group swept his own hat from his long fair hair with a flourish, revealing a handsome face, scarred by a sword cut. It was Gabriel's friend and groomsman, Hampshire gentleman, Lieutenant Francis Cuffaud.

CHAPTER 10

Will lay on the ground of an empty storeroom in the manor's undercroft. Blood had soaked through the left sleeve of his coat and Will felt faint. His head and right shoulder throbbed but he could not feel his left arm. The rebels had bound his hands. He squinted into the gloom at the two other captives. One was motionless, dead or unconscious. The other had been brought in struggling and was bound hand and foot.

'Water,' Will moaned.

'Expecting compassion from the rebels?' the other man snorted. 'You know what they have on one of their colours? *Only in Heaven!*'

Pain was muddling Will's thoughts. There was nothing but disconnected pictures and sounds.

'God with us!' Screaming the battle cry. A gust of wind as he emerged from the lane onto open ground. The scent of burning grass, mingled with the bitter, acrid smell of powder. Fighting men dimly seen through smoke-drenched air.

No, the battle had finished. He remembered now, the musketeer with the ear hanging off. 'Face them.' And Will had, with the poor remnants of his troop. Had any of them escaped? He remembered seeing the trumpeter fall from his horse under the hooves of the oncoming rush moments before the enemy officer charged Will.

Searing pain as a blade ripped through the sleeve of Will's buff coat. 'Take him!' A blow on Will's right shoulder from an unseen assailant

"

and the sensation of falling as he was dragged sideways off his horse. Jolting along in an empty ammunition cart, another captive lying across his legs. Closing his eyes in a vain attempt to shut out the pain and nausea. And, finally, being thrust into this room. The smell of shit and fear, the sweet odour of his own blood.

Sweating with pain, Will shivered as the light began to fade. He had dreaded being confined in the dark since he was ten years old.

It was Lady Day, 25 March. Father and the steward had been busy all day with tenant farmers and servants, as written contracts were made for the new year of 1630. While wages were handed out, and each servant received a new suit of livery, Will grew bored. He and Harry, in best doublets and breeches, had stood beside their mother for an hour or more while she greeted the arriving tenants.

Harry had put him up to it, of course, even though Will was the elder by three years. The grooms were indoors, celebrating another year in the service of the Lucie family.

'Shall I fetch the saddle, Will?'

'Too heavy and I need you to hold his head.'

First removing their shoes so they would not make a clatter on the wooden floors, the brothers crept through the door from the west wing into the stables. They were crowded with tenants' horses and wagons.

'Come on, boy. Come on, Thunder.' Will held out an apple. The stallion rolled an eye, his ears flattening against his head. 'Quick, Harry. Untie the halter when I mount him.'

The stall next to Thunder was empty. Pushing aside the swinging bar which separated it from the stallion's stall, Will climbed into the manger to reach the horse's back and then launched himself across the powerful hindquarters. Scrambling forward he wound his small hands in the silken mane.

'Now, Harry!' Standing on tiptoe, his brother released the slip knot on the halter. Sensing freedom, the stallion spun round on his haunches, knocking Harry flat on his back. Will flung himself forward on the horse's neck as Thunder reared and then made a dash through the

coach house into the stable yard. Clinging like a limpet, Will glimpsed his father's astounded face as he bade farewell to one of the tenants. Thunder pulled up short at sight of his master, his hooves skidding on the wet cobbles. Will shot over his shoulder, landing painfully at the feet of his father. From the stables came Harry's distant wails.

'You will go to my study and await me.'

There was a brief stay of execution while Sir Henry ascertained that Harry had suffered no worse than a fright and packed him off to the nursery.

'Valuable stallion . . . such behaviour from the heir to Chadshunt Hall and before the tenants.' Will stood bolt upright, his gaze fixed on the third silver button from the bottom of his father's best doublet. Small posterior stinging after the subsequent beating, Will blinked back the tears. But his father was not yet done with him. He rang the bell.

'Does the old brew house have a key for the door?' he enquired of the manservant.

'Yes, Master, but we have not used it since the new one was built.'

'You will lock Master Will in there until the morrow.'

'No, Father, please,' Will wept. The children believed it haunted and shunned it even on the brightest of summer days.

Timbers groaned and creaked all night, while smells of hops and barley mingled with a mustier odour. Will feared it was rats. He curled himself into a tight ball as if that might protect him from demons and vermin alike. When a servant came to let him out at dawn, he found the young master asleep, his breeches soiled, and the snail tracks of dried tears on his cheeks.

It was years before Will could abide the aroma of hops or barley. His fear of confined spaces had never left him. The sound of footsteps, a key in the lock. Light from the grey afternoon infiltrated the room and Will blinked, relieved that he was not to be left in darkness.

'How many prisoners in here?' Will heard.

'Four officers, Sir, some wounded.' Two soldiers entered, drawn swords in their hands.

'Murderers,' the other prisoner shouted. 'A turd in your teeth!'

Will mumbled a prayer and closed his eyes. He hoped death would be quick.

'Wait outside,' the voice ordered the two soldiers. An officer entered, carrying a lamp in one hand and a sword in the other. He inspected each of the bound and recumbent bodies before leaving the room. Darkness returned as the door shut behind him. Outside, the conversation continued.

'Remove the dead prisoner in the corner. Search him for any papers and have him buried.'

'Aye Sir.'

'Bring the quarrelsome prisoner to me for questioning. The other is bleeding heavily. Dress his wounds. God will decide if he lives or dies but he may not last the night.' The footsteps receded.

'So I'm dying,' Will thought. Slipping into unconsciousness, it no longer seemed to matter.

CHAPTER 11

Basing House

30 March

There was a missing piece in the leaded panes where the engraved glass should have borne the words 'Aymez Loyaute', love loyalty. 'ez Loyaute' was all that remained, and a chill breeze whistled through the gap. Gabriel picked at the glass and another fragment fell to the ground far below where he stood, leaning on a windowsill. Bellows of raucous hilarity, relief at survival, floated up from the Lower Court of the New House. Hopton's army was forming up.

'They saved the baggage train,' he thought. 'But not Will Lucie.' There had been no further news of Will. All he could do was pray for his safety. He set off for the Great Gatehouse where the Marquess of Winchester had a private chapel.

It was quiet in the once-beautiful chapel with its leaking roof, tarnished gold leaf and cracked stained-glass windows, their biblical scenes shining like jewels. The distant clump of tramping feet and shouted orders only deepened the peace in the marbled stillness. It brought a measure of tranquillity, allowing him the luxury of opening the flood gates of his troubled conscience.

Gabriel kindled a wax taper and knelt at a prie-dieu before a statue of the Virgin. He prayed for Will Lucie, for the recovery of the many wounded, for the souls of those who had died in the fighting, for the people of Alresford.

'I guessed that I might find you here, Gabriel.' The Jesuit known by the alias of John Allen was, as ever, unrecognisable as a priest. Attired in a red velvet doublet with yellow silk showing through the slashed sleeves, brown curls hanging to his shoulders, he could have been just another Catholic gentleman who had taken refuge at Basing House as war raged like the plague. 'I appear to have become your confessor.'

'I have none other. Only those at court have the luxury of choosing their confessor.' Bowing his head, Gabriel sank again onto the faded damask cushion. Now he could pray for God's forgiveness.

Father Allen removed the stole from his neck after pronouncing the words of absolution. Gabriel rose from his knees. He had hoped for the easing of a burden, but Alresford was too fresh in his memory. He kissed the priest's hand in farewell.

'Father, we must leave this haven and march on.'

'In God's time. Gabriel, I gave you a heavy penance, twelve years of twice weekly fasts and prayer, for the crimes you committed with Prince Rupert's forces in Birmingham. I might reduce that penalty if you perform some service for the Church.'

'Is this conversation still under the seal of confession?'

'It is not, but it must nevertheless remain between us two.'

'What service?' The hairs prickled on the back of Gabriel's neck.

'This house is a royalist stronghold, a Catholic haven. Yet there are many Protestants here.'

'That is so. They have done good service under Colonel Rawdon.'

The priest pursed his lips and picked up a book from a prie dieu. It was *The Exercise of a Christian Life.* 'There are those here who may not be trusted with such precious objects as this book. Did you ever see the singing knives from Italy?'

'No, Father.'

'The first Marquess bought them. Fine silver knives, the blades engraved with musical parts, with Latin prayers. They are a part of the birth right of the present fifth Marquess. They have disappeared and who would take them but one of the Protestants in the garrison, for their private gain?'

Gabriel was unconvinced and said so.

'Gabriel, this house is England's greatest Catholic stronghold for His Majesty, but the heretics here taint the glory of its present deeds.' Allen's voice became vibrant with passion. 'Imagine if in years to come, men could say that Basing House stood a pillar of the true faith, that it prevailed against the King's enemies through the force of prayer as well as force of arms. That men and women adhered to the faith even while mortars and grenadoes landed around them.

'You might play a further part in Basing's destiny. I have a feeling that Colonel Rawdon would listen to a proposition from you.'

'What proposition?' There was a cold feeling in the pit of Gabriel's stomach. It was thanks to Father Allen that Gabriel and Bess were now man and wife, for they could not marry until Bess became a Catholic. Gabriel was in his debt.

'Persuade him that the need for his Protestant soldiers has passed, that the time has come for Basing House to stand or fall by its own merits, with its own Catholic soldiers. There is, no doubt, important work for his regiment elsewhere.'

Gabriel stared through the window at the growing defensive earthworks beyond the walls. He thought he recognised his friend Captain Robert Amery supervising a group of muddy men with spades. A patch of blue behind them was a pile of discarded coats, the blue coats of Rawdon's Protestant regiment.

'Has Colonel Rawdon given you some reason to mistrust him? Have you spoken to the Marquess of this, Father?'

Father Allen had undeniable courage, the courage to live in a country where his presence was a capital offence. During the attacks on the House of the previous November, he had not taken cover but had been among the men of the garrison, a stole about his neck, hearing confessions and giving absolution to those about to fight and to those who were dying. This was the man to whom Gabriel had unburdened himself of the worst sins of his life but, for the first time, he feared him.

'A singular question. That is between the Marquess and me.' The priest's voice was as calm as it had been passionate moments before. 'What is your answer?'

'May I have time to consider this? Our forces are leaving for Reading today.'

'You may. Send me your answer when you have done so.' His tone was cool.

As he reached the bottom of the spiral stairs in the Great Gatehouse, Gabriel spotted the loose-limbed walk and auburn hair of Robert Amery, muddied from the works. Grateful for the distraction, Gabriel hailed him.

'I should have guessed that the night-time onslaught which woke me was your doing,' Amery grinned.

The two men embraced. 'It was fortunate, Rob, that Basing was within a few hours march, but we will not prolong our stay. The House cannot feed so many.'

'I hope you will prolong it until you have explained what brought our forces here in such bad case. Wild tales are circulating.'

Amery accompanied Gabriel into the Great Hall of the Old House. It was unchanged since Gabriel's last visit. The blue and white tiles on the floor, chipped and discoloured through a century of use, had not been scrubbed for some time, but the tapestry of Queen Elizabeth entering the Great Gatehouse hung in its place on the south wall, the faded colours of blue, green and red telling of Basing's greatest moment.

The lofty painted ceiling with its arched beams, colours dimmed by wood smoke, soared above the men, women and children gathered there. A few of the men wore the red coats of the Marquess of Winchester's Catholic regiment.

Gabriel and Amery seated themselves beside one of the hearths and a servant brought mulled ale. Gabriel gave a brief account of the fight at Cheriton and its aftermath. Amery's attention strayed.

'Is my tale so tedious, Rob?'

The older man grunted, pulling a clay pipe from his pocket. He glanced at the red-coated soldiers lounging around a long table. 'There is bad feeling. Catholics pray in comfort within Basing's walls. They may use the chapel for their devotions.'

'As I have.'

'As you have. Colonel Rawdon has made repeated requests that our men, Rawdon's regiment, should have the Great Hall set aside at certain times for their own prayers, the rites of the English church to which we are all legally bound. His requests are always refused. Some say it is at the insistence of the Jesuits. And so, we Protestants continue praying outside in the bailey, rain or shine.'

'These grievances are not new, Rob.'

Amery shifted again on the stool. 'It is rumoured that the forces who arrived here today will leave behind a chaplain for our use, but it may only inflame matters. Have you heard that Colonel Peake is under orders from the Marquess to strengthen the garrison?'

'That is a sensible move. Our ranks shrink through sickness, battle and desertion. Why are you mentioning this in the same breath as your chaplain?'

'Because it is only Peake who has such orders. And he must only recruit men who are Catholic. There is no attempt made to fill the gaps in our own thinning ranks.'

'No attempt to fill the gaps in Rawdon's regiment?' Gabriel's heart sank.

'No. I do not believe the Marquess fully trusts us.'

Gabriel was silent. Amery was well aware that he was a Catholic officer. 'Time draws on, we are marching to Reading.' He stood up.

The other man shook back his long hair and turned troubled blue eyes to Gabriel. 'Would you speak to Colonel Peake?'

'For what purpose?'

'Ask him to stop worsening the divisions here by his actions. Remind him that we are one garrison and that it was together we fought off Waller's roundhead army last November. He respects you. Without your help, and that of your wife, this house might well have been taken.'

Gabriel smiled, recalling Bess's wild ride to warn of the enemy army, approaching under cover of a heavy fog. Encouraged by the smile, Amery persisted.

'You will speak to him?'

'There is nothing that I would like to see more than this garrison living together in harmony, but if Peake is truly under orders to recruit only Catholics, what then? Do you think my word would sway the Marquess? If I were part of the nobility then perhaps he might. But I am no more than a lieutenant colonel, the son of a baronet. But I will think about the matter, Rob.'

Glum-faced, Amery stared about him, at the Great Hall of the Marquess's massive castle, at the Marquess's liveried servants. 'There may be another way, for the Marquess is presently away in Oxford with the King. He left his younger brother, Lord Edward Paulet, in charge, and his views are more moderate.'

'Then seize the moment. He may be more open to reason than his brother.' Gabriel clasped his hand and took his leave.

On the march towards Reading, he said nothing of what had occurred. He wondered if Father Allen knew of the arrival of the Anglican chaplain. Was it the spur for his approach to Gabriel? There was no one with whom he could discuss the conflicting demands of faith, friendship and loyalty which had been laid upon him in the space of one short morning.

CHAPTER 12

April

'His Majesty wishes to see you, Lucie.' Sir Edward Walker, Sir Henry's superior and Secretary to the King's Council of War, was looking displeased as he entered the audit office. 'As my second in command, and a gentleman who may be called upon to enter His Majesty's presence, you should take greater pains with your appearance.'

Sir Henry fought to master the rage rising within him unbidden, as it so often did these days. 'I am always ready to serve His Majesty.'

'I daresay you are. But look at your attire. Have you no servant or laundress to make you a presentable scarf?' Walker flicked at Sir Henry's crimson sash, then stalked from the room, his own crimson sash falling in shimmering folds from its neat, ornate bow.

Looking down at the crumpled and stained silk, Sir Henry felt the anger draining away, leaving sadness in its place. He remembered the first time he donned his new sash, its crimson colour a visible sign that he was loyal to the King. It was days before the battle of Edgehill, and the very last time that his family were all together in this life.

His man Ralph must give it to one of the maids to repair and launder. He must remember to submit more regularly to the man trimming his beard, combing his hair. But first he must see the King.

Within a short time, Sir Henry was bowing himself out from the royal presence chamber. News of the army's defeat at Cheriton in

"

Hampshire was a grave setback; and the King had determined to take the field in person once more. He wished his 'happy progress' to be set down in a journal. He had charged Walker with accompanying him and Sir Henry with composing a faithful and pleasing account. For the first time in many months, Sir Henry felt there might be some purpose in his life besides revenge.

He must show himself worthy of His Sacred Majesty's trust. And away from Oxford, Sir Henry stood a better chance of gaining tidings of his fugitive older son, and of Vaughan.

* * *

Hinton Ampner, near Cheriton

'Will, Will Lucie.' The voice in his ear was insistent as the buzzing of a horsefly. He wished to be left alone in the fevered pain-racked place he inhabited.

'It is you is it not? Do you not recall me? Francis, brother to Giles Blake, your neighbour in Warwickshire,' the voice breathed. 'I am a Captain with Parliament's army under General Waller.'

'What do you want?' The face floated into Will's field of vision, round and luminous as the moon.

'To help you. If I claim you as a kinsman they may release you into my care.'

Will shut his eyes again. Hands on his arm, competent, unyielding. Odours of vinegar and lavender as the crusted bandage on his arm was torn away. 'He is not strong enough for me to bleed him. I will return tomorrow.'

Another voice. 'Add his name to the list of prisoners of quality taken at Cheriton fight.'

Will drifted again into a feverish sleep.

* * *

'Will, can you hear me?'

Light filtered in, motes of dust dancing in the sun beams, through a barred window. He was no longer in the darkened tomb of the undercroft. 'I hear you.' His voice creaked from lack of use.

'They refuse to free you. You are to be sent to London under guard with other captured Royalist officers. The major has ordered the escort to be ready an hour after dawn. You must leave tonight. Let me think on the means.'

* * *

'Strip him. Leave the dressing on his arm.'

Two sets of hands eased him out of his doublet, the amber silk quite spoiled with blood and vomit, the green ribbons blackened and frayed.

'Cut away his shirt?' a second voice enquired.

'No, spare the knife.'

Will twisted away at the word 'knife'.

'Lie still. We mean no harm.' The hands were unbuttoning his breeches. Despite his fever, Will shivered at the cold air and the hands on his burning flesh. A rough blanket was slid beneath him, wrapping him in a parcel. The scratchy wool was comforting in its warmth.

'Lively now – lift!'

Will cried out and a hand clapped across his mouth.

'Dead men say nothing and neither must you.'

Swaying and jolting, Will's blanket was carried with shuffling steps. Chill night air penetrated the musty woollen folds.

'Brace yourself.' Will felt himself sliding into a knobbly, misshapen heap. An indescribable stench filled his nostrils, the stink of dead and bloated human flesh. He retched again.

'Keep silence for Jesu's sake!' A rag was tied over his mouth. 'There,' a voice panted, 'It is for your own sake.' Will realised it was the voice of Francis Blake.

Rattling and jolting told Will he was on a cart, bumping across cobbles.

'More dead? At this hour?'

'A half dozen cavaliers, Corporal. The Major says to pass them through the gate tonight. Some of them have lain for many hours. The flies . . .'

'Very well,' the corporal interrupted hastily. 'Are you burying them by moonlight?'

'Tomorrow, before we march.'

Imagining the mottled flesh and bloated bellies pillowing his head and the hatching maggots, Will retched again despite the gag.

'What was that?'

'A fox,' said Blake.

'Come to dine on cavaliers,' chuckled the corporal. 'You may have fewer to bury in the morning than are put to bed tonight.'

* * *

The cart trundled through the gate and the bar banged down behind it. A minute or so later there was a thud as the handles hit the ground. 'Make haste,' Blake said. Will was swaying in the blanket again and then he was lowered onto sweet-smelling hay. 'Lie still. I will leave you a bottle of water and my dagger. If all goes well, I shall return in the morning.'

But daylight arrived without bringing Blake. Will lay helpless and naked beneath the blanket. Hours passed before he heard footsteps.

'Captain Lucie?' Will relaxed his tight grip on the dagger's handle. The straw parted, revealing a young manservant in blue and green livery, a worried expression on his face.

'My master, Francis Blake sent me. The major's orders have taken him away. I am to dress you in these garments. As described in this paper of safe conduct, you are James Headley, gentleman volunteer, wounded in Parliament's cause. Help me, Goodwife.'

A woman with arms like tree trunks emerged from the doorway. Together, turning Will this way and that, they dressed him in a plain broadcloth suit of blue with more-or-less clean white ribbons. There was a fur-edged cloak in a darker blue and somehow Blake had reclaimed Will's riding boots and his sword with the Lucie family crest.

'My master said to keep this sword hidden. If questioned, you must say you took it from a prisoner. Goodwife Hannah will care for you at her cottage until you are well. She has been paid for her silence.'

CHAPTER 13

The Allt

Gabriel came riding down the valley, accompanied by Ieuan and two troopers, on a mild, sunny morning. On their arrival at Reading, his regiment had been dispatched to join Worcester's garrison, but he had taken a brief leave of absence. He had barely dismounted from his horse when Bess flew into his arms, heedless of grooms, servants and troopers.

'Have you seen Will?' she asked between kisses.

Gabriel broke away, turning to his manservant. 'Ieuan, find the men a bed. Twm will tend the horses.'

'Officer first,' she thought, scowling. 'His men, his horses, then his wife.' With an effort, Bess replaced the scowl with a smile. She had married a cavalryman and must not mind it.

'I saw Will at Winchester last month.' It was a part truth, but he would not disturb her with fears for Will. He remained missing, but his name was not on any list of fallen officers. Gabriel had written to Northampton's garrison at Banbury Castle and was hoping for news. Once there was certainty, he would tell her.

There was a sharp gust of wind. Gabriel wrapped a fold of his cloak around her shoulders. Nestling her head against him, Bess inhaled his familiar scent, damp wool, leather and horse.

That night, cocooned within the curtains of their bed, Gabriel untied the ribbons on her nightgown. With his fingertips, he traced the line of her body from her swelling breasts to her expanding belly and the fragrant bush of hair at its base. 'Cuckoo's nest,' he murmured, bending to kiss the softness of her inner thigh. Bess shuddered with pleasure.

But lying beside her later, Gabriel turned his face away. Did something trouble him? She reached for his hand. He squeezed hers lightly, then relinquished it.

'I am somewhat weary, my love,' he said, snuffing out the candles.

Gabriel's pensive mood lingered. Sometimes he got up in the night and Bess heard the faint click of rosary beads. Had he taken part in some military action of which he was ashamed but could not speak? She waited for him to confide in her, but he said nothing.

A few days after his arrival, Bess found Gabriel writing a letter in his father's study. He was tugging at the lock falling over his forehead. Seeing her at the door, Gabriel tucked the paper away in the desk and laid down the quill.

'I thought you were spending the morning with my mother in the stillhouse learning some of her remedies.'

'Old Goody Megan has taken ill and so she is gone there with physic. She would not take me because of the baby.'

'Ah.' His eyes strayed to the desk.

'Will you not trust me? I am your wife.' To her vexation, her voice was shaking.

A look of sadness passed over his face. 'There are good reasons why I may not talk of it to you.' Rising, he bowed and left the room. Bess glanced towards the desk in which he had hidden the letter, tempted by the thought that since he would not speak to her, she might take the step of reading it. Her feet had marched her to the other side of the desk before she heard footsteps.

'Ah, Bess. Were you, too, seeking Gabriel?' Sir Thomas smiled at her. 'Shall we wait for him in comfort by the parlour fire? I rarely trouble the servants to light the one here.' When she crept back later, the desk was locked.

* * *

It was Gabriel's third attempt at composing a letter to Colonel Rawdon that Bess had disturbed. He had seen the hurt in her eyes when he refused to say what troubled him. When she was asleep that night, he retrieved the letter he had written in accordance with Father Allen's wishes.

> '*Sir,*
>
> *You know that I hold you in the utmost esteem, as a brave soldier and a worthy man whose loyalty to His Majesty will never be in doubt. I hope that I will lose neither your trust nor respect for what I write.*
>
> *Basing had scarcely half a dozen defenders before your arrival with the regiment you raised. You built a garrison, a fighting force and have preserved the house with the aid of the Marquess's own regiment of Foot.*
>
> *Friends within the garrison have asked me to bring a request to you. It is that, since the King's superior forces are gaining mastery in the struggle for England, the Marquess's own regiment is sufficient for future needs at Basing House. You nurtured it, but the regiment may now stand alone, freeing you and your own men to take the fight to wherever His Majesty decrees.*
>
> *Your most obedient servant*
> *Gabriel Vaughan*'

He would rest for a few minutes while he considered whether he had made the right decision.

Pools of wax filled the drip pans of the guttering candles when Gabriel awoke. His dilemma unresolved, he locked the letter in the desk and returned to bed. Bess was sobbing quietly. 'My love, what ails you?'

'I dreamed of Basing.' She sniffed and sat up, propping herself against the bolster. 'I stood in the New House, in one of the towers, leaning against a casement. The leads were smoking. I lifted the latch, but it stuck fast, and I had to push hard to move it. The oak splintered, for it was charred. The whole side piece tumbled to the ground far below, leaving the bare metal frame.'

'The New House is in disrepair. Many years of neglect, following the ruinous expense of entertaining Queen Elizabeth. No wonder you dreamed of it crumbling.'

'It was more than that,' she whispered. 'The house was a smoking ruin. A fire had been set and nothing remained but an empty shell. Beds and bedding, chests, hangings, chairs, all gone. Silence, except for the sounds of popping glass and crumbling wood. And down below, worse than all that, I saw people, bodies, lying on the ground dead, burnt. Do you think something terrible has happened to the house and our friends in the garrison?'

'It is scarcely a week since I left there. Dreams are foolish things, *cariad*. Lie down and let me warm you.'

The church forbade relying on dreams or omens, but for all that, he was Welsh, his people a nation of dreamers, poets and musicians. It was harder to dismiss than he cared to admit.

* * *

There was a sharp wind and clouds scudded across the sky as Gabriel squelched across the old castle's bailey. Only a pair of mallards riding the tiny waves on the ancient moat watched him climb the steps of the circular tower.

Reaching the deserted solar, he sat down with his bag of writing materials in a stone window embrasure and reread his letter to Colonel Rawdon. He was no monk and had taken no vow of obedience to Father Allen. Weighting down a corner of the paper with the inkpot, Gabriel began writing a different letter.

'It saddens me to hear from others within the garrison that the seeds of discord are flourishing between Catholic and Protestant. It was my honour to serve with you, from the day we fought side by side to repel the enemy from the Grange until the day you drank the health of my wife and I on our wedding day.

You, who delight in your herb garden and your drawings more than in warfare, will surely pay attention to my plea for reconciliation. If it lies within your power, persuade Colonel Peake to turn aside from this dangerous path, courting only Catholic men to join the garrison, while Colonel Rawdon's Protestant regiment dwindles. It may break the House. I will add my voice to yours.

I am reluctant to write words which others may interpret as interference. You, my trusted friend, will surely see nothing but a wish that God preserves a house, its men and women, who are dear to me.

I remain your servant, Gabriel Vaughan. Destroy this letter.'

He addressed it to Lieutenant Colonel Thomas Johnson, Basing House. That left only one more letter to write, to Colonel Peake. He must tread carefully, for it was Peake who was carrying out the Marquess's orders. Gabriel did not have the same close relationship with him that he had with Johnson; and was concerned that his attempts at persuasion might have the opposite effect.

With no clear idea of how far the rift within the garrison extended, it was best that this letter arrived secretly.

'Sir, our paths did not cross during my recent, necessarily brief visit to Basing House. It gave me shelter, as it has done to many in these troubled times, standing strong, a bulwark against its enemies. But I have received disturbing news that there are those who are weakening it by thinning the ranks of its defenders, and that you are foremost among them. In the name of that true religion and the cause we both have sworn to fight for, I implore you to stop. Turn away from the path you have set your foot upon before it is too late.

Now, while the Marquess is away in Oxford, is the fittest time for action. Lord Edward's views are of a different colour; and you would do well to follow his advice.

Your obedient servant.'

He signed it with a drawing of a linnet. Peake would know who had written the letter.

* * *

Worcester, 3 days later

'They do not have the men to patrol every inch of that curtain wall, Sir. By hook or by crook I will find a way in with your letter for Colonel Peake.'

Corporal Foal's leathery face cracked into a smile. A corporal in Gabriel's own troop, the hardened veteran of the European wars had a talent for extricating himself and his men from tight corners.

'They do not. It is a full four miles round. Yet, take care it does not fall into the hands of others.'

The letter for Lieutenant Colonel Johnson had left with a convoy carrying supplies to Oxford, thence to Basing. But Gabriel had decided it was safer to send the letter to the Catholic Lieutenant Colonel Peake by private messenger.

'I am taking a patrol to Grimley collecting levies, but I will be back by dinner,' Foal said. 'I will leave for Basing House before the city gates close tonight, Sir.'

'I will provide you with the letter and means for your journey,' Gabriel said.

* * *

'Corporal Foal?' A clerk walked into the stable yard in Mealcheapen Street where Vaughan's cavalry kept their horses.

'I'm Foal.'

'This is the letter to be taken to Basing House from Colonel Vaughan. You are to wear this coat, and here is a purse for the journey.'

Trooper Alexander Foal turned over the letter. It was sealed with a plain wafer. There was neither name nor address. He opened the heavy purse. A note addressed to his father, Corporal James Foal, lay on top of the silver coins.

'You had best find your father without delay,' his friend and fellow trooper Charles said. Alexander ignored him.

'Wear this coat so that noone will take you for a soldier. There is a hidden pocket in the lining. Use it for the letter. Deliver it to noone but Lieutenant Colonel Peake. You must do so in secret. I leave it to your invention as how to manage it. This map may be some assistance. Note the low points and breaks in the curtain wall.'

There was a rough charcoal map of Basing House on the back. Alexander looked up, his face suffused with glee. 'Why should my father gain all the glory? I have been with the army two or three months and whenever there is danger, Father ensures that I am elsewhere.'

'Your father will have you flogged if you take a dispatch he is meant to carry.'

'He would never do so. Not a flogging. An hour riding the wooden horse, perhaps. It is worth the risk.'

Charles groaned. If his friend was happy to contemplate an hour astride the sharpened apex of the army's punishment device known as the wooden horse, heavy muskets tied to his legs, there was clearly no point in remonstrating further.

'I had best make haste then before my father returns from Grimley.' Alexander stopped only to pick up his uniform coat which was lying on a bench. 'Look after my gear, Charlie. I will be back in a week, unless more adventures beckon.' Donning the plain, dark coat, Alexander tucked the letter into the hidden pocket and bounded into the tack room to collect his saddle.

It was several hours later before Corporal Foal discovered what had happened. 'Have I permission to pursue him, Sir? Alexander is a green lad, sixteen last Candlemas Day, and the only son his mother and I have left to us.'

Gabriel shook his head. 'He is long gone. God willing, he will return safely.'

CHAPTER 14

Bess waved from the gatehouse as the carriage containing Elspeth Henderson, disappeared down the lane. Her stay had provided a welcome distraction from Gabriel's absence and a lack of news from her brothers. Harry had written once since he arrived in Ireland and she had heard nothing from Will since February.

'Did Miss Elspeth tell you of their journey, Mistress?' Gwyneth asked with a grin as she helped Bess undress that night.

'Only that the roads were dirty.'

The maid tied the strings on Bess's night gown and began combing out her hair. 'The coach stuck fast in a muddy rut on the Llangattock road. Twm had it from Miss Elspeth's coachman.'

'How did they free it? Miss Elspeth must have wondered how long she must sit there.' Bess could not resist a giggle.

'Oh, no. She called for the steps to be let down. Then she went to the horses' heads while the coachman joined the groom and manservant with their shoulders to the wheel. Twm said if she had not helped, the horses might have entangled themselves in the traces.'

'And she is only a little thing,' Bess exclaimed indiscreetly. She climbed into the great bed.

Gwyneth moved about the bedchamber, folding discarded garments. 'We always thought, Mistress,' she stopped short.

'Thought what?' Bess yawned. 'Close my bed curtains now if you please.'

'Some of the servants said, that once there had been plans for Master Gabriel and Miss Elspeth to wed.'

'Before he married Mistress Catherine?' Bess's heart gave a lurch.

'I should have held my tongue. It always did run away with me.'

'Too late, I think,' Bess said lightly. 'Proceed.'

'The Mistress will flay me alive if she hears I've said anything. To you, of all people.'

'Lady Alice will hear nothing from my lips,' Bess said to the dark shape faintly illuminated by the candle.

'Well, it was last year, after you travelled here with your brother. Once you had gone away again, the Mistress invited Miss Elspeth and her parents for a visit. Ieuan heard her tell Master Gabriel it was high time he thought of taking another wife; and she mentioned Miss Elspeth. But Master Gabriel left for Oxford not many days later and the next thing was he came riding back and we heard he was marrying you. You won't mention it? I wouldn't make trouble for Ieuan.'

'I have already said so. Goodnight.' Gwyneth went to her trundle bed in the closet, but sleep had fled from Bess. Now she knew for certain that Lady Alice had wished Gabriel to marry another woman.

A worse thought crossed her mind. Gabriel had written a letter of farewell to her in those days before he returned to Oxford.

'I believe it would be best for both of us if we agree to meet no more . . . for part we must. We cannot marry, Bess . . . You are of a different faith, while mine is outlawed.'

Refusing to accept his decision, she had told him she would adopt his faith. Later, she had seduced him; but Will had discovered them together. It was only after that dreadful confrontation that Gabriel had asked his parents' consent. Would he have married Elspeth if Bess had not interfered? She remembered Elspeth's joyous cry of 'Gabe!' on seeing Gabriel again the night the priest came.

Twisting the linen sheet between her fingers, Bess stared into the darkness. Her husband was loving, courteous, but above all he was honourable. Had it been solely to preserve her good name that he had married her?

By the time grey dawn spread clammy fingers across the rush matting and the last glowing pinpricks of light from the fire winked out, Bess had decided that Gabriel regretted marrying her and was writing secretly to Elspeth. For if not, why had he hidden the letter?

* * *

Basing House

Captain William Payne, a recent addition to Basing's garrison, removed his hat and scratched his head. He was in his mid-twenties, but there was already a crease between his eyebrows. It deepened as he listened to the excited soldier standing before him.

'Bring him in. He may be yet another of those conspiring with Lord Edward to betray us.' He reached for a fresh sheet of paper and a sharpened quill. The door opened again and a young man, scarcely more than a boy, was dragged in, his hands bound behind his back. Bright eyes in a flushed, dirty face met Payne's defiantly.

He wore a nondescript brown coat of kersey with cloth buttons, grey breeches and mud-splattered riding boots. Payne noted the boots resembled those worn by the average cavalry trooper.

'You found him climbing in over the wall, you say?' Payne's mouth twisted. These days men were more likely to be found climbing out of the House than in. Desertion was increasing along with the hardships of war and siege.

'Aye, Sir, not far from Garrison Gate. This letter was 'idden in 'is coat lining.'

Payne opened the letter. It bore no name. At the bottom of the paper, by way of a signature, there was a small drawing of a bird. He read the letter through twice. '*Lord Edward's views are of a different colour; and you would do well to follow his advice.*' It was clearly inciting the anonymous recipient to join with the traitor brother.

'To whom did your commanding officer tell you to deliver this letter?' Payne growled.

'I may not say.'

'Oh, but you will say, I think, with sufficient encouragement. You do not deny you are a soldier. Was this for one of those in league with Lord Edward Paulet?'

The boy did not react at the name, but neither did he deny it. Payne nodded at the soldier who had captured the boy. The man struck the boy hard across the face. He raised his hand for a second blow and Payne averted his eyes. In spite of his words, he had little appetite for questioning suspected spies. 'I ask you again, for whom was this letter intended?'

The boy's mouth was bleeding. He spat blood and then repeated, 'I may not say.'

'What is your name, soldier?'

The boy paused. Apparently, he saw no harm in this question.

'Alexander Foal.'

'Well, Alexander Foal, you are brave but foolish to have acted so.

'Lock him in the cellars with the others. If he does not talk further, I will add his name to the list of those of the garrison who will face justice once His Majesty has decided the Lord Edward's fate.'

CHAPTER 15

Worcester

____

April

Gabriel was hot with fury when he joined other officers at dinner. One of his own troopers had raped a fourteen-year-old maidservant in the house where he was billeted. He had visited the Provost Marshal to arrange the trooper's immediate arrest but, for the girl, the damage was done.

His fellow officers were discussing Sir Richard Grenville, a commander of Horse under General Waller who had left the rebels and joined the King at Oxford.

'And here's the best of it,' one man laughed. 'Grenville handed over secret papers. Vaughan, you spent time at Basing House, did you not? There was a plot to betray the House. By now the traitors will have been arrested.'

'Their names, are they known?' Gabriel asked, his thoughts jolted from the maidservant to Grenville's disclosures. 'Who brought this news?' Could it be true that men who had stood side by side with him defending Basing House had turned traitor?

'A company from Oxford collecting supplies. As to the villains' names, would you have had me record them on a roll?' Chortling he beckoned a servant for more wine. Gabriel clapped his hand over the empty goblet.

'Damn it, Vaughan, why glum looks?'

'Their names, any that you heard.' The words were polite but the look in Gabriel's eyes was murderous.

'It is said their leader was Winchester's younger brother, Lord Edward Paulet. As to his fellows, I cannot say.'

Gabriel remembered Lord Edward's charm and easy manner, so different from his overbearing older brother, the Marquess of Winchester. He had liked him. During his recent visit to Basing, he had heard things were different with Lord Edward as temporary keeper of the house. He was, it appeared, prepared to listen to the views of others. Gabriel had hoped that Lord Edward might place Basing House on a fresh footing.

'And so he did,' Gabriel muttered. But instead of making peace between the Catholics and Protestants in the King's garrison, Lord Edward had planned to hand the house over to the enemy, to Parliament. And if Lord Edward was a traitor, then Alexander Foal, bearer of the letter promoting his cause, was in mortal danger.

* * *

Oxford

'Traitor and ingrate,' Winchester spat. He had stood apart throughout the trial, curling his lip at the sight of his defiant younger brother.

'I only wanted to preserve our estates from sequestration or destruction and our family honour from ruin,' Lord Edward countered.

'What would you know of honour? You are no Roman senator defending the republic.' Winchester broke off at the sound of marching feet approaching.

'My Lord Marquess,' an officer was at the door. 'The court has reached its verdict.'

The verdict, death by hanging, came as no surprise to any of those clustered within the Great Hall of Christ Church College. Lord Edward turned a little paler. 'I claim the privilege of the nobility, death by the axe,' he shouted. There was a hum of conversation. The Marquess approached the table where the court sat and whispered urgently in the ear of the Advocate General. After a minute or so, the man nodded. Winchester bowed and swept out.

More than an hour elapsed before he returned. Many of the idlers had gone about their business. Lord Edward, apparently oblivious to the comings and goings, had not moved. He raised his head at being addressed by the Advocate General.

'Your request for an honourable death is denied. Yet His Majesty recognises the great loyalty of others in your family and has spared your life. You are sentenced to imprisonment at His Majesty's pleasure in Oxford Castle. Before you are transported there, you will return to Basing House, where you will execute justice on your fellow conspirators. You will hang every one of them with your own hands.'

* * *

Basing House

A despondent Captain Robert Amery watched the line of barefoot, battered prisoners shuffle between silent ranks of blue-coated soldiers towards the gallows. They were clad only in shirts and breeches. Their coats would be set aside for others, and boots were always in short supply. A drummer preceded them, beating a slow march. Six men were to die, three of them Lord Edward's own servants. There had been no further reprieves, no drawing of straws as sometimes happened, to see who would live and who would die.

Standing on the scaffold was the executioner. Instead of the customary hooded, anonymous figure, it was Lord Edward Paulet, his uncovered face pasty white. Attired in a shabby leather jerkin and kersey breeches in place of his usual silks and satins, his dark hair was partially covered by a Monmouth cap and his feet were bare. Basing's blacksmith, and occasional executioner, stood behind him, ready to provide assistance if called upon.

Amery had returned a day earlier from a week-long visit to Oxford. Captain Payne had the dubious privilege of overseeing the executions, of making sure that none of the shivering, condemned men tried to flee. Of making sure that the escorting musketeers were sparing with the butts of their guns and did not render the prisoners unable to mount the ladder. Amery ran a professional eye over the scaffold with its six dangling nooses. It was not the first time that men had been hanged at Basing, generally for desertion, but this was different.

The drummer neared the scaffold and the first prisoner in the line backed away.

'Where d'yer think yer going?' One of the escort jabbed the condemned man with his musket and he reeled, thrown off balance by the blow and his bound hands.

'Keep them in line,' Amery ordered, glancing apologetically at Captain Payne, a newcomer to the garrison and the business of executions. The sooner the hangings were over, the sooner the dreadful episode could be put behind them. The prisoner was chivvied up the steps to the platform.

'Men of Basing, I beg your forgiveness,' Lord Edward shouted suddenly. Payne nodded at the drummer, and he began a slow roll. Rawdon had been very precise in his instructions. The nobleman gestured with his hands, protesting. Then he knelt before the first of the men he was to hang and bowed his head. The prisoner spat at him.

* * *

'I hope I will never be tasked with such a duty again,' Payne said to Amery as they seated themselves in the Great Hall for dinner. He was green in the face and shouted at the nearest servant to bring him wine.

'Lord Edward had no notion of adjusting the length of the rope,' Amery said, spearing a slice of beef on his knife and munching hungrily.

'Nor the position of the knot.' Payne drained his goblet.

Instead of breaking their necks in the fall, the first two men had slowly strangled to death in front of their weeping families. After that, the blacksmith had stepped forward to help at Amery's silent gesture. There was no need to prolong their torments through the fumbling incompetence of a man whose hands were slippery with sweat.

'I pray that they may be forgiven in the next world,' Payne muttered, picking at the food on his plate, 'For being deceived by Lord Edward's silken tongue.'

'Were all of the men hanged soldiers of the garrison or servants?' Amery mumbled with his mouth full. 'I thought I knew every man's face here, but there was one who I did not recall.'

'All but one, a boy who slipped in carrying a secret letter on the very day intelligence was brought of the plot. He would not say who it was for, but when questioned, he did not deny it was for one of the plotters.'

'Guilty then. Who was the writer of the letter?'

'It had no signature, at least nothing but a drawing of a bird.'

Amery almost choked on a morsel of beef. There was only one person who used that signature. It was Gabriel Vaughan.

CHAPTER 16

Banbury Castle

May

'Eight riding horses, and two wagonloads of ducks and pullets taken from rebel-loving Newport Pagnell.' Will rotated his shoulder and winced. 'I wonder if I shall ever recover full use of this wounded arm.

'Why so grave, John?' he asked the servant.

'Major Compton left orders you were to see him as soon as you returned from the raid. A stranger came here asking for you.'

'Was I followed from Hampshire? It cannot be coincidence. It is scarcely a week since I reached here; and yet I did not think I had aroused the suspicions of other travellers.'

After spending more than a month hidden in the cottage, while Goodwife Hannah treated his wounded arm with her own herbs, and salves from an apothecary in Winchester, Will had recovered sufficiently to leave. Mounted on a stolid broad-backed bay cob that Blake's servant had delivered one night, Will had jogged through the lanes at the unhurried pace of his horse, avoiding Oxford and sleeping at alehouses in small villages where he was less likely to encounter army patrols.

This summons to his commanding officer Major Charles Compton had none of the informality that Will was accustomed to. Brushing ineffectually at the dust from the road coating his boots and breeches, he crossed the drawbridge over the inner moat, climbed the spiral stairs to the major's quarters in the keep and knocked.

'Enter.'

Will bowed and removed his hat. Charles was standing at a narrow window overlooking the inner ward. Beyond the castle the moat flowed into the nearby River Cherwell.

'A Welshman arrived at the gate today. He claimed to be from your sister, Mistress Elisabeth Vaughan, seeking confirmation of your death in battle at Cheriton. He carried a letter with the Vaughan seal. The sergeant on the gate bade the man wait and brought it to me. There was something about the man he said, and when I told him to fetch him, the man had gone. But here is the letter.'

Will frowned as he took the letter, sealed with the Vaughan emblem of the man with a serpent about his neck. He had sent word by the carrier cart to The Allt that he was recovering from a wound but was safe, but perhaps it had not got through. He broke the seal and unfolded the sheet of paper.

'That is not my sister's hand, Major. The seal is genuine, but this letter is a forgery.' He clamped his mouth shut while his mind raced.

'You seem less surprised than I would have expected, Will. I fear you are concealing something.' Compton leant against the wall, his arms folded.

Will stared at a puddle of sunlight on the flag-stoned floor. 'I am a fugitive, Sir, fleeing an arrest warrant issued on the orders of my father.'

'Your father? In God's name, why? And you thought to keep this from me and my brothers, your friends and neighbours in Warwickshire?' Compton coloured in anger.

'May I have leave, Sir to explain?' The light was fading, and a servant had brought candles by the time Will finished his explanation. 'I fear Father has lost his wits. It is the war, my mother's death and losing our estates.' He paused. 'Am I under arrest?'

Compton's face relaxed. 'No. I have strong objections to spies who come here carrying forged documents. I will have the guards on the gate hold the man if he returns. Continue with your duties. You are safe here.'

The major might have been less sanguine if he had seen the letter Jones penned that night to Sir Henry Lucie.

'One who you seek is returned to his regiment at Banbury Castle. Acquaint me of your wishes by the usual means if your very obedient servant may be of use to you again.'

* * *

Worcester

Despite the delay caused by a team of oxen wedging themselves in the central bridge gate, Gabriel whistled as he crossed the narrow bridge over the Severn. It was two days since he had received a letter from Bess saying that Will was safe; and he was in daily expectation of a letter from Harry, in Ireland. A clerk, sorting through the pile of letters and boxes which had arrived on a barge, handed Gabriel a letter. It was from Thomas Johnson, and there were so many agitated crossings through that it was barely legible.

'You do not know what you are meddling in. Your letter addressed to me at Basing House followed me to Oxford where I had returned with the escort for Lord Edward Paulet. Your anonymous letter intended for Colonel Peake arrived at Basing in time to be thought a part of the conspiracy. It came into the hand of a new officer. He arrested the bearer, who refused to speak and was hanged with the plotters. Rob Amery identified you as the writer and showed the letter to Colonel Peake. Your messenger being already dead, Colonel Peake could not question him further. I would not believe you complicit in the plot, yet how else can your meaning be construed? Stay away from Basing House or you will answer for the mischief you have wrought. I remain, Sir, a more loyal friend to the King's cause than you have proved, Thomas Johnson.'

'The bearer refused to speak and was hanged with the plotters.' Why had he thought he might intervene for the better? He had failed in his bid to stop the weakening of the garrison. His interference at Basing House

had done nothing but harm and had cost the life of a blameless young soldier.

* * *

'Alexander was ever a head-strong lad, Sir,' Corporal Foal whispered. The veteran soldier had aged in the weeks since his son disappeared.

'No, he was a brave soldier who kept faith, as he saw it. He went to his death without revealing for whom the letter was intended, or that I was its author. Had he done so, it might have saved him.'

'Do not talk of what might have been.' Foal's voice broke.

'Comfort your wife. I will make enquiry as to his place of burial. Your son deserves to lie near his home.' Gabriel could think of no other way of making amends.

'No, Sir. Let him rest. It will not bring him back; and making a great to-do in the midst of war about one young lad is foolishness, when there are thousands like him who lie in mass graves.'

CHAPTER 17

Worcester

'Why in Heaven's name does the city garrison need a plough for a day?' Perched on a stool in his Friar Street quarters, Gabriel was examining a ledger of expenses. A week had passed since Thomas Johnson's letter arrived. Burying himself in his work, Gabriel was able to forget for a few minutes what had happened to Alexander Foal.

'The men from the plough team, Sir, not the oxen. 'It was their village's turn to labour at the defences.'

A liveried servant appeared in the open doorway. 'The governor requests you attend him at your convenience, your honour.'

Gabriel grabbed his coat from a hook. He buttoned it and retied his sash as he walked. Sir Gilbert Gerard disliked tardiness. On arrival at the governor's house, Gabriel followed an aide. The usual huddle of servants and messengers awaiting orders outside the door of the great parlour was absent. In their place were a guard of two pikemen. Gabriel wondered if Gerard had heard of a threat to his safety.

'You will wait here,' the aide said. 'Sir,' he added. The soldiers uncrossed their pikes and the aide entered. 'Lieutenant Colonel Vaughan, Sir.'

'You have your orders,' Gabriel heard the governor respond. The aide's face was blank as he motioned Gabriel to enter and shut the door behind him. Gabriel heard the clash of pikes and felt a prickle of unease.

The tall, long-jawed governor was pacing up and down the tiled floor. Ignoring Gabriel's bow he seated himself on a high-backed chair at the long maple table. At the far end sat a clerk, a pen and inkpot at his elbow.

'I need every man I have, Vaughan, or by God you would have been marched here under guard. I determined to speak to you before reaching a final decision.' Snatching a letter from his desk, Gerard threw it to Gabriel. 'Stand there and read this. Think carefully what reply you make.' The clerk dipped the quill in the ink and pulled a sheet of paper towards him.

Belatedly, Gabriel understood the significance of the pikemen guarding the door. They were there to intercept him if he bolted.

There was silence in the room but for the crackle of the fire, sending smoke towards the blackened beams. An armed manservant slipped in through a side door, taking his place behind the governor's chair.

'May I read this at the window, Governor?' Gabriel heard himself say. The light beneath the windows was better, but it gave him a reason to step away from the table and turn his back while he read.

The letter was from Basing House, from Lieutenant Colonel Robert Peake.

'. . . Gabriel Vaughan, at one time a captain of cavalry at Basing House and now, I understand, a lieutenant colonel in your garrison . . . has incited treachery, leaving others to take the risks and pay the ultimate price. Lord Edward has been reprieved, the other conspirators hanged, but Vaughan himself has slipped the net . . .'

The words swam before his eyes. Alexander's death could be laid at his door, but he was innocent of the charges Peake made. Yet without proof, the letters written in Gabriel's own hand suggested that he was an instigator of the plot to deliver Basing House to Parliament's rebel forces.

He saw a bleak future – Bess giving birth alone and their son growing up fatherless. Would Sir Thomas be permitted to leave the child his estate when he died, or would it be forfeit as the property of a traitor?

He read on. '*Send him to Oxford for close questioning and for trial. It grieves me to think that one who fought gallantly in months past has acted basely, but so it seems. He must be stopped before he does further injury to the King's cause . . .*'

Once he would have welcomed death. After the loss of Catherine and Michael he had joined the army seeking an honourable end. But now there was Bess, their unborn child; and his love for her, and for life, burned like a flame.

He rolled the letter into a tight scroll, clenching it in his fist.

'Well, Colonel Vaughan? I understood that the guilty had been dealt with and the sorry business at an end. A pity to reopen the wound which has just begun to scab over, but I will not condone treachery. I have sent for a guard of Horse to escort you to Oxford. If you can satisfy me of your innocence before they arrive, they will be stood down and the matter will remain private between the two of us.'

The governor pulled a watch from his pocket, flicked it open and placed it on the table before him.

'I am no traitor, Governor,' Gabriel began, standing before the table.

'So says many a roundhead rebel. You must do better than that.' Gerard's grave expression hardened. '*Take counsel with Lord Edward while his brother is away.*' Do you deny you wrote these words?'

'I regret that I ever wrote them.'

'You should have considered what you did before inciting treachery.'

'It is not treachery that I regret, Sir, for I committed none.'

The governor slammed his fist against the table. 'You stand by your rebellion then? I must relieve you of your command!'

'Indeed, you misunderstand me. I regret the death of one of my men, a young trooper who carried the letter to Basing House and was thought a part of the plot. He was an innocent.'

The governor grunted. 'A lamb to the slaughter embroiled in your stratagems. It is a pity, but wars kill boys as well as men.'

There was a tap at the door and the aide came in. 'The escort awaits, Governor.'

'You may bring them presently.'

Gabriel saw his last chance slipping away. 'I knew nothing of any plot to betray Basing House when I wrote to Colonel Peake.'

'Then why not sign your name to the letter like an honest man? Why send the boy over the wall instead of through the gate with a pass?'

The door opened again, and a servant edged inside. 'The deputation from the city is here, Your Honour.' Gerard consulted the open watch and scowled.

'A moment more, Governor,' Gabriel pleaded. 'Basing House is split between two factions. That is why my messenger was sent in secret.'

'This is scarcely news, Sir,' Gerard snapped. 'The plot has shown it is split between traitors like yourself and those loyal to the King.'

'But it was a different split I knew of Governor. One between men loyal to the King and to the Church of England and those loyal to the King and the Church of Rome.'

'Hm, papists,' Gerard snorted. 'The rebels call it a nest of papists. It does His Majesty's cause no good being associated with such law-breakers. Are you numbered among them? Is that the true religion your letter referred to?'

Gabriel bowed by way of reply.

Gerard sighed. 'I imagine that Colonel Peake is also of your persuasion. It is not that which disturbs him then, but your advice . . .' He reached for the letter and unrolled it once more. '*Now, while the Marquess is away in Oxford, is the fittest time for action. Lord Edward's views are of a different colour; and you would do well to follow his advice.*' Those, Sir, are damning words. Well?'

'My wife and I spent some months there last winter. The men and women of that house showed us great kindness; and we fear for their safety if the Marquess continues on his path.'

'What path?'

Gabriel explained he had been warned of the plans to have only Catholics at Basing. Gerard tugged at his beard and reached for a pipe. He said nothing until he had filled it from a pouch in his desk and lit it at the fire. 'And this is what you meant by turning the House away and saving it?'

'It was.'

Gerard puffed silently for a minute or so while Gabriel wracked his brains for persuasive arguments. At least the governor had not dismissed his explanation out of hand.

'And as to following Lord Edward's advice? How do you explain that?'

This was the nub of the matter, and Gerard would either believe him or not. 'The Marquess holds strong principles, hardened in the fires of war. He does what seems right to him to protect his estates and uphold the cause of His Majesty while practising his Catholic faith. He may believe a rigid stance is the only way to combat the harshness of the times.

'His brother is younger and in a different mould. It seemed that he might be the best hope of restraining Colonel Peake and that by the time the Marquess returned from Oxford, steps might have been taken uniting the two factions.'

Gabriel held his breath while the clerk's pen scratched. From outside the room came a rising hum of conversation from the waiting delegation, the mayor's strident tones prominent.

'Did you have any direct dealings with the traitor? You must have had some grounds for your belief.'

'I met him a few times, Governor, in company, while I was there last year. I formed a favourable impression of his character. I was sorely mistaken.'

'Mistaken!' Gerard exclaimed. 'You could scarcely have been more so.' He turned to the clerk. 'That will do. Leave those here.' He indicated the neatly penned sheets of paper.

When the clerk had left, the governor rose from the table and knocked out his pipe at the fire. He glanced at Gabriel who was standing tensely, hat in hand.

'Very well, Colonel Vaughan. I will make your version of events known to Colonel Peake. We will see if he accepts them before taking matters further. For the present you may continue in your command, but have a care how you act, who you speak to. Now I must receive these merchants who, no doubt, have more complaints to make.'

It was a reprieve, Gabriel thought – for him and, perhaps, for Basing House. He might try once more to turn the tide before the garrison destroyed itself. Only then might he make amends to Peake and Johnson; and forgive himself for sacrificing Alexander Foal.

* * *

The merchants had departed with the usual empty promises from the governor. Gerard retrieved the notes the clerk had made of the examination of Lieutenant Colonel Vaughan. He read through them and compared them with Peake's letter. The young Welshman's explanation had the ring of truth about it. Should he write to Peake as he had said?

After a few minutes' thought he locked letter and notes in his desk. The villages in the local hundreds were sending only a fraction of the levies needed to keep Worcester provisioned and the garrison in arms. And on his ride that morning he had heard Massie, the governor of rebel Gloucester, was issuing pernicious demands to some of the same villages. Gerard had more pressing concerns than making peace between papists.

CHAPTER 18

The Allt

June

Bess threw down the needle and the tiny smock she was embroidering, leaving the silks in a jumble of colours spilling across the cushioned bench. Drawn by the sunny day, the fragrance of cut hay, and cries of men and women working in the fields she threw a wrap over her shoulders and wandered towards them.

During the many wet and windy days, busy with the housekeeper or in the stillhouse with Lady Alice, distilling waters and learning the uses of herbs for summer ailments, Bess suppressed her fears and longings with some success. But alone in the great tester bed at night she felt Gabriel's absence keenly. Running her fingers over her tingling breasts, down her belly and between her thighs, she made believe that it was Gabriel who touched her, conjuring up his voice, his eyes locking onto hers.

And it was at night that her fears about Elspeth recurred, swelling like a plague bubo even while her belly swelled with Gabriel's child. Hoping to resolve her anxiety, Bess had written to him, confronting him about the story. But, before the letter was finished, she lost her courage. Elspeth had not visited The Allt again, but Bess was constantly alert for any mention of her. Sometimes she pretended that she had imagined the conversation with Gwyneth. An hour later she would despise her own weakness.

Haymaking was in progress in the field known as 'deuddeg erw' or '12 acres.' Sitting under a shady tree, she watched rows of sweating men swinging their scythes. Women and children followed, calling to each other as they gathered the cut hay and bound it into sheaves. A rabbit shot out almost under her feet and ran towards the lane. Watched by a swaddled infant, placed by its mother for safety in the shady hedgerow, three bluetits squabbled over the spoils of spilled grass seeds.

'A fine sight, Mistress. Alas, in too many corners of the land, the war has left little to harvest.'

Startled, Bess scrambled to her feet, shading her eyes against the sun as she looked up. The lone horseman had no servant and his mount carried only a single bag tied to the saddle. His face was in shadow, a long nose and fleshy lips all that were visible beneath the wide-brimmed hat pulled low on his brow. He swung his leg over the saddle and dropped easily to the ground, brushing dust from his grey breeches.

'Do I know you, Sir?' Bess enquired coolly, taken aback to be addressed by a stranger, and a man, without her inviting him to do so. He had a Welsh accent.

'I have not passed through this fertile, well-tended valley before.'

Bess sensed his hidden eyes lingering on her swollen belly. Instinctively, she tugged the folds of the rose-coloured silk wrap tighter around her. 'There are many fine rides in these parts. Do you have business with Sir Thomas Vaughan or his steward?'

'Then that fine gentleman's house over there, with the ancient castle beyond it, must be Allt yr Esgair. Do I have the honour of speaking to Mistress Vaughan?' The man responded, without answering her question. Despite his courteous words, he had not removed his hat.

'Yes. But if it was my husband Gabriel you sought, I am afraid you have had a wasted journey. He is away fighting with His Majesty's forces. Sir Thomas is somewhere about the estates. I can send a servant for him.'

'No matter, Mistress Vaughan. I had intended to spend an hour reminiscing about old times with Captain Vaughan. We are former comrades. I have no reason to trouble Sir Thomas.'

'He is Lieutenant Colonel Vaughan now,' she corrected him, relieved that the man had explained his presence. 'He commands Sir George Vaughan's regiment.'

'Then my congratulations to Gabe. Well, I must take my leave.' He gave a slight bow and put his foot in the stirrup.

Thoughts of Elspeth banished for the present, Bess hurried back to the house. The encounter with the unknown Welshman had removed any desire to roam out of doors by herself. He had come and gone without giving either his name or where he came from.

Bess could not fathom the chief reason for her unease. Then it occurred to her that it was unusual for a Welshman in those parts to address a stranger in English. Perhaps he had already known her identity. It was odd that Gabriel had never made mention of this man who seemed to be a close friend. He was known as Gabriel to all but a very few. The man had called him Gabe.

CHAPTER 19

Gabriel was puzzling over an odd letter from Bess. She had scratched several sentences quite through, obliterating every word. The nib had punctured the paper in several places. It spoke of agitation. The letter concluded abruptly with, '*Elspeth has paid me a visit. It was very kind of her. Your mother sends her love, as do I, your wife E.V.*'

Had Elspeth upset Bess? Gabriel tugged at the lock of hair falling across his brow. He would have liked to visit The Allt, but there was not the time. He dashed off a letter to his parents, asking if anything had upset Bess. The letter to his wife took more than one attempt and even then it resulted in nothing but vague and tender reassurance. 'Ieuan,' he shouted.

'Master?' Ieuan stuck his head round the door. He had a cleaning rag in one hand, Gabriel's sword in the other.

'Find a messenger to carry two letters to The Allt without delay.'

'Aye. As we march after dinner, that will give me an hour, maybe two, to find someone.'

'I have not received any marching orders,' Gabriel objected.

'No.'

The sandy head withdrew but was swiftly replaced by one of the junior staff officers. 'Colonel Vaughan, here are your marching orders.' Gabriel chuckled.

The orders began with an instruction to follow the army from Worcester, taking the Oxford Road. Surely, this game of cat and mouse between the King's Oxford Army and those of Generals Waller and Essex could not continue much longer. They had been marching back and forth across the midlands for weeks. At first they were trying to evade Waller and Essex but now the King's army had increased in size and they had started searching for the enemy instead.

The remainder of the orders made him sit up. '*Once the army has passed through Pershore you are to pull down the bridge over the Avon. The engineers being required by the train of artillery, you will carry out your duties with the resources at your disposal.*'

Gabriel cursed. There were never enough engineers available. By the time Ieuan returned with the news the letters were on their way with a party of dragoons heading for Abergavenny Castle, Gabriel was drawing a sketch of the ancient bridge at Pershore.

'Shall I bring the new mare we captured in the skirmish? And there is a wagon outside for you, with an escort of five men – a sergeant and four firelocks.'

'Yes, bring all the horses including the grey. And find Huw Gwyn. He knows Pershore better than I do.'

Jumping to his feet, Gabriel went outside into a downpour. The wagon contained powder to blow up the bridge. Gabriel climbed onto the back of the covered cart and examined the wooden kegs for leaks.

'Sound as a bell, Sir,' the sergeant assured him. 'Manufactured only last month for the Train. No more powder that's been sitting for years, Sir. Not like when the war started.'

'Thank you, Sergeant,' Gabriel interrupted the flow. 'We will hope the rain has not seeped in. Keep everyone but your own musketeers with their firelocks well away. No lighted match or pipes.'

Huw Gwyn had arrived and was making alterations to the sketches. 'This is the only bridge, and the road to London. It is in need of repairs, Sir.'

'That will make our task easier. Have your troops ready to march by two o'clock.'

'I believe Corporal Foal would be the best man to assist us, Sir. He has done such work, fighting in the Low Countries.'

Gabriel winced. The veteran soldier had avoided him in recent weeks. 'He is mourning his son's death. I am reluctant to weigh him down with extra duties.'

'It may be a kindness to employ him, keeping his mind occupied for a few hours,' Gwyn said.

It would take more than the distraction of blowing up a bridge to forget the death of a son, as Gabriel knew only too well.

*　*　*

Pershore, Worcestershire

His leathery face grim, Corporal Foal walked across the bridge once more. 'The fourth arch, Sir, that'll be the one to blow,' he said to Gabriel's shoulder. That made sense, Gabriel thought. The arch was almost in the centre of the crumbling bridge straddling the river Avon, swollen by days of incessant rain.

Drawing his dagger Foal prodded at the stone and the edge broke off into fragments. 'Very poor condition.'

'Can you find it in your heart to forgive me some day?' Gabriel longed to ask, but all he said was, 'Thank you Corporal.' Gabriel leaned over the brick parapet to examine the pier supporting the arch. 'Will that pier take the weight of a man?' He was bracing himself against the top of the parapet when a line of bricks gave way.

An arm grabbed him by the sword belt, preventing Gabriel from following them into the river. 'Careful there, Sir.' The faintest glimmer of a smile crossed Foal's face. Gabriel stared at the muddy water racing through the arches of the swollen Avon. Broken branches, a piece of sacking and a dead dog performed a crazy dance as they were carried along on the flood.

'Disarm.' At least his voice was under control, Gabriel thought. With luck no one would notice that his narrow escape had left him shaken. 'Any sparks from the steel and we will reach heaven before General Waller sings another psalm.' He attempted a smile and there were sporadic chuckles at the feeble joke. There was a chorus of clinks and dull thuds as the group participating in the bridge destruction removed their swords, daggers and spurs; and laid them on a horse blanket.

It was mid-summer and plenty of daylight remained, even on such a day as this. Thankfully, the downpour had eased to a drizzle. Gabriel's lips moved in silent prayer as two of the musketeers, tasked with prising out stones to make space for the powder, were lowered on ropes, picks over their shoulders. It was a dangerous task for all concerned.

Two of Vaughan's sturdiest troopers stood on the bridge, feet braced and leather gloves on their hands, supporting the men standing on the piers above the foaming water. Gabriel and Foal stood beside them, the corporal directing proceedings. Gwyn had moved to the riverbank and was shouting a running commentary on the progress from down below. The sharp clang of metal on stone mingled with the sounds of rushing water in Gabriel's ears.

On the eastern side of the bridge, a larger group of officers and men stood waiting with the gunpowder. The remainder of the regiment were walking their horses up and down. A solitary rider, holding two horses, was stationary on the bank, anxiety showing in every rigid line of his body. Gabriel glanced towards Ieuan and gave a reassuring wave.

Spray splashed up at the toiling men with the picks. The river level had risen perceptibly in the time since they had arrived at the bridge. Watching closely, Gabriel realised that before long the holes being painstakingly gouged for the barrels would be covered.

A clang and a scrape were followed by a long pause from one of the picks. 'He is through,' Gwyn called.

'Got it,' panted the man. Leaning over as far as he dared, Gabriel could see a large chunk of stone being prised out. There was a splash as it fell into the river, followed by a shower of smaller pieces as the soldier scraped at the crumbling mass with his pick. The second man was redoubling his own efforts when Gabriel heard a sharp crack from below.

'Have a care,' he yelled. 'Heave them up.' He threw his own weight on one of the ropes and hauled. There was a scrabbling as the soldier on the rope grabbed for a handhold on the edge of the parapet. His head emerged and Gabriel reached out a hand, but as he did so there was a second sharp crack. The ground opened at Gabriel's feet and the middle of the bridge collapsed.

There were shouts behind him and then he was falling, still gripping the rope, towards the boiling torrent. Chunks of masonry rained down upon the figures floundering in the water. Gabriel hit the surface with a smack, and the rope was torn from his hand. He opened his mouth to cry for help, but foul water rushed in. He was going to drown. As brown, turbulent waves closed over his head, he thought of Bess, of how he would never see their child.

He surfaced, gulping air, and striking out desperately for the east bank. The current tore at his garments, spun him around and swept him along, but the weight of his long-sleeved leather buff coat and water-logged riding boots pulled him under again.

Lungs bursting, Gabriel surfaced for what must be the last time, near a snaking tangle of tree roots, half submerged. He grabbed at them as he was whirled past and missed, but a thick tendril of floating hair caught fast, wrapping itself around a root. Gasping, Gabriel clawed at the root with his hand while the force of the river tore at the hair.

Somehow, he found the strength to raise his other arm and catch hold of a low, overhanging bough. He clung to it, retching and coughing. As his vision cleared, he spotted something blue wedged below him, caught in another knot of submerged tree roots. It was a uniform coat, above it a lifeless face. The head was dreadfully battered by the falling bridge, but Gabriel knew that while he had survived, Corporal Foal was dead.

CHAPTER 20

Near Banbury

28 June

'Surely they must see us soon, Colonel,' Sayer said.

Gabriel nodded, his eyes on the brown dots in the distance. Scouting ahead of the King's army, his small regiment had spotted what appeared to be the rearguard of Waller's rebel army. The distance had closed to the point where the brown dots were recognisable through his perspective glass as buff-coated men, some with the tawny orange sashes worn by the rebels about their waists. The game of cat and mouse between the two armies was at an end.

There was a blast from a distant trumpet and the trotting enemy horsemen reined in sharply and faced about.

'Will we make a charge, Sir?' Sayer asked.

'No. Tell the trumpeters to blow recall.' But to flee openly went against the grain with Gabriel. A breeze had sprung up, ruffling the silk of the enemy cornets. Red, blue, green silk standards fluttered boldly. So far, they had not moved.

He felt the rush of exhilaration through his veins, banishing fear, which accompanied the prospect of imminent action. 'Let us see if they make a charge. If not, we will retire one troop at a time. David, send a man back to our brigade commander with our position and the news that we have discovered the enemy army.'

Too warm a day to don armour, nor was there time to go through the slow process of fastening back and breast plates. Gabriel went through the familiar routine of replacing his hat with the heavy metal helmet, loading his pistols, slipping his hand inside his shirt to touch his crucifix.

Vaughan's trumpets sounded. Three troops in three ranks, each blue silk troop colour held high by its cornet, Gabriel's with the motto '*Experto crede*', trust in experience. The stamp of hooves on grass, the swish of tails, ears flicking back and forth, the jingle of harness, the smell of warm horse flesh. Their riders, sweating freely, tightening chin straps on helmets and loosening swords in scabbards. Two recent recruits crouched behind the ranks, breeches lowered.

Gabriel's attention was on the enemy rearguard, shimmering in the heat. A trumpet sounded and the line began to move towards him, breaking into a trot. Waller's men were aiming to punish their temerity in approaching so close.

'Close up.' The moving ranks of horsemen closed the gap until each man's knee was tucked under the next man's. Gabriel, in the centre of the front rank, drew his sword and held it over his head. Each captain followed his example.

'The king and the cause!' Two hundred men bellowed the chosen field word, as Gabriel's sword swept down and the trumpeters blew the charge.

Gabriel repressed the automatic urge to duck as the parliamentarians fired their pistols in an untidy burst and clouds of smoke, moments before the two sides met with a crash. Despite the close quarters, as usual the pistols did limited damage. Out of the corner of his eye, Gabriel saw one of his men fall from his horse and another clap his hand to his shoulder with a silent scream. The remainder set to with their drawn swords, thrusting at exposed arms, necks and thighs before most of the enemy cavalry had lowered their pistols.

Gabriel faced a tall officer on an iron-grey horse. The man's mouth gaped in a ferocious snarl as he fought to draw and raise his sword. Gabriel swung his sword, but the sharpened edge of the blade failed to penetrate the thick hide of the buff coat. The man grunted and slashed at Gabriel's bridle hand, protected by his gauntlet. Gabriel dropped the reins and fired his pistol point blank. It shattered the man's jawbone, and he toppled sideways off his horse with a cry.

Gabriel risked a quick glance about him. The sharp blades had done their work, throwing the enemy front rank into disarray as saddles were emptied. A number of loose horses were becoming entangled in the enemy second rank, compounding the disorder. It was time to withdraw before Waller's men had time to recover and pursue them.

'Have a care!' At Ieuan's warning, Gabriel reached for his second pistol. He and the oncoming enemy trooper fired together. Gabriel felt a burning pain as the ball penetrated the scalloped edging to his glove, tearing a jagged cut in his left wrist. There was a scream from the other man's horse. Gabriel's own shot had hit the animal in the neck. It reared and took off at a gallop. Then Ieuan was there, his hand on Blackbird's bridle.

* * *

Gabriel flexed the fingers of his bandaged left hand. His wrist hurt like the devil. He rested his hand on the clay pipe and pouch of tobacco Ieuan had left beside his straw mattress but changed his mind. The stinking leaf might ease the pain in his wrist, but he needed a clear head. Blackbird had pulled up lame and his dun mare Llangenny was tired from the march. He would ride the new grey, Moonlight, on the morrow.

Moving quietly so as to not disturb the manservant, wrapped in his blanket at the foot of the mattress, Gabriel lifted the flap of his tent and went out into the night, where a soft warmth lingered. Most of the regiment slept, the captains in their tents, the others cocooned in blankets around the cook fires. Plucking a brand from the nearest fire to light his way, he wandered through the camp. A soft challenge from a picket, answered by Gabriel with the password he had chosen, 'Victory or the sword.'

'Sir!' the sentry doffed his hat, recognising his commander's voice. Gabriel moved on until the sounds of grunting, snoring men, of horses cropping the grass, the odours of wood smoke, leather, men and horses faded. Above him wisps of dark cloud trailed across the starry heavens. A shooting star caught his attention. Such a star might have led the way to a stable in Bethlehem. Did the angels watch over the sleeping armies, or were they weeping? It would be a fine day tomorrow, a fine day for killing or being killed. With a last glance at the twinkling lights far above him, Gabriel extinguished the remnants of the burning brand in a patch of mud. He sank to his knees on the soft ground, crossed himself and prayed that God would find the fallible men fighting on the side of the King worthy of victory, that He would not abandon them as He had done at Cheriton.

CHAPTER 21

Cropredy Bridge, Oxfordshire

29 June

Far down below, the river Cherwell sparkled in the sun. Will rubbed his eyes. Since Northampton's Regiment had been deployed to the King's Oxford Army, leaving their base at Banbury Castle, it seemed that every night was interrupted by the call 'To arms' and the sound of trumpets. By the time he had his boots on, the command 'Stand down' would be issued. Days of false alarms, but yesterday, if rumours were true, Colonel George Vaughan's Regiment of Horse, Gabriel's regiment, had tracked down Waller's rearguard and skirmished with them.

And now, for the first time since Northampton's had left the safe haven of Banbury Castle, the scattered regiments of the King's roving army had been gathered together in one place. The army, bolstered by the addition of troops from numerous garrisons, was ready for the long-awaited battle with Waller. It was a chance to even the score after Cheriton three months earlier.

But bringing the army together meant the King was not far away. And with him, in all probability, was the Council of War and Sir Henry Lucie. Only the sheer size of the army, and the strung-out line of march extending over several miles, was concealing Will from discovery if a search was mounted. Thank God, with a battle imminent, hunting down a single fugitive would surely be deferred.

With an effort Will dragged his mind away from the possible proximity of his father and began estimating rations for his troop. Feeding seventy three men now they were on a seemingly endless march criss-crossing the midlands was a constant struggle. One pound of meat a day, two pounds of bread. Even bread was becoming problematic despite the King having at least a dozen bakers on his payroll.

'Not a baker's dozen?' Will had quipped to the grumbling quartermaster, but the joke fell flat.

'Captain Lucie!' A messenger reined in beside him. 'We are under attack! Face about and await further orders. The word is 'Hand and Sword'!'

Will's stomach lurched. Two officers came cantering down the road. One was Charles Compton, the other was the 22-year-old Earl of Northampton, James Compton, brigade commander. The earl was bareheaded, the better for his men to recognise him.

'Major, what has happened?' Will called.

'Enemy Horse have forded the river at Slat Mill. They think to take us in the rear. We will send the beggars back whence they came.' Charles Compton raced after his brother past the other six troops of Northampton's regiment.

There was a sour taste in Will's mouth as the strip of dried beef he had eaten threatened to reappear. A trooper was vomiting over the side of his horse. It was Denton, whose brother had been mortally wounded at Cheriton. 'Seventh troop, walk march,' Will ordered.

A rumble of many hooves shook the ground. Waller's cavalry were thundering towards him, their streaming standards an artist's palette of different coloured silks, a moving tapestry come to life. Field mice shot from their hiding places and flocks of birds flew into the sky in alarm. The yellow ears of growing corn lay trampled into the earth.

* * *

'Colonel, message arrow! The King commands you turn back! We are under attack!'

Gabriel frowned at the breathless horseman. 'Who is under attack?' To his left, corn fields waved in the morning sun, deceptively peaceful. Ahead of him other regiments continued their march uninterrupted.

'My Lord Cleveland's brigade, Sir. To our rear. The rebels have crossed the Cherwell.'

'Face about!' Vaughan's Horse swung round. Back down the empty road, Gabriel urging the grey mare to greater speed. Her paces were good, he noted absently. Foam flew from the mouths of the horses on either side of him and the beasts flattened their ears.

He heard the sound of fighting cavalry before a bend in the road brought them into view. 'Hand and sword, hand and sword,' he yelled. Carbines banged and the higher-pitched pistols cracked. Smoke, flame and brief confusion as Vaughan's Horse joined the melee. 'Hand and sword,' Gabriel shouted again, parrying as a red-sashed trooper slashed with his blade.

'Your pardon,' the Royalist gasped, but now Gabriel was facing an enemy trooper levelling his pistol. The man fired, but there was only a flash in the pan, and he stared stupidly as Gabriel thrust his blade into his throat. He slumped forward and Gabriel wrenched his blade free.

A sword clanged against his helmet, and he twisted to meet the threat as his new adversary, a snarl upon his face, struck again. Gabriel threw his sword arm up just in time, but the flat of the deflected blade smacked into his elbow and the sword slipped from his nerveless grasp. Gabriel dropped the reins and snatched the pistol from his left-hand holster. There was a bang and the roundhead toppled from his saddle. 'My thanks, Cary,' Gabriel shouted at the quick-witted trooper who had fired the shot. He retrieved his sword, dangling by its strap from his wrist, and rubbed his bruised elbow.

'Oh, dear God.' An elegant figure wearing polished black armour and a silk sash whose extravagant bow almost covered his back plate. Curling hair cascaded over his deep lace collar and his head was bare. It was Lord Wilmot. With typical disregard for his own safety, the general had outstripped his lifeguard.

'Cary, with me,' he yelled. They spurred after Wilmot's pure white horse, but others had recognised a valuable prize. A spurt of flame from a pistol, a bang and a cloud of smoke. Wilmot reeled in the saddle, clutching at his shoulder. A trooper grabbed his bridle and within seconds a tight knot of men was trotting away with their prisoner. Standing in his stirrups, Gabriel stared in every direction for help. Three more troopers were galloping towards him. It was Will Lucie with two of his men.

'Will,' Gabriel shouted, 'Rescue General Wilmot. We will attack his guards.' He chased after the group holding Wilmot. Hampered by their efforts to keep the wounded commander in the saddle, they were moving slowly. Closing in, Gabriel hurled an empty pistol at the man holding Wilmot's bridle. Startled, he dropped the rein. Gabriel slashed at the next man's wrist with his sword while Cary engaged a third enemy trooper. Will had grabbed Wilmot's bridle. The horse reared, but one of Will's men grabbed the other rein.

The one remaining roundhead turned his horse's head and galloped away. Will and the rescued General had gone. Gabriel saw a fresh group of ten or twelve Horse, galloping towards him. Some of Wilmot's life-guard had belatedly spotted their General's predicament. He thought he recognised the white blaze on the black horse of the officer leading the group and rode towards him.

'The General is safe, gentlemen,' he hailed them. 'Northampton's have him.'

'And we, Sir, have you,' was the angry retort from the rider of the black horse. Gabriel's senses had registered his error, and he was already wheeling Moonlight as the roundhead's words reached him. He dug his spurs into her sides, and she leapt forward. Cary, safely ahead, reined in.

'Go, Cary,' Gabriel yelled, and the man obeyed, urging his own mount into a gallop.

The ground was a blur beneath the grey mare's hooves as she sped towards the bank of the river. Gabriel was making for the ford. There it was, the water sparkling in the sunlight. A shot from his pursuers pinged off his back plate. The mare's pace did not falter, but now a chestnut horse was streaking towards him, the rider hunched forward in the saddle. Horse and rider were between Gabriel and the shallow crossing.

Gabriel reached for his remaining pistol before remembering it was empty. He had only his sword with which to defend himself. The pounding of hooves behind him grew louder as he swerved to his left to avoid the chestnut on his right. A burst of movement to his left and a hand grabbed the bridle. It was the officer on the black horse. Moonlight snorted, pulling up sharply.

'You have given enough trouble, Sir,' the man panted, levelling a pistol at Gabriel's head. 'Your sword, or I will shoot.'

Gabriel dismounted and extended the hilt of his sword in surrender to a corporal. Two troopers seized hold of him. They wrenched off his bridle gauntlet to tie his wrists, worsening the pain in the wounded hand. Blood began seeping through the bandage.

'More than enough trouble,' the enemy officer said, swinging down from his horse. He nodded to the troopers, and they unfastened Gabriel's helmet. The man raised his own visor, revealing an engagingly boyish face, with blonde, curling hair. He smiled, exhibiting a fine, regular set of teeth, then struck Gabriel across the mouth with his gloved hand.

'That is for preventing our taking Lord Wilmot,' he said calmly. 'Search him, Corporal.' The man felt inside Gabriel's pockets and untied the purse from his belt. 'I said search him, Corporal, not toy with him. Must I give instruction on how the godly are to treat enemy commanders? You men,' he turned to the two troopers, 'Strip his armour.' He stood with folded arms while the men fumbled with the ties.

'That is better.' Drawing back his arm he punched Gabriel in the belly. He bared his teeth again as Gabriel gasped and doubled up. 'Now, search him properly!' He bellowed at the two troopers who hastened to obey. Capture at Edgehill had taught Gabriel to leave valuables with Ieuan or the baggage train. Their attempts, although considerably rougher, bore little fruit. Gabriel breathed a sigh of relief until one of the men untied the neck of his silk shirt, plunged his hand inside and gave a sharp tug.

'Major,' The man held out the silver crucifix on its broken chain for inspection. Gabriel suppressed a groan. They had found the one thing that was best kept hidden.

'A papist,' the officer stroked the glossy, black neck of his horse thoughtfully.

'Put him with the other malignant officers, Sir?' the corporal prompted, examining a louse he had picked from his own shirt.

'I think not. We have different ways of dealing with Irish papist savages.'

'Pardon, Major, do we know that he is Irish?' The corporal coloured under the officer's stony gaze and feigned a coughing fit.

'Are you challenging my authority, Corporal? If you do so a second time, I will break you,' the major replied conversationally. The corporal blanched. He flicked a troubled look at the captive royalist.

'Irish then, Sir, if you say so.'

'I do say so.' He smiled again.

Gabriel said nothing, though his heart was beating fast. His pride forbade him pleading that he was Welsh, not Irish.

'Well, Sir? Have you nothing to say?' the handsome officer smirked, inching closer until Gabriel felt the warmth of his breath on his cheek. Gabriel met his eyes resolutely and the officer shrugged. 'Irish papists are rebels, and this man is subject to summary execution. It is the Lord's work. Take him to the mill and wait for me there. We will shoot him as soon as I have leisure to attend to him.'

CHAPTER 22

Cropredy Bridge

'Lucie, is it not?' Lord Wilmot smiled; his customary charm undimmed by the pain which made him gasp.

'Will Lucie, General, Northampton's Horse.'

'Be still, My Lord,' the surgeon interjected, frowning as he attempted to cut away the torn and bloody silk.

'My thanks, Lucie. I believe we have won this fight, but His Majesty would consider it a high price if I had been taken.' Wilmot turned away, his rescuer forgotten, as the surgeon inserted a probe into his patient's flesh.

* * *

The royalists had driven Waller's cavalry back across the narrow, wooden Cropredy Bridge, but several hours later it was difficult to say if the fight was over. Both armies had regrouped and were facing each other across the Cherwell. Most of the men had removed their helmets and some were dismounted, allowing their mounts to crop the lush grass. With the approach of evening, clouds of gnats swarmed the riverbanks.

Swatting insects away from his face, Will wondered where Gabriel's regiment was. He wished he could speak to him. Now the battle had ended, at least for the time being, Will's thoughts had turned from relief that none of his troop had been wounded and that he was unscathed, back to his father's likely proximity. Would Sir Henry take immediate advantage of the lull? The Earl of Northampton was now a brigade commander, and it would not be difficult for the Assistant Secretary to the Council of War to ascertain the whereabouts of Northampton's Regiment of Horse.

Restless and unsettled, Will left his horse with his servant John and walked towards the riverbank to fill his water bottle.

'Are there you are, Captain Lucie. A messenger from the High Command is seeking you. He said the matter was urgent.' It was Charles Compton.

'Did he not say what the matter was, Sir?' Will asked, filled with dread.

'No doubt you will discover when you obey the summons. Make haste.'

'I must fetch my horse and my coat, Sir.' Will attempted a smile, but the colour had drained from his face and cold drops of sweat stood out on it.

Compton nodded and Will turned away, taking a circuitous route back to his servant and horse to allow him to think. Who had sent for him and why? Northampton's regiment was a good distance from the High Command where the royal standard flew. Nevertheless, Will feared that Sir Henry had spotted them during the battle. It seemed unlikely that a senior officer would have summoned Will, the most junior captain in the regiment, for any other purpose.

Oblivious to their captain's torment, Will's troop relaxed beside the river, some sleeping as only soldiers exhausted from fighting and marching can sleep. Once he realised his father would be there, he should have fled. His safety had lain in distance, and Charles Compton's willingness to shelter him at Banbury Castle by feigning ignorance of the arrest warrant. That would not protect him here.

Will glanced at the sun. The shadows were lengthening but it was just past the summer solstice, and it would not be dark for some hours. He might travel some miles before he was missed. 'Ready Samson for me, John,' he said to the servant. 'And fill my powder flask. I have received new orders. I may not return before nightfall.'

The servant did as he was ordered, showing no surprise. It was not for him to question the captain. 'Your blanket, Sir?'

'Yes, behind the saddle, and give me my purse,' Will added, looking about him. There was no sign of the messenger, but there was no time to send for victuals, or to retrieve his chest from the baggage train. He must leave without delay, with only his weapons.

Mounting his horse, Will passed through the ring of pickets at the edge of the King's army without challenge. He trotted steadily away as if on legitimate business, King's business, regimental business. There was no need to explain himself unless stopped by a more senior officer. He could turn around at any point, he reasoned. It was not desertion until he had knowingly ridden beyond the reach of patrols. He was still following the east bank of the Cherwell, where the royal army waited.

Will touched his legs to his horse's sides and the bay gelding broke into a canter. It appeared that, after all, he had made his decision.

'Captain Lucie did not tell you where he was bound?' Major Charles Compton asked Will's servant in perplexity.

'He spoke only of new orders, Your Honour,' John said.

'Very well, you may go. Inform me as soon as Captain Lucie returns.'

'Then we must send word to Lord Wilmot that he cannot be found,' said Compton's older brother the Earl. 'A pity, for who knows what favours His Majesty might have bestowed on him for his gallantry in rescuing the General.'

'I fear he has missed his chance,' Charles Compton said.

* * *

Will was quickly surrounded by bird song and cattle grazing in the fields. Men and women in the villages were going about their business as if a bitter struggle were not being waged closer than a man might walk in an hour.

At the second village he came to, he stopped at an ale house, watered his horse and went inside to slake his thirst and ask himself what he had done.

Will upended the empty pot over the upturned barrel at which he was sitting. A few drops trickled onto the scored surface, and he began tracing circles with a finger. An hour's drinking had provided no answers, but a slowly dawning realisation that, whatever his muddled thoughts had been, he had deserted the King's army.

'Supper, Sir? There's a fine rabbit stew in the pot,' the serving wench said, at his elbow with a jug of ale.

'Supper? No, I must be on my way,' The alehouse was filling with men who had finished their work for the day, and he was attracting curious glances. No doubt they were accustomed by now to the sight of soldiers in these parts, but in groups or patrols. A single officer was bound to attract unwelcome attention.

Riding on, Will realised that he was unconsciously making for his old home, Chadshunt Hall. It was no more than a few miles away, but the estate had been seized by the roundheads and he could not return there.

Where in Heaven's name could he go? He needed somewhere safe to hide, and someone to hide him. Bess would take him in but that might be the first place their father would seek him, and he could not bring that trouble on Bess and on Gabriel's family. He might go into exile, but to leave the country he needed a pass, and Parliament controlled the Channel ports. Besides, he had only the little money in his purse, not enough to pay for a sea voyage or lodgings in another country.

Turning off the Banbury road, Will dismounted and led Samson into a thick wood. While the horse cropped the grass, Will sat with his back to a tree and his aching head in his hands, thinking.

The sky was darkening. A few drops of rain fell and a chill breeze made him shiver. Standing up, Will removed his crimson sash and buff coat, untied his helmet from the saddle and unstrapped his holsters. Without them he hoped that he was no longer conspicuous as a soldier. Taking his officer's commission from his coat pocket he folded it several times and tucked it into the very bottom of his boot. His pistols and powder flask he placed out of sight in his saddle bag. The remaining bundle he hid in thick undergrowth after carving his initials on a nearby tree to mark the spot if ever he returned that way.

He was a deserter now, a hunted man, and there was only one place he could think of where a deserter from the King's army would be welcome.

CHAPTER 23

Near Cropredy

Leaving the horses with the dejected corporal, the two troopers marched Gabriel towards the mill, one holding him by the arm, while the other carried a drawn sword. Distant shouts, scattered shots and thundering hooves told him that the battle was not yet done, but there was no sign of any royalist troops who might come to his rescue. From the moment the major had declared Gabriel to be Irish he had guessed the officer planned to shoot him, either in revenge or as a Catholic, for he had made no attempt to discover his name. Gabriel had heard rumours of Parliament's forces executing Irish soldiers but had never imagined it would be his own fate.

'No more roasting children of good Protestants on a spit while their parents are forced to watch,' the trooper chortled. 'Nor pricking them on the point of a pike.' He unslung his carbine.

'Have a care, Jack,' the trooper with the sword cautioned. 'We may not kill him now without the major's command.'

'Have you not seen the tales from Ireland in the news sheets?' Jack protested.

'I have and they sicken me; yet the major will want him kept for the firing party.'

Wild thoughts of escaping by throwing himself into the river passed through Gabriel's mind, only to be rejected. With his hands bound he would drown.

'I said nothing of finishing him. I thought only to spend a half hour readying him for his end.' He clubbed Gabriel across the shoulders with the carbine, knocking him to the ground.

'Enough, Jack! Another of those and he will not stand upright against the wall. No more.'

The other muttered something but dragged Gabriel to his feet and the trio continued toward the tall, timber-framed mill. Waterfowl floated on the still waters of the millpond. The water wheel turned with a rhythmic thud and the sound of gushing water spoke of everyday industry and more peaceful times.

Two dogs ran towards them barking, but a whistle called them back. A white, spectral figure filled the doorway. It was the miller, coated in flour from head to toe. Dark eyes flickered a question in the mask-like face.

'Stay inside. This is Parliament business, and none of yours,' the other trooper ordered. The ghost grabbed the dogs by their necks and closed the doors behind him.

'And yet, we might spare the major the trouble of shooting him,' Jack grunted. He pointed to the hoist high above them where sacks of grain disappeared into the darkness of the uppermost floor, and his breathing quickened.

The pain in his wrist and shoulders forgotten, Gabriel's stomach knotted. He could smell the man's excitement, the rank odour increasing as he contemplated hanging his prisoner from the top of the mill.

'Why have you brought this prisoner here?' An officer trotted up. He dismounted unhurriedly from his horse. In his early thirties, he wore a gold-laced buff coat straining at its laces. The coat bore the stains of travel, but the absence of fresh blood stains suggested that he had only recently arrived; and had not taken part in the battle.

'Captured officers are being confined in that barn.' He pointed in the opposite direction.

'Major's orders, Sir. Summary execution as an Irish papist rebel, Sir.'

'Ah,' the officer tightened his mouth. 'I have no truck with papists, yet I am myself Irish, and it is a harsh judgement. What is his name?'

'I cannot say, Sir, but he was wearing this.' Jack retrieved the silver crucifix from his purse. The officer's lip curled. 'A papist indeed.' He took the crucifix between a leather-gloved finger and thumb then dropped it to the earth and ground it deliberately beneath his heel.

'And yet, that is no proof that he is Irish.' He turned to Gabriel.

'Your name, Sir, if you please? I am Colonel Nicholas Devereux.'

'Lieutenant Colonel Gabriel Vaughan, officer commanding Sir George Vaughan's Regiment of Horse,' Gabriel said wearily. *This man must be kin to Essex himself.*

Devereux frowned. 'But that is surely a Welsh regiment, as is your accent. Do you carry your commission?'

'It is in the pocket of my coat.'

Devereux jerked his head at Jack. The man, sulking at the loss of his silver prize, retrieved the paper from Gabriel's pocket with a bad grace and handed it to Devereux.

'Lieutenant Colonel Gabriel Thomas Vaughan,' the colonel read aloud. 'Very well.' He refolded the commission with a nod, returning it to Gabriel's pocket.

'Give me his sword. Put him with the other prisoners in the barn. If your major questions why you have not followed his orders, refer him to me.'

'Thank you, Colonel.' Gabriel inclined his head. Devereux nodded stiffly and walked away, carrying Gabriel's sword.

CHAPTER 24

Cropredy Bridge

Riding behind Sir Edward Walker with a delegation from the King to the rebel General Waller, Sir Henry's thoughts were of the fugitives. When the main field army was on the march, he was rarely certain which regiments were present. But today, he had discovered that both Northampton's and Vaughan's Horse were engaged in the battle. Thanks to the spy he knew that Will had survived Cheriton and returned to Northampton's regiment.

Walker turned in his saddle. 'Lucie, before I send a trumpeter to Waller, I think it would be wise to obtain a safe conduct for myself. It might be perilous to trust my life to those who have cast off their allegiance. You will go to Waller and seek one for me.'

Sir Henry reflected that his own peril was evidently unimportant.

'Once you have concluded that,' Walker continued, sublimely unaware of his subordinate's thoughts, 'Your part is done. Have a man on a fast horse held in readiness to carry word of Waller's submission to His Majesty. I feel sure that after his defeat today, Waller will be ready to accept the King's generous offer.'

Having carried out this mission, Sir Henry had no qualms approaching the brooding Secretary the moment he emerged from his tent early the next morning. Walker wore fresh garments. His boots gleamed and he was shaved. The army had limited what officers might carry, for the baggage train slowed down the main body, and drained resources for guard duty. Sir Henry, restricted to one chest, suppressed his resentment with difficulty.

'Sir Edward, there is a private matter I must speak to you about, concerning two officers who have disgraced their colours.'

'Has someone given offence to you? It must wait for we have more urgent business. Waller refuses to submit. Your task is to attend the Council of War and to set down the account of yesterday's great action.

'But first, find Birkenhead, the editor of Mercurius Aulicus. Ensure any mention he makes of my approach to Waller is couched in suitable terms.'

'Conceited popinjay,' Sir Henry thought as he went in search of the editor of the royalist news book. After that, he was determined to discover if the two fugitives were on the field. He beckoned to a passing musketeer.

The Council of War was assembling by the time the selected musketeer returned. Sir Henry set down his portable writing desk on a convenient drumhead. 'Did you find them?'

The man bared his head, but then turned the cap upside down. 'Aye, yer honour.'

Sir Henry dropped a handful of coins into the cap. 'Their whereabouts then, quickly.'

'Captain William Lucie's troop ain't seen 'ide nor 'air of 'im since before sunset. Then an officer come along. Ordered me to return to my colours.'

Soldiers deserted daily but officers rarely so. If Will had deserted, his commanding officer might be tempted to conceal the fact. He felt a burden lifting and was angry at himself for the weakness. 'And Vaughan?'

'Ah, there you are, Lucie.' Walker's cultured tones had an edge to them.

'Do not stir,' Sir Henry muttered to the soldier. For the next hour, he endured the debate as to the rival merits of pursuing the remnants of Waller's army or marching west in search of Robert Devereux, Earl of Essex's army.

The soldier was waiting outside the tent, under the watchful eye of two sentries.

'And Vaughan?' Sir Henry continued.

'Never 'eard of 'im.'

'You tell me that Vaughan's regiment has never heard of one of their own officers?'

'Nossir.'

'Did you speak to a horse boy or one of their trollops?'

'A corporal in their pike division and another in their muskets division. Neither 'ad 'eard of 'im.'

'God's teeth,' Sir Henry exploded. 'It was Sir George Vaughan's Regiment of Horse I ordered you to approach, not Sir Henry Vaughan's Foot regiment. Half-wit!'

Surrounded by fools, Sir Henry fumed. And Walker was evidently in a black mood after the failure of his embassy to Waller. Arresting Vaughan in Oxford had been simple. In the field, soldiers had duties more pressing than rounding up their own delinquent officers.

* * *

Gabriel shifted, trying for a more comfortable position on the earthen floor of the barn. Light flowed under its barred doors. It must be morning. The night had been punctuated by what sounded like reinforcements arriving, the tramp of many feet and the shouting of orders. The strands of match binding his hands behind him cut into his wrists. His bandaged hand throbbed, and his mouth was swollen from the blow. With his tongue, he explored the damage. One loosened tooth, maybe two.

'What will happen to us, Sir? They will not execute us?' The young ensign sitting on the ground beside Gabriel enquired, his voice wobbling.

The code of war said that a man whose surrender had been accepted was safe from death, but it was only thanks to the roundhead Colonel Devereux that he had been saved. Looking at the wan face, pale beneath a layer of grime and blood, Gabriel decided on a half-truth.

'They have given us quarter. To kill us now would bring them dishonour.' The boy's eyes scanned Gabriel's face in search of further reassurance. 'We may be imprisoned for a time. Warwick Castle is less than twenty miles away.'

'The rebels will not wish for that trouble,' an older officer said. 'Twenty miles with the King's armies close at hand? And diverting half a troop of Horse to guard us.'

'So, they will release us?' the ensign asked.

'Believe that if it comforts you,' the officer murmured.

'When will they bring us meat and drink, Sir? I am so thirsty I can scarcely speak.'

'Then spare your breath, lad,' a middle-aged sergeant advised. 'They've more urgent matters than our victuals, or our other needs. Nothing to them if we pisses down our legs.'

Attracted by the smell of blood and urine, flies had found a way into the barn and had settled on every exposed inch of skin of the bound men, adding to their discomfort. Gabriel's own hunger and thirst were considerable, but the cramp in his arms and the growing pain in his hand was worse.

The officers exchanged apprehensive glances as the regular tramp of marching feet approached the barn. One began reciting the Lord's prayer. There was a thud as the heavy bar across the doors was lifted. Blinded by the sudden light, Gabriel could see nothing at first, but the acrid smell of burning match reached him. Musketeers – bile rose in his throat. Then his vision cleared. Standing in the doorway was the roundhead, Colonel Devereux. Gabriel breathed more freely.

'Colonel Nicholas Devereux at your service, gentlemen.' Devereux beckoned to two soldiers standing behind him. They drew their daggers and there was a moan from the ensign.

'Cut them free. The King has sent a trumpet requesting you all be exchanged.'

There was a collective sigh of relief from the prisoners. An escort of red-coated musketeers marched them across the fields towards the river and Cropredy Bridge, where a larger group of prisoners waited. A knot of gold-laced rebel officers stood nearby, talking.

A growing clatter of hooves, the hum of voices and the uneven tramp of men marching without the beat of a drum. Trumpets sounded from the other side of the bridge. Senior officers met in the middle of the narrow bridge and bowed ceremoniously. Within minutes the exchange was over. As Gabriel passed the group of roundhead officers, Devereux stepped forward carrying his sword. 'You might find a better use for it, Colonel,' he said.

Gabriel's first wish was to find Ieuan before he carried word to The Allt of his capture. The news could endanger Bess and the child. There was no time to waste. He paid scant attention to the words of their welcoming escort until he heard, 'This way then, gentlemen. His Majesty wishes to thank you for your trials.' Much against his will, Gabriel was swept onward with the rest.

CHAPTER 25

Cropredy Bridge

Sir Henry pulled the watch from his pocket, flicking open the case. He had not yet given up hope of persuading his superior to allow him to arrest Vaughan on the field. Now there was a further delay while the King, in full armour and carrying a commander's baton, addressed a parade of released prisoners. Common soldiers had been sent back to their regiments, but the officers were drawn up for inspection. Standing at the back of the crowd of staff officers, Sir Henry caught little beyond the King's opening words of 'Loyal and well-beloved men, we greet you.'

At the end of the speech, a herald proclaimed, 'His Majesty's officers above the rank of captain, step forward.'

Followed by an aide, the King passed down the line of kneeling men. Sir Henry stiffened as the King paused next to a young officer. Beneath the dirt and blood obscuring the man's features, Sir Henry thought he recognised Gabriel Vaughan. He was speaking to the King. Charles inclined his head graciously and the aide made a note. When the King and his entourage withdrew at the end of the inspection, the baronet pounced on the aide. 'Let me see that paper.'

'By what authority?' The youth shook back the silken ruffles protruding from his coat sleeves.

'My own, as Assistant Secretary to the Council of War!'

Pursing his lips, the aide handed over the paper. Sir Henry scanned it, searching for one name. He found it. 'Lt Col Gabriel Vaughan, Sir

G Vaughan's Horse', with a scribbled addendum, 'Liberty to depart for attending to urgent family matters.' Thrusting the paper back at the aide, Sir Henry forced his way through the crowds. But when he reached the spot where the officers had paraded, they had dispersed. Vaughan was gone.

CHAPTER 26

The Allt

July

There was a saying in Crickhowell that if you could not see the hills it was raining, and if you could see them, it was going to rain. It was a rare day of soft sunshine in the south Wales valley, with a mackerel sky of pale blue laced with white. The barley was turning gold. Gabriel and Bess picked their way along the paths between strips of swaying waist-high stalks.

Gabriel had been at The Allt several days, time enough to recover from his pursuit of Ieuan. Bess carried a small basket with a whole cheese tart and slices of honey cake. Field mice scuttled across their path and Gabriel chased marauding blue tits away. He waved his arms to attract the attention of the two boys whose task was to act as bird scarers, more pleasantly engaged in whittling sticks with their knives.

Reaching the top of a knoll overlooking the peaceful expanse, Gabriel spread his cloak on the damp grass. Panting, Bess flopped onto the fading and carefully repaired yellow silk lining of the elderly green woollen cloak Gabriel wore at home. He pulled the wrap from around her shoulders, released her silky hair from the coif and slid a warm hand beneath the lace of her falling band. She closed her eyes as he pressed his lips to her neck and shoulders. 'We are on the top of a hill, Gabriel,' Bess mumbled between kisses. Warmth was spreading through her body.

'Indeed we are,' was the muffled response.

'We will be clearly visible from the fields, against the skyline.'

'Then I will declare my love to the sky.' He sighed and sat up, 'I should appoint you as a scout, Bess. You have a keen eye for danger.' She plucked a leaf from his hair, then pulled the cloth off the basket. Turning his attention to its contents Gabriel reached for the knife at his belt.

Gabriel had spoken very little since his arrival. No, she corrected herself, he spoke to his parents, joked with Ieuan and was unfailingly polite and considerate. Yet the watchful look in his eyes which she had noticed in the spring rarely left them. During the days he spent hours closeted with his father, with Lewis or riding the estate visiting tenants. When he was with Bess, they were surrounded by servants, or his parents were present.

At night, as she lay in his arms, she tried to muster the courage to mention Elspeth's name, but those minutes were too precious to mar with possible discord. Sometimes he picked up his lute and played. He would move from music to kisses to the gentlest of lovemaking, thence to sleep. Night after night she fell asleep promising 'Tomorrow.' She knew he would not remain at The Allt much longer. Today then must be her opportunity.

Bess's heart thumped. She had rehearsed this conversation many times. *Did you ever love Elspeth? Do you regret that you wed me?*

'Did you ever . . .,' Bess began and stopped. She felt she could not breathe. Had Gwyneth laced her more tightly than usual? The stays were pressing on the baby. Or was it fear?

'Did I ever?' he prompted, handing her a generous slice of cheese tart.

'Did you ever see an elephant?' No, she dared not ask *'Did you ever plan to marry Elspeth?'* Because what would the rest of her life be if he said 'yes'?

'Why do you ask?'

The baby kicked, providing a ready response. 'Because I think I am carrying one within me. Are they not huge beyond imagination?'

Gabriel laughed. 'My father took Michael and me to London when we were children, five or so. We had just been breeched. We rode all the way, taking turns to ride before Father on his saddle and before the servant, Ieuan's father, Dafydd. We visited the Tower and the King's menagerie. The King of Spain had presented him with an elephant. They say it drank nothing but wine. Michael and I longed to see it, but to no avail. Maybe it had died from drinking too much wine.'

Encouraged by his light tone, Bess decided to try again. She rolled away from him and plucked a few grass stalks at random so that she did not need to look at him.

'Did you ever plan to marry Elspeth?' This time the words came out in a rush and she felt blood surge to her face. Gabriel said nothing and Bess was filled with terror. Why had she said it?

His hand was stroking her hair. 'Look at me Bess.' His voice was gentle. It felt like a hundred years until he spoke again. 'No, I did not, never in this life. She is like a sister to me, but nothing more. I suppose the servants have been gossiping about my mother's former plans?'

When she raised her eyes she saw pain in his.

'My mother admires you, Bess and loves you. It was not so to begin with for at first she saw only a young woman of the wrong faith and who was English, not Welsh. But now she knows you. I am very sorry that this foolish notion of hers came to your ears.' He bent and kissed her. 'Shall we return to the house?'

He changed the subject, talking cheerfully as they walked back down the hill of the expanding yield from barley, which thrived in wet conditions.

'Gabriel, do the rebels send out people in these parts gathering intelligence?' Bess interrupted the reassuring flow of 'might reach twenty five bushels per acre'.

'It is possible. Oxford is full of spies, you will recall.'

'The spies on their way to execution. I cannot forget them, nor the jeering crowds.' She shuddered. 'I believe I should tell you of something that happened. Although it is probably only my imagination that the man was not what he claimed to be.'

'What man?' The words sliced through the air.

Bess fiddled with the cloth on the basket to cover her confusion. 'A stranger who came here three or four weeks ago, asking for you.'

'That is odd. None of the household mentioned him.'

'It was only I who spoke to him,' Bess mumbled.

'I think it might be wise if you tell me the whole story.'

Her husband's voice was controlled, but she noticed the emphasis on the word 'whole'. Quickly she told him all she could remember of the Welshman who had claimed to be an old comrade from the army.

'His name?'

'He did not give one.'

'And yet he called me Gabe.' Gabriel fingered the hilt of his knife. 'I will have Lewis enquire if anybody else saw him, or knows of such a man, a returning soldier or deserter perhaps. There may be no harm in him; but listen Bess. Next time you go walking, take one of the men servants with you.'

He took her hand. Bess noticed his other hand remained on his knife.

* * *

As they neared the gatehouse, Gabriel reproached himself for occupying his thoughts solely with the dangers to those at Basing House; and not thinking that his own family might be at risk. Could the man be a spy? Repairs to stone walls would not repel an enemy who slithered in like a snake.

They were met in the hall by his mother's maid.

'Your lady mother sent me to find you, Master Gabriel. She is in her chamber.'

'Thank you, Betsy.' Wondering at the formal summons, Gabriel took the stairs to his mother's chamber two at a time. Lady Alice was seated on a padded upright chair next to the open window. She held a book of hours in her hand, tilted towards the light, and her face had the serenity which it rarely attained other than through prayer.

Gabriel glanced at the book, open at one of the scenes depicting the life of the Virgin Mary. His own favourite, as a child, had been the picture of the Tower of Babel, its beautifully illuminated miniature figures in orange, blue and red toiling with weights and pulleys at a white tower.

Lady Alice laid down the book. 'You do not say when you are leaving, but I know it must be soon.' She opened the tall press and took out a familiar wooden box decorated with the Vaughan coat of arms. It contained her jewels and other precious things such as a small missal, the red velvet cover faded and its pages yellow with age that had belonged to her own mother.

'My son, I was distressed to hear that your silver crucifix had been taken when the rebels captured you. It is dangerous to wear one.'

Gabriel smiled, 'Since I have it no more, there is no danger, but I am sorry for its loss. *Tadcu* gave it to me, I should say to us, for Michael also had one.'

'Yes, I remember the day your grandfather gave it to you. When Michael died, I took his crucifix as a keepsake. He has no use for it now; and would not begrudge his twin wearing it.'

Selecting a tiny key from the bunch at her waist, Lady Alice unlocked the box. She lifted out a scrap of silk and unfolded it. The silver crucifix, scarcely larger than Gabriel's thumb nail, and the slender chain, gleamed as if they were newly brought from the hands of the silver smith. Michael had worn them for no more than a year before he died.

There were tears in his mother's eyes as she placed the crucifix in Gabriel's open palm, closing his fingers over it.

'Go now. May God and all the angels keep you safe.'

CHAPTER 27

The Allt

———

'Are you leaving?' Bess sat bolt upright in bed at the sight of Gabriel booted and spurred, his cloak slung over his shoulder and his sword belt strapped on.

'I must, my love. I have lingered here a week.'

'Will you return for my lying in?' Bess's voice wobbled. Gabriel placed his hand on the mound of her belly in its embroidered night gown. 'If it is in my power, nothing will keep me from you.' It was not quite a promise. A hundred things might prevent him returning in time, or ever.

A messenger had arrived at first light. Parliament and the Scottish Covenanters had routed Prince Rupert's cavalry and the northern army of the Marquess of Newcastle during a huge battle outside York at a place called Marston Moor. Gabriel knew he must leave at once.

'This is a sudden departure. There is something important to discuss first,' Sir Thomas said when Gabriel found his parents at breakfast. One eye on the growing light, Gabriel followed his father from dining room to study.

'Tell me, Father.'

'How many more months can this accursed war continue?' Sir Thomas asked, busying himself with the tinder box, pipe and tobacco pouch. 'This is the third summer, the third harvest that we have prepared for under its shadow. When it began, all the talk was that it would be over by Christmas.'

'I wish I could answer you.' Gabriel began to pace, his spurs jangling. Much of the floor space was taken up with neat piles of ledgers interspersed with fleeces, samples from the different hill farms.

'Oh, *eistedd i lawr*, sit down. Your spurs make my ears ring. When so many lives are being lost, I hesitate to talk of money matters, but the demands upon the estate increase by the month. The taxes we must pay the King to support the war, the levies to support his garrison at Abergavenny Castle, Raglan Castle too. Requests for cheeses, sacks of flour from our mill, a fully equipped horse for a new trooper. The Allt cannot go on like this.'

'Then it is fortunate the pursuivants and the sheriff are too busy with the war to add to our woes as recusants.'

'No words of comfort for me?'

'We lose men through death and desertion, as water runs into sand. Yet it is the same for Parliament's armies. The King may triumph in the end. That is all the comfort I can give you.' Gabriel sank to one knee before his father, drawing the conversation to a close.

PART 2

THE
TAWNY
SASH

CHAPTER 28

Mid July

Leaving his horse Samson tethered to a branch, Will crept to the edge of the tree line and lowered himself onto his belly. Below, enfolded by a curve of the River Exe, stretched the enemy camp of the Earl of Essex's army, where Will planned to take refuge. A handful of tents with flags marked the positions of the commanders. The remainder of the camp consisted of makeshift shelters of branches, bracken, greenery, some draped with blankets. They were interspersed with cook fires, where soldiers were tending pots or roasting meat on improvised wooden spits. Linen drying on bushes flapped in the breeze. Female camp followers wandered here and there. The horses, tethered in neat lines to portable stakes, were guarded by sentries, not just horse boys. It would be difficult to slip into the camp unchallenged, even on foot.

Waves of misery rolled through him. Was he ready to forsake everything he held dear in order to save his own skin? Was turning his coat and joining the enemy the only choice that remained? It might have been better if he had perished at Edgehill in that first glorious charge when the war was new, and victory lay at the other side of the battlefield.

The shadows were lengthening. He must come to a decision.

Without warning a booted foot thumped down on his back, pinning him to the ground.

'I do believe we've caught a spy,' a voice rasped. 'Rope!'

Will's wrists were seized and bound behind him. Hands hauled him to his feet and turned him to face his captor. Sandy hair thrust its way from beneath the soldier's cap and a tawny orange sash was knotted carelessly across his chest. He looked Will up and down and whistled. Despite long days of travel, sleeping in woods and hedgerows, Will could not be anything other than an officer from his bearing to his scuffed and muddied but expensive leather boots.

'So, the King is using gentlemen to gather intelligence these days. A fine weapon.' He unbuckled Will's sword belt.

'Fine beast too, Corporal.' Will caught sight of another soldier holding Samson.

'Move! You will be questioned in the camp you are so eager to see.'

'I am not a spy,' Will blurted. 'I am turning my coat.' This was not the welcome he had expected. Sir Richard Grenville had been welcomed warmly by the King when he left Parliament and changed sides.

'A turncoat, not a spy? Then come with me, Master Turncoat.' The corporal gave a mock bow. 'It is not for me to say if you live or die.'

'Caught another one?' a man cleaning his musket jeered as the patrol entered the camp. They marched Will towards a tent. Inside, a middle-aged officer sat on a stool, a cup of ale in his grasp.

'Prisoner for interrogation, Captain. Says he's a turncoat. King's spy more like. Watching our camp from the hill.'

'Sir, I must protest,' Will urged. His bound wrists were already sore and he was thirsty.

The officer put down the cup and pulled on a pair of leather gauntlets lying on top of a leather-covered travelling chest. He made a slow circuit of Will before pausing in front of him.

'Your name, if you please,' the officer barked. 'And what you are doing here.' He slapped Will hard across the face.

'Buckley,' Will muttered, 'William Buckley.' He had brought enough shame on the Lucie family.

* * *

Would the beating never stop? One eye was swollen half shut. Blood streamed from Will's nose. The captain punched him again.

'Who sent you?'

'No one,' Will groaned, spitting out a mouthful of blood. He had bitten his tongue during the interrogation.

'Where is the prisoner?' a voice barked. Will felt a draught of air as the tent flap opened.

'Colonel,' the captain bowed.

An officer with a haughty face and a long straight nose came into Will's limited field of vision. Gold lace gleamed on his buff coat.

'At least tell us your name, man, before we hang you. You appear to be a gentleman and your family would wish to receive news of your death.'

Will said nothing. He prayed his family would never learn of his ignominious end.

'He says his name is Buckley, Colonel,' the captain interjected.

'Any proof of that? It is rare that a spy gives his true name without some encouragement. Was he properly searched?'

The captain inhaled sharply. 'My corporal searched him, Sir.'

'And now you will search him, Captain,' the colonel ordered. Removing the blood-splattered leather gauntlets, the captain ran his hands over Will, fingering the lining of his coat and breeches. Finding nothing, he folded the wide bucket tops of Will's boots as far down as they would go and felt inside. A moment later he straightened up, clutching a scrap of oiled cloth. It contained a small piece of grimy parchment, the creases well embedded. Red-faced, he handed it to the colonel who snatched it, glaring at his subordinate.

'Now he has been properly searched! Commission as captain, Earl of Northampton's Horse, William Charles Lucie. Is that your name?'

Will nodded without raising his eyes.

'Clean him up!' the colonel snapped. 'Then send for Colonel Lucie. If this man is a kinsman, he will be able to identify him.'

The remaining colour drained from Will's battered face. It had not occurred to him that his uncle Hugh, estranged from the family since he chose Parliament's side in the civil war, might be there in Essex's camp. The rigid, uncompromising Puritan was unlikely to welcome him or believe his story.

The captain untied the ropes binding Will's ankles to the three-legged stool. Will rose to his feet with difficulty, his hands still bound behind his back. The captain shouted an order at the guard outside the tent. A few minutes later a tall camp follower sidled in, bearing a bowl of water and a towel. She was lame. One hip rose higher than the other. As one leg moved forwards strongly, the other trailed in its wake. Her hair was hidden beneath a coif, but well-marked dark brows emphasised a pair of sea-green eyes.

Her breath was warm on his neck.as she cleaned away the worst of the blood with water and cloth. It was quite some time since Will had been this close to a young and attractive woman, longer still since he had bedded one. Battered and bruised as he was, Will felt far removed from life, from the insistent calls of the body.

Glancing at him she smiled, revealing strong teeth, a tiny chip at the front drawing attention to the gap between it and its neighbour.

'That will do, wench!' the captain snarled. She bobbed a clumsy curtsey and picked up the bowl. As she left the tent, the girl gave Will a second, fleeting smile of compassion.

* * *

'That is my nephew, William Lucie.' Hugh Lucie stalked into the tent. He was attired in his customary black, but his collar and his folded boot tops were edged with rich lace, and the buttons fastening his doublet were gold.

'Untie his hands.' Hugh cast a look of distaste at Will. Despite the girl's ministrations, Will's appearance could not be described as any-thing but disreputable,

'I will continue the questioning myself, alone. When last I heard, he was fighting with the King's forces, as were his father and brother. My nephew will give his word as a gentleman not to run in the meantime. Is that not so, Will?'

Will nodded, mortified. Without a backward glance to see that his nephew followed him, Hugh strode through the camp. They were attracting curious glances. Little wonder, Will thought, the one elegantly and richly dressed, the other bloodstained, ragged, battered. Hugh led the way into a larger tent, a grey-cassacked halberdier on duty outside.

'Withdraw ten paces,' Hugh snapped. 'I will call if I need you.' He seated himself behind a table.

With a supreme effort Will pulled his shoulders back and lifted his chin. He licked dry lips. Hugh stared at him and then offered him a leather flask. Ale had rarely tasted so good.

'Thank you, Uncle.'

'You will address me as Sir or Colonel. Now what is the real reason you are here? An artful attempt to win your freedom by claiming you are a turncoat. Is this some strange new family custom to visit the enemy camp seeking favours? If I had not intervened when your father made the same foolish mistake, he could have been our prisoner for many months. Did Henry send you with a message?'

'No, Sir.'

'Were you observing the camp as they say?'

'Yes, Sir.'

'Then if you did not come here as a messenger, you came as a spy.' Hugh pronounced. 'You will be placed under guard until tomorrow. You will hang at dawn. I will give orders that you are to be treated as an officer. A chaplain will attend you and provide spiritual comfort. Do you wish to send a last letter to your father?'

Will was struggling miserably for words. 'It was true, Sir.'

'What?'

'I came to join the rebels. The army of the Lord General,' he amended hastily.

'You expect me to accept that?'

'Whether you accept it or not, Sir, I speak the truth. I have broken with my father. I would rather not say why, but he seeks my arrest. My only hope of safety is . . .'

'Joining a pack of traitors, it seems.' Hugh seemed at a loss. Steepling his fingers he cast his eyes upwards. 'Wait here. Guard! This man is not to stir until my return.'

Hugh returned carrying a brass-bound bible under his arm. 'Place your hand on the bible.'

Reluctantly, Will did as he was bidden, the calfskin cover cool and smooth beneath his hand. He had lied to the captain interrogating him. He might have continued lying to his uncle, but not if he was forced to swear to the truth of what he was saying. Only the most hardened of men would imperil his soul by lying under oath.

'Now swear that you are telling the truth and that you have come to join the army of Lord Essex.'

'I swear it,' Will mumbled.

'And do you undertake to be a faithful soldier to Parliament, remaining so until released by our commanders or by death?'

Will hesitated, but there was no going back now. 'I swear.'

CHAPTER 29

Will lay wrapped in a rough blanket on the floor of a barn, surrounded by the anonymous shapes of snoring men. A silent, red-haired officer had shown him to it as darkness fell. There was no longer a need to hide his tear-stained, damaged face. Pulling the blanket over his head he fell asleep.

He awoke in pain to the first day of whatever remained of his existence. Trudging through the open doorway he heard 'Good morning, Lucie.' It was the red-haired officer. Will stared down at the man, who he overtopped by half a head. 'Good morning, Sir,' he replied, glad to hear a normal greeting.

'Captain Robin Lawrence, at your service.' He swept the blue silk Montero cap off his head and made a jaunty bow. Automatically, Will reached for his own hat, before remembering that it had been lost during his capture.

'Are you a captain in my uncle's regiment? Colonel Lucie's regiment,' he corrected himself.

The officer chuckled. 'Colonel Lucie has no regiment. He's on Old Robin's staff. The Earl of Essex, Robert Devereux, the Lord General,' Lawrence explained, seeing Will's confusion. 'What do you cavaliers call him? Rebel in Chief, I suppose.'

Will flushed.

'Colonel Lucie is a reformado,' Lawrence went on. 'He retains the rank of Colonel, but no longer has men at his command. Well, Lucie, I will leave you to contemplate your many sins. I am to take you to Major Hamilton when he returns at noon. Break your fast first. My servant will bring you bread and cheese.' He dropped his voice. 'And take heart. You are not the first gentleman to see the righteousness of our cause, and to abandon his mistaken allegiance. God grant you will not be the last.'

Munching with difficulty on the bread and cheese, Will wandered unhindered through the camp until he reached its western extremity. A wide stream, tributary to the River Exe, formed a natural boundary and secured the camp from attack.

Traces of the army's occupation showed in muddied banks with animal droppings, wisps of hay trampled by foot and hoof. A mound of refuse, broken buckles, scraps of leather and shoes torn and worn beyond repair vied for space. Half a dozen dogs were snarling and tussling over bones.

Will scratched his head, discovering a few lice. Well, he could at least clean himself before facing Major Hamilton. Stripping off his torn, stained clothes he plunged naked into the waist-high waters. The ripples flowed across his bruised and aching body. It felt like a new beginning, but as what? A renegade and a rebel. Without his royalist attire he was a snail without a shell.

* * *

Hephzibah stood on the riverbank holding a basket of soiled shirts. There was the tall officer whose blood she had washed away after his interrogation. Purple bruising covered his face, back and belly. But she also read mental anguish in his face, even in his body.

It was in the way he straightened his sagging shoulders with a visible effort after touching the purple patches; and it was in the way, after shaking water from his trailing flaxen hair, that his head drooped.

He dragged the torn shirt over his head, wincing as he moved. As he climbed the bank and trudged away, Hephzibah followed him with her eyes.

* * *

'Come in, Lucie.' Major Hamilton was grey-haired, with a scholar's stoop in his shoulders. 'Do you mean to take root where you are?' His accents marked him as an educated man from Scotland. Will made a hasty bow and took a seat on a stool.

Hamilton studied Will's disfigured face. 'I perceive your welcome was over-warm. Colonel Lucie tells me you wish to join our cause.' He listened without comment to Will's halting tale of his wholly imaginary change of heart.

'And your father and brother?'

'Remain with the King. Father seeks my arrest.' At least that much was true, Will brooded.

'Unhappily, there are many families such as yours, where the godly are seen as miscreants. One of our lieutenants died two days ago. I will request the General give you a commission in Colonel Sir Robert Pye's Regiment of Horse.'

* * *

A few nights later, Will was woken by a soft footstep with an uneven tread. He fumbled for the dagger he kept beside him, before remembering he had been disarmed. 'Who's there?'

'epzibah, Sir. 'ush, I means you no 'arm.'

It was the camp follower. Aromas from cooking fires, woodsmoke, meat, fresh baked bread mingled deliciously with a faint whiff of onion and the intoxicating musky smell of a woman. The first time he crossed paths with her after his arrival, he thanked her for her kindness. After that he found that wherever he was in the camp, she seemed to be there too, cooking, or washing shirts, or just brushing past him, lifting his gloom with her infectious laugh. She had taken his torn shirt for mending and returned it to him washed and smelling of rosemary.

'What are you doing here?' he whispered, wondering if he were dreaming.

'I would 'ave thought that was plain enough, Sir.' There was a hint of laughter in her voice. She touched him. 'Leastways, plain enough to your cock.'

Will gasped. Fingers trembling, he tugged the hem of his long shirt out of the way as she straddled him, bundling her skirts above her waist. If it were truly a dream, the stirring in his loins was more than pleasurable and he succumbed to it gladly, tears streaming down his cheeks as he joined his body hungrily with hers. For a few hours he could forget he was Will Lucie, traitor and turncoat. In the faceless dark he was just another man lying with a woman.

* * *

Will whistled as he emerged from the barn's dimness into the milky light of daybreak. Hephzibah was gone, but her musky scent clung to the rough woollen blanket. Her boldness had startled him. It was a confidence arising, he accepted, from having lain with other men, other soldiers. Her arts had, perhaps, been hard won in the constant search for a protector or, failing that, the means to keep body and soul together. The tribe of women and children who trailed behind the armies depended on their men for food and what passed for shelter.

'Feeling better, Lucie?' Captain Lawrence grinned. Despite the aching mass of bruises and contusions from the beating, Will realised that he was indeed feeling better. Simultaneously came the realisation of the officer's meaning. Darkness might have hidden his frantic couplings from sight, but he had not spent many months encamped without becoming familiar with the sounds of other men taking their pleasure.

Did Hephzibah pity him? Had the girl with the malformed hip sensed in the turncoat and traitor another damaged creature? Later that day, Will found her waiting at the barn.

'Got summat to show you, Sir.' Curious, he followed her to a corner of the camp where tumbled the remains of a cottage. Ivy and brambles fought for possession, thrusting their stalks through window embrasures and the sagging roof into the single room, empty but for dried leaves and a blackened pot, hanging from a hook in the fireplace.

'I c'ld clean it up, Sir for you, for us.' She gazed at him hopefully. 'They says it's haunted by a man who killed his wife 'n run mad.'

'You are not afraid of ghosts, Hephzibah?' He stumbled over the unfamiliar name, but she glowed with pleasure.

'It's men as walk the earth that I's affeered of, not those cold in their graves.'

'The army may not remain here for more than another day or two.' Her face fell. 'But it will do very well for us two on one condition,' he hurried on.

'What, Sir?'

He smiled. 'That when we are alone, you call me Will.'

'Will it is, Sir.' She spat in her hand and grasped his to seal the bargain. Her palm was roughened from work.

'And shall you come to my bed again, tonight?' His heartbeat quickened at the prospect.

'Aye, Will, after I have cooked your supper and brushed your coat.' Grinning, she bobbed a curtsey and walked away, determination in every line of her body.

CHAPTER 30

'Master?' Sir Henry's servant Ralph appeared in the farmhouse kitchen holding a letter. 'A messenger brought this.'

Sir Henry put down his knife and pushed the platter of roast pork aside. There was no seal, nothing but a plain wafer, but he knew the hand. As usual it commenced without a greeting.

'The dog that sired your bitch's litter will be near you by and by. He remains with his cousin's Horse.'

He had heard at the Council of War that Sir George Vaughan's Horse would join them as they moved west, as part of Prince Maurice's Western Army. So, Gabriel Vaughan remained in command and had not gone home to see the birth of an heir. Maybe he had already tired of the girl. It was time to raise the subject of the felon with Sir Edward Walker once more.

An opportunity presented itself the next day on the march towards Exeter and a rendezvous with the Western Army. A gentle sun warmed Sir Henry's bones and lifted his spirits as he rode. Stubble in the fields showed where crops had been harvested prematurely in the quest to feed hungry soldiers. Here and there surviving herds of the red Devon cattle stampeded in fright.

Sir Henry reined in beside the Secretary's showy chestnut stallion. 'Good morning, Sir Edward.'

Walker nodded. 'Lucie.'

Fearing interruption, Sir Henry plunged into his prepared speech. 'Sir, are you aware that among Prince Maurice's forces is Sir George Vaughan's Regiment of Horse?'

The Secretary raised his finely arched brows. 'What of it?'

'They are under the command of a felon.'

'A felon? You astonish me.'

'Lieutenant Colonel Gabriel Vaughan is in command. There is an arrest warrant for him awaiting execution.'

'And what has this officer done that has earned your enmity?' Sir Edward's voice hardened.

Sir Henry had gone too far to stop. Briefly, he listed Gabriel Vaughan's crimes, ending with a plea that he should be arrested on their arrival in Exeter.

Walker flicked away a horse fly. 'Thank you. You have made yourself quite clear.'

Relief flooded Sir Henry. 'Then you will support me, Sir, in sending guards to arrest him?'

'Are you quite deprived of your wits? I meant that I am now in command of the facts or, I should say, the facts as you choose to portray them. You are aware that we pursue the rebel army to bring them to a final battle?'

'Yes, Sir,' Sir Henry muttered, clenching his teeth.

'Yet you believe that we should stop to convene a court martial and try this Lieutenant Colonel Vaughan who has had the temerity to cross you, the baronet and landless gentleman.'

'His Majesty himself has said he has no home,' Sir Henry retorted in vexation.

'Stop wasting my time, Lucie. Does His Majesty have so many regiments of Horse at his command that he can afford to alienate one by arresting its commander shortly before we engage the enemy? If you can perform some extraordinary service to His Majesty, you may approach me again. Until then, do not test my temper.'

Sir Edward spurred away. Seething with impotent fury, Sir Henry followed. If only an extraordinary service would secure Walker's support, then he must perform one.

CHAPTER 31

The Allt

One night, Bess dreamed of Jacob's ladder. It had been a recurrent dream in childhood. Cherubim and seraphim with folded wings and flaxen hair, their faces indistinct, or their backs turned. This time, as the figures reached the top, they descended once more and now they turned towards her.

Their faces were of those she had known, but who were no longer alive. Her mother smiling at her, a young lieutenant, victim of camp fever in Oxford, others who had perished during the siege at Basing House, their bodies miraculously whole again.

Bess was filled with a sense of peace. She woke, wriggling her bare toes and revelling in the feeling of warmth. A moment later peace turned to panic. The warmth was liquid flowing between her legs. 'Gwyneth!'

'Mistress Bess?' The maid emerged from her trundle bed in the closet at once.

'I think the baby is coming. The midwife did not expect it yet.'

'Babies are born when God wills it,' the maid reassured her, pulling aside the heavy bed curtains. Her night cap sat rakishly on one side of her head over her red plaits. In the dim gloom of the bed chamber a line of faint grey light under the door to the long gallery meant that the start of this late summer day was not far away. Soon, there would be familiar sounds as farm workers, and all those from the household who could be spared for the all-important task of bringing in the harvest, headed for the fields.

On a frosty January morning, lying in their marriage bed at Basing House, Bess had told Gabriel, 'I will bear you a child at harvest time.' She was about to keep her promise, but he was not there.

'Why is Gabriel not returned?' she pleaded as the maid helped her into an old night gown. The birthing chair stood ready. Other maids were arranging a straw mattress on the floor, covering it in worn linen and much washed towels. 'Let's make you comfortable, *fy cig oen*,' Gwyneth soothed, sponging Bess's face and hands with water.

Sir Thomas's page arrived with a bowl of the blackberries and cream Bess had been craving lately. She gave a tearful chuckle that ended in a gasp as her belly contracted suddenly and painfully, the unwelcome sensation travelling downwards towards her thighs. She did not want blackberries, she wanted Gabriel.

Another contraction tore through her. While the maids fastened the shutters and stuffed rags into key holes, Bess prayed for a healthy child, a son, and for her own life. The flickering candles seemed to throb in time with the pains pulsating through her belly with increasing frequency.

Goodwife Nan slipped through the door. As round as a barrel, the village midwife came only to Bess's shoulder. The arms she bared to the elbow were brawny as those of a blacksmith. Lifting Bess's night gown she felt first her belly and then between her thighs. Bess winced and arched her back as another pain came.

'Up,up!' Nan muttered something in Welsh to the maid, then switched to English. 'You must walk, walk.' She clapped her hands.

Bess groaned. 'If I am to be torn apart by pains, I would rather remain lying down, Goodwife.'

'Up, up,' Nan repeated. Bess found herself on her feet, leaning on the arms of Gwyneth and the shorter Nan. From the bed to the window, then to the door, past the empty fireplace, a press, the entrance to Gwyneth's closet, back to the bed. In the uneven shadows cast by the yellow glow of candlelight, the bed chamber took on an air of unreality. Carved beasts and birds on the panelling stirred and danced in the flickering flames. Beside the fireplace, the miniature of Gabriel's twin smiled encouragement.

When Bess could walk no more, Nan grudgingly permitted her to rest a while. There was a quiet tap at the door. Lady Alice's maid Betsy entered, carrying clean cloths and a steaming bowl of rosewater.

'Not rosewater,' Bess gasped, retching. Throughout the pregnancy she had not been able to abide that sweet odour. The surprised Betsy was bundled out of the door again.

Next came Lady Alice herself, carrying a bowl of warm caudle. 'Will you take a little, Bess? I made it with my own hands.'

The smell of cinnamon was comforting. Bess permitted Gwyneth to spoon spicy oatmeal into her mouth until a stronger contraction gripped her, and she cried out.

'*ydy hi'n iawn?*' Lady Alice asked, her face drawn and anxious. She said something else. Bess thought 'too early' was a part of it.

'Yes, indeed. All is well, My Lady,' the midwife replied. She winked at Bess.

That day had many hours. Time and again Bess was coaxed to her feet to walk and walk. By the time the elderly physician arrived she was seated on the birthing chair, braced against the leather-covered back and clutching the arms. Nan, on her knees, was busy with goose grease, massaging the opening to the birth canal.

'Master Morgan,' Nan greeted him. Furrowing her brow she returned her attention to the labouring woman. The physician's dark eyes, undimmed by advancing age, crinkled as he regarded Bess.

'Well, Mistress Vaughan, I believe with God's mercy we will see the birth of your child shortly.'

'A son, it will be a son will it not?' Bess's plea ended in a shriek as she was wracked by a fresh pain.

The candles burned down and were replaced. Bess groaned and prayed with unaccustomed fervour. Once, she clutched Gwyneth's arm and begged her to tell Gabriel she loved him. She was starting on what to name the baby, for she was about to die.

'You may tell Master Gabriel yourself, Mistress when he returns,' Gwyneth said with a smile.

Bess, intent only on freeing the baby trapped within her body, did not hear her. By now she cared not if it were boy, girl, angel or devil. She only wanted an end to the torment. At last the midwife's calm was replaced by excitement, urging Bess to push.

It was some time after nightfall when Bess and Gabriel's daughter was born. Wreathed in smiles, Gwyneth washed Bess, dressing her in a fresh night gown and propping her up on pillows. After swaddling the tiny infant, Nan handed her to Bess. A mass of dark, spiky hair emerged from the blanket and a pink fist waved angrily in the air.

She traced the contour of the heart-shaped face with a tentative finger. The closed eyes tilted upwards like Gabriel's. Taking hold of the tiny fist, she gazed at the miniature fingernails, all complete. The baby grabbed her finger with surprising strength and Bess laughed as the door opened again. It was Lady Alice.

'Well, child, has God blessed you with a son?'

Bess was filled with dismay. The baby was perfect, and yet she was a girl, not the longed-for heir. It must all be gone through again if she was to give Gabriel a son. 'Madam, I have borne Gabriel a daughter,' she snapped. 'I know that he will love her as he would a son.'

'Let me see.' With a rustle of silk, her mother-in-law sank to her knees beside the straw mattress. Gently, she took the swaddled bundle from Bess, clucking over it. Her lips curved into a wide smile. 'She looks like her father. You have done well, Bess. Rest now.' Within minutes the wet nurse had carried the baby away and the midwife had left for her own house. As Bess fell headlong down the slope of sheer exhaustion into sleep, she thought she heard, 'Only a baby girl, but she is young and strong and may yet bear him an heir.'

CHAPTER 32

'Cursed be he who withheld his hand from blood.' For once the sun was shining as the troop rode through the narrow Cornish lanes with their high hedges; but remembering the words that the regiment's preacher had taken as his text, Will shivered. A chill of foreboding went through him as though the man had placed a cold hand inside his shirt. His stomach clenched at the thought of coming face to face with Gabriel in battle, but it was too late to turn back. He had made his choice. Thank God his brother Harry was in Ireland.

'I doubt we will find a finer billet for the night, Lieutenant.' The ruddy-faced quartermaster, William Ardington twisted his beard between his fingers as he pondered.

Will pushed his own worries aside. Scouts had spotted a small farm as likely overnight quarters for the troop. There was smoke from the farmhouse chimney. It was not abandoned. He turned in his saddle towards the dozen troopers. 'Have your dags at the ready, loaded and resting on your thighs. The people here are unlikely to be friends to Parliament.'

The farmyard was deserted, but for poultry scratching at grass sprouting between the stones. They scattered at the sound of hooves. There was no other sound but pigs grunting in their sty. At a signal from Will the men dismounted. Each trooper threw the reins over the next horse's neck and one man remained holding all. Will gestured for them to fan out. In a line, they crept across the yard, carbines and swords at the ready, but the farm had no armed men lying in wait. A trooper was dispatched to inform Captain Pyle that it was safe to advance with the remainder of the troop.

Next, Will sent two men in search of provisions. The brewhouse contained nothing but empty wooden barrels and a trail of scattered barley.

'What shall I do with this wild cat, Lieutenant? Found her hiding in an empty cow byre along with barrels of ale.' The trooper was dragging a woman by the elbow, screaming, spitting and kicking. The other men fell whooping on the ale.

Will stared at the woman. The empty cow byre spoke of hard times, famine, or cattle sold to pay the King's crippling taxes. By the time the roundheads had taken the new year's crop of hay for their horses and carried off the few pigs and poultry, the woman and her family would be destitute. Will felt doubly wretched at the thought that he was plundering a woman loyal to the King. Yet he had done the same for those whose only crime was rebellion against crippling taxes. His guts twisted.

'Sir?' the trooper queried.

'Oh, lock her up, Baxter, until we leave.'

'And the brats?'

Will turned his attention to the boy and girl of some ten or eleven years, yelling and kicking at the shins of another trooper who held them easily by the scruff of the neck.

'Them as well if they will not keep quiet.'

'Aye, rebel, lock us up,' the woman snarled at the tall, flaxen-haired officer in the tawny sash. 'Rape me too, I shouldn't wonder. Enjoy the day, for the King will hang you all and send you to Old Nick where you belong.' She twisted in Baxter's grip, biting him on the hand.

'I'm not a rebel,' Will wanted to scream. Instead, he slapped her hard. He glanced down at the new leather glove with its scalloped edges, bought from a sutler at the camp with his new-found wealth, in surprise, as if it had acted of its own volition.

The two children wailed at the sight of their dishevelled mother, her coif trampled in the mud and her dark plaits fallen to her shoulders.

'Noone will take you against your will, woman,' Will barked. 'The Lord General forbids any man to rape a woman. Now, hand over those keys at your belt if you do not wish my men to rip your doors off their hinges. And, for pity's sake, be quiet.'

She hurled the bunch of iron keys at Will's feet, where it landed in the mud with a splash. The scanty number of keys to chambers, stores and chests told of the size and poverty of the farm. The regiment would kill one or two of her pigs so that they might eat tonight. Smoked hams that would not hang from her rafters, joints of roast pork that she and her family would not eat with apple sauce, pigs' trotters that would not make a tasty supper for her man.

'Is all secure, Lieutenant?'

Captain Seymour Pyle reined in effortlessly, pistol in hand. He managed his horse as he did his troop, with an easy grace.

'Yes, Sir.'

Spotting the bunch of keys in Will's hand, Seymour's eyes lit up. 'You have done well. Thanks be to God, this place will feed us for one night.' He swung down from the saddle, unfastened his helmet and rubbed his aching neck. 'Here you, lad!' He beckoned to the woman's son, now skulking in a corner of the farmyard between barn and pigsty. 'Have a care for my horse. A penny for you if you do so well. If you mistreat him or try to steal him,' he pointed at the gable end of the barn, 'You will be swinging from there by nightfall.'

Turning his back, he winked at Will. 'Never fails. My beast will be well cared for.' He patted the roan gelding and handed the reins to the child, who had edged closer at the promise of a penny. Whistling, he strolled towards the farmhouse.

* * *

Will bedded down in the straw of the ramshackle barn with his men. He might have passed the night in the greater comfort of the house, sleeping on the floor, or sharing a bed or palliasse with another officer; but he preferred to earn the respect of the troopers.

Outside, it was pouring. He wished he were home in his own country of Warwickshire, where he understood the weather. The glory of war! Reality was mud, rain, the noise and stench of tightly-packed men in sodden, filthy garments, curled around each other like wet puppies, snoring and farting.

At least his belly was full for once, he comforted himself. Undeterred by the rain, the men had been cheerful at supper, roasting two pigs over flaming wood. Despite Will's implicit promise to spare the farm buildings, the blaze had been created by chopping up doors from cow byre and pigsty.

Sucking fingers burnt by pulling strips of hot, crackling fat from the pork, the men washed down the meat with barrels of ale. At first Will hung back from the boisterous throng, but when Seymour Pyle led the men in a rousing rebel song, Will edged forward. Soon, his fine voice mingled with the others.

'When cannons are roaring
And bullets are flying,
He who will honour win
Must not fear dying.'

He tugged the damp woollen blanket tighter about his neck. It was pungent with his sweat, musty from nights sleeping in dripping fields, from days strapped in a tight roll behind his saddle. More alluringly, Hephzibah's musky scent clung to it. He missed her, but she was safer in rebel-held Devon with other women and children.

'Twas Da who made me as I am,'

Will was propped on an elbow on the bed of bracken, covering the floor of the tiny cottage. He had been admiring her body, the small, firm breasts, the long legs like a colt, the dirty toes with pink toenails. Hephzibah ran her hand matter of factly down the ungainly shape of the crooked hip.

'When 'ed ad a skinful ed give Ma a hiding; and so I wor born like this. Some women said it wor a witch put a hex on me, but the only

hex was in the drink Da took. Fell out of the hay loft one day and broke 'is neck. Good riddance, Ma said but squire put us outer farm. See a woman couldn't take lease. So we left then Ma died of the flux.'

'I see.' Will could see only too well. It was not unknown for wealthy widows to own property in their own right, but for the poor widow of a tenanted farm it was natural that she would be cast out in favour of a man. 'And you?'

'Tried work as a servant. I come cheap being crook'd. But en said I were clumsy and beat me every time I came back from market, so I run away after en paid me at Quarter Day. Makes me a thief I suppose.' Will pulled her to him.

'Noone will beat you or mistreat you, Hebzibah while I am here.'

Remembering her words, Will's heart bled for the orphaned girl who had become a camp follower of the poorest kind. Despite rain trickling down his neck from gaps in the broken tiles, the exhausted Will fell asleep.

Morning brought a rare dry spell. Will hung his half-dry coat over a branch, pushed back the linen sleeves of his shirt, untied the strings at the neck and sloshed water from an overflowing rain barrel over face and arms. The men were bleary-eyed from too much ale, scratching at lice in their garments. Two hunting terriers tussled over discarded bones from the previous night's feast.

'Be silent,' one of the troopers growled, aiming a kick at the smaller dog. It leapt into the air, snapping at his hand. He gave a howl as the animal's teeth sank into his wrist. 'Bested by a mangy cur, White?' grinned another man. White glared and drew his dagger. Grabbing the dog by the back of the neck he slashed it across the throat, severing an artery.

Will frowned. He disliked unnecessary cruelty and there had been no need to deprive the farm of a useful working dog. 'Why did you do that?' he snapped. 'Must we make enemies more than we need?'

'I beg your pardon, Lieutenant,' White sneered. 'Have you yet some sympathy for a Cavalier dog, Sir?'

Other men stopped what they were doing to watch how the new officer dealt with this challenge to his authority.

'Minstrel, no!' The child of the night before rushed across the yard and flung himself across the dog's twitching body. Pulling his hand away from the dog's fur he looked at the crimson stain on it with horror.

'Blackguard, murderer, th'ast killed him,' he screamed. With no desire to start the day with a disciplinary matter, Will took advantage of the distraction, walking away towards the farmhouse. He would seek out Captain Pyle for marching orders. The sound of a sickening thud stopped him in his tracks. He turned, to see White beating the lad over the head with the butt of his pistol.

'Stop that!' Will sprang forward, horrified, as the two-foot-long wheel lock pistol descended for a third time. He wrenched the weapon from White before he could raise his arm again, but it was too late. Kneeling in the mud, Will placed a shaking hand on the small skull, cracked like an eggshell. The child's eyes were open, fixed in their last look of rage.

'Lieutenant Lucie, what is the meaning of this outrage? Corporal Potter, place this man under close arrest.' Seymour Pyle flicked White a glance of loathing and jerked his head towards the farmhouse. Forlornly, Will draped a saddle cloth over the dead child and followed the captain inside. Pyle folded his arms.

'Are you not fit to be in command of men? Why did you not prevent this? Now, you will send my clerk to make arrangements with the regimental chaplain for the boy to be buried and prayers said. And give the boy's mother.' He thrust out his lower lip and delved into his purse. 'Give her this in recompense for her loss. If I can get the pay due to White, you will send it to her. I must speak to Major Hamilton without delay.'

It was a subdued troop that descended the steep hill into the town of Lostwithiel. The streets were choked with half-starved infantry, shepherded by harassed officers in scarcely better case than their men. Will rode at the rear of his troop, holding a halter attached to White's bound wrists. The trooper was on foot. His face was ashen, his coat and breeches covered with dirt from the roads, torn from the times he had fallen. Will was shocked, not only by the events at the farm, but at his captain's reaction. Such swift and decisive retribution was rarely meted out in the King's armies. Will had the uncomfortable feeling that, had the episode occurred in Northampton's Horse, it might have been overlooked.

CHAPTER 33

'That was an inauspicious start. Granted, the child was of no account, the family poor and insignificant.' Hugh Lucie paced the floor in the parlour of the town's principal inn, his face stern. 'Well, what have you to say for yourself?'

Will's mouth felt dry. He had scarcely handed over his prisoner to the Provost Marshal when one of Hugh's servants arrived to fetch him. Standing, hat in hand, he told of the dog fight which had led so swiftly to the child's death. 'If only I acted sooner, I might have saved the boy.'

'It is not the death of one brat which troubles me, but your failure to maintain discipline. I had heard that the King's troops were a rabble. Now I perceive it is true.'

Hugh's eyes dropped to the cheap tuck hanging from Will's side. 'Do you not have your own sword?'

'It was taken when I was captured.'

'Doubtless it was. Describe it.'

'A fine broadsword, Sir. The Irish hilt is inlaid with a silver engraving of the Lucie arms.'

'It will be recovered. I will not have you carrying the weapon of a common soldier. You have brought sufficient disgrace to the family name.'

Ears burning, Will left the inn. He remained with his troop while White and a series of recaptured deserters were tried by Council of War.

'Death by hanging, Lucie,' Captain Pyle said soberly. He had found Will staring at a sheet of paper headed 'Deficiencies in troop's equipment'. 'Missing spanners 7' was the only entry.

'The Lord General is anxious to preserve the goodwill of the country people. White will be an example to the men.'

Riding out of the town on the Bodmin road early next morning with a patrol of scouts, Will passed the hanging tree. White dangled from one of several boughs heavy with their ghastly human fruit, his tongue lolling and the odour of faeces filling the air. Small boys hooted with glee while they pelted the corpses with mud.

On the other side of the street stood the dead boy's mother, her thin body convulsed with sobs. Thankfully, he could not hear her wails above the jeering from the townspeople who had gathered to watch the spectacle. Will marched his silent troop away. Some of the men gave backward glances to their erstwhile comrade, already food for crows, but Will faced forward and resolved to pass that way no more.

CHAPTER 34

Gabriel finished the postscript to his letter to Bess, sanded and folded it. He held the stick of sealing wax to the candle flame and stared at the molten blood-red drops falling onto the sheet of paper. The signet ring with the Vaughan emblem was pressed into the soft wax.

'I wish that I might return to you, my love, but it is not possible. We have pursued Lord Essex to the very ends of the realm. Soon he will be trapped. The local people, who bring us intelligence of the rebels with no thought of payment, say that they are close by. The regiment cannot spare me until this is over, for Sir George continues lame. And so, my darling, my most beloved wife, I will not have the joy of being at your side to see our child born. I pray daily to St Margaret who intercedes for all pregnant women, for your safe delivery.'

In this fashion men broke their most sacred promises, Gabriel thought. Replacing the wax in its case he closed it with a snap. He had sent Ieuan to bed, telling him he did not need him again that night. A gust of wind blew a flurry of rain drops against the narrow window of the house in Pound Street. There would be many soldiers lying under hedges wrapped in their cloaks. The ancient castle on the hill was too far decayed to provide shelter.

He pulled on the linen night shirt and pinched out the candle. His conscience pricked him, for there was something he had deliberately omitted from his letter to Bess. Now that the King was in the field, so too were his staff. Sir Henry Lucie would be among them. Fate, and the course of the war without an enemy, was bringing them together again.

* * *

Lostwithiel, Cornwall
____

'It seems My Lord Robartes was mistaken,' the quarter master grumbled to Will in the taproom of the alehouse beside the bridge. 'Him being a great landowner in these parts, he believed the local people would flock to our standards, but instead the scoundrels are pleading poverty. They feed our men nothing but pease pottage and small beer; and swear they have no corn to feed our horses.'

'As to horses, Ardington, I had hoped to find a spare mount. My own will not be fit for the field if I use him without respite.'

Ardington grimaced. 'If the landlord waters this ale any further we might save our pennies and drink it direct from the Fowey.' He spat on the floor. 'You would have been wise to buy a second nag before we crossed the Tamar. The Cornishman would sooner put a bullet in his horse's head than sell it to Old Robin. I believe the Lord General would be better advised to march back into Devon, where Parliament has friends. Here, we have only the sea at our backs.'

'The local people hate us,' Will said, thinking of the mother of the murdered child.

'Do you hate us?'

Will's throat constricted. 'No,' he muttered, 'I do not.'

'I am relieved to hear it.' There was a twinkle in Ardington's brown eyes.

'Are you accusing me of spying?' Will protested. 'I have been cleared of that.'

'Indeed, I do not dare,' Ardington laughed. 'I have no wish to duel with a man whose reach with his sword far exceeds mine.'

170

Will dropped his hand from his sword hilt. He usually restrained his wilder impulses, but the upside-down world he inhabited was affecting his behaviour.

'Yet I wonder,' Ardington continued, 'whether, when we form up in line of battle, you will not be tempted to flee rather than fight your former comrades.'

'I will not flee. I have sworn an oath to serve Parliament.' Will had once sworn to serve the King, but that must be forgotten.

CHAPTER 35

Entering the tavern in Bodmin north of Lostwithiel one afternoon after another day of scouting and foraging with his troop, Will was tired and wet through. The cavalry had been billeted in the town for several days, so Will found the taproom crammed with cavalry drying steaming cloaks before glowing turves of burning peat. Will spread his own damp cloak to dry. His attention was caught by an angry hail. 'Clodpole, treating my cassack like that!'

'Your pardon, Sir.' Will retrieved the coat from where he had knocked it.

The coat's owner glanced at Will. 'Well, well, the clodpole is the turncoat I questioned. Have the blows I gave you spoiled your sight?'

'I beg you, Sir, consider your words,' Seymour Pyle said.

'What would you have me consider? If clodpole irks you, I will call him stupid. I may not replace turncoat, unless, as one who has run from his colours, he prefers to be called a coward?'

A sudden hush fell in the packed room.

'Sir, I think you are drunk,' Pyle placed a cautionary hand on Will's rigid shoulder.

'Am I drunk because I say a man is lily-livered?'

Cold fury surged through Will at the public slur on his honour. It was all he had left, or what poor scraps remained. He grasped the hilt of his sword.

'Duelling is forbidden, Will, especially with an officer senior to you,' Pyle warned, but the words were lost in the scrape of steel as Will drew the sword.

'I cannot be expected to endure such an insult, Captain.' Men from the troop sprang forward to help him remove the heavy boots and spurs, tie back his long hair with a piece of twine, undo the buttons on his doublet. Stripped to shirt, breeches and knitted stockings, Will led the way outside. The grass was wet and slippery, but it was the best option for his stockinged feet.

There was a buzz of excitement. Moments later the taproom was empty, but for the tapster in his greasy tunic, thriftily emptying ale dregs into a jug. Whatever the outcome, the soldiers would soon be back, toasting the victor.

A gust of wind blew fine drizzle in Will's face, coating his flaxen hair with a sheen like dew on a corn field. The chill air, after the fug of the tavern's smoky interior, made him shiver. He had never fought a duel before.

'Are you frightened?' his opponent taunted. His face was flushed from drink, but his stance was that of an old soldier whose body knew what to do, even while his tongue led him astray.

'Not at all, friend. The air is sharp, but my blade is sharper, and our discourse will warm us.' Will rubbed his thumb over the Lucie crest and slipped his hand into the familiar leather lining of the basket hilt. His uncle had retrieved the sword as he had promised.

'Try not to get yourself killed,' Seymour Pyle requested. 'And no mortal wounds to your opponent, or I will lose an officer I prefer to keep.'

Will bowed, favouring Pyle with a sunny smile. Surveying the harsh lines on the scowling face of his adversary, Will wondered what he had done to earn his enmity. Until he remembered what he had heard through the haze of pain. *Now he has been properly searched!* By hiding his commission in his boot, Will had made the captain look a fool before the haughty man in gold lace he now knew to be Lord Robartes, one of the most influential men in the Earl of Essex's inner circle. Will was facing a man in deadly earnest.

'Well, Sir, have you finished dawdling?'

He must not allow the other man to rattle him with his barbs. 'I am quite ready, Captain?'

'Harding, Lieutenant Lucie.'

Will bowed his head formally and then raised his sword. He balanced his weight evenly on both feet while he assessed his adversary. The man was shorter by several inches but more powerfully built.

Harding paused for a moment and then rushed at Will. The blades met with an overhead clash and Will stepped back, giving ground. The other man snorted, detecting weakness, but Will was considering his position. He lunged high, then low, testing the other man's reflexes. Harding parried easily. Continuing the offensive, Will made a sidewise swipe at his ribs which his opponent narrowly evaded. Will dropped to one knee to parry the reply, and the blades met overhead once more.

It felt odd to be fighting on foot with his heavy cavalry sword, rather than the lighter, flexible rapier. A loose strand of hair brushed Will's face, diverting his attention. Harding dived forwards, falling to one knee and striking upwards. The blade's sharp side cut through shirt and flesh, scraping against a rib. Will cried out in pain. A line of red was spreading across his shirt. Harding laughed and lunged again. Will tore his eyes from the wound just in time to twist sideways. The movement saved him; but intensified the pain. Pyle was at his elbow.

'Carry on,' Will panted.

'Very well.' Pyle stepped back.

Will was in too much pain to fight much longer. He must finish it. Will watched Harding's eyes and feet. While the captain feinted this way and that with his upper body, he betrayed his intentions through his eyes and through shifting his weight before moving his feet. Will feigned a stumble. Harding's eyes gave a tell-tale flicker to one side and Will, instead of falling to one knee, twisted quickly and painfully to the other side.

Wrong-footed, Harding fought to retain his balance. Will's sword flashed through the air, on through leather and flesh. Harding screamed as the sword severed muscles and sinews. He sank to his knees, clutching his bleeding arm.

* * *

'No gentleman could have borne the insult, Sir,' Seymour Pyle assured Major Hamilton.

'That may be so,' the major interrupted, an edge to his cultured Scottish accent. 'Yet since Lieutenant Lucie has joined us, our forces have lost two more men without the assistance of the enemy, the first because he did not act when he should, the second because he acted when he should not. Captain Harding will not be able to fight again for many weeks.' The rolling of each letter r emphasised his irritation.

'I believe Lucie is a good officer, Sir, nevertheless.'

Hamilton grunted and turned his attention to Will, standing motionless, hands by his sides.

'Well, Lieutenant, you have heard the generous words of your captain. Do you have anything to add?'

'No, Sir.'

'No, Sir, and there you stand as if butter would not melt in your mouth. Does your wound pain you?'

Will touched his side where a tight bandage covered the shallow wound. 'Yes, Sir,' he gasped.

Hamilton laced his fingers together, the stoop to his shoulders becoming even more pronounced. 'My duty is clear. Insubordination should be punished. Nevertheless, I need every man, every officer. I cannot fault your horsemanship and it appears you are also a swordsman. It remains to be seen if you can command men. Very well, you are dismissed.'

Will followed Pyle from the room. His respect for Pyle had been growing since the incident at the farm; and now he was grateful for his captain's support. For the first time, Will knew an impulse, however weak, to fight at Pyle's side.

CHAPTER 36

'Halt. Password.'

'Duchy.'

The guard lowered his sword. Gabriel strained his eyes to identify the mounted man emerging from the gloom. Like the remainder of the regiment, the horse had cloth over its hooves and muffling the bridle to stop the bit jingling. It was Lieutenant Hooper.

'The gate is closed, Sir, but there are no guards outside.'

'Could you see or hear anything of what goes on inside?'

'Nothing. The outside is all blank wall, except for arrow hoops. The windows must all face inward.'

Sir George Vaughan's Regiment of Horse advanced down the slope between high hedges sitting atop stone-faced banks towards where the ancient, fortified Boconnoc House crowned a plateau. Surrounded by a deer park, it nestled between wooded hills. Thick banks of dark cloud hid moon and stars. It was the perfect night for an attack – unless it had been foreseen.

Parliament's troops had taken advantage of its owner's absence to occupy it. Now Gabriel had been ordered to retake Boconnoc House. A boy had brought news to Liskeard that the officers were sitting at table carousing and the house was unguarded.

Dim, wraith-like shapes were grazing not far away. One of the animals lifted its head and galloped away, closely followed by two others.

'The deer are restless. Dismount. Pass the word for Rilstone.' The men tethered their horses under the cover of the trees, leaving two men keeping watch.

'I am here, Colonel.' Accompanied by the lad who had brought the message, the estate steward's younger brother approached. The tall, broad shouldered Cornishman was head game keeper.

'Wait here with me, Rilstone. Captain Gwyn, surround the house and silence any guards who are without. And remember, do not give fire. Use your swords. When all is secure, send me word, and Rilstone will approach the house openly.'

Captain Gwyn and his troop slunk away. The mass of the house, a tower at each end, loomed as a dark and silent presence in the night.

'Message from Captain Gwyn, Sir. There are no sentries outside the walls of the house.'

'We attack then. Tell him to remain on guard.'

With the lad leading the way, Gabriel and the remaining men crept in single file up the southern slope from the deer park. Rilstone mounted his horse. He was to make a wide sweep and approach the house by the main entrance on the west side.

Once at the base of the house it was difficult to see their way without torches. Each man kept a hand on the wall so that he did not stray from the path. Boconnoc stretched monotonously before them. Gabriel had the dream-like sensation that the walk around the house would never end. The boy tapped him on the arm. 'Corner of south tower, Zur.'

'Wait here, lad. Your part is done.' The gatehouse then was around the corner. Gabriel waited until he heard the hoofbeats of a single horse. Followed by the other men, and staying in the shadow of the wall, Gabriel edged towards the gatehouse. Rilstone reined in with a clatter of hooves and dismounted. There was a sharp challenge from the gate. Drawing his dagger, Gabriel crept closer.

'I have an urgent message for the steward,' Rilstone hollered. 'Soldiers have broken down the fence and the deer are escaping.'

There was a thud as the wicket gate was unbarred. A creak was the gate opening. Leading his horse, Rilstone ambled towards it.

'Enter then, what are you waiting for? Hey, John, hold this beast.'

Gabriel sprang from behind the animal, hurling himself on the sentry. The man grunted in surprise, then collapsed to his knees inside the gate, gurgling as Gabriel's dagger buried itself in his throat. Rilstone sped past him and by the time a second man, presumably John, emerged from the stables, the main gate was swinging open on its bars. More dark shapes crowded through, drawn swords in their hands. The man was felled by a blow to the head from a pistol butt.

Motioning Gabriel to follow, Rilstone jogged across a cobbled court-yard. He indicated a row of candle-lit windows. 'The family dining room where the officers are having supper. That door leads to a service passage. Follow it and you find the principal rooms in use by the rebels.'

The narrow wooden door was unlocked. Taking a half-dozen men, their swords drawn and pistols loaded, Gabriel groped his way along the stone-flagged unlit passage. Several times he felt the outline of a door set in the wall, but all were dark and locked until, rounding a bend, he heard voices and saw light streaming through an open door.

'More wine for the officers, girl. Quickly now.' The unmistakeable flat tones of a man far from his home in London.

'And more for honest soldiers like you and me,' slurred a second voice. The glow from lanterns and hearth revealed to Gabriel the shad-owy shapes of his men, hunched against the wall.

'Make ready,' he muttered. 'Now!' The seven men burst through the open door to the kitchens. A red-coated soldier stood, arms folded, near the door while the other sat splay-legged on a bench, propping his back against the smoke-blackened wall. A long table was covered with dishes bearing the congealing remains of roast meats, carcases of fowl and a half-eaten salmon, the bones of the fish on one side laid bare. A tortoiseshell cat sat on a windowsill, its eyes fixed on the dish of fish. At the other end of the table, two women were busy, one arranging sweet meats on a platter, the other peeling oranges. A third woman was lifting a tray of pies from a modern bread oven.

The three servants and two soldiers froze in a tableau reminiscent of a court masque. Two of Gabriel's troopers seized the drunken soldier, gagging him with a dish clout offered by one of the women and prop-ping him in a corner, trussed like a turkey. The other soldier opened his mouth to call for help, but Gabriel silenced him with a blow from the butt of his pistol.

'How many men?' Gabriel addressed the question to the woman who had provided the cloth. She bobbed a curtsey.

'No more 'n twenny men, Zur. Five, no, six officers, at table.'

'Sadly, they may not have time to enjoy the fruits of your labours.' He nodded at the pies and sweetmeats.

At the sound of running feet, the roundhead officers in the family dining room scrambled for their weapons. The sight of many pistols being cocked persuaded them of the futility of it.

'Stay where you are,' Gabriel thundered, his Welsh lilt gone in the momentary stress of imposing his will on a group of unknown enemy officers. 'Surrender and you will be given quarter.' The answering silence vibrated with hostility. Gabriel scanned their faces, seeking any interchange of glances that might signal a concerted move.

'I am Colonel Edward Aldridge, Governor of Aylesbury. To whom are we surrendering?' one of the officers enquired. His words were calm, but his colour was heightened beneath a thatch of dark hair liberally streaked with grey.

'Lieutenant Colonel Gabriel Vaughan, Sir George Vaughan's Regiment of Horse.' Aldridge gave a short bow and laid down his pistol. An audible sigh swept the room and the other officers followed suit, adding their weapons to the clutter of plates and dishes strewn with bones and pastry cases on the linen-covered table.

With the surrender of the officers, there only remained a handful of soldiers to find. While his men collected the discarded weapons and searched the officers, Gabriel counted heads.

'Five, no, six officers,' the servant had said. Only five men stood around the table. 'Hooper,' Gabriel whispered. 'Go to the kitchens. Ask the tall, darkhaired woman if she is sure there were six officers, not five.'

Lieutenant Hooper returned with the unwelcome confirmation that an officer was missing. Gabriel frowned. If the man had fled it did not matter, but if he remained, he might be organising resistance. And where was Lord Mohun's family, who must be prisoners in their home? He had forgotten about them. This time Gabriel left the room himself, breaking into a run towards the kitchens. The three women were seated patiently on stools at the table, evidently awaiting orders.

'Where are my Lord Mohun's family?' Gabriel demanded.

'I'll take you, Zur,' the darkhaired woman responded, jumping to her feet. 'Milord is with the King, but Milady and her child are here.'

Leaving the officers under heavy guard, Gabriel collected the remainder of his two troops and followed the maidservant back into the courtyard and towards a tower topped with the dim outline of a dome. They tramped swiftly up a winding staircase, its stone worn smooth by centuries of passing feet. Halfway up the tower, the stairs widened, and a passage led away into the rambling house.

'Which door leads to the lady's apartments?' Gabriel asked the maid. She pointed to a nearby door just as it opened. By the light of the candles in silver sconces to either side of the door, Gabriel saw the missing officer. Dressed with careless elegance in green satin doublet and breeches, fine lace showing at the cuffs, he was grasping the neck of a slim young woman. She was wearing only a pale, loose night gown, and a nightcap. Her face was contorted with terror.

'Oh, My Lady,' from the servant confirmed that it was Lord Mohun's wife, Lady Catherine.

'Do not come any closer or you will regret it.' Despite the confident words, the cultured voice shook. Gabriel realised he was only a boy. His face was flushed with wine, but the sheen on his brow was sweat.

Gabriel took a step backwards. 'Is there another way to the lady's chamber?' he muttered to the servant. She nodded, and he thrust her behind him, telling Lieutenant Sykes to go with her.

'Help me.' The words were spoken in a light, silvery voice. Gabriel took a deep breath. He must somehow calm Lady Catherine and keep her safe from the frightened boy who held a pistol pressed to her temple.

'Do not fear, My Lady, you will be safe. I pledge my life,' Gabriel spoke quietly but firmly. 'Sir, do not be foolish. Release her and no harm done. Your fellow officers have all been given quarter.' He edged closer.

'Lay down your weapons, and tell your men to withdraw, or she dies.' Lady Catherine swayed. Gabriel hoped she would not faint. There was no telling how the young officer might react.

'Do as he bids you,' Gabriel ordered. 'Withdraw until I summon you.'

Reluctantly, Gabriel's men retreated towards the stairs.

'Why did you come to this part of the house? Were you searching for the lady?' Gabriel was playing for time.

'I heard your men as I returned from visiting the privy. I was hiding,' the boy blurted. He squared his shoulders. 'Your weapons, Sir,' he repeated, his voice cracking under the strain. There was a click as he cocked the pistol.

Gabriel bent and with infinite care, placed his own pistol on the ground. 'Release her. No one will harm you.'

'And why should I trust the word of a cavalier?' the youth spat. 'I will not be taken in chains to Oxford like my elder brother.' Tears of rage coursed down his cheeks. 'Your sword too. Remove your sword belt.' The barrel of the wheel lock pistol shifted towards Gabriel.

Slowly, Gabriel unbuckled the leather sword belt and inched forward, carrying it.

'No closer,' the officer snapped, the pistol swinging back and fore like a pendulum between Gabriel and the girl.

Gabriel laid down the sword belt, succeeding in advancing two further paces. If he could entice the boy's attention away from the girl, he was near enough to risk flinging himself at him and grabbing the gun. Most firearms had a tendency to fire high, so if he dived low, he should be safe enough. 'Be a sensible lad and give it up,' Gabriel urged. As he guessed, the boy scowled, and the barrel swung back towards him.

'You insult me, Sir. I am an officer, an Ensign of the Lord General's Regiment of Foot.'

Gabriel steadied himself to jump. 'Don't shoot.' His plea was ostensibly directed to the young officer, but his eyes flickered to the towering figure of Lieutenant Sykes padding silently on stockinged feet behind the pair.

Sykes, a pistol in his left hand and a dagger in his right, nodded his agreement. He plunged the dagger into the ensign's back, thrusting upwards under the rib cage. The boy gave a cry of agony and staggered. The pistol in his hand exploded as he fell to the floor, the ball embedding itself harmlessly in the wall.

'You did well, Sykes,' Gabriel sighed as he knelt beside the two figures, for Lady Catherine had fainted at his feet. Sykes had misunderstood his words. There was a sucking noise, followed by a gush of blood, more black than red in the dim light as Sykes freed his dagger. He wiped it clean on the boy's doublet.

'Carry the lady to her chamber and find her personal maid. She should not be left alone tonight. I will deal with – this,' Gabriel said. Sykes bent his long body, lifted the girl in his arms with ease and carried her through the open door into her chamber.

There was a groan from the dying officer, whose face was growing deathly pale as his blood soaked into the rush matting. Gabriel grasped his hand, hoping to comfort him. Blood bubbled from the boy's lips, staining the hairs of his scanty moustache and dribbling down his smooth chin. 'Bury me,' he broke off with a gasp of pain.

'I will see you interred in the church yard. What is your name? I will inform your family.'

'Robin Cambridge.'

'Be easy then, Ensign Cambridge,' Gabriel said, 'And may God have mercy on you and on your brother.' He crossed himself. Cambridge was dead.

* * *

Guards posted around the grounds, and a message dispatched with news of his success, Gabriel fell asleep in Lord Mohun's study where open drawers and scattered parchments told of the invading troops' search. He was making a hasty breakfast when a trooper arrived with a message from Liskeard. The King was moving his headquarters to Boconnoc within a day or so. Gabriel was ordered to guard the house until the King's Lifeguard arrived.

Next came a maidservant with a message that Milady wished to see him. Sighing, he pulled the comb from his pocket and dragged it through his tousled hair. Lady Catherine awaited him in the cheerless Great Parlour. In a gesture to modern comforts, the windows were glazed, but they were overshadowed by heavy wooden shutters. She was reclining on a daybed, a small spaniel in her lap, while a motherly servant fluffed pillows.

'I wanted to thank you, Colonel Vaughan for your bravery. I am often frightened, with my husband being away from home with His Majesty. Will your men remain here until his return?' Despite her words, the silvery voice was calm and controlled.

'Until I have further orders, My Lady, I cannot answer that, but I will do what I can while the rebel army remains close by.' Gabriel bowed.

Next was a survey of the outer walls and doors with the house steward, the older of the Rilstone brothers. In daylight, exploring the massive, rambling house, he found it was built in the shape of an s. It boasted two towers, each of different shape and size. There were narrow slits in the tower walls intended for archers to fire arrows. It might be possible to enlarge some of them into musket loops if he were permitted.

The steward was making notes of shattered windowpanes, and broken doors when they came upon a gaggle of small boys filling their caps with lead shot from the ground and gathering flattened pieces embedded in the wall like some strange form of lichen. 'Only a penny each piece, Sir,' one of them offered. Rilstone chased them away. Dispatching a corporal to collect all the shot for melting down and reuse, Gabriel hoped he would soon be relieved of guarding the house.

CHAPTER 37

Less than five miles from Boconnoc House, the red silk bearing Pyle's troop motto, '*sola salus salutis in domino*,' the only safety is safety in the Lord, rippled in the breeze. Will sneezed three times and clapped his hand to the wound, fearing to strain the sutures. As if the injury from the duel were not enough, he had woken with an ague.

Their goal was Beacon Hill above Lostwithiel, to report on the practicalities of siting a battery there. On reaching the crest, Captain Pyle called a halt. The men rummaged in their packs for hunks of coarse cheat bread and pieces of cheese while their horses grazed.

A movement behind a bush caught Will's eye. A flash of long, black-tipped ears as the brown hare, disturbed, lolloped away. They were good eating, if you could catch them, he thought regretfully. The hare vanished over what Will realised was an unseen ridge in the hillside.

A moment later something else appeared, close by where the hare had disappeared. He gaped at it puzzled before identifying it as the moving tip of a lance. A flapping cornet came into view, red, bearing a picture of the House of Commons adorned with severed heads. It was a colour of the royalist Lord Spencer's Horse.

Will had imagined this encounter, his first as a soldier of Essex's rebel army, many times. Yet he had always envisaged himself on some great battlefield, the comforting anonymity of thousands of enemy, half obscured by cannon smoke. He would know battle was about to be joined; and there would be time to decide if he could fight former comrades.

Numbness creeping through his veins, Will stared transfixed at the row of helmeted heads bobbing into view. Then discipline, and the habits of two years in the army, made his body respond. Running towards his troop, pain shooting through his side with every step, he yelled a warning to Pyle. 'The enemy!'

Hoisting himself painfully into the saddle, Will gestured towards the rise, where the first rank of the troop of royalist Horse was visible. A trumpet sounded. There was a tightness in Will's chest. He had used the word 'enemy' many times but until this day he had always meant the roundheads.

'Take position,' Pyle ordered. 'Lieutenant Lucie!' With an effort, Will tore his eyes away from the approaching cavaliers.

'For God and Parliament,' Pyle urged, his face troubled.

'For God and Parliament,' Will croaked.

'Good man, then do your duty,' Pyle cantered away to take his place at the head of his fifty six men.

Trotting at the back of the troop, Will watched his own hands checking the primed and loaded pistols, loosening his sword in the scabbard, pulling down his visor. He heard his voice barking commands, 'Third rank, close up. Make ready.'

His words were drowned out by Pyle, unfamiliar harshness in his voice as he bellowed a psalm.

'Whom do we fight?'

'The Amalekites!' the troop roared.

'Where do we strike them?'

'Hip and thigh!'

Trumpets blaring, the two small forces converged. A ragged volley of shot before the opposing sides mingled, entwined in a deadly dance. A red-sashed trooper was charging at Will, his pistol raised. The man's mouth gaped wide, mouthing unintelligible words amid the din. Without conscious thought, Will fired. Smoke and flame, but the ball went wide, as did his adversary's. Breathing out, Will knew a moment of guilty relief.

Another man now, tall with a luxuriant ginger moustache, sword in hand. Will reached for his own familiar blade. He parried the first overhead blow, slashed in his turn, which his opponent parried, and then made a lightning thrust into the neck of the trooper. The sword stuck fast between chin strap and lace-edged collar. A scream, a liquid gurgle of blood from thick, red lips and the blade was torn from Will's hand as the man fell forward on his horse's neck, impaling himself further, and spraying Will with blood.

Will grabbed the hilt and twisted viciously to free it. He stared in disbelief at the royalist blood staining his blade. His face was wet, and he scrubbed at it with his glove, spitting repeatedly. He could taste the man's blood on his tongue.

'Withdraw!' His captain's cry, reinforced by a trumpet call, recalled Will to awareness of where he was. The troop was reforming, the two sides drawing apart in an instant. It was the end of another skirmish, leaving a handful of men on the ground, a horse thrashing in its death agonies while another galloped away in panic, riderless. Pyle's men were cantering, in more or less ordered files, from the field.

One of Pyle's fallen troopers scrambled to his feet unhurt looking wildly around for his horse. 'Here, Moor!' Reining in beside him, Will extended an arm and pulled the trooper onto the saddle behind him.

At the bottom of the hill, Pyle counted heads. Another man was missing, his loose horse galloping alongside the others, trailing a broken rein. Two men had minor sword cuts to the face, and one had a wrist grazed by a bullet.

'We cannot stay for Cooper,' Pyle said sadly of the missing trooper. 'You did well, Lucie.' He regarded Will's crimson-streaked face. 'You are blooded in the cause. Now we must seek intelligence of the enemy's movements. If they are this far south, then the King's main force must be closer than our scouts reported.'

Will rode back surrounded by an embarrassing wave of camaraderie. They did not know what was going through his head. The face of the man he killed remained fresh in his mind, gaping red-lipped mouth, expression of hatred, then horror. A stranger but, for all that, a soldier of the King, and Will had slaughtered him.

CHAPTER 38

News of the skirmish, and Will's part in raising the alarm, soon spread. 'What an odd fellow you are, Lucie,' Robin Lawrence laughed. 'Here is Moor hailing you as hero for snatching him from beneath the hooves of his fallen horse, heaving him onto your beast and preserving him from capture or death. Yet from your countenance you might have seen the death of your favourite hound.'

'Best of all, the enemy is at hand,' Quartermaster Ardington crowed over the hubbub of the crowded alehouse by the bridge over the Fowey. 'I am weary of sparring with women and servants, for the goods they hide in holes in the ground.'

'Aye, let us fight, and make an end to it with one good battle,' Lawrence agreed. He smiled at the pinch-faced girl approaching with wooden bowls of pottage. She placed them on the scarred and rickety table and scurried away.

'Your charm has deserted you, Robin.' Ardington retrieved a horn spoon from his purse and stirred the murky surface.

'As to one good battle ending matters,' Will answered, 'Men said as much before Edgehill.' He grimaced at the mixture of stale bread, scraps of fatty meat and onion.

'And were you there, killing rebels?' Will caught a flicker in Lawrence's eyes.

'Let us not quarrel with the hero of the hour,' Ardington scolded. 'You spoke the truth, Lucie.'

'Of what?'

'Of yourself. You said you would not flee, and you did not.'

Will was saved from replying by a summons from Colonel Robert Pye to the Talbot Inn. Seymour Pyle was with him. It was the first time that Will had been interviewed by his twenty two-year-old colonel. From a distance his iron composure, and the haughty impression conveyed by a long, hooked nose, were forbidding. Close at hand, his composure seemed shyness; and the way he constantly rumpled the untidy brown hair sticking out at the back like a duck's tail, softened Will's former impressions.

'You are quite certain as to the troop colour you saw, Lieutenant?' Colonel Pye asked.

'Yes, Colonel. The colour was well known, a jest in poor taste, for it portrayed the Commons with severed heads upon poles. It was Lord Spencer's regiment.'

'And you last saw this regiment?'

'Fighting with the King's Oxford Army, at Cropredy Bridge.'

'In that case I have a task for you.' Pye stood up, stretching his legs. 'A half dozen of our senior officers, Colonel Aldrich, Colonel Barclay and others of the Lord General's lifeguard, with a handful of men, occupied Boconnoc House two days ago for Parliament. It lies five miles east of here. The two colonels failed to arrive for a council of war this morning. We fear something has gone wrong. Your skirmish has given fresh cause for concern. Take two men and approach Boconnoc House covertly. Bring me word by sunset as to whether the colonels are safe.'

'I am honoured, Sir, but I do not know the country hereabouts. Is there no man more suited to this task?'

Pye smiled. 'We might ask the Lord Robartes, I suppose, but I fear he is too great a personage to use as a scout. No, you have been chosen for your knowledge of the enemy forces. You may recognise further colours, or even officers, and, if challenged, might pass more easily as a King's officer.'

Will bowed, 'Thank you, Sir, for the trust you are placing in me.'

He stared correctly over Pye's shoulder, fearing his commander might read in his eyes how paper-thin was his loyalty to Parliament.

'May Jesus go with you,' Pye said.

'Have a care,' Seymour Pyle added. 'It would go badly with you, should you be taken.'

'I will, Sir.' He needed no reminder that, having deserted his colours, he would be shot if captured by his former comrades.

Wary of losing himself in the narrow lanes, Will engaged a guide, after some difficulty. Although most Cornishmen could speak English, they looked blank when addressed by a roundhead officer. He was rebuffed several times before the promise of a shilling secured a child from the Talbot's kitchens.

Following the boy's gestures, Will and his men trotted down the hill through Lostwithiel. Three more urchins ran alongside, hooting with glee. Their guide, seated in front of Will, chattered in the strange Cornish tongue, thumbing his nose at his friends. When they reached the bridge with its sentries, the impudent escort abandoned them. The boy fell quiet, indicating with his hand the road they should take. Shut in on either side by high hedges, Will could see little of their surroundings as they climbed, but then the road dropped away. Standing on a plateau, facing west, an old, turreted house came into view.

* * *

Boconnoc House

Gabriel sat in his chamber at the bottom of the house's second tower, writing. Its walls were covered in hangings and tapestries of an earlier age. The only light came from windows high in the wall, and candles in wall sconces.

He was anxious to quit Boconnoc House, yet as senior officer there, he could not leave until the servants and staff of the high command arrived to make it ready for the King to take up residence. It would be a close-run thing, for the entourage might include Sir Henry Lucie.

Like the throbbing of an abscessed tooth, Gabriel could not ignore the threat from the implacable baronet.

There must be a way to resolve this. If he could clear himself from the charges laid by Sir Henry, he might turn his attention to removing the cloud of suspicion that hung over him at Basing House. If only he had someone more powerful than Sir Henry Lucie, to intercede for him. Then he recalled his own part in rescuing Lord Wilmot at Cropredy Bridge. It was not the first time he had met the General, and Gabriel thought Wilmot might remember what he had done for him.

Going cap in hand to Lord Wilmot was not an appealing prospect, but he had Bess to consider, and their child.

CHAPTER 39

The boy pointed.

'Boconnoc House?' Will confirmed. He extracted a silver shilling from his purse. Snatching it, the boy slid nimbly to the ground. A moment later he had vanished into the woods. Will swung himself out of the saddle. 'Look after my horse,' he said to his two men. 'If I do not return by sunset, tell Colonel Pye that I have been taken, and that Boconnoc House is in the hands of the enemy.'

Despite Colonel Pye's belief that Will might pass himself off as a royalist officer, Will's hope was that he might reconnoitre unobserved. If the house remained in the hands of Parliament, he could be truthful about his mission. If he encountered royalists, his best chance might be passing himself off as a visiting gentleman.

He removed his sash and buff coat, together with the belt attached to his carbine. Wearing his cloak and a dark blue Montero cap, a loaded pistol concealed beneath the cloak, he climbed over the low wall surrounding the park and crept towards the house. Rain was falling again, leaching the colour from the landscape as he crouched in the bushes near the gatehouse. The gate opened to allow two men, servants by the look of them, to leave, and then shut again.

Will gazed in frustration at the blank face of the wall surrounding the medieval house. The jangle of harness and rattling drew his attention to three covered wagons trundling over the bridge across the river. As they began to ascend the steep slope towards the gatehouse, their pace slowed. Emerging from the bushes, Will clambered onto the low back of the last wagon, full of tightly packed hay. He burrowed into it with some difficulty. The driver of the first wagon hailed the gatehouse and the wagons jolted through the gate. Will held his breath. What he might have done if the hay was immediately unloaded, he did not know, but his luck held.

A bell rang and he heard, 'Put the nags in the stable. The men will help you with unloading once they have had their dinner.' Jingling as horses were unharnessed, the clop of hooves as they were led away, then silence.

Will stuck his head out. The wagon was drawn up in an extensive courtyard, surrounded on all four sides by stone buildings, some with glazed windows. Staying close to the wall, Will edged towards the nearest door. He heard the hum of conversation and the clatter of plates. It must be the Great Hall, where dinner would be in progress for the household. Whoever was in command, the life of Boconnoc was going on as usual. Will headed in the opposite direction until he found a service passage. He passed a pantry and then a buttery where a servant was filling blackjacks with ale. The man looked up.

'If you seek the Colonel, you'll find un in his chamber, most like.' He pointed down the passageway behind him.

'Thankyou,' Will mumbled. The man returned to his task. Will walked on, heart thumping. If he found this colonel, he would know one way or the other what had happened. If he were one of Essex's missing colonels, all was well, and Will himself was safe; but if the colonel was a royalist and realised the intruder was a spy, Will would need to kill him to make good his escape. It was many weeks since he had deserted, and word must have got around by now that a captain in Northampton's regiment had deserted. He could not use the cover of his former rank and regiment.

At the end of the passage, the wall curved into the base of a tower. The interior was dim, but candlelight glowed beneath a door. Will pulled out his loaded pistol and checked the priming. Looking at the curving wall, he realised firing a shot would create an echo. He could not afford the risk of raising the alarm. Thrusting the firearm into his boot, making sure it was only at half cock, he drew his sword and pressed his ear to the closed door. There was no sound of voices. Will eased the latch upward.

The man was seated at a table, his back to the door, reading a letter. His cloak, buff coat and sword belt were hanging from pegs hammered into the wall, but the red sash around his waist told Will all he needed to know. Boconnoc had been recaptured by the royalists.

Gabriel turned his head. 'Will!' He leapt to his feet, a smile lighting up his face for a brief moment. It vanished, and Will realised that Gabriel knew he was a deserter and had guessed he was a spy. Only a few paces lay between them, but neither attempted to cross the tiled floor.

'Why are you here?' Gabriel asked, his lilting voice wary. 'Were you seeking me?'

Will gave a tiny shake of his head. Gabriel's eyes swerved towards the sword belt hanging on the wall.

'Let it be, Gabriel,' Will ordered. 'I mean you no harm.'

Gabriel inclined his head, a gleam of amusement in his eyes.

'Where are they? What has become of them?' Will asked.

'Do you speak of the rebel colonels who were here?'

Will winced at the emphasis Gabriel laid on the word 'rebel'. 'I am speaking of the officers of the Lord General's regiment, who must be either dead or under lock and key, since you have evidently supplanted them.'

Gabriel grimaced. 'Since this house is the lawful possession of Lord Mohun, who is with the King, I believe it is your forces who supplanted him, but we will not quarrel over words.'

'Are they alive?' Will pursued.

'We slew one of them, Robin Cambridge, an ensign. The others are prisoners, but not here,' Gabriel replied. He nodded at the naked blade in Will's hand. 'Do you intend to fight me? If not, I suggest you sheath it.'

Will stared at his brother-in-law whose cat-like green eyes returned his gaze candidly. While Will held the sword, he had Gabriel at a disadvantage. Will loved and respected him, but they were now enemies.

'Are you alone?' Gabriel probed.

'Let us not waste more time. You will see me safe out of this place.' There was a tightness in Will's chest.

'And if I do not?' Gabriel asked politely.

'Then I will do whatever is necessary to secure my withdrawal, for my duty is to Parliament.' Will sheathed his sword, then bent to retrieve the pistol from his boot.

Out of the corner of his eye, he saw Gabriel springing for the sword belt. Will reacted quickly, but by the time he drew his blade once more, Gabriel had freed his from the scabbard. Sword in hand, the two men faced each other across the table.

'Check?'

The use of the chess term exasperated Will, as did the half smile on Gabriel's lips.

'Had I not helped you escape from Oxford last winter, you would not be here now,' Will said hotly. 'Do you owe me nothing for that?' He lunged at Gabriel, who parried. The steel blades met with a loud clash which reverberated off the tower walls. Will flinched at the sound.

'Is the earl so short of officers that he must send one whose loyalty is suspect?' Gabriel's tone was playful. Colouring at the taunt, Will tugged the dagger from his belt. Gabriel looked deliberately from the dagger in Will's left hand to the sword in his right.

'I see this is no jest.' Snatching his cloak from its peg, Gabriel hurled it at Will.

'Is that how the Welsh fight?' Will growled at the unorthodox move.

'The Welsh fight as they must. Am I the one with a dagger in his hand?'

Will disentangled his dagger from the folds of the cloak, but Gabriel had used the time to edge towards the door from his position near the wall. Will moved quickly, intercepting him before he reached it.

'You will never leave this place without my aid,' Gabriel said calmly. 'Surrender and return to the right side. Your conscience will be clear, and His Majesty may be merciful.'

'And who will plead for me?' Will snapped. 'You, who live in daily expectation of your own arrest?'

The barb struck home. Gabriel's voice was cold when he answered. 'Not I. Your old commander, the Earl of Northampton may be able to intercede.'

'It is too late.' Desolate, Will lowered his blade and Gabriel pounced, knocking the sword from his hand. Will jumped backward, tugging the loaded pistol from his boot. 'That was a low trick.'

Gabriel eyed the pistol. 'If you give fire, you will bring a hornet's nest about your ears.'

'I must take that chance. You will escort me past the gatehouse and give me your word that you will not have me pursued. Lay down your sword.'

'If that is your wish.' Gabriel laid the weapon on the table and picked up his hat. 'Well, Sir, I am ready.'

Wrapping the pistol in a fold of his cloak, Will gestured for Gabriel to precede him. 'Do not play me false.' Twice they encountered servants in yellow and black livery, who bowed respectfully to Gabriel, tugging the caps off their heads. Finally, they reached the courtyard. There were the wagons, standing unattended. Dinner was still in progress. Will breathed an audible sigh of relief.

Gabriel turned his head. 'There is the gatehouse. It is fortunate for you that you made your visit today when there are none but my own troops here.' His voice was clipped and disdainful now, that of an aristocratic officer. He did not explain his meaning, but Will was intent only on passing the gatehouse.

'The gate?'

'They will open it for me, never fear.' Gabriel passed between the wagons. For a few moments they were out of sight of the gatehouse and its troopers standing guard. There was a blur of movement and Will found the point of a dagger pressed to his throat.

'You drew on me once before, Will. Had it not been for Harry and Bess we might have spilled each other's blood. And again today. Let there not be a third time, brother.'

Gabriel replaced the blade in his belt, beneath his doublet. 'I have not forgotten your help in removing me from Oxford Castle. You have walked into a trap by coming here.'

Will shuddered. 'Myself, or the army of Lord Essex?'

The green cat-eyes narrowed. 'Both, but I will not lead you to the scaffold.' Emerging from behind the wagon he shouted, 'Morgan, Blake, open the gate so this gentleman may leave.'

'How is my sister?' Will muttered.

'Bess is well, and with God's blessing she will be a mother when I see her next.' A hint of warmth crept back into Gabriel's voice.

'Tell her I love her and think of her every day.'

Gabriel only nodded. As Will passed through the gate, he thought he heard 'I will pray for you,' but when he turned around, Gabriel was gone, and the heavy, iron-studded door of the gatehouse was swinging shut.

CHAPTER 40

The Allt

———

'What will you name your daughter?' Elspeth Henderson enquired.

Bess was holding court, sitting up in the high bed, an embroidered coif covering her dark hair. Mistress Henderson and Elspeth were wearing their smartest silk gowns for the important ritual of visiting the new mother and baby. The wet nurse sat beside the oak cradle, rocking it with her foot, while Gwyneth handed round steaming goblets of caudle, spiced with cinnamon and nutmeg. A cool breeze blew through the half open casement, opened at Bess's insistence. With so many women present, and a fire smouldering in the hearth, she felt suffocated.

Bess sipped the caudle. 'I wish to name her Frances.'

Mistress Henderson twitched at her deep lace falling band. Small and plump, she reminded Bess of a hen pheasant fluffing her plumage. 'Has Gabriel given his consent?' Irritated by the question, Bess stifled a retort.

'The army is gone into the west,' Lady Alice said. 'They were at Exeter when last we had any news of Gabriel.'

'Why, whatever are they doing so far away?' Mistress Henderson squeaked. 'How will they protect us from this Colonel Massey in Gloucestershire that I hear of, if he comes calling?'

'I feel sure that if there was danger to us here, Gabriel would have sent a warning. He has not done so, and therefore I believe we are safe.'

Bess's vehement tone earned her a look of surprise from Mistress Henderson.

'Might I have another of those sweetmeats?' Elspeth interposed. 'The honey is quite delicious.'

'It is from our own hives,' Lady Alice said.

Bess stifled a yawn. Elspeth and her mother took the hint.

'We will leave you to sleep, Mistress Vaughan. May Our Lady bring you and your daughter many blessings,' Mistress Henderson smiled. Lady Alice ushered her swiftly from the room. The word 'baptism' floated back.

'How many more days?' Elspeth whispered.

'Fifteen more before my month of lying in is done and I am free of this chamber. Visit me again when I am no longer a captive.'

Elspeth bobbed a curtsey and hurried in pursuit of her mother. Bess had warmed to her afresh now that she knew there had never been more than friendship between her and Gabriel.

'Go, Bron, and rest while the baby sleeps,' she said to the plump wet nurse. Climbing from the bed Bess crossed the rush-matted floor to the window and threw it open wider. The scent of roses, their petals battered by wind and rain, drifted from the gardens. She wondered what the 'baptism' conversation had been about.

A few days later, that question was answered. 'The baby is healthy,' Lady Alice began. 'Yet we should have her baptised before long.'

'We cannot do so without Gabriel,' Bess protested. She had set her heart on naming her daughter Frances Anne in honour of her own mother, but Gabriel might have other names in mind.

'We cannot allow her soul to continue in a state of sin much longer,' was the tart response. 'Would you condemn her to limbo?' Bess sighed, remembering the newly-learnt Catholic doctrine of the fate of babies who died before baptism.

'We might have your churching on the same day as the baptism,' Lady Alice said. The churching ritual, giving thanks for her safe recovery from childbirth, could not come soon enough for Bess. It marked the end of her confinement. And during those remaining days, Gabriel might return.

CHAPTER 41

Sir Henry Lucie dismounted outside the three-storey, grey stone town-house in Barras Street where the King was staying with the town's Mayor. He tossed a coin to a boy to hold Fleet, his high-spirited grey stallion. Some of the gentlemen of the King's Lifeguard were outside with their fine animals and costly equipment. A crown and royal cypher adorned a crimson cornet edged with a wide gold fringe. Lord Bernard Stuart, the flamboyant 21-year-old commander of the King's own troop strode through the archway into the street, flinging back his blue velvet cloak to display the fine lace and matching blue of the silk doublet beneath. He was followed by Sir Edward Walker.

'Ah, Lucie. Not before time.' Walker jerked his head and Sir Henry, puzzled at the unexplained summons, followed him into a neglected formal garden. The hedges dividing the walks were untrimmed, and a carpet of sodden blossoms had turned gravel paths to mud underfoot. Walker brushed at a stone bench before seating himself. 'Gardeners all gone of course. His Majesty needs every man who can hold a musket.'

Sir Henry remained standing while the Secretary toyed with a gold and ruby ring. 'His Majesty has an important commission for you. You must carry a letter to Devereux in secret at Lostwithiel where the rebel army lies.

'His Majesty's advisers are convinced the Earl has lost his appetite for the fight. Now that the tide has turned so far in our favour, the time is ripe to pressure him to return to his proper allegiance. You have authority to negotiate, but make no promises that may embarrass His Majesty, or it will be upon your own head.'

The heavens were smiling on him at last. 'If I succeed in this, Sir, may I have Vaughan arrested?'

Unexpectedly, the Secretary smiled. 'If you succeed in this today, we may have peace, and there will be no further need for field armies and Lieutenant Colonel Vaughan. In which case I will personally see the man arrested. But remember you go in secret, not as an emissary of the King. You must find a way of seeing Devereux that does not arouse suspicion.'

There was a way, providing Hugh Lucie remained on Essex's staff. Sir Henry would swallow his pride and beg his assistance. 'Needs must when the devil drives,' he thought.

Fleet snorted as Sir Henry approached the old bridge over the Fowey on his way to Lostwithiel. The once great river had silted up from centuries of tin mining and was no longer deep enough for any shipping larger than a barge. Nevertheless, the rain-swollen waters surged brown and opaque between the arches.

A company of rebel Foot was on guard. Ahead of him were two women carrying heavy baskets, a pedlar with a wagon laden with everything from pots to trinkets and a soberly dressed man on horseback.

The precious letter from King Charles to Robert Devereux, Earl of Essex and commander of the rebels, was sewn into the red silk lining of Sir Henry's coat. He had done his best to avoid suspicion by dressing as a civilian in a dark blue woollen cassack, buttoned to the neck; and carried no weapon but the sword which all gentlemen wore.

'Your business?' yawned a bored, tawny-sashed corporal, scratching his crotch. His eyes lingered on the grey stallion's glossy coat and proudly-arched neck, but he scarcely glanced at the middle-aged gentleman rider until Sir Henry said he had urgent family business with his brother, one of the Earl's staff. The corporal woke up with a jolt.

'Wait here.'

Pulling his cassack tighter against the driving rain, Sir Henry feigned nonchalance while the man sent for an officer. The reality of his mission, the trust which the King had placed in him, was a weighty burden. Sweat trickled down inside his fine cambric shirt. He raised a hand to tug at the lace falling band about his neck and dropped it again. He must avoid signs of nervousness.

The officer was not long in arriving. His coat was stained, his sash tattered, and his boots covered in mud.

'Dismount, Sir.'

Keeping a tight grip on the stallion's bridle, Sir Henry complied.

'What is your business with His Excellency's staff?' The officer's gaze was keen. 'And why have you come alone?'

'Alone?' The unexpected question confounded him.

'Unattended by any servant.'

'My man is sick with the flux.'

'I see.' The officer signed a piece of paper and handed it to Sir Henry. 'I cannot promise that this pass will gain you admittance to Colonel Lucie, but it should ensure that you are not barred from entering the Lord General's headquarters at Lanhydrock.'

Sir Henry remounted Fleet with relief and crossed the bridge into the town. He clicked his tongue in annoyance at the necessity of enlisting his younger brother's help. Hugh's Puritan foibles had caused tension long before they chose opposing sides on the outbreak of war in '42.

Lanhydrock, was a further three miles ride. Sir Henry made way for a smart troop of cavalry splashing out of its gate. The flag was tawny orange, with a motto *Comes Virtutis Invidia*. He guessed they were part of the earl's personal lifeguard.

Producing the pass, Sir Henry was waved onward towards the main house, whose fine new granite buildings trumpeted the wealth and power of its owner, Lord Robartes. He dismounted in a vast courtyard. A spiky-haired groom ran out, a sack draped over his shoulders, to take the horse. The stallion shied.

'Have a care, fool,' Sir Henry snapped, his nerves fraying like the tattered edge of the sack. Shaking himself like a wet dog, he followed a servant in red-and-yellow livery into the house.

* * *

'Is Colonel Lucie expecting you, Sir?' The young aide wore an officer's military leather buff coat. Its sleeves were hooped with bright silver lace and the sash about his waist was perfectly folded.

'I have only recently arrived in Cornwall and have had no time to advise him of it,' Sir Henry lied.

'Your name?'

'I am Colonel Lucie's elder brother, Henry.'

'Wait here please, Sir.'

Left alone, Sir Henry walked to a deep window overlooking rain-drenched gardens. Drooping blooms and battered shrubs bore testimony to the bleakness of the season. The room itself was warm and pleasant, a bright fire burning to keep summer chill at bay. The sound of approaching footsteps was followed by a few words between two speakers.

'He is in here, Colonel,' in the well-bred tones of the aide and 'You may return to your duties.' That was Hugh's voice. It was a step forward – Hugh had not refused to see him.

The door opened. It was nearly two years since they had met. There were harsher lines carved into Hugh's face, darkened from campaigning to a hue more suited to farmer or labourer than gentleman. His attire however was unchanged, black silk and velvet, a tall-crowned hat and the tawny sash about his waist.

'Well, Henry what brings you to see me this time? Is it Will?' Hugh's tone was icy.

'Will? My son? No, Hugh, why would I wish to see you about Will?'

'No matter. I told you last time when you approached me in the midst of the army that I could have you arrested as an enemy officer. What foolishness makes you risk a second encounter?' Hugh closed the door behind him and seated himself in an elaborately carved chair. He drummed impatient fingers on the arm.

'Are you trying to sit in judgement upon me?' Sir Henry snarled, before recollecting he was in sore need of Hugh's good offices. 'Forgive me. I spoke hastily. I need your help in arranging an urgent meeting with His Excellency. Is he here?'

'The Lord General is very busy. Why should he consent to see a malignant officer?'

'I have a letter for him. I may deliver it to none but he.'

'You expect me to be satisfied with that? You must do better than that, if you need my help.'

'But it is imperative you help!'

'I bid you good day.' Hugh opened the door.

'Wait, Hugh. It seems I must confide in you. The letter is from His Majesty.'

Hugh froze, one hand on the door handle, then he nodded abruptly and stalked from the room. For the first few minutes Sir Henry stood facing the door expectantly, but then reproached himself for foolishness. He removed his hat and draped his damp cassack over the back of a chair before the fire. By the time he heard slow footsteps approaching, the heavy cloth was almost dry. The man who entered was recognisable from news sheets. Robert Devereux, third Earl of Essex, was no more than three or four years older than Sir Henry, but his greying hair and weary face told of strain and ill health.

'I trust you are not wasting my time, Sir. Colonel Lucie tells me you have intelligence which is for my ears alone.'

Sir Henry bowed. 'Your pardon, My Lord while I retrieve it from its hiding place.'

The Earl grew restive while Sir Henry slit open the stitches in his coat with a dagger. He extracted the letter, sealed only with a plain wafer for greater secrecy. Devereux took it and broke the seal. Turning his back, he perused the words. There was no sound in the room but the Earl's ragged breathing and the thumping of Sir Henry's own heart.

If there were peace, with Parliament's rebel commander submitting to the King, that grateful sovereign would see Sir Henry's confiscated lands restored. Other honours might follow.

Devereux folded the sheet carefully and held it out. 'My answer is no.'

Sir Henry stared at him. 'It is from His Majesty.'

'I am aware of that,' Devereux replied. 'I know his hand. And my answer is no.' His voice was firm.

'And is that your only reply to His Majesty? Will you not write to him?' Sir Henry saw his mission crumbling before his eyes. 'Do you not wish to consider his generous proposals, My Lord? He will restore you to his royal favour if you return to your obedience to him.'

'My answer remains no.' The Earl lifted his chin, his face haughty. He had not raised his voice, but Sir Henry sensed his growing impatience, that of a nobleman accustomed to command. 'And putting the words on paper will not change them. You may tell His Majesty I will not negotiate with him. He should go to the parliament at Westminster. There is no more to say.' Breaking off in a fit of coughing, Devereux quit the room, a handkerchief pressed to his mouth.

Left alone, Sir Henry stared out of the window, but the leaden sky held no answers. Burying his rising despair, he stamped back to the stables. England had missed its chance of peace; but Sir Henry's thoughts were on his own dashed hopes.

CHAPTER 42

Fleet was skittish on the return journey. Jogging sideways through Lostwithiel's crowded streets, his hooves slid on the greasy cobbles. Sir Henry was relieved to reach the end of the long street leading to the bridge over the Fowey. Only one obstacle remained, a busy inn hard by the bridge. Drunken soldiers spilled from its doors. So much for the godly reputation of the rebel army, he gloated. A heavily bearded cavalry trooper was wobbling his way across the street. Sir Henry clamped his legs more firmly to the horse's sides. If he trampled the sot under Fleet's hooves, it would be a short-lived triumph.

Emerging from the inn was a tall soldier. Walking briskly, he thrust the drunkard out of the way. He wore a tawny sash knotted across his shoulder which marked him as one of Essex's officers. Only his back was visible to Sir Henry, but the angle of his head, the way he carried himself and the corn-coloured hair falling to his shoulders from beneath his hat, were unmistakeable. It was his son Will.

'Wait! Will! Come back!' The father's anguished cry went unheard in the hubbub of the street. Sir Henry tried to keep Will in sight, standing in his stirrups, but within moments of recognising him, his son was swallowed in the crowds.

'Is it Will?' Belatedly, he understood Hugh's question. He had banished his son from his mind, or so he believed. The last news had been Will's disappearance following the battle at Cropredy Bridge nearly two months earlier. Will had abandoned his father and his family. The discovery that he had also turned traitor should not matter. And yet, somehow, it did. He longed to see Will's face and hear his voice.

A mile or more remained before he reached Liskeard. Instead of formulating excuses to give the King, Sir Henry slumped in his saddle, thinking only of Will. Inattentive to approaching hoofbeats, he was taken by surprise when a royalist cavalry patrol surged into sight around a bend. The leading riders swerved to avoid him, but the startled Fleet reared, slipped on the muddy road and fell, pinning Sir Henry beneath him.

CHAPTER 43

Liskeard

'My Lord Wilmot is very occupied with business, Colonel. I will inform him that you wish to see him, but . . .' The aide spread his hands apologetically.

'Would you say this to him, 'Lieutenant Colonel Gabriel Vaughan seeks to remind you of Cropredy Bridge.' Gabriel coloured.

'Those words alone?'

'Just those words.'

Gabriel squeezed past the crowd of cavalry officers thronging the steps into the street. As Lieutenant General of royalist Horse, Wilmot was lodged in a modern brick house not far from the mayor's house. A few minutes later he appeared, resplendent in white silk trimmed with deep ruffled lace cuffs more suited to court than to battlefield.

His eyes alighting on Gabriel, Wilmot stared for a moment as if testing his recollections, but then he strode forward. A wide smile lit up his face in the way that kept the Horse enthralled. He held his wounded arm stiffly, but no longer wore a sling.

'Colonel Vaughan, I am honoured to renew our acquaintance.' Gabriel bowed and Wilmot returned it. 'I have not had the opportunity to thank you for the great service you rendered me at Cropredy Bridge,' Wilmot continued smoothly. 'If I believed my life was more important than my honour, it would not need brave men like you to rescue me.' The boastful words were softened by an unabashed chuckle. Gabriel felt himself succumbing to Wilmot's famous charm. 'Now that we meet, I hope I may do you some slight service in return.'

'My Lord, I would not have approached you if I had seen an alternative,' Gabriel confessed, wondering how it was that this man had made enemies of other Generals.

'Then let us walk,' Wilmot said, 'While you tell me what is troubling you.'

Gabriel's carefully chosen words sounded hollow and unconvincing to him as he described his predicament. When he finished, Wilmot pursed his full lips.

'I will hope to speak to His Majesty before nightfall. There are weighty matters of state in hand which will, if successful, bring me high in his favour. I am confident that he will make light of, if you will forgive me, such a trivial matter and have it dismissed from your record, should I request it. Today, my enemies are still powerful enough to challenge my wishes.'

'Thank you, My Lord on behalf of myself and my wife.'

Wilmot nodded, but from the expression on his face his mind was already returned to the 'weighty matters'. 'Come and see me again tomorrow morning, at nine o'clock, and I will tell you what success I have had. Good day to you, Colonel Vaughan and my best wishes to your lady for a safe delivery and the birth of an heir.'

CHAPTER 44

Liskeard

---

8 August

Barras Street was a hive of activity when Gabriel and Ieuan arrived in Liskeard the next morning. Cavalry filled the wide cobbled street, adding piles of horse droppings to the general detritus which strewed the stones, despite the efforts of the overnight scavengers who cleaned the streets. Officers barked orders, while laggards flung saddles on their horses' backs. The command to mount sounded repeatedly from a dozen bugles.

Leaving Blackbird with Ieuan, Gabriel was squeezing his way through the crowd when Wilmot emerged from the house. His face was tense and preoccupied. He caught sight of Gabriel and paused. Annoyance flitted across his face, swiftly replaced by a charming, apologetic smile. 'Colonel Vaughan.'

'Good morning, My Lord.'

'You have arrived in good time, Sir, but I regret I have no news for you today. Circumstances are not yet favourable.' Wilmot spread his hands.

Gabriel knew better than to question the General in front of his troops. 'Then I will return another day, My Lord.'

'Good man.' Wilmot flung his cloak back over his shoulder, displaying its scarlet lining, and leapt into the saddle with ease. Gathering the reins in his left hand, he swept the feathered hat off his head in homage to his troops.

'Good morning, gentlemen of the Horse.' There were close to 1,500 men gathered, but there was an immediate hush, broken only by the jingling of harness and the stamping of hooves. Gabriel halted to listen. 'Gentlemen, today we ride . . .'

'My Lord Wilmot,' a strident voice interjected. A score of musketeers were shouldering their way between the ranks of horses. At their head, Gabriel recognised the tall, thin form of Sir Edward Sydenham, the Knight Marshal, the officer of the King's household responsible for preserving order in peace as well as war. Wilmot turned pale.

'Henry, Lord Wilmot, you are accused of high treason for conspiring and seeking to bring comfort to the King's enemy, Robert Devereux. Guards, seize him.'

Angry murmurs rippled through the mass of cavalry; and a loud rasp of steel as sword blades emerged from their scabbards. Gabriel held his breath. If the troopers attempted to intervene, it would amount to mutiny.

'Hold! Gentlemen of the Horse,' Wilmot's voice rang out, shaking with emotion. 'I am innocent of these charges. Yet His Majesty's commands must be obeyed. Sir,' He turned his head towards the Knight Marshal. 'I will go with you.'

Wilmot swung himself down from his horse. He adjusted his hat, smoothed his collar and walked with measured tread towards the men who had come to arrest him. Head held high he took his place in the midst of the escort. The Knight Marshal had the good sense not to lay hands on the commander. He gave a quiet order and the men marched away. Gabriel watched in disbelief. Wilmot's arrest had brought the King's cause inexorably nearer to its end.

* * *

Later that day, the King's Lifeguard arrived at Boconnoc and Gabriel was finally relieved of responsibility for the House. But that night, back in his old quarters in Liskeard, he lay sleepless, thinking of Wilmot's predicament and the effect on his own future. Any prospect of Gabriel receiving a pardon had melted like snow in May.

Eventually he rose and kindled a light. Ieuan appeared, sandy hair tousled, yawning. '*Ydych chi'n llwglyd, Meistr?*'

Gabriel chuckled. Ieuan's first thought was always that he might need food. 'No, thank you, Ieuan. Go back to bed.'

Gabriel rummaged for his half-written song, *How fair is she I love.* He hummed a few notes under his breath, but the melody remained elusive. Instead, he took a fresh sheet of paper and a piece of charcoal. The light from the single wax candle burned clear. It was the last of the supply he had brought from The Allt.

With sure and certain strokes, the outline of a face took shape, large eyes with long eyelashes, full lips, straight dark hair spilling loose over bare shoulders. The sketch of Bess complete, Gabriel licked his fingers to pinch out the flame, but instead found himself staring longingly at the face of his beautiful wife. Imagining the swelling of her breasts and belly as they might be in these last weeks of pregnancy, there was a familiar stirring in his body.

The church said that sexual pleasure must be confined to congress between man and wife, but his wife was many days travel from him, and Gabriel hungered for her. Resigned to the fact that he was already condemned to a lengthy period in Purgatory for his many sins, Gabriel's hand dropped lower, a smile lingering on his lips.

* * *

Gabriel set out the next morning for a farmhouse outside the town. After his sleepless night he had woken with the inkling of an idea. When Ieuan held out the travel and blood-stained buff coat, Gabriel shook his head. 'Not today. Bring me the embroidered baldric for my sword – and my Dutch coat.'

'Does my heart good, seeing you turned out as a proper gentleman for once.' Ieuan grinned, fetching the fine wool blue coat with alacrity. He buttoned it over Gabriel's doublet and turned back the wide cuffs, displaying the white silk lining.

'Hmm,' was Gabriel's non-committal answer.

Many of the Royalist cavalry officers crammed into the modest parlour of the farmhouse appeared apprehensive. Beside the fireplace stood a tall officer with shoulders crooked over like a heron. His long legs encased in riding boots pulled tightly up his thighs as if for battle reinforced the idea of the water bird. It was Aymes Pollard, second in command of Wilmot's own regiment of Horse. When the flow of arrivals had eased to a trickle, Pollard consulted a silver pocket watch and flicked it shut. 'Gentlemen, we are come together in defence of an honourable gentleman, Henry Wilmot.'

'We must free him without delay!' shouted a man with fierce blue eyes whose face was scarred by a sword cut. 'If we ride hard, we might yet overtake his escort on the road to Exeter . . .'

'And thus leave ourselves open to charges of treason,' an older man growled.

'I believe there may be another way,' Gabriel interrupted. After introducing himself, he explained his plan.

* * *

'Humbly beg His Majesty to let us know what fault Lord Wilmot has committed, that we may implore the King's pardon for it.' His eyes red-rimmed with weariness, Gabriel laid down his quill. The grey light of dawn was inching through the cracks in the shutters. Agreeing the wording of the petition to the King had taken many hours.

The other two men got to their feet, stretching stiff limbs and knocking out their pipes in the cooling embers of the fire. An empty jug of ale and wooden platters bearing scraps of cold meat and a solitary heel of cheese sat forgotten on the flagstone floor. Gabriel smiled at their shadowy faces, indistinct in the dim light and the fug of tobacco. 'What do you think?'

'I do not say it will win his freedom, or restore him to his former command, but if we put our names to it, we must hope the King will spare his life.' Aymes Pollard's face was grey with fatigue. 'I will take this petition and seek the signatures of as many officers of Horse as I can find. But first, let us put our own names to it.'

There was a long pause as the three officers considered what they were about to do. Then Pollard seized the quill and signed his name, writing his rank and regiment beside his name. He handed the pen to Gabriel. The first three signatures on the parchment, Pollard gave a deep bow, took the petition and left the room, followed by the other man.

Yawning, Gabriel threw open the shutters, drawing sweet morning air into his lungs. The table was covered with sheets of paper, much smudged and crossed through. Writing in Gabriel's neat hand was accompanied by additions in the margins from his two companions. The ink pot was almost empty, and the drip pans of the candle sticks were full. Gathering the discarded papers together, Gabriel coaxed the glowing embers, feeding them with kindling until they began to flame, then he pushed the bundle into the fire. The dangers of their various rejected attempts, and their thoughts, being discovered, made destruction a necessary precaution. When nothing remained but ash, Gabriel picked up his own cast-off clothing, closed the door behind him and trudged towards the stables. He was looking forward to an hour or two of sleep.

It was two days later that Gabriel received a letter. He did not recognise the hand, nor the seal. Opening it, he read,

'Sir, our efforts have borne fruit. My Lord Wilmot's life is spared. He is to be exiled.'

'Good news, Master?' Ieuan had been watching his expression.

'Good and bad. The petition was of some use, and I thank God. My Lord Wilmot is banished. But it leaves the royalist cause the poorer.' Gabriel was disturbed that the King did not reciprocate the loyalty he expected from his supporters, and his people.

'Might a petition be raised in your defence?'

'Mine?' Gabriel laughed. 'The fate of an unknown Welsh lieutenant colonel of Horse will never merit such action. No, I must shift for myself.' But he knew it was no joke, for he had lost the one man who would have championed Gabriel's cause.

214

CHAPTER 45

Respryn Bridge, near Lostwithiel

'Solid, and much of it is granite.' Will peered closely at the arches of Respryn Bridge and poked at the stones with his dagger. 'We need an engineer.'

The bridge was barely two miles from Lostwithiel and Captain Seymour Pyle had decided to demolish it, hoping to delay the enemy crossing the Fowey. The army was being pushed nearer and nearer towards the sea.

'We are delivering our heads on a plate as Salome did with that of John the Baptist.' Pyle smacked his hat against his thigh in frustration.

'Might we send for an engineer?' Will repeated.

'You are very eager to hold this bridge against your former comrades.'

Will's feelings were confused. While he had succeeded in his mission at Boconnoc House, resentment at Gabriel's actions lingered. Will's brief report had omitted the encounter with his brother-in-law, stating only that the house had been captured and the missing officers taken. Was he seeking further success as an officer to justify to himself his change of allegiance? 'We have not marched all this way, Sir, to tamely surrender that which we have taken,' he replied.

'An admirable sentiment, but unless Waller's reinforcements arrive, our forces are too small to fight the united armies of the King in open battle.' Pyle was interrupted by the arrival of a messenger.

'Captain Pyle, I bring new orders.'

'You are required to bring your troop with all speed to Lanhydrock House,' Pyle read aloud. *'The Lord General is moving his command to*

Lostwithiel. You will provide escort for his staff and their personal goods.' I believed we did the Lord's will, but now I perceive it is that of venal men who care only for themselves and their possessions.' A look of disgust on his face, Pyle screwed the letter into a ball and tossed it to the ground.

Will placed a cautionary hand on his arm. 'My advice is to keep it, to show cause why you abandoned the bridge.'

'You think I may need to prove my orders?' Pyle enquired in disgust, picking up the scrunched up letter and thrusting it into his purse.

Lanhydrock's entrance and spacious central courtyard were humming with activity when the troop arrived. Servants and soldiers were loading barrels of beef, beer, wheels of cheese and sacks of other provender onto wagons. A middle-aged man, a silver chain of office around his neck, bustled forward. 'Sir, what is this intrusion? The household is engaged in packing His Lordship's valuables.'

Will did not hear Pyle's measured response, but it evidently mollified the steward. A servant took Pyle's horse, and the officer vanished through a distant doorway.

An empty carriage stood waiting, the open door displaying crimson velvet cushions. Four matched greys were already in the traces. Two gold-braided senior officers issued from another doorway. A servant hurried to let down the step and the older of the pair climbed in. It must be the Earl, Robert Devereux himself, Will thought. He was followed by a younger man who Will recognised as Lord Robartes.

Next came a lady, accompanied by a maid carrying a prayer book. Catching sight of Will, mistress gestured towards him, and the maid hurried forward. 'My Lady wishes to speak to you.'

Lucy, Lady Robartes' beautiful face was drawn and anxious. Her black silk bodice and petticoats accentuated its pallor. 'Sir, what is your name?' she enquired in a clear voice.

'William Lucie, My Lady, lieutenant.'

'My three children are remaining here, Lieutenant. The two younger have measles, and the eldest refuses to quit their side. I charge you to keep them safe for a day or two until our physician agrees they are well enough to travel. He fears exposing them to damp humours would be bad for them. They . . .'

'Lucy, my love.' Lord Robartes stepped down from the carriage. 'His Excellency waits for you.' The mild words were accompanied by a look demanding immediate obedience.

'May Lord Jesus keep my children safe, and you who guards them,' she whispered, before following her husband. Essex's Lifeguard of Horse took up their positions to either side, and the carriage rolled out of the courtyard as Pyle reappeared.

'Our task begins. The Lord General's staff will follow within the hour. We are escorting them, their servants and whatever baggage is ready.'

'Sir, I must remain here.' Will quickly explained.

'Then you must stay.' Pyle frowned as more servants appeared, staggering under the weight of heavy wooden chests.

The steward was shouldering his way through them. 'Remove those barrels of beef. Take this chest with the tapestries, the carpets from Flanders, this one with My Lord's books. Dolt!' His voice rose. 'I will have you whipped.' A hapless lad had dropped a painting, splintering the frame.

'Sir, there is not time for this,' Pyle said.

The steward glared at him. 'My Lord's treasures must not be plundered. This house may be new, but My Lord has many possessions of great antiquity.'

'My orders are to arrange safe conduct for the Lord General's staff, their own servants and such personal goods as can be conveniently transported, that is all,' Pyle responded.

Leaving them arguing, Will went in search of the Robartes children. A servant directed him through the long gallery. Gaps on the wall below the vaulted ceiling showed where servants had removed paintings. A distant wail suggested he was on the right track. Pushing open a door he saw a young maidservant bending over a fractious small girl in a bed. The child's cheeks were flushed and covered with a red rash. A second woman, plump and middle-aged, was seated in the window sewing. Catching sight of Will she snatched up a chamber pot and brandished it.

'And who might you be?'

'I mean you no harm. My Lady Robartes wishes me to remain behind with the children until they are well enough to travel.' Will spread his hands to emphasise his peaceful intent.

The child in the bed sat up. 'Oh, do put that pot down, Nan,' she piped, scratching at a spot on her face.

'By whose authority are you in the apartments of my brother and sister?' An older boy of eleven or twelve, was standing in the doorway of an interconnecting room. Fully dressed, he held a rapier. The long straight nose and well-marked brows told Will that this was the son of Lord Robartes. Given his age, he was, presumably, the heir.

'Don't be silly, Rob,' the girl countered. 'Cannot you see his scarf? It is the same hue as Father's officers.' She pointed at Will's sash.

'I am Lieutenant William Lucie of Pye's Regiment of Horse, and you, I assume, are Robert.'

'I am Robert Robartes. You must address me as Master Robert, as the servants do,' the boy pronounced.

'He is not a servant,' his sister protested. 'Father's officers are gentlemen. I have heard him say so.'

Will suppressed a grin. It hardly seemed the moment for a dispute about etiquette.

'Be quiet, Anne,' Robert frowned. 'Mother said you were to listen to me.'

'My head hurts,' came a muffled voice from the other bed and a tousle-haired boy surfaced from beneath the covers.

'Master Hender,' The servant Nan dropped the chamber pot on the floor with a thud and hurried over to the boy.

'I will make my bed here, if you will provide me with a closet,' Will said to the younger maidservant.

'Oh, Sir, will you sleep across the threshold?'

Glancing at her bright eyes and heaving bosom, Will guessed that here was another wench in search of romance. There would be little opportunity in Lord Robartes' strict Presbyterian household. 'Too draughty,' he joked. 'A trundle bed will do. Now I must see that my horse has been stabled.'

He passed a door, standing open. It was a bedchamber, more richly furnished than any Will had slept in. The tester bed was hung about with green and gold hangings. Will stepped forward, tracing a tree of life with his finger, the stem twisting downwards through a pattern of leaves and buds, interspersed with butterflies. A half-filled chest of linen stood beside the bed, the task abandoned in the frenzy of departure.

It dawned on Will that, for the first time in weeks, he was left to his own devices. There might be fifty servants remaining at Lanhydrock. Yet noone was watching him. Few commanders were more detested by the royalists than Lord Robartes. What might Will not seek as recompense if he delivered Lanhydrock into the hands of the King's army now that fate had left him in possession? The Robartes children would be valuable hostages; and the King would forgive his crimes, as he had done for others who had returned to their allegiance bringing troops or valuable intelligence.

By the time he reached the stables, Will was almost dizzy at these prospects. One of the troop was there, waiting for him with a note.

'To Lieutenant William Lucie. You are hereby detached from the troop at the request of Lord Robartes. You may retain the messenger to do your bidding. This is your authority. Seymour Pyle.'

'Thank you, Archer.' Will folded the paper carefully away. Pyle had not forgotten that without it, Will might be taken for a deserter. The trooper might be useful, less so if Will succumbed to the temptation of handing the house to the enemy.

'Sir, this too is from the captain.' Archer handed Will a scrap of paper. Unsigned, the message read, *'Our quarter master knows how poor I am at reckoning. Therefore, you may discover I have overlooked a man or two when I took my leave.'* Archer gave a conspiratorial grin. A scar running from mouth to cheek puckered one side of his mouth and gave him a sinister expression.

'How many men has Captain Pyle mislaid?' Will asked noncommittally.

'Six, Sir. You will find the others in the stables.'

'Return to the men, Archer until I bring further orders.'

Speaking to the steward would be the quickest way of discovering the layout of the house and what arms remained. The man favoured Will with a sour glance, before returning to the ledger he was inspecting. Fingering his sword hilt, Will stepped forward and closed the ledger. 'Enough, Sir,' he said.

The steward bit back an angry retort. Fingers clutching the chain of office like a talisman, he grumbled his replies to the young officer's questions. 'As to arms, the store is long gone. The gardeners have their spades and stakes, the men in the fields their scythes, their pitchforks.' A gleam of satisfaction appeared in his protuberant eyes. 'Now if you will forgive me.' He bent his head to the ledger.

Will pelted from one end of the house to the other. The servants, by and large older men, young boys, women and girls, paid the tawny-sashed cavalry officer little attention. The master and mistress might have departed but beer must be brewed, butter churned, floors swept. It was as the steward had said – Will found no arms remaining and the only armed men were the half dozen troopers Seymour Pyle had given him. The house and its occupants were at the mercy of the royalists, as he hoped, or feared.

The aroma of roasting meat wafted towards him. Realising he was hungry, Will followed his nose and the smell of roasting meat to the kitchens. A black cat was licking cream from a pan and a haunch of beef was burning on an unattended spit.

On seeing Will, a rotund cookmaid dropped the fowl she was plucking, hurled a wooden spoon at the cat and directed a torrent of abuse at a skinny kitchen boy in a faded tunic. 'You'll be wanting your dinner, Zur. Mr Barrett, the cook, the butler, the pantler and most o' the footmen are gone with 'is Lordship.'

'No matter, bread, cold meats are all I need and no ceremony. Send a tray to the stables for six of my men.' Will made a hasty meal standing at the one board remaining on trestles while considering his next move. Could he find means of sending a message to Gabriel at Boconnoc House offering Lanhydrock and the Robartes children in exchange for a pardon from the King? Would Gabriel trust him after their last encounter?

He rummaged in his pockets, pulling out the scrap of paper from Seymour Pyle. Hoping to find space for a message, he flipped it over, but there was already writing on the back. Pyle had torn it from what appeared to be a letter. '. . . *much missed at the harvest home. Your mother and sisters count the days until you return, but it is God's work you do, my son and I must not hasten that day before your own harvest is complete . . .*'

His feet carried him back to the nursery, to the children and nursemaids. He realised that there had been no sign of the physician whose opinion was to determine the children's departure.

'Gone, Zur, rode away like the devil was on 'is tail,' the older woman, Nan shook her head. 'Milady left these from the stillhouse, camomile and elder with a spoonful of honey for the fever, witch hazel, chamomile and lavender for the itching. Lie still, Master Hender.' She began smearing a thick paste on the boy's angry red rash. Hender whimpered. Anne was sleeping.

Will inhaled the fragrance of the crushed herbal salve. His own mother's physic had cured him, Bess and Harry many a time. She had died of fever before the first winter of the war was done, and the contours of her beloved face were blurring in his memory. 'An excellent remedy,' he mumbled. He thought of the words on the paper, 'It is God's work you do, my son.' God's or the devil's? Will asked himself. Pyle's fervour, his care for the mother of the dead child, his belief in Will . . . Seymour Pyle trusted him, had done all he could to help him. Pyle, he knew, was a good man.

Sweat trickled down inside Will's shirt. He could smell the rank odour of his own body, stale sweat, the bandage over his wound in need of dressing.

For a few moments more he clung to the dream of his own restoration to the King's favour and, through that, his father's. But it would be the devil's work to hand these children, sick or healthy, to their father's enemies. He could not do it. Shrugging his shoulders, Will began planning how, with only six troopers, he might defend Lanhydrock against the King's men.

CHAPTER 46

Despite a clean, dry bed, Will slept uneasily. He had set a watch of three of his men around the house, while the other three slept, but twice he snatched up his sword and padded out into the passage, convinced he heard footsteps. Waking for a third time, he lit a candle at the banked fire in the hearth, pulled on breeches and doublet and strapped on his sword belt. The closet opened into Robert's chamber. From behind the bedcurtains came the sound of his steady breathing. Carrying boots and cloak, Will left the nursery.

'Archer, it is I, Lucie,' he called softly to the dark shape standing in the shadow of the gatehouse.

'Lieutenant,' the soldier relaxed his grip on the carbine.

'Go and rest. I am wakeful and will stand guard the rest of your watch.'

Will gathered his cloak more tightly about him. A mass of scudding, grey clouds obscured the moon. He was no stranger to night watches, but it took some minutes to school himself to see and to hear only what was there; and not what his imagination conjured. That shape was a bush, not a man, and if it moved it was only the wind. The stealthy steps in the grass, were the plough horses, grazing a field's length away from him, the sounds magnified in the night air. He sniffed, but detected only the nighttime fragrance of growing things, that and his soiled linen. Imperceptibly the sky lightened, revealing nothing worse than dark green leaves on the bush and the shaggy-coated horses ambling along the hedge. As dawn broke, another man came to take over the watch. Yawning, Will took himself back to the nursery and threw himself across the trundle bed fully-dressed. Moments later he was asleep.

He awoke with a jolt, knowing that all was not well. From the nursery came the murmurs of the two servants, a plaintive cry from Hender. No, that was not the source of his unease. It was the absence of the early morning bustle, the to-ing and fro-ing of servants drawing curtains, taking out the night soil or wielding brooms that made up the early hours of any great house. A dog barked, but then subsided into yelps, whines and silence. Will snatched up his sword belt and edged his way to the nursery window, attracting curious stares from the two servants. He eased back a damask curtain and peered through the glass.

Beneath the window a gravelled path led around the side of the east wing. Lying in a pool of blood, was the body of the dog. A liveried servant lay beside it, face down. He turned from the window to see Robert standing there, dressed in shirt and breeches. Will made a small motion with his hand towards the boy's chamber. He disappeared and returned moments later carrying his rapier.

Running footsteps, and the nursery door burst open to admit Weller, another of those left on guard. 'The enemy, Sir, below,' he panted.

'How many?' Will snapped.

'Too many for us to fight.'

Will could hear the distant tramp of many feet. In a few minutes they would gain the long gallery. 'Is there another way from the house, besides the long gallery?' he asked Robert, keeping his voice calm.

The boy nodded. 'My father does not like to see the servants as they go about their work. A service passage leads down a back stair.'

'Wrap the children in blankets.'

There were shots from below. Will looked about him for inspiration. 'Weller, help me drag that great table into the gallery.' A relic of an earlier time, banished to the nursery, it was long, dark and heavy. Between them the two men dragged the heavy table through the door and manoeuvred it sideways, so that it blocked passage through the gallery.

'Now, over with it,' Will gasped. Turned on its side, the table might serve to hold off the enemy for a few vital minutes. He ran back into the nursery for his carbine. The two younger children were on their feet, blankets wrapped around them, their eyes wide as saucers.

Robert Robartes was standing by the improvised barricade clutching his rapier. 'I will stay with you, Lieutenant and defend my father's house.'

'Brave words, but it cannot be. Take your brother and sister and the women and lead them to safety. Hide in the woods,' Will urged. 'It is your duty.'

The boy hesitated. 'Very well. Come Hender, come Anne. Quickly.' The three children and the two women disappeared through a narrow door. Will pushed a chest in front of it, hoping the servants' door might be overlooked.

Joining Weller, he crouched behind the table, fingers a blur as he rammed powder and shot down the barrel of his gun. There were more running footsteps. It was Archer, his legs pumping. They heaved him over the table as the first soldiers burst into the gallery. The royalists paused at the sight of the wooden barrier, the three men kneeling behind it, the muzzles of the cavalry carbines protruding over the edge.

'Make ready,' Will muttered.

'Hold!' A hatchet-faced officer, wearing a scarlet sash over a muddied buff coat, stepped forward, doffing his cap in mock homage. 'A brave gesture, gentlemen, but you can scarcely prevail against so many.' He waved a gloved hand at the group of armed, blue-coated men behind him. 'Stand aside, for we mean His Lordship's children no harm. They will be kept safe enough.'

'Indeed, they shall, Sir, for that is our duty,' Will answered, wondering if he was about to die in defence of the children he had so recently considered betraying. He steadied the barrel against the wooden edge of the table, his heart thumping.

The officer's smile faded. He barked an order and ten or twelve men from the group dashed forward.

'Give fire,' Will ordered and the three carbines belched smoke and flame in unison. Two of the men fell, but the others ran on. A few fired their heavy pistols wildly as they ran. Splinters flew from panelling and table. Will clutched his cheek where a jagged sliver of wood had embedded itself like a dart. A shot caught Archer in the throat. He tumbled backward with a gurgling cry, blood pulsing through the small hole. Will clambered over the wooden barrier, sword in one hand, empty carbine in the other.

'Come, Weller.' At least they had provided a distraction, giving the Robartes children a chance of escape. The two men met the oncoming rush, swords raised. Will parried one sword blade, crunched his hilt into the man's face and saw him stagger back, his cheek laid open to the bone. A second man took Will off balance and sent his sword flying. Will reversed the empty carbine and swung the butt hard at the man's head. It made contact and came away coated in blood and hair. Weller was down, a heaving mass of men kicking and pummelling him into the wooden floor.

'Enough!' shouted the officer to his men. Blood flowing down his cheek, Will struggled in the grasp of three soldiers.

'Captain, we found the brats.'

'How many?'

'Three, Sir, two boys and a girl.'

'Is that the whole brood?' The officer touched his sword tip to Will's throat.

'Yes.'

'Bring them here.'

The two younger children clutched the blankets defensively about them. Hender's night gown dripped urine, but Anne's heavy brows were knitted. Robert was dragged in struggling. He aimed a kick at one of his captors and caught the soldier a blow on the kneecap. 'Devil's spawn,' the man spat and twisted the boy's arm behind his back. Robert clenched his teeth in pain.

'Take them back to their apartments. Let him go.' The officer nodded at the man holding Robert. The boy gave Will a stiff little bow as the children were escorted from the long gallery.

'Be brave, Master Robartes as your noble father would expect,' Will said.

The boy turned his head. 'You may call me Robert,' he said.

'What do you want with young children?' Will protested to the royalist officer. 'You may hold me as hostage instead. I am an officer of Parliament.'

The man ran his eyes over Will's linen shirt and kersey breeches, made for him in Tiverton at short notice and modest cost. He stared for a few moments at the leather boots, of a far higher quality, though much worn. 'Your rank?'

'Lieutenant of Horse.'

'As I thought,' sneered the royalist, 'And a gentleman, no doubt, but not of noble birth, or you would not be playing nurse maid. These are the children of a rebel commander, while you are nothing but a lieutenant. No, I will turn you loose so that you may carry a message. You may take your horse and your sword, nothing else. Fetch me writing materials.' The last was directed to the servants. The older woman glared, but the younger bobbed a curtsey and returned with pen, ink and paper.

'And what of my men?' Will looked down at Archer and Weller, neither of whom were moving. Weller's head was at an unnatural angle and Will thought his neck was broken. The officer prodded them with the toe of his boot. 'Dead or dying.'

When the soldiers marched Will to the stables he saw three of his troopers lying dead side by side, their spilled blood soaking into the straw on which they had been tossed. The fourth was not there, so perhaps he, at least, had survived.

An hour later, accompanied by Colonel Pye, Will was ushered into the parlour of a gentleman's house in Lostwithiel where Lord Robartes was waiting. The missing trooper had evaded the royalists and reported that Lanhydrock was taken. It was a relief to Will that he did not have to break the news. Lord Robartes snatched the letter from Will. He scanned the few lines and rubbed his face.

'The villain says he will not harm my children if we leave my house in Grenville's hands. Has the gall to sign himself my most obedient servant. Did they take Lanhydrock by surprise?' he snarled at Will. 'Did you not set a guard?'

'My Lord,' Colonel Pye interjected. Lord Robartes silenced him with the wave of a hand. 'He may answer for himself, Pye. What is your name, Lieutenant? I seem to know your face.'

'William Lucie, My Lord.'

'Hah,' Robartes exclaimed. 'Colonel Lucie's turncoat nephew. Perhaps it was nothing but a ruse. What proof have you of this man's loyalty, Colonel? Did he hand my house to Skellum Grenville?'

'My Lord, he gave warning of an attack some days past, else his troop would have been taken unawares.'

'As were my house and children,' Lord Robartes snapped. 'How many men did you have at your command, Lieutenant? And what became of them? Did they flee at the first sign of trouble?'

'Six, My Lord, all killed save for the man who brought the news.'

'And yet you survived.' Lord Robartes' cold eyes bored into Will. For a few moments Will wished that he had suffered more than a torn cheek to prove he had defended Lanhydrock. 'How were you taken?'

'Before the doors of the children's apartments, My Lord. A score of the enemy stormed the long gallery and called for our surrender. They attacked when we refused. The two men with me died bravely where they stood.'

Crumpling the letter in his hand, Robartes scowled at Will. 'Pye, send for the surviving trooper. I will question him about the lieutenant's actions.'

Brought into the presence of his captain, his colonel and the unknown august personage Lord Robartes, trooper Moor was pale with fright.

'His Lordship has a few questions for you Moor,' Colonel Pye said.

'Yessir. Am I under arrest?' Moor blurted, risking a direct glance at his colonel.

'Indeed not. You have nothing to fear.' Pye gave an encouraging smile. Will, hearing the emphasis on the word 'You', was not reassured.

'Very well,' Robartes snapped at Pye. 'What was your lieutenant doing the last time you saw him and when was that?' he asked Moor in quieter tones.

Moor swallowed and licked dry lips. 'Last night Sir, Milord. Lieutenant Lucie had told me to guard the gate. He come by the gate-house as it was getting dark. Said that come what may, I must not fall asleep on guard.'

Robartes snorted with disdain. 'Of course not, you would be court martialled.'

Moor stared at the floor as if hoping it would swallow him up. 'Yessir. But he said the lives of us all, including three innocent children depended on us all doing our part. And he said if the enemy came I must not stay to fight them for I was but one man. I must bring word to him.'

'And where were you to bring this word?'

'To the house, Sir, the nursery. He said he must remain there to protect the children as best he could. Then he checked the bars on the gate, that they was all in place, and that the postern gate was locked and bolted too.' After this long speech, Moor clamped his lips together, darting a worried look at Will.

'And when the enemy came, what happened?'

'I didn't hear them arrive, Sir,' Moor admitted.

'You were asleep!'

'Nossir, the bars and bolts, they was all in place still. I heard noise from the house. Shouting, screams. They must've come over the wall beyond the woods. So I knew it was too late to warn the Lieutenant, but not too late to help mebbe. I had my sword and pistols, Sir.' He paused.

'And then?' Robartes prompted impatiently.

'I never got there. I was creeping along the outside wall of the house near the kitchens when I nearly fell over the body of one of our men. Then I heard voices, so I hid behind a bush.'

'Whose voices?'

'The enemy, Sir. They were laughing fit to burst. 'Fine pickings in the house. Leave that rebel's filthy body to the dogs,' they said. 'He'll have nothing to give you but lice or the pox. Even the officer we captured had nothing but a handful of silver. Tried to trade himself for the three brats as if he were worth something.'

'What was that?' Robartes interrupted sharply. 'Trade himself?'

'As a hostage, Sir, that's what I heard. One of them was telling the others that Lieutenant Lucie had offered himself as a hostage in place of the children. They thought it a great jest, Sir.'

A clock ticked loudly in the hush that followed. Will could hear his own breathing and the blood pounding in his ears.

'Have you any more questions for Moor, My Lord?' asked Pye.

'He may go.' Robartes rubbed his hand across his face again. Will saw that when he removed it, his cheeks were wet with the traces of tears. 'How did you come by that gash, Lieutenant?' Robartes' tone was warmer.

'A wood splinter when a ball hit the panelling.'

Robartes turned his back, walking to the window which overlooked a neglected garden, a stable beyond it. Will waited. His cheek was stinging.

'How are my children?'

'The two younger have not yet recovered, My Lord, but they are unharmed.'

'And the eldest, Robert, what of him?' His voice trembled.

'His spirit is not broken, My Lord. He would have stood shoulder to shoulder with me had I permitted it.' Robartes took a shuddering breath and turned around.

'He will rain down upon the wicked blazing coals and sulfur,
A scorching wind shall be their lot.

The Lord will prevail. You had best have a surgeon look to your wound.'

Sitting on a stool while Pye's surgeon cleaned and stitched together the edges of the jagged tear, Will thought about Robartes' children. He could only hope that the royalist officer would honour his word to keep them safe. There was nothing further that Will could do for them.

CHAPTER 47

21 August

Standing on the walkway at the top of the keep, Will watched the marching files of enemy bluecoats, red colours dipping and swirling in the hands of the ensigns.

'Strength, Lucie?'

'Six, seven, eight, colours, Sir.' Will lowered his spyglass.

'Seven or eight hundred soldiers, then,' Seymour Pyle said. 'Skellum Grenville's men without a doubt.'

The taking of Lanhydrock House ten days earlier had been only the beginning of the royalist offensive. Bodmin town had fallen, the Horse retreating south towards the sea. The rebels' cause was waning. Today there had been concerted royalist attacks around Lostwithiel and Pyle's troop had been sent to defend Restormel Castle.

The sound of gasping heralded the arrival of the portly Captain Mudge, in charge of the garrison.

'How many men remain within the castle?' Pyle asked.

'Eighteen men, and a gun crew. Women and children too.'

'Send the women and children down to the town. Now. Then draw up your men below. We have not much time.'

Down in the courtyard the group of women waited, faces set and petticoats tucked up. Half a dozen children clustered beside them, sobbing and blowing noses on smocks. The moment the wooden drawbridge touched the ground they broke into a run. The mechanism creaked into action again, but before it was more than a few inches off the ground, five men burst from the meagre ranks of infantry and hurtled after them.

'Halt!' Mudge yelled, but the men did not pause. There was a crash from above as the castle's single gun fired. The beat of the royalist drums was growing louder.

'We have too few men, Lucie, to fight them,' Pyle said. 'We must abandon the castle.'

* * *

'I summon you to surrender the castle for the use of the King and of Sir Richard Grenville, here present,' the royalist trumpeter proclaimed. He had arrived under a flag of truce, leaving Grenville and his royalists some distance away, awaiting his return with an answer.

'Grenville! Traitor,' Pyle muttered. His mounted troop was waiting in the courtyard, two files of infantry behind them. 'They will give us an hour to consider their proposals. During that hour we must destroy everything that may be of use to them. What stores do you have?'

'Barrels of beef and beer, sacks of grain and peas in the cellar beneath the Great Hall. Powder and shot are in the magazine,' Mudge replied.

'Leave them to me, Captain.' While Pyle ascended to the top of the wall to bellow a reply to the summons, Will ran towards the cellar. It was filled with barrels. A hot iron had burnt a single word on each, identifying the contents.

'In the name of King and Parliament,' Pyle was commencing his reply. With no time to retrieve the victuals it was better to burn them. Where was the magazine? Will needed powder.

He was standing on top of the piled barrels when a trooper ran in.

'Captain Pyle has ordered you to join us, Sir. The Foot have marched out. Only our troop of Horse remains.'

'Tell him I will join him presently,' Will panted. He jumped back down to the beaten earth floor. There was a crunching sound beneath his boots. Will froze. He was standing on a trail of gunpowder. Where had it come from? Following the trail, he discovered the magazine in an adjoining room. It contained only three barrels of powder, one of them leaking. With infinite care he walked to the door of the cellar and then ran back to the gatehouse.

After a brief consultation with Pyle, Will tore off his sword belt, carbine and leather-soled boots, for fear of sparks. Accompanied by a trooper carrying a torch in each hand kindled from the brazier in the porter's lodge, Will returned to the cellar, where he halted on the threshold. A rhythmic metallic clanging from far above was the gun crew spiking the gun so that it could not be used to fire upon the retreating troops. His heart was banging in time with the hammer. Then came the running footsteps of the gun crew making for the gatehouse.

'Are they gone?' he mumbled out of the side of his mouth, as if talking plainly might ignite the gun powder prematurely.

'Aye, Sir,' the trooper responded. Will swallowed. Despite the chill of the cellar, sweat was trickling down his back under his shirt. He padded softly in his stockinged feet across the blue-grey grains scattering the ground and into the magazine. Prising off the lid of the leaking keg, he filled a ladle with powder, then poured it around the base of the barrels in the cellar.

'Lucie!' Pyle called.

'Go. Ask the captain to take the troop and ride out. Leave my horse.'

The trooper handed the two burning torches to Will and backed away. Will stood at the cellar door, waiting, until he heard the clatter as the troop trotted across the drawbridge. He breathed a sigh of relief as the vibration of iron shoes on wood was replaced by the softer drumming of hooves on grass. Better to be alone lest it go wrong. Leaning through the doorway he hurled first one and then the other torch at the powder.

The flash as the powder ignited knocked Will flat on his back. 'Thank Jesus it was but the scattered powder,' was his thought as he scrambled to his feet, shaking. The flames would reach the keg any moment.

His horse was standing where he had left it, tethered to a post.

With no thought but to get clear, he threw himself into the saddle and dug his bare heels into the horse's sides. Once over the drawbridge and ditch, he flattened himself against the horse's neck, his flaxen hair mingling with the pale mane. Memories of boyhood races with Harry came to him as he galloped. 'Last one to the great oak is a booby,' his brother's voice whispered in the wind.

Safely across the bailey, he drew rein, pulled on boots and sword belt and listened for the second, louder, bang as the keg exploded. It did not come. A cold certainty grew within him that the powder in the keg was damp. He remembered the roof over the Great Hall had collapsed, the faint sound of dripping. The victuals were spoils for Grenville's men. He had failed.

Turning his horse's head, Will pushed him into a canter. Gun smoke drifted lazily upwards from the wooded slopes. Next came the sounds of scattered shots, drums, horses neighing and wild screams of men fighting. In wretched suspense he pushed his mount harder around another bend in the hill.

There before him was a square of bristling sixteen-foot pikes with four company colours sheltering in its midst, around half of the Royalist force Will had seen approaching through the spyglass. The drums were beating the order for them to retreat, but Pyle's troop was blocking their attempts.

Circling the penned-in royalists, Will's heavily outnumbered troop was firing pistols and carbines into the screaming, defiant mass of men. Hundreds of musketeers crouched beneath the protection of the long pikes.

Pyle's horse was dancing and weaving in response to his rider's knees while the captain, waving his sword, shouted encouragement.

Out of the corner of his eye, Will saw a raised gun and recognised the shape as a fowling piece, not a musket. A game keeper turned soldier, one who knew how to aim a firearm. Half hidden in the centre of the pikes a tall, hatless officer was pointing out Pyle. Will screamed a warning and waved his arm violently as his horse covered the remaining few paces between him and the captain.

Amidst the clamour of hooves, yelling, drums and trumpets, Seymour Pyle acknowledged Will's return with a cheery wave. Smoke and flame blasted from the long barrel of the fowling piece, transforming Pyle's neck into a crimson fountain. Somehow Will was on the ground in time to catch his captain as he slipped sideways from the saddle, face, hair, coat and breeches all drenched in spurting blood. Blood bubbled from his mouth, glistening drops coating his chin, but he was fighting to speak. Will gripped Pyle's hand and bent his head to hear the dying words.

'Take over – Will – Captain – now.' Pyle's body convulsed. There was a final gush of crimson before he went limp, sightless brown eyes fixed on Will.

Lowering the corpse to the ground, Will became conscious of the continuing tumult about him. The attack had faltered, as Pyle's troop became aware of their captain's fall. Grenville's musketeers took advantage of the momentary lull to reload their pieces. Flying balls of lead found homes in two more men before Will mastered himself sufficiently to climb back into the saddle. Grasping the reins, they slipped through his wet gloves. Shuddering, he wiped his hands on the saddle cloth.

'To the standard' and 'Withdraw' were his first hesitant commands. The bugle echoed his words and the men gathered in an untidy, ragged group, following Will as he cantered into the nearby woods. He was pursued by jeers and a flurry of parting shots. Panting, he drew rein and wheeled his horse. 'Now, men, while they believe us beaten, one more charge, this to our captain's memory. Are you with me?'

Faces streaked with smoke, blood and dirt glared back at him from beneath their three-barred helmets. 'Aye, Sir, for Captain Pyle.'

'Go hell for leather then,' Will ordered. 'Run them through and the devil take the hindmost.' He had no softer feeling in him.

In tense silence, the troop reformed into two tight ranks with a precision that would have gladdened their late captain's heart. The red cornet with Pyle's motto flapped against its spiked pole. A wood pigeon's throaty call punctuated the stillness. Will drew his sword and held it over his head.

'Charge!' The trumpet rang out as Will's sword swept down and the troop burst from the tree line in a thunder of hooves. The hollow square of royalist infantry had reformed itself into a marching column, the vanguard already out of sight, advancing towards the castle. Bent on revenge, Will cantered past the bodies of the fallen. A cry of alarm, a shout from an officer and a handful of men at the back faced about, a dozen musketeers fumbling to reload. The remainder ran for the safety of the castle where Grenville's standard already flew.

Will had spotted the tall, hatless officer whose order had spelled death for Pyle. Sword in hand, the man was screaming orders at his fleeing men, spittle flying from his mouth. By the time Will reached him, the officer stood alone, but for a giant of a man brandishing a pike. At a word from the officer, the pikeman dropped the butt to the ground.

'Well, Sir, are you offering quarter, or are you intent on murder?'

The words shamed Will. There was neither lace nor braid on the officer's plain brown kersey suit and his breast plate was in the fashion of the last century. Another yeoman or a tenant, who had followed the call of the Grenvilles to defend the Duchy of Cornwall against the foreigners from across the Tamar. Yet Will was not in a forgiving mood. 'One of your men killed my captain at your command.'

'And if I did? You might have performed the same office for me.'

Will climbed deliberately from his horse and sheathed his blade. Then he knocked the officer to the ground with a punch to the jaw. 'And now you may have quarter. Your sword,' Will held out his hand. 'Take him,' he barked to a corporal.

Turning his back, Will led his horse towards the still form of Seymour Pyle. Two troopers waited, bareheaded, a few paces away. Will stood beside Pyle's body for a moment and bowed his head. 'Help me,' he said. Together, they lifted the limp, warm body and draped it across the saddle of Will's horse. Removing his cloak Will covered the face of the man who had welcomed him, overlooked his past and enabled him to face the future.

CHAPTER 48

'Skirmishing below Restormel Castle, Sir, near the ford,' a scout reported to Gabriel. 'But Grenville's flag still flies from the keep.'

'Have Grenville's Horse arrived?'

'No, Sir. I saw only a handful of Foot.'

Gabriel removed his helmet and ran his hands through sweat-drenched hair. Essex had counterattacked and the royalists were in danger of losing all the ground they had won since their coordinated surprise attacks at dawn.

'We must hold the ford,' he told Sayer. 'It is the only place to cross the Fowey within easy reach of Lostwithiel.'

Bodies strewed the ground to the north of the castle, many wearing the blue coats of the Grenvilles. A flock of crows pecking at the corpses rose into the air as Vaughan's Horse thundered towards them. Bile rose in Gabriel's throat.

On a small strip of beach, a handful of Grenville's blue-coated Foot wielded swords and the butt end of muskets against red-coated rebels. Two men struggled in the shallow waters. One was tall, an officer from his tawny sash. A blow from a musket dislodged his hat and long, corn-coloured hair flowed freely in the wind. The officer lunged with his sword but missed his footing and fell to one knee. When the musket descended again, he collapsed face down in the water, hair drenched in blood.

The sound of hooves scattered the fighters around the ford. A final hack with sword or musket and Essex's men ran, pursued by derisive shouts from the royalist blue coats.

Plunging down the steep incline on his surefooted Welsh mare, Gabriel dropped the reins and leapt from Llangenny's back. He waded into the river, water pouring over the tops of his boots and trailing weed tugging at his spurs. Time and heartbeat seemed suspended as Gabriel battled against the current to turn the body over. Lifeless blue eyes stared at the sky and the corn-coloured hair floated on the water.

It was not Will. Panting and retching, Gabriel stood, hands on his knees while the dead parliamentarian officer bumped gently against his boots, the river tugging at the latest piece of flotsam in its path.

'Sir?' He turned to see the snub nose and anxious black eyes of Sayer.

'I feared he was a kinsman,' Gabriel blurted. With a final glance at the dead stranger, he squelched his way to the beach where Ieuan was holding Llangenny at the water's edge.

Looking back, Gabriel saw that the dead officer had drifted downstream, and his body was stuck fast against a boulder. To Ieuan's surprise, Gabriel plunged again into the river. Tiny fish darted away as he took hold of the dead man's shoulders, dislodging him with difficulty. Dragging the body, he staggered to the beach, and deposited it at the top of the bank, straightening the limbs and closing the staring eyes. For a long moment, Gabriel stood, head bowed, before remounting Llangenny. The ford was theirs, but the encircling royalist line was thin. That line must hold.

* * *

'We must halt their advance. If the enemy breach our ring of defences here, they will pour through like water.'

There had been no sign of Grenville's Horse, but scouts had reported a large body of enemy Foot approaching. Vaughan's were on their own.

Gabriel's officers digested his words. 'Carbines from a distance, then pistols?' Sayer asked.

'No, forget the books on warfare. Tell your troops to leave their pistols in their holsters. Our horses and our swords will be our weapons.

We must break them with the force of our charge. It is our only hope.'

It was too late for speeches to inspire the troops. Drums and the regular tread of marching feet were growing louder. Gabriel unfolded the sodden leather tops of his boots, the boot hose clinging uncomfortably to his legs. Followed by the cornet, the blue standard flapping, he trotted out in front of the regiment. Ieuan hurried towards him, scowling.

'Those boots are ruined, Master.' Seizing the offending articles, Ieuan peeled them from Gabriel's legs and tipped muddy river water onto the ground. 'The hose too.'

Boots replaced, Gabriel handed his helmet to Ieuan.

'For Mary's sake, Master, put that on. Would you make yourself a target?'

'Unless their shooting is improved since the morning, they will be hard pressed to hit the castle walls. The men must see me. Now cease your *cwynion* and tie my hair back in a tail.'

* * *

The head of the infantry column marching up the hill towards the castle wavered at the sight of Vaughan's Horse. Drawn up knee to knee across the bailey, the troopers sat their horses in complete silence, naked swords in their hands. Roundhead officers bellowed orders, the drums quickened their rhythm, and the soldiers in red coats and grey coats trudged forward once more.

'They look half-starved,' Sayer said.

'Do not underestimate them. We are pushing them slowly but surely into the sea and they know it.'

Gabriel had never faced worse odds than this scarecrow army, but there was no choice. The blood pounded in his ears. Vaughan's two hundred troopers must smash through the toiling ranks of infantry. If they faltered, the many hundreds of Foot would pull them from their horses. Every man would be taken or bludgeoned to death. He clicked his tongue to Llangenny and signalled to the trumpeters. 'For

Cornwall and for Wales!' Gabriel's sword swept down, and Vaughan's Horse charged.

Across the bailey and down the slope, nearer and nearer to the enemy. Llangenny, ears pricked, eating up the sloping ground with her smooth, long stride. Groups of musketeers kneeling in fragmented lines, facing him. A ragged burst of musket fire. Now a more organised volley, a ball flying past Gabriel's ear. Officers bawling orders, the front rank, half hidden in clouds of smoke from their own muskets, frozen in position, standing or kneeling. A bare-headed officer, black hair streaming, brandishing the long shaft of his partizan, his men clutching their empty weapons for dear life.

The line of infantry shivered, trembled, men cowering away. Stumbling backwards, muskets in the second rank exploding haphazardly, hitting some of their own men as they turned to flee. Gaps appeared in the infantry line, but others stood their ground before the oncoming rush of cavalry. Some had reversed their empty muskets, and a few had drawn their tucks.

War cries in English and Welsh rang out as the solid line of horses slammed into increasingly fragmented groups of infantry. Twisting and turning their beasts, the regiment engaged in a surge of heaving horseflesh and flailing hooves. The infantry broke and scattered, many abandoning their weapons and taking to their heels, pursued by thundering horses.

Screaming defiance, the black-haired officer struck out at Gabriel with the spear- headed polearm.

'Llangenny, hup!' At Gabriel's command, the mare reared. Her front hooves caught the enemy officer full in the face, but the sharp tip of his partizan scored a red furrow across her shoulder.

The mare was squealing. 'Hush, girl,' Gabriel soothed, his attention distracted from the fighting by the urgent need to prevent her bolting. He slashed downward with his sword as two soldiers sought to pull him from his horse, emboldened by her wound. Maddened by pain, the mare reared again. The soldiers took to their heels, following the rest of the running infantry.

'Take command, David,' Gabriel shouted. 'Sound recall. Llangenny needs attention and I must find myself another horse. Secure the bailey.' Fighting for mastery, he rode away on the plunging, injured mare.

The remains of ancient buildings dotted the bailey. Something was not right. 'Flush out any men who may have taken refuge in those ruins,' he called to Sayer over his shoulder. 'I think I saw something.'

Waiting nearby on Blackbird, Ieuan raised his arm to Gabriel to show he was there and urged the gelding into a trot. There was the crack of a carbine. Ieuan saw Gabriel's head jerk, watched him topple from the saddle. The terrified Llangenny reared again, her hooves narrowly missing Gabriel. The manservant pushed Blackbird into a canter, praying he would reach the frightened mare before she trampled her fallen rider, lying motionless on the ground. He drew his sword.

CHAPTER 49

'You will gain the promotion then that you spurned.' Hugh Lucie's words were stern, but Will believed him pleased that his nephew was to be commissioned captain of Pyle's troop.

The long day's fighting was over, leaving Essex's army with nothing but Lostwithiel and a small corridor of safety to the town of Fowey. Will regarded Hugh Lucie's immaculate black silk doublet and breeches and his snowy white lace falling band with distaste. The sight of Seymour Pyle's blood-drenched garments and tangled hair was fresh in his memory. His uncle's composure only sharpened his grief.

'What will you have on your troop cornet?' Hugh continued. 'It need not be the three fish of the Lucie coat of arms. It is your personal colour.'

'I hardly know, Sir. The three fish leaping through the air may satisfy my wishes. I am a fish out of the water when all is said and done,' Will said bitterly. A new flag for the troop was furthest from his thoughts.

Hugh narrowed his eyes. 'You seem overwrought. I will send my personal chaplain to pray with you.'

Will clasped his hands tight behind his back. 'May I go, Sir? There is the matter of a new lieutenant, besides seeing Captain Pyle buried.'

'Yes, go. No doubt you want to change your garments.' Hugh Lucie waved his hand at Will's buff coat, stiff with Pyle's blood, his sodden breeches with their filthy ribbons. 'You are a captain now, who may rise further if this war continues and the godly prevail.'

Not trusting himself to answer, Will made his uncle a slight bow, replaced the damp Montero cap on his head and departed. Pyle must be buried here, in the churchyard, today, with the minimum of ceremony; but Will would return his sword to his family. It was the only service he could render them.

* * *

Liskeard

'You will oblige me, Colonel, by remaining in your bed. The wound will heal more quickly, and the dry stitch will hold fast where I have glued it to the skin. And do not make sudden movements of your head. You were most fortunate the ball did not hit a vital blood vessel in your neck.'

The regimental surgeon finished his inspection of his previous day's handiwork, replacing the linen bandage covering the stitched buckram with swift, practised movements. His plain, dark suit was splattered with stains and there were dark smudges under his eyes. Gabriel suspected he had been tending the wounded all night.

'I am afraid my brigade commander does not share your views. Colonel Bennett sent a servant an hour ago asking if I would be present at today's council of war. What is the news on our wounded?' Gabriel probed, swinging his legs carefully to the floor while attempting to keep his head still.

'Sword cuts. Both men will recover.'

The surgeon's footsteps receded and Gabriel called for Ieuan.

'Shall I bring you some caudle, Master?'

'No caudle, I am not a woman in child bed. I am tired of listening to remedies for rest when I am needed in the field. Bring me a cup of ale, and a scarf I may wind about my throat.'

Ieuan swelled with indignation like a pig's bladder about to burst but Sayer arrived at that moment. Gabriel seated himself once more on the bed, grimacing as pain shot through his neck.

'News, Sir. The rebels have abandoned their offensive and fallen back on Lostwithiel. All the talk is of how our charge saved the day,' Sayer enthused. 'Though Colonel Bennett has claimed the credit. His Majesty sent for him and gave him a jewel.'

'Well, I wish him good fortune,' Gabriel said philosophically. Fate seemed to conspire against him gaining the King's favour.

'I heard another piece of news, Master,' Ieuan said as he dumped the requested mug of ale on the table. 'You might say it is good.'

'Well?' Gabriel raised the mug carefully, trying to drink without moving his neck.

'Sir Henry Lucie has fallen from his horse and has been carried back to Oxford with a broken leg.'

'How did you hear this?'

'One of the servants of the King's Lifeguard.'

Gabriel felt a guilty relief. It would be some weeks before Sir Henry was fit enough to take further action, weeks in which Gabriel might find other means of earning a pardon from the King.

* * *

Lostwithiel

'What became of the spy who took a match to the ammunition wagons yesterday?' Will asked Robin Lawrence, more to take his mind off the contents of the bowl of potage they were sharing than from any real curiosity.

'The man who posed as a deserter from the cavaliers? Fortunate that the match was damp. He is already dispatched to His Maker,' Lawrence flicked a penny into the air and caught it in his Montero cap.

Will smiled faintly. 'We should report to Major Hamilton.' He wiped the worst of the mess off his spoon and replaced it in his purse.

'He would have wanted it, you know,' Lawrence said, as they set off for the Talbot Inn.

Will patted the pocket where his new commission as captain lay, signed by Essex himself. 'I hope so. He was a good man and a good officer.'

The Talbot was a scene of confused activity. A handful of sullen inn servants were providing maddeningly slow service to frantic staff officers who were calling for their horses. Major Hamilton met them in the courtyard. 'Gentlemen, not before time. The King's army is heading west.'

Will did not hear him, for standing in a corner was a tall, gawky figure. Her hair was tucked respectably beneath her coif, her body concealed by the thick grey woollen cloak that he had procured for her in Tiverton. Its hem was sodden, and thick with dirt from the roads. An absurd grin spread across his face before the flash of joy was banished by cold, hard reality.

'Will you grant me a quarter hour for some personal business, Sir?' Will interrupted. 'My servant is here.'

Hamilton grunted assent, his eyes following Will as he crossed the courtyard.

'Hephzibah! How did you get here?'

'Walked mostly, rode on wagons when I could.' She bobbed a curtsey, lowering her eyes. 'Major's a'watching us.'

'Do not think I am not pleased at your arrival, but it is badly timed. Our troops are suffering one misfortune after another. Captain Pyle is dead, and I fear we will soon be in full retreat. How will I provide for you so that you do not starve?'

She lifted her chin. 'You needs't not do so. Scrubbing floors, helping in the scullery, tha's what I'll do.' She ran her eyes over his bloodstained coat, and his mud-encrusted boots. 'Poor Will, tha's nothing but skin and bone.'

Her concern brought a lump to his throat. If he had eaten less than his fill in recent weeks, the same could be said for her. 'Sit a while and rest yourself. Your boots are worn quite through. When did you last eat?'

Affecting not to hear his question, she lifted her petticoats and examined the soles of her boots, the holes stuffed with rags. Glancing over his shoulder at the waiting major, Will shouldered his way into the kitchen.

'My servant has walked many miles and she needs meat,' he demanded.

The cook glowered. 'Give his honour a platter of sausages,' he growled at a maid.

'No sausages,' Will said. He pointed at fowl roasting on a spit. 'One of those.'

At the cook's surly gesture, the woman took one of the fowl, the golden skin glistening and dripping fat; and placed it on a platter. It was the smallest of them all, but Will's mouth watered.

'She'll be chacking?'

Will stared at the maid. She pointed at a jug of ale.

'Oh, thirsty, yes.' Will fished a shilling from his purse. It had lightened considerably since he received his lieutenant's entertainment money, his first pay with the army of Parliament. There would be no more until the long-awaited supply ships arrived with the army's pay from London.

Hephzibah stared in disbelief when the inn servant approached her with the jug and platter. Smiling, Will pantomimed eating with his hand. He left her with the bounty in her lap, taking a cautious bite of meat.

'You had best send her back to Devon,' Lawrence warned. 'We are to retreat again.'

'We will end in the sea,' said Will, his smile fading.

'Pray that we reach it. If we are shut off from the sea then Lord Essex's army is lost, and without old Robin, so is the war.'

CHAPTER 50

30 August

'Are we to fight, Captain?' asked the cornet. Will Kent was a dependable yeoman in his thirties. The fraying troop standard that he gripped was that of Seymour Pyle. There had been no opportunity to replace it, but in some obscure way Will felt it a tribute to the dead officer who, in another life, might have become a friend.

'Our orders are to cross the Fowey to the east bank and wait.' They were leaving Lostwithiel.

Women stood in doorways, arms folded, watching the cavalry whose clothes, ragged from constant marching, skirmishing and scouting in incessant rain, hung loose on their emaciated bodies. With too little rest and not enough fodder, their horses were in no better case. The usual gang of children ran alongside, hooting.

Will's troop began the descent towards the strongly guarded bridge over the river. Ahead, led by Sir William Balfour, a line of cavalry regiments stretched into the distance. Will's troop was bringing up the rear. The swelling crowd of boys was growing restive. Smaller ones were falling back or being tugged away. Behind and beside the troop marched rising numbers of youths, some swinging their arms in mockery. Will glanced at the loaded carbine resting on his thigh.

A few of the bolder boys lobbed stones. One hit a horse in the eye. The injured beast screamed and kicked out. Hearing the commotion, Will turned in his saddle. His newly appointed Lieutenant, Trenchard, was pointing his carbine at a boy. 'Hold,' Will cried, wheeling his horse. One trooper had blood streaming from his cheek while others were reaching for the pistols in their saddle holsters.

'Hold your fire,' Will cried again. 'Close up,' a corporal ordered. As the march resumed, two troopers swooped on the smirking youth whose own stone had begun the attack; and carried him off. Without their leader, the boys lost courage. Will pushed back hair damp with sweat. It had been a close-run thing.

Once over the bridge, the cavalry made camp. It was a desolate scene, for the nearby suburb of Bridgend was in flames. Burning embers dropped from roofs and floated on the wind. Dispossessed inhabitants wandered, clutching blackened pots and singed bedding. Shaken by the recent incident, Will reported the near-riot to Major Hamilton and Colonel Pye.

'What of the boy?' Hamilton asked.

'Unharmed, Sir, but for a few bruises.'

'He must be punished, but a whipping will suffice.'

Pye exchanged glances with Hamilton. 'We are leaving here tonight, Lucie. Our Horse must break through the enemy lines.'

'The regiment?'

'The whole body of Horse, under the command of General Balfour.' Pye spoke with an energy far removed from his usual quiet composure.

'And the Foot?' Will asked.

'The Foot will fall back to the sea for My Lord Warwick's ships to take them off,' Hamilton intoned, cutting off further questions.

'I knew something was in the wind. Our Horse has been dispersed about the villages. Suddenly we are all gathered together in one place,' Will muttered to Robin Lawrence later. They were sheltering in a make-shift tent that Lawrence's servant had constructed. 'Defeat is coming. We are left with escape or surrender.'

'And so, this final, desperate throw of the dice to preserve the cavalry,' Lawrence agreed. 'Yet we are encircled by the royalists. It will not be easy.'

'Do you believe the fleet will come?'

A pair of boots became visible in the gap beneath the blanket wall. 'Captain Lucie?' Will poked his head out. The man thrust a letter with the three fishes seal of the Lucie family into his hand. Will's face darkened as he read.

'Bad news?' Lawrence enquired.

'My uncle invites me to try my luck with him and the high command tonight. He talks of a boat.'

Lawrence snorted. 'He, too, believes in Warwick's ships arriving in the nick of time.'

'I am not sure he means the fleet, though. He has written "boat" not "fleet".'

'A private venture then?'

'Or rats leaving a sinking ship. I need to think.' Stuffing the letter into his pocket, Will wriggled his long body out of the shelter. He wandered through the grey, smoky drizzle amid the reek of smouldering timbers. He had run once to save himself. If he did so a second time, he would lose those shreds of self-respect he had nurtured painfully in recent days.

What would become of the three Robartes children now? And there would be no place in such a boat for Hephzibah. Hugh would laugh at the very notion. She was safe at present, working and sleeping at the Talbot while the army remained. Once they left, that doubtful protection would be removed. The Cornish servants of the Talbot, loyal to the King, would have no reason to shield her from victorious royalist soldiers. He must find her.

'Robin,' Will stuck his head inside the shelter. 'Will you cover for me? I will be an hour, no more.'

'Making arrangements with your uncle? Or are you giving warning of the flight of the Horse to your former comrades?' He rolled, reaching for his dagger.

Will's longer arm reached it first. Grabbing the hilt, he pinned Lawrence down with his elbow. 'Don't be a fool. Do you not trust me even now? It is Hephzibah I must warn.'

Lawrence relaxed. 'Ah, I had forgotten her. But there is scarcely time. And besides, who is to say she will not raise the alarm herself?'

'I say she will not! She walked alone from Devon to reach me. And all the thanks I give her is to leave her to the mercies of the King's men. She will never betray us.'

'Make haste then. I hope she may warm your bed again in days to come. But not today,' he grinned. 'There is not time for that.'

CHAPTER 51

Braddock Down, near Lostwithiel

31 August

The messenger arrived before midnight, bringing with him the fragrance of a summer night, mingled with the scents of horses tethered close by. Thanks to the wound in his neck, Gabriel was lying sleepless in the two-room cottage. He threw off the blanket, groping for breeches and boots. They were drenched in smoke from the smouldering coals in the grate, but at least they were dry and warm. Gabriel saw the flicker of the messenger's lamp beyond the narrow doorway. Ieuan, curled up in the inglenook like a dog, leapt forward to kindle rushlights and help him dress.

'Sir, a message from Boconnoc House. The rebel Horse intend to break out tonight. You are to intercept them.'

'All the Horse?'

'Aye, Sir.'

'At what hour? And by what road?'

'The two deserters who brought the news could not say. They knew only that it is to be tonight.'

'Then I will do what I can.' Gabriel groaned inwardly. 'Rouse my captains,' he continued to the trooper who had brought the messenger, 'And tell them their troops must be ready to march within the hour.' He had shifted the regiment westward from Liskeard earlier that day. The army was closing in on Lostwithiel and the Earl of Essex's trapped forces.

Minutes later the trumpeters were blowing the command to saddle up. There were shouts, the thud of running footsteps, the whinnying of the horses. Most of his men were billeted close by in the church of St Mary the Virgin. He peered at the time on his pocket watch. If the tale was true the breakout would be in the next hour or so, taking maximum advantage of the short summer night. Essex's Horse would want to be clear of the area before daybreak. They would probably make for Plymouth. Ieuan handed him a hunk of cheese and a cup of small beer. Gabriel ate and drank, his mind visualising the roads to Devon and the scattered locations of the royalist outposts.

Footsteps announced the arrival of their local guide. Using a stool as a desk, he knelt, Gabriel beside him, and sketched a rough map of the area east of Lostwithiel by the feeble illumination of a rushlight. 'That road now, yer honour, that'll be their path.' The man stabbed at the completed sketch with a stubby finger.

Getting to his feet, Gabriel sent for his officers. 'All the outposts are being alerted,' he explained to them. 'The King's Lifeguard are close at hand, we can count on them, maybe others. But we cannot wait until our forces are gathered together. The enemy may have passed beyond our reach.

Mend the light, please,' he added to Ieuan, who reached for another of the tallow-coated strips of rush hanging from the rafters.

Gabriel traced the line of the likely route with his long, slim, musician's fingers. 'If we follow this path across Braddock Down, we may intercept them close to Liskeard. Our guide says it is the fastest road by far for moving so many men and horses. They will not take the risk at night of sinking into moorland bogs.'

Briefing over, Ieuan hooked Gabriel into his buff coat and strapped on his armour while his master fidgeted. 'Rust,' Ieuan grumbled, rubbing at a spot on the back plate. 'Much more rain and the ties will rot away.'

Gabriel grinned, 'Then I will ride without armour, my friend, be more cautious and less valiant.' Twitching at the bandage on his neck, he walked out into the night, where a light mist drifted across the down. Following at his heels, Ieuan snorted.

Lanterns bobbed in the hands of the horse boys, casting faint pools of light. Behind them loomed the tower of the church, fading into blackness. The breeze had died away with nightfall. There was a softness in the air. It clung to Gabriel's hair and beard. Tension filled his body. Reluctantly, he donned his helmet. The weight increased the pain in his neck. He always detested being strapped into the constricting steel armour, would rather ride in leather alone.

Tonight he needed that protection, for if they were successful in intercepting the massed Horse of Essex, his regiment would face two or three thousand desperate men. Gabriel was so tired. So were they all. Since the forced march through the west country in pursuit of Essex's army the army had barely rested. His men had an impossible task tonight.

'You all know our purpose,' he said. 'To stop the rebel Horse. They must not escape. The watchword is 'the duchy and the King'. And God grant that I do not lead you all astray into the nearest marsh.'

Gabriel took up his place at their head for the march, their guide riding alongside, mounted on a shaggy moorland pony. Each troop carried a dark lantern at the front, and their white shirts pulled out at the back made each man faintly visible to the one in front.

Ribbons of cloud trailed across a sky fitfully illuminated by a new moon. A faint glow a few miles to the southwest was the fires of Bridgend. The mist thickened as they descended from the Down. By the time they reached the road from Lostwithiel to Liskeard, it took the guide's 'Here is the highway, Zur,' and the changed sound of the horses' hooves from grass to stone to understand they had found it.

Ahead were pinpricks of light, the glow of dying cook fires. Shrouded in oatmeal grey, they had the eerie appearance of the marsh gases known as will-o'-the-wisps. Gabriel remembered their nurse saying the unearthly lights were ghosts or fairies as the five-year-old twins listened wide-eyed. 'Lost souls,' she had concluded. 'Then I will kill them,' Michael said, waving a wooden sword. 'Poor, lost souls,' the child Gabriel said sadly. 'I hope the angels will pray for them.'

For a fleeting moment, Gabriel pictured Michael alive, at his side, a leader of men, a flaming sword in his hand like the archangel he had been named for. 'Those fires must be one of our outposts,' he said to Sayer. 'The King's army should be camped on that side of the road and Prince Maurice's on the other.' Raucous laughter issued from a shelter. A soldier appeared, brandishing a musket. The knot of men at his back, toasting their hands at a fire, were passing blackjacks of ale from hand to hand.

'Who goes there? Password,' the man slurred the challenge.

'The duchy and the King,' Sayer shouted.

There was a pause while the musketeer scratched his crotch. 'King Charles,' he said. 'Advance.' He lowered the butt of his musket to the ground. 'ere, Lieutenant, Horse arrived.'

'Whose?' The officer sounded as if he did not greatly care.

'Colonel George Vaughan's Regiment of Horse. Who commands here?' Gabriel shouted.

'Captain Beck of Colonel Baker's dragoons.'

'Summon him, now.'

'Captain said he was not to be disturbed as he is very busy – Sir,' the officer said. The musketeer guard sniggered, attempting to turn it into a cough.

'Summon him, Lieutenant.' Gabriel dismounted and paced impatiently until a bobbing lantern heralded the appearance of the yawning captain. He shook his head when Gabriel warned of the approaching Parliament Horse.

'Begging your pardon, Colonel but you're jumping at shadows. The rebels would not venture out in this mist. Night marches are the very devil. Take it from an old soldier.' The lantern illuminated the unkempt beard and weary features of a man who had reached his fortieth year without great distinction and who wanted nothing more than to sleep undisturbed. 'The night is quiet. There has been no one on the road, or my officers would have fetched me. Is that not so, Lieutenant?'

'That's right, Sir. Not a soul on the road, except the regiments of Prince Maurice's Horse. They passed by an hour ago.'

The hairs stood up on Gabriel's neck.

'You did not think fit to inform me?' Captain Beck snapped.

'You said not to disturb you before dawn, Captain,' the lieutenant protested.

'What numbers of Horse?' Gabriel asked with dangerous calm.

'Well, Lieutenant?' Beck urged.

The lieutenant hesitated.

'They was passing by for some while, Cap'n even though they were in a tearing hurry,' the musketeer interjected helpfully.

'I kept no tally, Captain, but two thousand, no more like three,' the lieutenant added, glaring at the musketeer.

'Who was in command of them?' Gabriel asked, more for confirmation than because he hoped his worst fears disproved.

'Ah, that I do know, Sir,' the lieutenant brightened. 'It was the Prince's Lieutenant General of Horse, Sir John Digby.'

Gabriel took a sharp breath. 'Sir John Digby was taken prisoner some days ago. As to the Prince's Horse, he has scarcely fifteen hundred. Essex on the other hand has twice that number if reports are correct.' Turning his back, Gabriel swung himself back into the saddle.

'I fear we are too late. How far to Liskeard by this road?'

The guide rubbed his chin. 'Matter of seven mile from here.'

'Is there some way we might head them off?'

'Sheep tracks, no more,' he shrugged. 'There might be one place, if we pick up the pace.'

CHAPTER 52

The mist clung to the fleeing horses and their riders, muffling the sounds of the three thousand. It wrapped about them like a cocoon. Will's troop were the rearguard, behind them only a single company of dragoons. Should he have accepted his uncle's offer of a place in a boat, insisting that Hephzibah accompany him? He feared what might become of the fiercely loyal girl if this mad venture of breaking through the ring of royalist forces did not succeed.

Hephzibah was on the road back to Devon. In that one stolen hour, Will had attempted to buy her a pony or a donkey, but there were none to be had. All he could procure was a pair of boots, not much worn, from a pedlar. To Will's relief, he had found her at the Talbot. He forced her to accept a handful of coins, enough to buy bread and find herself lodging better than a haystack.

'God be with you, Hephzibah. If all goes well, we will meet again at Plymouth. Take this.' He held out his dagger. She raised her head from lacing up the new boots. 'No, Will.'

'Please,' he begged. 'It is all the protection I can offer you.' She frowned, tucking it away in the small bundle she carried.

'If you need to use it, do not pause.'

'Come with me, Will. 'twill go 'ard with you if King's men catch you.' She stroked his unshaven cheek, her sea-green eyes wistful.

'Silly girl, it will take a faster horse than any the King's men have to catch Will Lucie.' His words were mere bravado, for she was right. If he were captured again it would be the noose. Yet, he could not bring himself to abandon his men in order to save himself. He would not dishonour the memory of Seymour Pyle.

'Close up! Keep to the colours!' The call jolted Will back to the present. Sir William Balfour, the General of Horse, had forbidden trumpets, but the beat of hooves and the jangle of harness shook the ground and left the air vibrating in their wake. Fused into a solid mass by darkness and fear, the troops needed few reminders to keep close. Before them lay Devon and the hope of freedom.

'Captain, Lieutenant Trenchard needs your advice.'

A horse was on its knees in the road.

'Moor can continue no further, Captain. Shall I mount him behind me?' Trenchard suggested.

Will shook his head. 'A double-laden beast will fall behind.'

'I'll manage, Cap'n. Bit o' a rest and Willow be fit for anything,' Moor said hopefully.

'Fall out then and make for the rendezvous at Plymouth.'

'What is wrong?' It was Captain Abercromby, in command of the dragoon rearguard.

'One of the horses has foundered. We have no choice but to leave the trooper behind.' Will dropped his voice. 'He must take his chances.'

'Aye, that is so. You know our orders, Captain,' Abercromby muttered. 'And remove his armour.'

'In God's name why?'

'Without armour he has some chance of passing for a civilian. If the Cornish find one of our soldiers by himself, they may tear him limb from limb.' They left Moor leading his beast off the road in search of shelter and a hiding place. Will doubted he would see him again alive.

A faint lightening in the grey pall to the east hinted at the coming of day. They had covered half the distance to the Tamar and the friendly shores of Devon. Once beyond the sleeping town of Liskeard, General Balfour called a short halt. They watered their horses at the gushing upland streams. Standing with their horses' bridles over their arms, they devoured their meagre provisions, watching and listening for a warning from Abercromby's men.

'Back in the saddle.' The order passed from one regiment to another by waving the colours.

Will rubbed bleary eyes. He must keep alert. The road was winding upwards between steep, banked lanes. An uneasy feeling pricked his dulled senses. It was a good place for an ambush. Was that a faint movement above him in the threatening dimness of the lane? He listened, but there was no sound except the slow hoofbeats of the horses toiling up the hill, the creak of leather and the jangle of harness. His tired imagination must be playing tricks on him.

Faster hoofbeats approached from behind. It was Abercromby. 'Look back, they are coming for us. Ride on, for our ways part here. God speed.' A break in the mist revealed a party of Horse on the crest of a hill. There was as yet no colour in the pale light, and the horses and riders on the skyline were washed with shades of grey and white, but there was precious little doubt that they were King's men.

Abercromby's mounted infantry were flinging themselves from their horses and forming three ranks across the road. They shouldered their muskets with practised movements, their ensign unfurling their blue guidon. The sound of distant trumpets carried on the air; and the motionless horses, framed against the sky, charged.

'Make ready,' Abercromby ordered as the first rank of royalists came within range.

Was that the shape of a crown on the enemy standard Will glimpsed? If he was correct, it was the elite troop, the gentlemen of the King's Lifeguard on their superb warhorses. Abercromby's company of dragoons could do no more than buy the fleeing roundheads a little time. If Will supported him, it might gain Balfour's force further precious minutes.

'Face about and dismount,' he ordered. 'Unfurl the standard.' Will Kent shook out the tattered silk, smoothing it with his hand.

More trumpets blared, but this time from the opposite direction. Will stared wildly about him, uncertain as to which threat to face. 'Stay in the saddle. Face forward. Sword and pistol,' he screamed.

Abercromby and his dragoons must deal with the King's Lifeguard. His own troop must face the other regiment, whoever they might be. The trumpets blared once more, and the second enemy force dashed from a nearby copse. Will dropped the reins on his horse's neck, cocked his left-hand pistol, and drew his sword. His heart was thumping, but the suddenness of the attack left no time for sweating palms or loose bowels. He signalled the trumpeter to blow the command to fall on.

'For Captain Pyle,' he shouted.

'And for Captain Lucie,' a voice responded. Robin Lawrence had doubled back. No time to question the merits of another troop disobeying their orders to flee, but Will was grateful. The front rank of the enemy was plunging down the slope; an anonymous body of men clad in buff and steel, a waving blue standard. These were not the gilded aristocrats of the King's troop. The royalist Horse were fresh, or, at least, fresher than the half-starved men and beasts of Pye's regiment. They charged, submerging the troops of Will and Lawrence in a vortex of trampling hooves, clashing swords and grunting men. Balfour and the rest of the Horse would be long gone. Had Will not stopped to help Abercromby, he, too, would be safely away.

The two troops slashed and hacked with their swords, seeking a way through the royalist attackers, but they could make no headway against these determined men blocking their path to Devon and safety. Three men were captured after their horses fell. After the initial charge, the royalists had not pressed their advantage, despite their greater numbers. The royalist commander seemed content with pinning them down as if awaiting reinforcements. Pistols cracked intermittently.

A stocky figure on a bay stallion menaced him, the horse flailing its hooves. Will thrust with his sword at its neck and the rider swerved away, yelling. The man was speaking Welsh. It was not Gabriel. Why should he think it? Will muttered. There were many Welsh regiments on the royalist side.

Shouted orders in Welsh were followed by a surge towards Pyle's standard. In the melee, Will had become separated from his cornet. 'Protect the colours,' he cried, urging his horse towards where the fight was thickest. Kent was fighting gallantly to save the rallying point and symbol of the troop. In one hand he whirled the standard, threatening the circling riders with its steel tip, while in the other he brandished a sword. Will battered his way towards the cornet, but the riders were closing in. One, bolder than the rest, reached for the horse's bridle. Kent jabbed viciously between the bars of the helmet and the lance point pierced the royalist's cheek. The man let go, but Kent had overreached himself, and another royalist snatched the standard from him before he could regain his balance. A third man struck at Kent with his sword and the cornet, blood pouring from a wounded arm, raised the other in surrender.

'No!' Will screamed as he watched Will Kent and the standard, Seymour Pyle's personal colour, receding into the distance escorted by jubilant horsemen. Tears of rage and humiliation coursed down his cheeks. Leaving the skirmish, he urged his horse after the captured flag. The rider carrying it reined in before an officer. Bowing from the saddle he presented the colour. The officer inclined his head in acknowledgement. To Will's fevered imagination, he was gloating over the silk trophy. Kent vanished over the hill with his escort, but Will was lost to anything but the need to regain the colour. He could not bear the shame of its loss.

Alone, he cantered towards the group gathered around the officer with the captured colour. Momentarily surprised by the hopeless charge of the lone captain, the riders whirled, swords drawn and then began moving towards him. Will reined in, the madness ebbing away. Alive, he might advance the cause and pursue revenge, while dead he could do nothing. He wrenched his horse's head around. A quiet order halted the blue-cloaked troopers, and they drew rein.

'Wait!' The single word was spoken in English. The Welsh commander was hailing him. Ignoring the cry, Will urged his beast into a canter. Glancing over his shoulder, he glimpsed the bare-headed enemy commander. Long dark hair flying, the man was holding his helmet in the air in salute. It was Gabriel.

* * *

'It was a lucky chance there were so few of the King's men pursuing us,' Robin Lawrence mused. 'Our preachers will surely tell how the Lord cloaked us in darkness, hiding us from our enemies. They will certainly mention our poor, naked troops. Our clothes have rotted on our backs. The weather is wet enough for Noah.'

He was standing elbow-to-elbow with Will on the packed deck of the horse ferry, towing their horses behind them across the Tamar into Devon. Saltash, and Cornwall, was slowly receding into the distance like a bad dream. They had survived.

'Did you recognise any of their colours?' Lawrence asked, getting no response. Will turned away so that his fellow captain could not see his face. 'The King's Lifeguard to our rear, the red standard with the gold crown.'

'And the others?' Lawrence prompted.

'One of the Welsh regiments. Sir George Vaughan's, I believe. They were at Cropredy Bridge.'

Will said no more. He would never speak of how close he had come to throwing his life away, had he not been saved by the good sense and humanity of Gabriel Vaughan.

PART 3

THE FLOODED MARSH

CHAPTER 53

Devon

September

'It's not right, Master,' Ieuan scolded, squeezing a bed of cloaks and blankets for Gabriel into a corner of a tent they were sharing with Vaughan's three troop captains. 'General Skippon sleeping in his coach while you are crammed head to tail like a plain trooper. And rebel colonels sleeping in your own tent like lords.'

There had been no ships to rescue the trapped Roundhead Foot. Robert Devereux had escaped in a small boat with Lord Robartes and a handful of the army staff. Most of the Horse had escaped but, for the thousands of Foot, there was only surrender, and the doubtful promise of protection by Sir George Vaughan's regiment as they marched through hostile Cornwall to rebel-held Devon.

Leading the funereal procession past the fire-blackened buildings of the Stannary Palace in Lostwithiel, had been a coach with drawn curtains, containing Devereux's General of Foot, Philip Skippon. There were angry murmurings when the watching crowd discovered they had been cheated of their lawful prey, the Earl of Essex.

Clutching remnants of sodden and threadbare uniforms about their thin bodies, the rebel soldiers trudged along, eyes on the ground. Scuffles broke out and swords flashed as royalist infantry officers attempted to restrain their own men from attacking the roundheads and rifling through their handful of belongings. Horn spoons, eating knives, odds and ends of match and ribbon, tattered blankets, even a few Soldiers' Catechisms, all strewn in the mud.

Once beyond Lostwithiel sporadic attacks by Cornishmen seeking vengeance continued. Gabriel's attempts to find food and shelter for his charges were rebuffed day after day. Towns refused them entry, and villages had not the means to provide for so many.

After more than a week on the forced march, Gabriel was too tired to argue with Ieuan. Clutching a hunk of salt bacon in one hand he thought of the thousands of enemy soldiers under his protection who had nothing to eat, and the many who had dropped by the wayside from exhaustion and starvation. Giving up his tent had been all he could do to salve his conscience. He had no food to give Skippon's troops. Gabriel's own regiment was surviving on the dwindling supplies of bacon and biscuit in their snapsacks. Thankfully a messenger had arrived from the roundhead regiment taking over the escort duty that it would be the next day. Gabriel held out the untouched bacon. 'I'm not hungry tonight, Ieuan.'

There was a sharp challenge outside the tent and a short exchange.

'Colonel, Captain Gale wishes to see you,' the trooper on guard said.

'Admit him.'

'Colonel,' the captain from Skippon's staff bowed and handed Gabriel a letter. 'Tomorrow we reach safety, and it is your own regiment who will be in danger. This letter of safe conduct will see you through those places controlled by our forces. Every senior officer has signed the letter as a tribute to your constancy.

'General Skippon wished me to give his thanks. You have lain in the cold fields with us; and if we have gone hungry, you and your men have scarcely fared any better.'

Lost for words, Gabriel could only bow. Gale turned to leave but hesitated. 'You spent some time at Basing House, I heard.'

'Last winter.'

'I am glad you left there, Sir. The place is surrounded by Colonel Norton's forces. He has culverin and has battered down a tower with his great guns. Escaped prisoners say the garrison has neither beer nor wheat and are making their bread from peas and oats. The messenger who brought the news of our escort told us of it. Basing House has been a thorn in Parliament's side, but not for much longer.'

* * *

Somerset

'Not far to Bristol now,' Ieuan said happily. 'If we cross the River Severn by the ferry, we might be home in two more days. Would you have me take a fresh horse and ride ahead to give word of your arrival?'

Like Moses staring towards the Promised Land, Gabriel gazed longingly westward towards the rain-laden clouds gathered over the Bristol Channel. In their brooding outlines was all the softness of Wales.

'I will not be returning home.'

'Master? *Ydych chi'n wallgof?*'

'No, I am not crazy. There is something I must do first. You will return to The Allt alone.' It was no use trying to explain his compulsion to come to the aid of the besieged fortress, Basing House. He had left it in order that Bess was safe. His departure had made a gap in the small garrison, a gap that had only worsened with the religious divide. And he had not helped matters with his foolishness. Now the House was surrounded, under siege once more. Only by helping the garrison in this fresh hour of need could he clear his conscience.

Gabriel stood by Llangenny's head while Ieuan, his movements jerky and angry, strapped the sack of necessaries, and fodder for the mare, to her back. In the sack were hidden Gabriel's pistols and two sashes, one red, the other tawny orange.

'I will take good care of Llangenny. Her wound is healing well, and Blackbird deserves a rest.'

'It's not the mare that troubles me, Master. What am I to say to the young mistress? That you have ridden towards a siege without so much as a buff coat?' Ieuan kicked the sack at his feet and there was a metallic ping from Gabriel's armour.

'Say nothing. Give her this.' Gabriel reached into the pocket of his coat and produced two sealed letters. 'The other is for my parents.' As to what he intended to do once he reached Basing House, he had no more than a hazy idea. If Governor Gerard had written to them exonerating Gabriel, all might be well, but there was still the matter of how to make his way through the parliamentary siege lines. Dark clouds matched Gabriel's mood as he mounted Llangenny. His officers swept their hats from their heads in farewell. Gabriel raised his own hat and turned eastward.

The second evening, he sought a night's shelter in the market town of Calne at the edge of the Wessex Downs. Gabriel almost missed the chalk marks on the rain-washed doors of the houses until a flaring torch outside a house illuminated the words 'Captain Harris 5'. Five soldiers within, allocated by a quartermaster. With no way of knowing which army 'Captain Harris' fought for, Gabriel had no option but to ride on.

He was crossing a lonely stretch of common, south of the enemy town of Newbury the next day when he heard the jangle of harness and the thunder of many hooves. Retreating into a copse, Gabriel tethered the mare, removed his spurs and crept forward. A troop of tawny-sashed cavalry were watering their horses at a stream. Inching backwards, Gabriel disturbed a rabbit. It bolted from the trees towards the troop.

'Huzzah, a rabbit for the pot.' A shot rang out. 'Should be more o'them about.' Troopers walking his way, one of them dangling the small body from his hand. Gabriel ran for Llangenny.

'Halt!' The men had seen him and were crashing through the undergrowth in pursuit. He ducked behind a tree trunk, picked up a stone and hurled it into a bush in the opposite direction. Rewarded by a cry of 'That way,' he straightened up.

'Don't move,' came from behind him, and he felt the barrel of a gun pressed against his back.

'Found more than a rabbit, Sir,' the trooper called cheerily. The officer he addressed turned his head from examining his horse's hoof.

'We cannot be delayed by taking prisoners, Corporal Fowler.'

'He was following us, Captain.'

'That is for me to ascertain. If he is here by chance, we might release him. If not . . .'

Gabriel mentally finished the sentence with, 'Then we will hang him.'

'And if he is with the rebels, Captain?' Fowler persisted.

Gabriel's head whirled at the words. 'Whose forces are you, Sir?'

'I will ask the questions,' the officer snapped. 'And since my corporal has already asked the question, I will repeat it. 'Are you with the rebels?'

'I am an officer of His Majesty. My name is Gabriel Vaughan, lately commanding Sir George Vaughan's Regiment of Horse.'

'Have you proof of this?'

'My commission is in my coat pocket.'

The officer studied Gabriel's commission and then nodded. 'My apologies, Colonel Vaughan, but why are you riding unattended?'

'I might ask why your troops are posing as rebels,' Gabriel replied.

The officer waved an apologetic hand at the tawny sash around his waist. 'We are from the garrison of Wallingford and we are riding to relieve Basing House. It is surrounded by rebel forces, hence this masquerade.'

'Then well met, Sir. I have the same purpose.' As they rode, Gabriel explained to the officer, Captain Walters, his previous service with the garrison.

'The situation there is desperate, Colonel,' Walters said. 'A messenger got through to Oxford. If the garrison does not receive supplies of ammunition within days, they will be forced to surrender. More men under Colonel Henry Gage will rendezvous with us at Aldermaston. Our horses are carrying as much as they can.' Behind the horses plodded a string of heavily laden pack mules.

'Has Colonel Gage arrived before us, Captain?' Gabriel asked as they approached the bridge over the River Kennet at Aldermaston. A group of cavalry with tawny sashes or ribbons in their hats were watering their horses. They glanced up at the sight of the approaching troop.

Reining in, Walters eyed the horsemen. 'I fear not,' he murmured. 'We must act our parts as rebels.' He walked his horse forward. Gabriel, a tawny sash about his own waist, followed. There was a sudden bang and a cry. Corporal Fowler had fired his pistol. 'The King and the cause,' he yelled and charged the surprised roundheads.

CHAPTER 54

The Allt

Daylight had not yet penetrated Bess's bedchamber when she was wakened by distant knocking from the courtyard. Instinct told her it must be Gabriel. She threw back the heavy, embroidered covers.

'Gwyneth,' she called. 'Master Gabriel has returned.' The maid ran in, her feet bare. 'Dear Gwyneth, bring me my best gown, the black and gold with the fleur de lys. Never mind my hair.'

Torn between the desire to see Gabriel without delay, and the wish to look her best, Bess crammed her night-time plaits inside a coif. Her petticoats remained on the chair, and only one sleeve was attached when there was a knock at the chamber door.

'Good morning, Bess,' Lady Alice smiled. 'Ieuan has returned.'

'And Gabriel?'

'Gabriel is well, but not yet here. If you come down, I will call Ieuan to speak to you.'

A quarter of an hour later Bess, now attired in an older gown, entered the Great Hall. Ieuan was standing by the fireplace. Less than three months since he had left with Gabriel, but his face was leaner and the expression in his eyes wary. He bowed.

'I am pleased to see you home, Ieuan. Have you broken your fast?'

'I have eaten, Mistress, thank you.'

'Why is he not with you?' The question would not be suppressed.

A gleam of sympathy appeared in Ieuan's eyes before he adopted the respectful expression of a manservant. 'I would have stayed with him, Mistress but he would not permit it. He has gone to Basing House.'

Bess felt a tightness in her throat. 'With his regiment?'

'Alone, Mistress. This is for you.' Ieuan pulled a crumpled letter from his coat.'

'Thank you, Ieuan. Go and rest.'

The manservant bowed. As he straightened up, she saw in his stance a flash of the comrade in arms and companion, who only her husband knew. Why would Gabriel return to Basing without his bodyguard? She broke the seal.

'My beloved wife, I hope to see you before many more weeks have passed. Basing House is under siege once more and they have neither bread nor ale. I cannot return to you while the men and women of Basing starve, for I have done them wrong. I will tell you all when we are together. I pray for your safety every day. Your devoted husband.'

Bess seated herself in a highbacked chair and bit her lip until it bled. Cradling the precious letter, she told the servant lighting the fire that she was going to the stillhouse and did not need breakfast.

Standing over the stove in the stillhouse later, Bess tried to recall how long her mother had steeped goldenrod flowers. Should she add the leaves? Twm's elderly father suffered from backache and the brew might ease it.

'Ah, Bess. Is that goldenrod you are soaking? I always add honey.' Lady Alice gave one of her rare smiles. Once steam was rising from the brass pot, she turned to business. 'We have sent to Cwm for a priest so that the baby may be baptised. We will begin preparations in secret. If word spreads too widely that a child has been born to you and Gabriel, wagging tongues may report the family again.'

'Report us? Why?'

'For not having the child baptised in the parish church and her birth entered in the register.'

Bess remembered Father Allen's warning. '*Your marriage will be valid in the eyes of God, but in English law it will be a crime. If it comes to the attention of the authorities, you may be arrested. If your children are not baptised as Protestants, you may be arrested again.*'

Lady Alice left the stillhouse in a brisk swish of skirts. Bess sank onto a stool while the brew steamed beside her forgotten. She had overlooked this further consequence of her daughter's birth. Civil war had neither changed the law nor lessened the hatred of Catholics in King Charles's England.

CHAPTER 55

Basing House

The attack on the roundhead patrol at Aldermaston had effectively destroyed any element of surprise, for some of them had escaped. It left the relief force with no alternative but to march all night. Then, in the darkness before dawn, came the fog, rising from the Loddon, obscuring the valley from view.

'Can you tell us our position, Colonel Vaughan?' Gage asked. 'We might be anywhere from Cirencester to Hull for all that I can see.'

'Chineham Down, Sir, no more than two miles from Basing,' Gabriel said. 'We have passed between two hills and from the feel of the ground, I would say we are on part of the old Roman road running to the coast.'

'Will you carry a message to the house warning the garrison of our approach and requesting a sortie in support? You are best placed to find a way through the enemy's siege lines; and they will trust a message if you are the bearer.'

Gabriel hesitated. If the garrison had received a letter from Governor Gerard they might well trust him, but if not . . . There was only one way to find out. 'Yes Sir. I will have them light a beacon to guide you in,' he said.

* * *

The wall of the Grange emerged, ghostlike, as Gabriel stumbled from the reeds barefoot, mud coating his shirt and breeches, droplets of fog curling his hair. Drawing his sword, he emptied muddy water from the scabbard and wiped the hilt clean.

Beyond it was the massive outline of the Great Barn, all that remained of the farm buildings after Lieutenant Colonel Johnson, Gabriel and a small group from the garrison, had burned them to the ground in a deadly game of hide and-seek with the enemy.

'*Far enough, I think. Throw down your weapons.*' Gabriel shuddered at the memory of the enemy officer ambushing him inside a barn on that November day. To the accompaniment of choking smoke and crackling flames, they had fought while tongues of fire shot up the wall until a blazing beam trapped his opponent.

'Watch the gate while I relieve meself.' The voice brought Gabriel back to the present. It sounded as if it were no more than feet away. He stooped and the hilt of his sword clanged against the brick wall.

'What was that?'

'One of those pesky cats, most likely. No one out in this. Give me the smoky, black air o' London any time.'

'Make sure you relieve yerself downwind.'

Beyond the Grange Gabriel could see the outline of earthworks thrown up by the roundhead Colonel Norton since his previous visit. Gabriel felt his way around the outside of the curtain wall to the small postern gate which lay close to the Great Barn and rapped hard.

'Stand away, or you will be fired upon from above.' Gabriel recognised the voice of Francis Cuffaud.

'Francis, it's Gabriel, Gabriel Vaughan.'

'Gabriel? Are you alone?' He sounded agitated.

'I am.'

'I will open the gate but lay down your arms before you enter. There is a guard of musketeers behind me who will shoot if you have lied.'

So, Gerard had not kept his word, or Rawdon had not accepted it. Cursing inwardly, Gabriel placed his sword and dagger on the ground. There was a scrape and clatter as bolts were slid and the bar was raised.

The gate opened a fraction. A lantern illuminated Cuffaud's face, throwing the long scar from a sword-cut into grotesque relief.

Lowering his blade, Cuffaud spoke over his shoulder to the man holding the lantern. 'Bring his weapons and secure the gate.' He pulled Gabriel inside.

'You do not trust me, Francis.'

'Not a bit. Why are you here?'

Gabriel stared at the friend who had been his groomsman. 'I am with a relief force bearing supplies, but they cannot make their way through this miasma. They sent me with a message. You must light a beacon as a signal.'

'Colonel Rawdon will be the judge of that. I must blindfold you.'

'You do not wish me to see how many men are left?'

'I do not.' Cuffaud tied a kerchief over Gabriel's eyes and guided him into the Great Gatehouse, where he knocked at a door.

'Enter,' came the familiar voice of Lieutenant Colonel Thomas Johnson.

Cuffaud led him inside before removing the blindfold. Johnson's face had grown haggard and thin.

'What the devil is this, Francis? Did you capture him?' Johnson asked. He ran his hand through his hair, releasing, as always, the aroma of herbs from his garden.

'He claims he is a messenger from a relief force who await our signal.'

'Why not send a trumpeter?'

'I alone knew the way. I swam the Loddon.'

'That at least is true. You stink of the marshes. Francis, find Colonel Rawdon and have a servant fetch Colonel Vaughan fresh attire. If we must hang him, at least he will not meet his maker smelling like a jakes.' He wrinkled his nose.

Gabriel shivered in his wet clothes. The fireplace was empty; and the cold struck through the soles of his feet from the worn blue and white tiles.

Johnson regarded him quizzically, arms folded over the buff coat which hung loose on his frame. 'I would send for mulled ale to warm you but, as your spies may have told you, we have neither ale, nor barley to brew more.' He turned his attention to a list he was making. It appeared to be an inventory of the stores. Seeing Gabriel scanning it, he turned the paper face down. 'What is your purpose? If you seek forgiveness, you should ask your confessor. Do you believe your crimes can be washed away in the Loddon?'

'I know it is not the River Jordan, Sir,' Gabriel countered.

'I see your wit has not deserted you. You stand accused of conspiring with Lord Edward to betray this place. Your letters, written in your own hand, signed with your own name, or with that ridiculous bird, condemned you. Why should I not sentence you to summary execution? If we string you up from the top of this gatehouse, it will be a sign to others that those who betray Basing House may expect no mercy.'

They had every reason to doubt his word. Gabriel had no proof that the relief force even existed. If they hanged him, the relief force might sit upon the Down until Colonel Norton discovered them. The supplies would be lost, Basing House's last chance with it. And all because he had not explained to Gage that he was the last person in the world he should send as a messenger.

'I ask only that I may prove my loyalty by fighting at your side today as I have before,' Gabriel said, his teeth chattering.

'If you perish from cold, you will neither fight nor hang,' the herbalist sighed. 'Strip off your wet attire and wrap this cloak about you.'

His fingers stiff with cold, Gabriel fumbled with the tie on his shirt and the buttons on his breeches. When he pulled the shirt over his head, Johnson peered at his neck. 'What is that clout about your neck? A wound?' Sniffing, he untied the muddy bandage covering the partially healed bullet wound. 'There is no odour of corruption, but I believe those sutures should be removed.' Johnson tugged gently at the stitches. 'Loose, as I thought. Sit.'

By the time Johnson had finished removing the waxed linen thread, Cuffaud was back, with Colonel Rawdon and a manservant carrying a towel and a pile of garments. There was a worn and mended doublet, a Monmouth cap, coarse linen shirt, patched breeches, a pair of shoes.

'I wonder that you concern yourself with this man's state of health,' Rawdon said to Johnson.

The herbalist spread his hands. 'I am a healer first, Colonel, a soldier second.'

Rawdon grunted. 'Lieutenant Cuffaud has told me your tale,' he said to Gabriel. 'That you want me to light a fire on the roof of the Great Gatehouse as a beacon to our forces.'

'I do, Sir. Unless the fog clears, they will not find their way.'

'And why should I believe you? Without doubt it is a signal, but for whom?'

'Sir, what assistance would a beacon bring the enemy? It is our friends who need a sign to find their way here from Chineham Down.'

'I fear it is a trap,' Cuffaud interjected.

Rawdon silenced him with a gesture. 'Take him outside. I will call you in when I have made a decision.'

He shut the door firmly behind him. Gabriel and Cuffaud waited, an invisible barrier between them. The muffled sounds of Rawdon's gruff voice and Johnson's lighter tones rose and fell. Finally, the door opened.

'Very well,' Rawdon growled. 'We will take you at your word. Lieutenant, have men carry logs and faggots to the roof. Fix a cage upon an iron pole and fill it with them, then fire it. We must hope that Colonel Gage, if he is indeed there, will see its light.' Cuffaud bowed and ran from the room.

'Thank you, Sir,' Gabriel breathed more freely. 'When you hear Colonel Gage's drums and trumpets, you must make a sally from Garrison Gate and take the enemy in the rear.'

Johnson cleared his throat. 'Sir, what of?' he nodded at Gabriel.

'Colonel Vaughan will lead the attack. If he speaks the truth and our friends are close by, he may redeem himself with the blood of the enemy or his own. If he is lying, I leave it to you to see that justice is served.'

'I will follow your orders Sir,' Johnson said.

CHAPTER 56

'We must arm you.' Johnson, comfortable while dealing with the bullet wound, had relapsed into his former distant manner. 'I will accompany you and familiarise you with the present positions of the enemy. They have built four forts about the house.'

Gabriel stopped in the act of hooking up the front of a blood-stained buff coat. 'There is no need, Sir. I saw their works myself.'

'Nevertheless, I go with you. I will give orders to return your sword and find you a carbine, but you have no need of a horse. We are going on foot with three score cavalry, those who you commanded last winter. We shall attack the fort on Cowdray's Down and seize the gun.'

Outside the Great Gatehouse, the fog was dense as ever. Its dank odour mingled with the lingering traces of decaying vegetation and marsh water on Gabriel's skin. He peered towards the roof. Was that a glimmer in the dimness? Like dye spreading through cloth, a soft red glow flowered high above them. It grew rapidly, the smell of wood-smoke drifting toward them. He wondered how many men remained in the garrison, if none but dismounted cavalry could be spared to attack the fort. The troopers were standing near Garrison Gate, in the curtain wall of the house on its north side.

'Gentlemen, most of you remember Captain Vaughan,' Johnson said. 'He has returned to lead you in one more sortie.'

'Our part is to attack the enemy's works on Cowdray's Down so that a relief force may cut their way through,' Gabriel explained.

The men loaded and wound up the wheel locks on their carbines, their faces impassive as they listened.

'The beacon is lit. It is time,' Johnson said.

'Wait!' Francis Cuffaud was galloping towards them. He reined in sharply and dismounted. 'I will join you.'

'As you wish.' Johnson looked unhappy; and Gabriel guessed that his arrival had not been sanctioned. 'You will need this.' He proffered a white kerchief. 'Tie it about your elbow so that Colonel Gage's party will know you.'

Despite the chill morning air, sweat prickled Gabriel's skin beneath the fresh shirt. He loaded his carbine and slung the strap over his shoulder. The borrowed buff coat was tight. He rotated his shoulders, hoping he had sufficient room to raise his sword arm above his head. Two men were lifting the heavy bars from the locking mechanism on Garrison Gate.

'Trumpets?' Johnson queried.

'No. Colonel Gage will use them. Our own is to be a surprise attack.'

'Then let us be about it.' Johnson's eyes scoured Gabriel's face as if searching his soul. They led the way through the gate and crossed the lane towards the Grange. Its farm gate lay in splintered fragments.

'I will go first,' Gabriel said.

'I will go with you.'

'Do you fear that I am going to fetch the enemy?'

'Believe what you will. We go together.'

Sword in hand they picked their way past the Great Barn, its bricks scarred by cannon balls and between blackened timbers, ashes and patches of nettles until they reached the encircling wall. Gabriel placed his weapons on the ground, put his foot in Johnson's hand and scrambled to the top of the wall.

'Nothing, but I heard two men earlier. There might be a regiment concealed this side of the Loddon and we would not see them.'

'We must trust to our ears then,' Johnson shrugged. The troopers swarmed after them over the wall, passing up the heavy carbines. There was a cry as a weapon landed on someone.

'Muttonhead, I'll have yer hide if that wheel lock is broken,' the corporal snarled. 'Who did it strike?' he added as an afterthought.

Me, Sir, Meldon. I am not much hurt.'

Gabriel remembered the accident-prone trooper. If a stirrup leather broke, or a clay pipe set a heap of straw afire, Meldon was sure to be there.

Beyond the wall, Johnson led the way across spongy ground towards the reeds of the marsh. 'I will show you a better place to cross the river. There are remains of a narrow causeway near the mill. The water will be no more than a foot or so deep.'

Shoes hanging about their necks and carbines across their shoulders, the sixty men waded through knee-deep water and began the climb to the invisible top of Cowdray's Down.

'How many are likely to be there?' Gabriel whispered.

'Not enough to trouble us, if God is with us. At this hour most of the Horse should be asleep in their billets in the villages.' Johnson pointed to a curving shape looming out of the mist. 'Here is the front of their works, facing the House.'

'I think I hear voices,' Gabriel gestured to halt.

'Warming themselves maybe?' asked a voice from the fort.

'Dunno, Dick. Might be up to something,' another voice answered. 'Reckon we should tell the cap'n Basing 'ouse is ablaze.'

'Never find 'im in this soup. Besides it's our turn for a warm.'

The voices receded.

'Let us fall on.' Johnson said.

'Sir, no, wait for Colonel Gage's drums and trumpets, signalling his attack. Let me make contact. Storm the fort too early and our attempt will be wasted.'

'You want to creep away? How do I know it is not to warn the enemy and lead us into an ambush?' Johnson's voice was harsh and desperate.

'I have no proof of my honesty. Yet if I am lying, may I never see my wife again, nor live to see my newborn child.' Gabriel pulled Michael's crucifix from his shirt and kissed it. Johnson hesitated then nodded.

'Go then.'

The fort was no more than a gun emplacement, mud walls capped by wicker gabions crammed with earth, chalk and flints. Gabriel edged along the shallow ditch in the lee of the wall, pausing often to listen. The men on watch were evidently confident the fog would prevent a royalist attack, but there must be more than the two he had heard. The acrid scent of burning match drifted across the wall. Loaded muskets ready to fire, and the saker, the gun which they must capture.

He had reached the back of the battery. Beyond an expanse of open ground, more than a hundred paces away, a brooding line of hedges was faintly visible. If the fog lifted, the men within the fort would spot him immediately.

Squatting in the shelter of the wall, Gabriel prepared to make his dash. There was a sudden chorus of trumpet blasts, followed by the thud of drums. Gage's signal that he had arrived. But moments later came a second outburst of drums and trumpets, this time from behind the hedges. The fog lifted, revealing a body of Horse and Foot emerging from their hiding place. They must be Norton's men. It was an ambush. Widening rents in the drifting fog revealed Gage's men. Poised like players on a stage, the two sides faced each other, then charged.

Gabriel raced back towards the crack of firearms, coming from below the fort. He skidded to a halt beside Cuffaud, who was leading a frontal attack. The first few men had crossed the shallow ditch and were swarming up the wall, under fire from a handful of musketeers.

'Keep going, men,' Cuffaud shouted, adjusting his own sword belt in preparation for climbing.

'To arms,' an officer called from inside the fort. More heads popped up above the parapet.

'St George!' cried Cuffaud, throwing himself at the wall. His leap took him halfway to the top. Gabriel followed, jumping for the parapet. He found a foothold on the roughened wall and scrabbled up the last few feet, his scabbard banging against his leg. Clinging to one of the reinforcing gabions, Gabriel saw Cuffaud throw a long leg over the top and disappear from view, sword in hand.

There were more shots as Gabriel dropped to the ground; but there were too few men to repulse their attack and the defenders quickly fell back. From the other side of the fort came more shouts as Johnson attacked.

'Bring ten men,' Gabriel ordered a corporal. 'We will disable the gun.'

A tall, thickset man with a patch over one eye blocked the top of a short flight of rough steps, wielding a long halberd. Gabriel ran up the steps, throwing himself beneath the outstretched arms, and thrust his blade into a meaty thigh as the man swung the axe blade hard. The halberdier roared in pain and fell on Gabriel, toppling him down the steps and trapping his sword arm beneath his body.

Winded, Gabriel fought to free his dagger with his left hand. The wounded man had dropped the halberd but had drawn his own dagger. Grunting, he pinned Gabriel with his elbow. Drawing his arm back to strike, he screamed and collapsed face down on Gabriel's chest. Wriggling from beneath the dying man, Gabriel saw Cuffaud's scarred face above him. The lieutenant twisted the blade of his sword to release it from the halberdier's back and it came free with a sucking sound.

'At your service, Sir,' he grinned. 'I will leave the saker to you.'

Pounding towards them came the corporal with the ten men. 'This way,' Gabriel said.

The gun crew strained at the ropes, labouring to rotate the saker to meet the attack on their rear while the gunner, an older man dressed in good broadcloth with silver on his sword hilt, screamed orders.

'Drop your weapons,' Gabriel commanded the gun crew. One man grabbed the long rammer and held it before him like a club while the gunner shouted, 'You shall not take my gun from me!'

His gallant resistance was short-lived. Rushing at Gabriel, sword in hand, he tripped over a pail of water set near the guns to cool them and the weapon flew from his hand. His men dropped their makeshift weapons.

'Spike the gun to disable it,' Gabriel ordered the grinning corporal. 'Our task is done.' The saker could not fire on Basing House while the relief force reprovisioned the garrison.

But the fight was not yet over. Turning his back on the corporal who was hammering a steel spike through the touch hole, Gabriel saw a knot of men stumbling about next to a pile of withies and half-finished baskets. Cuffaud was battling a powerfully-built man with muscular arms like a smith who was forcing him back against the baskets. Swinging his heavy cavalry sword above his head, Gabriel flung himself at the roundhead.

'Oh, would you?' the man snarled at Gabriel, disposing of Cuffaud by smashing the hilt of the sword into the side of his head. Dropping his sword, the lieutenant fell like a stone. The roundhead lunged at Gabriel, who parried the blow. His weak ankle wobbled, and he righted himself with difficulty. The morning had taken its toll. He must stop the fight.

'You are too much for me, Sir.' Gabriel lowered the point of the sword and unclipped his carbine from its sling. His adversary looked at the weapons dangling from Gabriel's hands.

'Are you begging for quarter?' He lowered his own blade as Gabriel trudged towards him.

'Beg?' Gabriel answered slowly, 'No.' Swinging the butt of the carbine at the man's head he knocked him off balance. A second blow rendered him unconscious. Panting, Gabriel hurried to the prone Cuffaud, and picked up his sword. He bent over him.

There was a click behind him. 'Drop that sword, Vaughan,' Johnson screamed. 'Touch him again and I shoot.'

Gabriel turned his head. The colonel was pointing a pistol at him. 'You disgust me. The enemy were lying in wait for our forces because you planned it with them. Have you killed him?'

'The enemy were alerted by a patrol of their own men. Neither was it I who attacked the lieutenant, Sir,' Gabriel protested. Johnson stalked towards him, levelling the pistol. Gabriel dropped Cuffaud's sword. Appearances were against him.

'Throw down your own weapons and turn around. Hands behind your back!' Johnson ripped the white kerchief from Gabriel's arm and pinioned his wrists.

'I may be a healer, Vaughan,' he spat, 'But by God above, I swear at this moment I would cheerfully run you through with my sword and consider justice well served. Cornet, get him out of my sight. Take him back to the House to Colonel Rawdon. See that he does not escape.'

CHAPTER 57

Fury pounding through his veins, Johnson squatted down beside Cuffaud. He must do what he could for him. How could he have been duped so easily by the traitor's renewed assurances of honesty? He felt Cuffaud's neck for a pulse and found it, beating strongly.

'Alive, then,' Johnson breathed. 'I arrived in the nick of time.' He had forestalled Vaughan from striking the fatal blow. There was a wound on Cuffaud's temple. Untying his own kerchief, Johnson gently wiped away the blood to see what lay below. Beneath the deep lacerations, a bump was swelling. Johnson probed gently, fearing damage to the brain within. He beckoned to two troopers. 'Rig a stretcher with your coats. We will carry the lieutenant back to the House.'

Gage's larger force had repelled the roundhead attack and were busy unloading their ammunition supplies when Johnson, after dressing the wound on the unconscious Cuffaud, joined Rawdon and Peake in the Great Gatehouse. He found Gage with them.

'I confess myself surprised that Colonel Vaughan is guilty of such perfidy,' Gage lamented. 'What could be his motive?'

'I say hang him now,' Peake growled.

'Not before questioning him,' Rawdon said. 'There has been one conspiracy and there may be other men caught in his web. Besides, there is not time to deal with him now. We must provision the House from Basingstoke market before the enemy regroups. It was no more than a small part of their forces who ambushed us.'

'What have you done with him?' Johnson asked. The pain of betrayal was almost physical.

'Locked in the cellars of the New House,' Rawdon said. 'Safe enough for the present.'

* * *

'Villains, papist thieves!' Market traders grabbed at their baskets of cheeses, herbs or ribbons. Eggs smashed as stalls overturned. Shop keepers yelled at their apprentices to get the shutters up. Those with livestock vainly tried to herd their startled beasts from the square. Two loose bullocks added to the confusion.

Running up the outside stairs of the dilapidated Mote Hall, a group of youths began pelting the troops with loose tiles from the roof. One of the horses reared. Several troopers reached for their pistols.

'Hold your fire,' Johnson ordered. 'Take those lads into custody before they kill someone. Then block the square at Mote Street.'

A handful of women were disappearing with their merchandise. 'Shall I go in pursuit, Sir?' an eager corporal asked, pointing at a stout woman with a struggling duck tucked under each arm.

'Let her be, it is the carts and the livestock we need. And find the powder store. It will be in one of the churches or the cellars of an inn.'

Gage's musketeers were shoving traders into lines for inspecting their goods. Grain, cheese, bacon and malt were being loaded into carts. The market square gradually emptied as loaded carts carrying powder and food stuffs creaked and lumbered towards Basing. They were accompanied by the livestock the royalists had rounded up. Behind the carts walked a score of men and boys under guard for resisting the seizure of their goods.

The mayor hurried up to Johnson, very red in the face. 'Sir, I must protest at the removal of the powder which is needed for the defence of this town.'

'The powder will be perfectly safe at Basing House, Sir,' Johnson assured him, straight-faced. 'The garrison is here for your protection. His Majesty will be pleased to hear of the town's loyalty.' It was no less than highway robbery, however he might dress it up in fine words. Johnson feared that one day the King, and Basing House, would pay a terrible price.

Arriving back at Basing, he went to check on Cuffaud's condition. The lieutenant's face was ashen and his eyes were closed, but he moaned when Johnson gently checked the bandage.

'Francis? Can you hear me?' he asked, relieved.

'Head hurts,' Cuffaud mumbled, opening his eyes. He tried to sit up, but Johnson placed a firm hand on his chest.

'Lie still. You have a wound to the head.'

Cuffaud groaned. 'What happened?'

'The villain attacked you, but we have him safe. He will work no more mischief in this world; and will soon find himself in the next.'

'Good.' Evidently exhausted by talking, Cuffaud closed his eyes again. 'But what became of Gabriel?' he asked a moment later.

Johnson's relief evaporated. His patient could not remember words from one moment to the next. 'Under guard, Francis, as I have said.'

'What are you talking of, Sir? Where is Gabriel? He saved me.'

* * *

'Forgive me. I thought . . .' Thomas Johnson tore the kerchief off Gabriel's wrists. Gabriel massaged them and flexed his fingers.

'I might have thought the same in your position. How is Francis?'

'A sore head, but no lasting harm.' There was an awkward pause. 'Colonel Gage is briefing the senior officers in the Great Parlour of the New House. We should join them.'

Like most of the house, the Great Parlour had suffered neglect from the falling fortunes of the Paulets. Gaps in the lead panes had allowed rain to cause further damage; and soldiers had carved their names below the family coat of arms in the fireplace's overmantel. But its distance from the busier courts and kitchens suited Gage's purpose.

'At nightfall tomorrow, we leave for Oxford,' Gage was saying as Johnson and Gabriel squeezed into the room.

'A hard task to pass through the siege lines,' Peake said. The enemy will have regrouped.' He broke off suddenly, 'What is he doing here? Why have you released him?' he asked Johnson.

'A grave misunderstanding has now been put right. It was I who was at fault. Gabriel Vaughan has done nothing.'

Peake looked as if he wished to argue but turned his attention back to Gage, who was waiting politely.

'We will don once more the orange scarves of parliament,' Gage said. 'But tomorrow we will deliver messages to all the villages hereabouts ordering them to bring provisions here the following day. They will not expect us to break out tomorrow night.'

* * *

'Will you leave with Gage?' Johnson asked Gabriel later.

'It is time I returned to my home in Wales.'

'I hope you will forgive the things I said.'

'You were in the right rebuking me for meddling,' Gabriel replied. 'It caused great harm, the death of a promising young trooper.'

The breach was mended, but Johnson wished to restore the greater degree of friendship they had known. 'Gabriel, before the war I published writings of the plants I discovered in travelling through Snowdon and Anglesey. When peace comes, I hope to continue my work in a tour of the southern parts of the principality. It might be a companion volume to the first. Would you grant me the honour of dedicating it to the Vaughans of Allt Yr Esgair?'

'The honour would be mine,' Gabriel said.

How long would it be, Johnson pondered, before the war ended, and he could substitute pen for sword? Only God knew who would die, and who would remain alive to enjoy the blessings of peace. In the meantime, there was a good supper for once awaiting in the Great Hall. He had eaten nothing all day and Johnson realised he was famished.

PART 4

HOMECOMING

CHAPTER 58

Chadshunt Hall

Will's heart quickened its beat as the well-known gate house came into sight. He had not visited his home since a night-time sortie with his father in August '43 to retrieve valuables. Would all the old servants be there? How would they receive him? Hugh Lucie had taken a dozen troopers with him. As they approached the gatehouse, Will took up position behind his uncle. The gates were closed, as they would not have been in the days before the war. The horses clattered to a halt. Jacob the gatekeeper opened the gate slowly, a trooper on guard beside him.

'Colonel Hugh Lucie!' Hugh barked. Jacob swung the gate open. Will saw his mouth gaping in surprise as he caught sight of Will in the midst of the group. They broke into a trot once more, leaving the gate house behind them. Now they were approaching the top of the lane. Will was relieved to see that both the main house and the west wing of the L-shaped Tudor mansion showed no obvious signs of damage. He wondered if the damage to the interior, caused by enemy soldiers searching the previous year, had been repaired. With a jolt, he realised that he, too, was now one of that self-same enemy. He found himself reining in with the rest in the cobbled courtyard. A groom emerged reluctantly from the stables.

'Ben,' Will hailed. Ben stopped short, recognising his master's son. 'Master Will!' His face broke into a grin, but then he frowned, looking at Hugh and the other troopers. As Will swung down from the saddle, Ben approached, his face anxious.

'Master Will, you are a prisoner? How were you captured?'

Will turned his face away, reluctant to reveal the truth. There was a tightness in his chest.

'Fellow, take Captain Lucie's horse away and mine,' Hugh barked at Ben. 'Come, Will, the servants will see to our horses and those of our men.'

If Will had arrived flourishing the cornet of his enemy troop, he could not have felt more hideously conspicuous than he did now, the tawny orange sash of Parliament about his waist. His uncle's arm resting lightly on his shoulder was a lead weight. He fixed his gaze upon his booted and spurred feet as Hugh marched him up the short flight of steps between the arches of the stone portico, below the Lucie family motto 'I am shut to envy but always open to a friend.' The door had opened, other servants were there.

During the preceding weeks Will had grown content with his lot as a soldier of the parliament. Now the fragile armour he had built for himself crumbled. Chadshunt's loyal servants were learning that he, the eldest son and heir to the estates, was returned there only because he had joined the rebels. It made a mockery of their own loyalty.

Hugh had said nothing on the long journey from Devon of why they were coming to Chadshunt. He had sent for Will a few days after the cavalry arrived in Plymouth at the end of their flight from Cornwall, and told him to prepare for a visit to his old home. Astonished, Will had pointed out he could not leave his battle-worn troop to fend for themselves, but Hugh had said only that Colonel Pye had agreed and that Major Hamilton would take temporary command of Will's troop until he rejoined them.

* * *

Will surveyed his old chamber, clearly left untenanted since his departure. The bed was neatly made, the embroidered counterpane stiff and straight, the brocaded curtains tied back with tasselled ties, and an absence of dust on the wooden chest, the table and chairs, suggested that the servants had kept it ready for his return. He opened the chest and discovered to his surprise that all his apparel was neatly folded in linen bags as he had left it the previous year.

Like a child, he sat on the floor and untied the necks of the bags, rediscovering what he had abandoned. Spare night caps, a Dutch coat, a heavy velvet cloak not suited to the field, a worn doublet or two and spare linen lay within the chest. No sign of moths nor mould. The servants must have been airing them in some defiant belief that he would return. He felt around at the bottom of the chest. A pair and a half of silk stockings, and one of wool, tidily rolled. Even a broken pair of silver spurs, intended for repair at the silver smiths, lay there untouched. The soldiers who had occupied the house must have been under strict command if there had been no looting.

Damage to the panelling showed where the troops had searched in vain for the King's campaign plans many months earlier. Will ran his hands over the splintered panels, none of which had been repaired. He knew them so well that he could enumerate the carved birds and flowers which were missing.

Will tugged off his dusty riding boots unaided, unbuttoned his doublet and flopped down on the high bed, sinking into the remembered softness of the feather beds and exhaling with relief. He was on the verge of sleep when the door opened without warning. It was Jack, his father's former page. The lad must be all of fourteen now, still a boy but no longer a child. Will sat up and smiled at the freckled face and unruly mop of dark curls.

'It is good to see you, Jack.'

A pair of brown eyes stared fixedly over Will's left shoulder. 'Colonel Lucie wishes you to attend him in the library, Your Honour.' He turned on his heel, leaving the room without bow or any further acknowledgement.

Will frowned at the insolence. He had half a mind to call the boy back. 'To what purpose?' he muttered. 'Should I punish him that he is more loyal to this house, this family, than I?' Despondently, Will reached once more for his dirty boots.

There were gaps on the library's high shelves, marking where

Parliament's soldiers had destroyed books in their search the previous year. Hugh was waiting, a book of prayers open in his hand. He smiled genially as his nephew entered. 'Do you wish for a pipe, Will?' He indicated a jar of tobacco on a side table.

'If you will join me, Sir,' Will said politely.

'Devil's weed,' Hugh responded, 'Dulls the senses, but there are many of the godly who partake of it. No matter.'

Nervous, Will perched on the edge of a high-backed chair and twitched at the pearl buttons on his doublet. Despite Hugh's friendly manner, he felt like a hare before the hounds.

'You are happy, are you not, Will, to be back at Chadshunt in your own home?'

'I am, Sir, although it no longer belongs to me.'

'You may call me Uncle. While we remain here, let us set aside formality.'

Will relaxed to the extent of pressing his tense shoulders against the padded chair back.

'I brought you here so that you might spend a week or two in your home and so that the servants may see and accept that it is you and not your father who is now master here. Now that you have joined the army of Parliament, I no longer need a tenant here.

'After your stay here you, and Colonel Pye's regiment, will join Lieutenant General Oliver Cromwell and his Eastern Association forces in East Anglia. But when the war is over, Chadshunt will once more be your home.'

Will stared at him with a mixture of disbelief and hope. 'How can that be, Uncle? The Committee for Sequestration,'

'The Committee for Sequestration,' Hugh interrupted, 'Seized these estates as the possession of a known malignant.'

'My father has not changed his allegiance, Uncle,' Will muttered.

'Regrettably, he has not. And that is why you are master here now, or will be in coming months, whether your father lives or dies.'

'And Hephzibah, Uncle? She is following behind with the baggage cart.'

'Your strumpet is your affair,' Huw said, betraying some impatience. 'Though she will need to go when you take a wife. But she may remain for the present.'

'Then may I go now? The baggage may have arrived.'

'Very well.'

Will pushed the door open. As he did so, the boy Jack, entering with a jug of ale and cups, knocked against him, spilling the ale over Will's doublet. He cast a triumphant look at him.

'Boy! Come here.' Hugh said. Will realised that he had seen the incident. 'You served my brother, no doubt.'

Jack nodded sullenly.

'Well, now you serve the parliament, and me. You will treat Parliament's servants with respect. That includes my nephew, Captain Lucie. Will, take this boy to the steward. Have him whipped.'

'Flog me then!' Jack shouted, tears in his eyes.

'Flog you?' Hugh curled his lip. 'A man is flogged upon his back. Insolent children are beaten on their bare buttocks. See to it, Will.'

Having reluctantly delivered a subdued Jack to the steward, Will went in search of the baggage, and Hephzibah, in a daze. He had never expected Hugh to hand him Chadshunt Hall on a platter.

* * *

In the stables, horses blew at him gently, rustling the straw with their hooves as they turned their heads to see who was there. Most of the beasts were unknown to him, save the one he rode. No, there was Lady! The draught horse which pulled the wagon had been brought in from the fields and her massive head stared placidly over the half door. She whinnied at Will, and he foraged a handful of grain from a sack, rubbing her between the ears. He heard a step behind him. It was Ben. The groom picked up a pitchfork, turning away. Will hesitated, shifting from one foot to the other. He could think of nothing to say to the groom, now climbing the ladder to the hay loft without showing any acknowledgement of his presence.

Will left the stables with dragging feet and was greeted by the clipclop of trotting hooves and the rattle of wheels on the cobbles. 'Hephzibah!' Finally a person who did not judge the new Will Lucie, Captain Lucie of Pye's Regiment of Horse. He ran towards her.

* * *

The girl's eyes widened at the sight of Will's bedchamber. Though the evening light was failing, and Will had not yet called for candles, there was light enough to see the rich panelling, the carved bed, the tapestry.

'Is this your chamber Will? Did you share the bed with your brother?'

Will chuckled. 'It was my own. Harry had his own bed, in his own chamber.'

Hephzibah was silent as she digested this evidence of wealth and luxury.

'And where..?'

'Enough. Come here and no more words until I see you in your shift.'

'You've such a beauteous voice, Will.' Hephzibah lay half- naked on the high bed, while Will, seated on a stool in his shirt, hummed an air and strummed his lute.

'Not I,' he chuckled, pulling the heavy bed curtains aside to see her. He laid down the instrument and ran an exploratory fingernail down her body, tracing a line from her throat, darkened by the sun, to the springy nest of dark curls at the bottom of her belly.

'Will,' she scolded Hephzibah. 'I was talking of your voice.'

'Mm,' came Will's muffled voice from between her thighs. He sat up reluctantly. 'It is nothing compared to that of Gabriel. He has the voice as well as the name of an angel.'

'Gabriel?'

'My sister Bess's husband.' At the thought of his last encounter with Gabriel the old, closed look clouded Will's face.

There was a rap at the door and Hephzibah reached for her abandoned shift with an air of resignation. Jack entered, his eyes flickering briefly towards the naked girl pulling the crumpled linen over her head with a pair of strong, brown arms. He smirked, and Will was savagely glad to see that the boy stood awkwardly, clearly in pain from the whipping.

'Well?'

'Goodwife Sarah wishes to know where you wish your servant to sleep, Your Honour?'

The faintest emphasis on 'servant', but there was nothing to be done about it, short of having the skin flayed from the boy's back.

'Who is Goodwife Sarah?' queried Will, stalling for time.

'The new housekeeper, your Honour.'

Will stared back into Jack's countenance, now carefully blank. A new housekeeper who neither knew him nor cared for him. She had not seen him grow to manhood, unlike old Marjorie.

'Tell her that I will make my own arrangements.'

'Yessir,' Jack bowed, duty personified, and withdrew. Turning to see if his woman was content with the arrangement, Will missed the gleam of malicious satisfaction in Jack's eyes.

CHAPTER 59

Will had been happy when Hephzibah had found him again at Plymouth. It was not just her physical attractions which appealed to him. His change of heart, of allegiance was in some part due to her. He had come upon her one day in his quarters, laboriously spelling her way through a psalm in the battered soldier's bible he had procured for himself. Surprised that she had some mastery of the written word, he could not repress a chuckle.

'Are you mockin' me?'

Will cursed himself when he heard the pain in her tones. 'Indeed not. I had not realised you could read. Who taught you?'

'Colonel's chaplain said women should know the Lord's word for 'emselves.'

'Colonel Pye's chaplain?' Will was astounded at a rebel preacher treating a camp follower with respect instead of ale dregs beneath his feet. The chaplains in the King's army solved the problem of camp followers more easily, by pretending they did not exist.

'He said more, as ow I could be saved as one of the 'lect. Parson in our village told me I 'ad sinned, and so 'ad Ma, 'n that was why I was born like this.'

'We are all sinners surely,' he had smiled into the sea-green eyes, 'But you no more than I or any man or woman for that matter. And as I, this minute, suffer from the sin of covetousness, so let me have my sin again.' He had pulled her to him, grinning as he reached for her laces. It was not until he was lying back on the narrow bed, his lust sated, that he thought about what she had said. It had been another step in understanding Hephzibah and in shaping his loyalty to Parliament.

* * *

Next morning, Will woke to Hephzibah curled beside him asleep. He reached out and stroked the hair which she had begun to wash with rosemary and lavender to please him.

Hephzibah sat up and smiled at him. 'Wait 'ere while I goes to the kitchens and bring victuals for you to break your fast.'

Will opened his mouth to object that she need not wait on him here, where there were servants, but shut it again. The servants were ignoring him where they could. There had been no knock at the door with hot water to shave, nor to kindle the fire. At dinner and supper, he ate with the rest of the household, seated beside his uncle. Direct requests were attended to with scarcely veiled contempt, although since Jack's whipping, none had insulted him to his face.

'My thanks, Hephzibah.' He lay there watching her lace her stays and don stockings, skirts and bodice. She tied on her apron, hastily braided her hair and pushed it under her coif.

'We must see about a new gown for you, Hephzibah. I cannot have the servants taking you for a beggar.'

She chewed her lower lip, glancing down at the coarse woollen kersey of her skirts, the hems stiff with mud from the roads and speckled with different shades of green and brown where spikes of gorse and sticky burs of seeds had meshed with the twill until they were almost a part of the weave. She had donned a fresh shift and apron from her small pack, but these, too had suffered from rain which had seeped in during the journey and there were spots of mould dotting the pale linen.

'Do I shame you?'

'Indeed you do not, love. Now go.' He smacked her lightly on the rear end, missing the delighted smile on her face, for he had called her his love for the very first time.

* * *

Will, staring from his casement window at the heaps of golden leaves in the deserted flower gardens, wondered at Hephzibah's lengthy absence. There was a hesitant, mouse-like scratching at the panelled door. She entered, empty handed but for a small loaf which she held out in a trembling hand. Will took it unthinkingly, staring in puzzlement at her tear-stained face and wet patches on her skirts. He sniffed. 'Have you broached a barrel of beer and then bathed in it? And what has become of your coif?'

'The groom, Ben.' Her shoulders heaved and she burst into tears. Patting her back and soothing her as he would a panicked filly, Will extracted the tale of the last half hour.

Hephzibah had found her way down the front stairs and, after a couple of false starts, through the service passage to the kitchens, empty but for a pair of grooms, lounging at a long well-scrubbed table sharing a platter of bread and cheese. The loaves were still warm from the oven and Hephzibah's stomach growled as the aroma of fresh bread wafted her way.

She hesitated as one of them, a young man of modest height with dark hair tied back in a tail, glanced in her direction.

'Well, well and what do we have here?' There was a note of malice in his voice.

'I'm here to get some victuals for Master Will, Cap'n Lucie that is.'

'Master Will, Cap'n Lucie,' the groom mimicked. Hephzibah attempted to pass him, but her ungainly gait made him burst out laughing. He shot out a booted foot and tripped her neatly. She crashed heavily to the tiled floor. Before she could recover, the groom leapt to his feet and pushed her flat. 'That's where a trollop belongs, on her back.'

'Oh, leave her be, Ben,' the other groom interjected, his mouth full of bread and cheese. He turned his attention to a jug of small beer and refilled his mug.

'And why should I?' spat Ben.' He made a grab at Hephzibah coif and dragged it off her head with a laugh. 'Coming in here wearing a coif and apron like an honest woman.'

'Give me your hand and up with you,' the other groom said, 'Now be off.'

The apron had become twisted round her hips, and her uncovered hair was spilling from its braids, but Hephzibah stood her ground. 'I's come for victuals for Cap'n Lucie, and that's what I'll go with.'

A cookmaid had appeared and was shaking her head. 'Come along, then. You can take him a jug o' small beer and a couple of loaves with some cheese.'

By the time the food was ready, Ben was gone. Hephzibah mumbled her thanks and carrying a laden tray she shuffled back down the service passage. She had gone no further than the hall at the bottom of the stairs when Ben leapt from behind a door and shoved her backwards hard, pulling the tray away as she fell. Sitting in the midst of the ruined breakfast, surrounded by shards of earthenware and rivulets of small beer, Hephzibah dashed tears from her eyes and scrambled to her feet again.

The crash brought the housekeeper running. 'Clean up that mess, clumsy wench!' she ordered.

* * *

'Flog one of the servants because of some imagined slight to that crippled baggage of a whore? You jest.' Hugh Lucie snorted in disgust.

'Well?' for Will had not moved from his posture just inside the door. His face was a mask of disdain and fury and his whole body radiated tension.

'If you will not have him flogged, Uncle then I will fight him.'

'A Lucie duelling with a servant! Would you make the family ridiculous?'

The two men glared at each other. Finally, Hugh shrugged his shoulders and leant back in his chair.

'Why you allow that girl to be your follower makes me fear for your reason. She must be a most accomplished strumpet for she has nothing else to recommend her. But no flogging, it will make him a hero. No,

I will instruct the steward to give him extra work. Keep that girl out of the servants' way.'

* * *

Will lay awake long after Hephzibah slept that night. When the rising chorus of bird song told him that dawn was not far away, he had come to the hard-won decision that he would only return to his home as its master.

But now was not the time. He had a place to go where he was respected and had friends. He would waste no more days dealing with recalcitrant servants who insulted him and the woman he loved, nor in going cap in hand to his uncle.

When Hephzibah awoke shortly after dawn, Will was packing his gear to rejoin Colonel Pye and General Cromwell's Eastern Association in East Anglia. 'Time to leave,' he said.

CHAPTER 60

The spy known as Sergeant Jones emptied his purse into his hand and pursed his lips. Winter was not far away, and with it, an end to the movement of the field armies. There were slim pickings for men like him over winter. The European wars had not made him rich; and he had returned to England, determined to make his fortune.

He divided the coins. Half he knotted in a kerchief and pushed into the thatch above his head, the other he took with him to the tap room. He fingered the special dice hidden in his pocket.

Alas for Jones, his attempts to cheat were spotted by a sharp-eyed man whose threadbare coat with yellow facings marked him as a probable deserter. The spy bluffed his way out, but the evening ended with even fewer coins. He climbed a ladder to the attic room where two other men lay snoring. Stretching out on a dirty straw palliasse, knife and purse in the bundle beneath his head, he came to a decision. He had invested many weeks in Sir Henry Lucie. It was time to have another throw at Vaughan.

In the chaos of those last days in Cornwall, Jones had lost sight of his quarry and the trail was cold. News of him would surely be forthcoming at The Allt but it was a long journey and he needed a better horse. He loitered at the posthouse next morning, but a suspicious postilion pointed him out to the ostler. Jones turned away.

At the town of Crickhowell, four interminable days later, he met with his first piece of luck. His decrepit beast cast a shoe, and he was forced to find a smith. The man, busy with a plough share, told him he could not shoe the horse for an hour or so.

'Not even for a fellow countryman?' Jones wheedled, speaking Welsh.

'Especially for a Gog, a northerner. Black Mountains here, bach, not Snowdonia,' the smith chuckled. 'Tie your animal up over there. Come back for him at three o'clock.

'Put your hand to those bellows before I put mine to your backside,' he barked at his apprentice.

'Damnation,' Jones thought. In England he was merely another Welshman but here they could tell which valley you were from. He must be careful. Entering an inn, he ordered ale and a small loaf. He could not afford the extra tuppence for cheese or a pie and the serving wench sneered at him. Taking his frugal dinner to a bench in the cobbled yard, the spy watched the comings and goings of other travellers.

Two horsemen gave their horses to the ostler. The older, wearing a silver chain of office, must be a gentleman's steward, the younger, wearing blue and orange livery, was presumably a humbler servant. Leaving his pack with a child hovering in the hope of employment, the younger man entered the taproom first while the steward stood back and dipped his head.

Jones's nose twitched like a dog scenting a hare. Why would a steward, a man of importance, inferior to none but the family he served, show deference to a menial? The manservant was ordinary in appearance, aged around thirty. His livery was neat and clean save for the usual dust of travel.

There was also something about his pack. Covered in coarse brown cloth, fastened with leather straps, it was unremarkable, but the man had handled it as if it contained something precious. If he were transporting gold or jewels for his master, he would surely have them in the pouch on his belt.

Jones sauntered back into the taproom. The men were seated at a table, a jug before them. Satisfied, he approached the child minding the pack. 'Gentleman who owns this has entrusted it to me. This is for you.'

The child scampered away with the silver penny. Satisfying himself that no one was watching, Jones undid the pack. Pieces of loosely folded fabric, linen, wool, silk. Nothing of interest, yet his instincts rarely misled him. He thrust his arm inside. Beneath the cloth nestled a pewter cup, a small plate and two candlesticks. Rather fine for a servant, but scarcely of great value. Squatting down, he felt around the bottom of the pack. There was the outline of something unyielding below the cloth. He poked and prodded until he uncovered a tiny row of buttons under a narrow fold. Moments later, he was looking at a slim volume, the corners of its leather cover faded with wear. He turned the pages.

Domine Deus, Agnus Dei, Filius Patris,
qui tollis peccata mundi, miserere nobis

Latin prayer – he whistled softly. Carefully he returned book, cup and candle sticks to their hiding places. He now recognised them for what they were – papist trappings for saying Mass. The manservant was a Romish priest, disguised in what Jones now recalled was the Vaughan family livery. Fastening the straps, he left the pack beside the door as if the child had abandoned it.

'Very clever, priest,' he thought. 'Now, how best to profit from your treasonous presence at The Allt?' He mulled over the question while he continued his journey. There was money to be made from the capture of a Catholic priest, from the reward for his arrest to the hangman selling off lengths of the rope used in the execution. Jones guessed that he had a few days before the priest went on his way. Once in the safe haven of a gentleman's house, they were loath to leave.

First he needed information about the routine of the estate. Strangers in rural neighbourhoods attracted attention; and Vaughan's wife might remember him, although his hair and beard were longer now. He mulled over the question while he waited for his horse and then rode the remaining distance to the village near The Allt. When he saw the house in the distance, he turned off into a wood. He loosened his hair about his face and donned his other suit of clothes, brown instead of grey. His hat was taller in the crown and his shoes had higher heels. It changed his gait as well as his appearance. Comfortable in his disguise, Jones sidled into the alehouse in the village.

Hunched over his ale, Jones listened. The shadows were lengthening, and the taproom filling with men finishing their day's labours, when he heard a conversation which made the cost of twice refilling the pot worthwhile.

'Baby's fair to look upon they say. Resembles her dam.' A man carrying a shepherd's crook seated himself on a stool.

'Her lady mother,' the woman wiping a table reproved him. 'Lady Elisabeth Vaughan she'll be some day.'

'If she lives longer than the young master's first wife,' a man with a thin, solemn face added.

'They say he dotes on her.'

'The baby?'

'Now how could he do that, numskull, when he hasn't clapped eyes on her yet? Young master is away with the King.'

Jones had heard enough. He paid his reckoning and left. It was raining but for the spy the day had just improved.

* * *

The Allt

'The priest is ready for the churching ceremony, My Lady.' The housekeeper's round face was flushed with excitement.

'Thank you, Isobel. You may escort him to the upper room.' Lady Alice stood at the window staring towards the road.

'He will not arrive in time, Mother,' Bess said. The shining prospect of leaving the house after the long weeks of her confinement was dulled by sadness that Gabriel had not returned.

'It is not Gabriel I am on watch for. The sheriffs of three counties are continually searching for the Jesuit house at Cwm. They know it exists.

And if the priest is followed here then the danger trails after him, as contagion spreads in tainted air. I have lived all my life with this reality, but now there is you to think about, and Frances too.'

Pulling a white lace veil over her head, Bess felt suddenly nervous. Lady Alice followed her to the hidden room where the door was ajar, Ieuan on guard.

Brisk footsteps approached. The priest still wore the Vaughan livery, but he had an embroidered stole around his neck. He smiled at Bess. 'Kneel, my child.'

'Inside the room, Father?'

'Outside the room, by the doorway. By rights we should be within the porch of our church, but this must act as our porch until the King sees fit to let us worship again in freedom.' He sprinkled her with water from a small bottle. 'The sun will not harm you by day, nor the moon by night,' he began in English. 'The Lord will watch over your coming and going both now and forevermore.'

The psalm was comforting in its familiarity. The Gloria and the Kyrie prayers which followed were in Latin, but Bess had grown accustomed to hearing Gabriel sing them, and they were no longer strange to her.

Lifting Bess to her feet, the priest put the end of the stole into her hand. 'Enter into the temple of God, that thou mayest have eternal life.' Carrying a candle, Bess followed him.

'I pray this is the first of many such occasions for you,' Lady Alice said afterwards, 'Giving thanks for your safe delivery.'

Bess suppressed the fear that if Gabriel did not return alive from Basing House, there might never be another churching ceremony.

CHAPTER 61

Lewis mopped his brow as the last carriage rolled away after the celebrations of the baby's baptism. The gate onto the highway, which that day had been guarded by two armed servants, was closed. Only the priest remained. There had been no alarms. Dressed in a cap and long gown of pale satin, trimmed with lace and embroidered with tiny seed pearls, the baby had been named Frances Anne. She had howled on cue, poked her finger in her eye and howled even louder.

For days the household had been occupied with preparations, the bakehouse busy at first with manchet bread and then with pies of meat and fruit. There had been partridges and pullets with artichokes and asparagus, a cold venison pie cooked with cloves, fish from the River Severn, ale, wine and mead, custards and jellies.

'It seems no more than a few years since Master Gabriel was rolling down a bank with his brother while they were yet in gowns. Please God, I will live to see him take his father's place,' Lewis confided to Ieuan as they strolled back towards the gatehouse.

'And more days like today. Did you ever taste anything like the baked sturgeon?' Ieuan smacked his lips.

'Perhaps there will be if God sees fit to end this war.'

'At least we are at peace here.'

'But you never know where a spy is lurking. With so many here today, who knows?'

'Among our neighbours?' Ieuan protested. 'They are known to us.'

'But not all those who fetched and carried from Abergavenny. Spices and wines, favours for the servants, that box with the silver apostle spoons. More than one man I had never clapped eyes on before.'

Lewis looked up and down the lane. There was no one to be seen but a man from the home farm walking beside the ambling herd of cattle; and no reason for the prickle of unease he felt.

* * *

There were no guarantees that the parish constable would not keep the whole reward for capturing a priest for himself. Jones believed he had hit upon a surer plan to fill his purse. Accordingly, the spy merely watched as the priest, now in the sober broadcloth of a farmer, rode away to his next assignment. Jones sketched an ironic sign of the cross in the air to his prey's departing back.

Scouting around The Allt, Jones discovered a ramshackle two-roomed cottage hidden deep in a copse. From the condition of the rotten thatch and crumbling wattle and daub walls, it had not been used for years; but the water in the well was clear. He could ill afford paying for lodging, and he was weary of dogs chasing him away from barns.

There were many strangers in Abergavenny on market day, and his purchases did not attract attention. While his horse grazed behind the cottage, Jones stuffed crevices in walls with straw to keep away draughts. The door to the second room was hanging off its hinges, but he repaired it with wood and nails and a strong bolt. There was a tiny, unglazed window, over which he nailed more wood.

Claiming to be a masterless man, his livelihood taken away by the war, Jones returned to the alehouse near The Allt.

'Try the big house,' the tapster suggested. 'Sir Thomas Vaughan is a good master. He owns all the land here about. Might have to wait a few days, mind. Steward's away with the master and mistress; and the young master is with the King's army. His wife is at home but hiring a new man now – best wait for the steward. He'll be back before Michaelmas Day.'

'Might he not go there tomorrow?' The woman paused in her task of replenishing the fire. 'They feed the poor after dinner on Thursdays. Gate'll be open.'

It was a perfect opportunity. The next morning, he rubbed ashes into his beard and wrapped himself in an old cloak. Pulling the hood over his face, feet bare and muddied, Jones mingled with the poor outside the gates at noon. The door in the gatehouse opened and an elderly porter appeared. 'Stand back now. Plenty for all,' he called.

Once the crowd had shuffled a half step backwards, two men came out, lugging baskets of cold meats and cheat bread. Behind them walked a young woman. It was Mistress Elisabeth Vaughan. Distributing coins, she moved between the paupers, speaking to each one. Purse and baskets empty, servants and mistress withdrew to a chorus of 'God bless you's', and the gate was closed.

Jones slid out from behind the corner of the wall where he had been standing half-concealed. So, it was true. The Vaughans were absent, all but Gabriel Vaughan's wife. Staring at the closed gate, he debated how best to obtain entry to the house. Then he remembered something. Laughing, he aimed a genial kick at a dog licking up crumbs. The cur yelped, and Jones turned away, content.

* * *

Earlier that week

'We will return in good time for Michaelmas, Bess. There are two leases of farms to assign, and Lewis wishes to show me a new strain of sheep. Goodwife Isobel will manage the servants, the kitchen.'

Sir Thomas Vaughan breezed into the nursery and pressed his lips to the sleeping baby's brow. He was dressed for a journey, his dark green woollen cassack buttoned down the front against autumn showers. The tooled scabbard of his sword belt was visible beneath the hem, a series of fleurs de lys intertwined with tendrils of leaves.

'Now that my confinement is over, I will continue riding Faerie each day,' Bess forewarned him.

'Be sure to take a servant with you.' Sketching a bow, he turned on his heel. Bess knew that he was looking forward to visiting his

312

Nantgarw estate near Caerphilly before autumn winds and rain made the roads impassable.

That afternoon, and for the next two days, Bess rode Faerie, accompanied by a groom. But on the following afternoon, Twm had ridden to Abergavenny. Searching for the younger groom, Dafydd, Bess found him at the bottom of the ladder to the hay loft, his face screwed up in pain.

'Stupid tumble, Mistress. Turned my ankle.'

'Stay there, Dafydd.'

A quarter of an hour later the groom, ankle bandaged, was assisted to the house. Thick banks of cloud were building over Table Mountain but if Bess saddled Faerie herself, she could ride for an hour. She would be back before anyone missed her.

Most of the village's inhabitants were at work in the fields as Bess passed a small girl with purple-stained mouth gathering blackberries; and splashed through the ford across the Usk. Only the rhythmic clang of metal on metal from the smithy and a wagon laden with sacks trundling towards the mill disturbed the peace. A red kite circled far above, its feathers glowing in the rays of the sun. Faerie bucked.

'Bothersome nag,' Bess scolded, hugging the chestnut neck. Leaving the cottages behind, horse and rider began the climb up the valley into the Black Mountains.

CHAPTER 62

Perched on a hill behind the church, Jones watched The Allt through a perspective glass. Jackdaw-like he collected scraps of useful information and he had remembered Mistress Vaughan's expressed enjoyment in riding. On the first afternoon of his vigil she appeared, riding a fine chestnut mare and followed by a mounted servant. The next day he saw them again.

On the third afternoon she came alone. Jones hurriedly mounted his horse. He waited out of sight of the village, hiding the animal behind a hedge. When he heard hoofbeats, he positioned himself face down in the lane, one arm thrown out as if he had met with an accident.

The trotting hooves came closer. There was a firm 'Stand, Faerie.' He heard footsteps and felt a hand on his shoulder.

'Sir, can you hear me?'

Jones was more than a score of years older, but he had surprise on his side. She kicked out, her boot catching him a fine blow on the knee as he pulled her to the ground.

'Fight, would you?' he grunted, twisting her arm behind her back. She gasped in pain. With his free hand, he pushed her face down into the mud, secured her wrists with a rope and gagged her. Whinnying, the chestnut mare galloped away in fright.

'If you want to see your child again, Mistress Vaughan, you will do as I say,' he panted, throwing her across his horse and roping her face down. The mare would cause a hue and cry, but with luck, the girl would not have given word of her intended road.

Keeping watch for any pursuit, he chivvied the double-laden horse back to his refuge, hustling the girl inside. Wide grey eyes surveyed the dingy room with its mended door, the blanket and heap of fresh straw, the empty pail. She kicked out again, but this time he was ready, slamming his fist into her jaw. The girl went slack in his arms. Depositing her on the straw he lifted her skirts.

* * *

Women lacked sense at the best of times Jones chuckled, bolting the door. Thanks to the unexpected absence of the groom, capturing the girl had been easy. It had proved too difficult to ensnare Gabriel Vaughan by fair means. His new plan depended on the preposterous code of honour of a gentleman.

Returning to his post on the hill, Jones settled his back against a tree and took his perspective glass from its leather case.

* * *

Her jaw felt swollen to twice its usual size and she felt sick. Where was she? The only sounds were bird song, rustling leaves and rain pattering on the roof. It took Bess a few moments to remember what had happened. Her wrists burned like fire, but the rope was gone.

Clutching her head, she found that her linen coif was still in place. At least he had not shamed her by uncovering her hair. Relief turned to horror as she discovered her petticoats had been folded back, baring her legs above her stocking tops. She thrust her hand under her shift, feeling between her legs. Dry and neither soreness nor stickiness. He had not . . .

But the linen pocket tied about her waist was missing. That was why her skirts were raised. She tried to remember what she had been carrying. A handkerchief, hairpins, a piece of ribbon and Gabriel's last letter to her. What could be the use of it to the man?

The crack of daylight beneath the door had faded into blackness when hoofbeats returned. The man unbolted the door. He held a lantern, a dagger gleaming in its light. Apparently reassured, he thrust the

315

weapon into his belt and returned a moment later with a pitcher and a bag.

'Food, Mistress,' he said cheerfully, 'Soldiers' fare. No custards or capons for poor men like me, and you must share in my fortunes.'

Swollen jaw and fear left no room for hunger, but Bess was parched. Raising the pitcher, she sniffed it.

'Water, not poison. Why would I kill the goose that will lay me a golden egg? I will send you home, once your husband agrees with my request and your father sends me my money.'

Bess's stomach lurched at the mention of her father. The man helped himself to a morsel of cold mutton.

'Not grand enough for you, Mistress? Perhaps hunger will teach you better manners.'

'Might I have a light left for me, Sir?' Bess pleaded, looking at him through her lashes. 'I have never slept without a servant in my chamber since I was a child, and there may be demons lurking in the dark.'

'Then take care you do not set the straw afire, for I have business elsewhere. Here is your pocket. There was no weapon in it.'

He fetched a rushlight in a holder, tossed the linen pocket inside the door and bolted it behind him. Sweating, Bess crumpled up. What was his purpose in taking her prisoner? Why had he mentioned her father? She unfastened her cloak and took a few deep breaths. Panic would achieve nothing.

The rushlight faintly illuminated the dark corners of her cell. She had been hoping for something she might use as a weapon, but there was not so much as a discarded broom, and he had given her neither knife nor spoon to eat with. That reminded her of the food. She must keep up her strength. Ignoring the pain in her jaw, Bess chewed her way slowly through mutton, cheat bread and hard cheese, forcing herself to swallow.

However much she worried at the problem, she could see no connection between her father paying this man money and Gabriel agreeing to some demand. The rushlight was burning low, so she squatted over the bucket and then curled up under the blanket, hugging her knees for warmth. To the accompaniment of creaks and rustles from roof and straw, Bess drifted into an uneasy sleep.

* * *

Nantgarw Manor, Caerphilly

The Vaughans were breakfasting at a heavy oak table made in the time of Sir Thomas's grandfather. Two chairs with high backs and cushioned seats were a concession to modern comforts. Patches on the white-washed walls showed where tapestries had hung. For such a short visit, the family had not taken the trouble of transporting such luxuries with them.

Sir Thomas Vaughan wiped his fingers on his napkin. 'We may return home tomorrow, my dear. The leases are signed, and everything is in order for the new tenants to take possession at Michaelmas.'

'Then I must speak to the gardener straight away about drying some herbs,' his wife replied. 'The marigolds here are more vigorous and I never have sufficient for making tea when the colder months bring agues.'

'I leave such matters to you, Alice. It is you who physics our household.'

There was a knock at the door. 'Twm is here, from The Allt. He says he must speak to you urgently, Master.'

The Vaughans exchanged apprehensive looks. 'Send him in.'

'What is the matter, Twm?'

'I am sorry, Master.' Twm pushed back his dripping hair and kneaded his wet cap in his hands. 'The young mistress has disappeared.'

Lady Alice clutched at the table edge.

'We searched every nook and cranny. When we could not find her by evening of the second day, I rode here through the night. We thought at first she had fallen from the mare when Faerie returned alone.'

'Never tell me that Mistress Bess went riding by herself?' Lady Alice cried. Twm swayed on his feet.

'When did you last eat?' Sir Thomas asked. He strode to the open door and shouted for a servant. 'Bring meat and drink for Twm. And tell Mr Griffith to make ready to depart to The Allt. We will leave within the hour. Not you Twm. You may follow when you have slept.'

'Let me come with you,' Lady Alice pleaded. 'The servants may follow later with the baggage. I cannot remain here in ignorance.'

Taking two armed servants and a bag of provisions for the journey, they rode hard, stopping only to rest the horses, for there were no post houses where they might change horses on their road through the wild Brecon Beacons.

The gate to the private road was closed when they arrived at The Allt. 'Shutting the stable-door after the horse has bolted,' Sir Thomas muttered. 'What news?' he bellowed as Ieuan opened the gate.

'None, Master.'

Lady Alice hurried away to question the servants but Sir Thomas was waylaid by the elderly porter, his face doleful.

'This was lying inside the gatehouse, Master.' He produced a damp sheet of paper. It was sealed with a plain wafer, and the ink had run, but the direction 'To Sir Thomas Vaughan, Baronet, of Allt Yr Esgair', was legible.

Alone in his study, Sir Thomas opened the letter. He had little doubt that one discovered in this manner would be from whatever person had taken Bess; for taken she had clearly been.

'Your honour, we have your son's wife in safe keeping. If you wish her release, you and your son will do what we bid you.'

Sir Thomas read the instructions twice, but there was no mistake about the decision he faced. He stared at the miniature of the boy Gabriel hanging on the wall. Dusk had fallen by the time he was roused from his anguish by the door opening. It was his wife bringing candles.

'I have questioned every servant, but noone can add anything. They have been searching throughout the day again but in vain. What is that in your hand?'

'Read,' he cleared his throat. 'And know the choice we have.'

Drops of hot beeswax trickled onto his wife's hand as she read. She rubbed at them absent-mindedly. 'We must not heed their demands. Gabriel will die.'

'But we cannot leave Bess in the hands of these men. If Lucie does not get his way, we may never see her again. In any event, this is not our decision. She is Gabriel's wife, and it is Gabriel who Lucie seeks. We must send a message to Worcester. He may have returned there by now. Our son must decide this himself, but I know what his answer will be.'

Lady Alice stroked her husband's hand. 'One more day of searching for Bess with every single person we can muster, before we send for Gabriel.'

'But what if we do not respond to their demands?'

'I did not say that. We will hang out the sign announcing our agreement.'

'You are ever resourceful my dear. One more day then. The game keeper shall lead the search. I will give the orders now.' With new energy, he sped from the room.

Lady Alice stood motionless until she could no longer hear his footsteps. Then she knelt and pulled a rosary from the pocket about her waist. 'Mother of God,' she whispered, 'Michael is lost to me. Not Gabriel too.'

CHAPTER 63

The Vaughans would find her. Faerie would make her way home and they would mount a search. But on the second day Bess's hope of rescue faded. It was time to take action herself.

Tied face down on the man's horse, she was uncertain as to her whereabouts, but it was probably beyond the Vaughan estates. It was unlikely that Lewis would have left a tumbledown cottage in an overgrown thicket.

'Do not set fire to the straw,' the man had warned. But if she dared do so in his absence, searchers might see the smoke. Flames would be seen more clearly at night, but there were few abroad after dark. She listened for the closing of the outside door, hoofbeats.

Bess counted slowly to one hundred before piling the straw in a heap and, hands shaking, touching the small flame of the rushlight to it. A handful of straw darkened, curled at the edges and smoked, but there was no sign of flame. Bess prodded the smouldering strands with the rushlight, but it sputtered and died. The straw was damp.

The odour of smoke lingered when the man returned. He sniffed, examined the singed patch of straw by the light of his lantern and grabbed one of Bess's soot-covered hands.

'Demons in the corners,' he muttered, striking her across the mouth. 'You will remain in darkness now.'

A further day and night passed. The man had been surly since her failed escape. Bess was becoming desperate, for she had no way of knowing what plot he had hatched with her father. She eyed the dagger he wore at his belt.

When he appeared with a platter of food that evening, she was squatting over the bucket, skirts raised. With a semblance of politeness, he turned his back. Bess pounced, snatching at the hilt. Twisting, he pinned her to the wall with his elbow.

'Now daggers are sharp things, Mistress.' He grabbed her right wrist in an iron grip and slashed the blade across the base of her fingers, cutting deep into the flesh. Bess screamed. He held onto the hand until a rivulet of red trickled onto the straw. 'A little further and you might lack a finger or two.'

Bess heard his words through a haze of white stars. He caught her and lowered her to the ground. She felt him bandage the hand with a kerchief to staunch the bleeding. That done he stormed out.

Stupefied by pain, nausea and the shock of his swift, brutal reprisal, Bess lay half conscious, cradling her injured hand. Hours later she heard a distant blast on a horn, then a second. Could it be The Allt's huntsman? Bess scrabbled to her feet. 'Help!' she screamed.

A few moments later she heard galloping hooves. 'Help me,' she screamed again. There was a final blast on the horn, but it was further away. The huntsman was gone.

* * *

With every mile closer to his home, Gabriel's heart felt lighter. He sang as he rode.

> *'How fair is she I love*
> *I saw her 'ere she came.*
> *From this sad world she took my cares*
> *And with a glance she banished them.'*

Would Bess's body retain the fullness of pregnancy now that the child was born? Desire flamed in him.

Was it cloud, that wisp of grey, or smoke from the chimneys of The Allt? There was something billowing from the high, round tower of the castle. Why in the world was a bed sheet suspended like a banner?

Llangenny whinnied as she approached her stable. There was an answering call from one of the horses, but no one appeared. 'Well, girl, we must fend for ourselves.' Leading the mare into a vacant stall, Gabriel unsaddled her, watered her and rubbed her down, whistling. He filled her manger with sweet hay, inhaling its fragrance. Hay from the home farm was like none other.

He heard a dragging footstep. 'Master, it is you.' Dafydd hobbled towards him, leaning on a stick.

'Dafydd, you are injured.'

'Master, forgive me. It is all my fault.'

'What is your fault?'

'Mistress Bess went riding alone. Had I not taken a tumble, I would have been with her.' His voice broke. 'Everyone is out searching. She has been abducted.'

'By whom?' Gabriel fired back at the stricken groom, grabbing him by the arm. With an effort, he let go. 'Tell me everything.'

* * *

The man's face was cheerful as he pushed back his wet hood. Briskly, he placed food and drink on the straw and removed the full pail. He returned with it empty and put it down with a thump.

'The Vaughans have agreed to our demands. If your husband gives his word of honour, I may rely on him to keep it, is it not so?' A faint trace of uncertainty entered his voice. The rising Welsh inflection, so much like Gabriel's, sickened her coming from this man. Bess stared at him, terrified.

'Is it not so?' he repeated, an edge to his voice.

'Yes,' she whispered.

'Then, Mistress, you may not have too many more days in these poor lodgings.' He left the cottage, whistling.

Bess moved her swollen fingers. They felt as if they were on fire and the cloth had adhered to the wounds. What had Gabriel given his word to do? If he were in danger, it was because of her. Bess had been warned not to ride alone, but the advice had come between her and an hour of idle pleasure and she had ignored it.

* * *

Gabriel stood by the nursery window with his infant daughter in his arms, marvelling at the likeness to her mother. Her eyes slanted like his own, but the long lashes and the heart-shaped face were Bess. As he pressed his lips to her soft brow, the baby gave a tiny belch.

'She does you credit, Goodwife.' Gabriel's voice cracked and Bron reached for her charge, tactfully replacing the baby in the cradle so the young master could hide his tear-stained face.

'They will find her, Sir.'

Gabriel tried to answer, but the effort was too great. He grabbed his cloak; and went to find the search party.

Like beaters flushing out the game, a line of men and women advanced on foot across the valley. Liveried servants mingled with tenants from the estate clad in leather jerkins. Ahead of them on horse-back went Huw, the game keeper and Aled, the huntsman, with the dogs.

When Gabriel, alerted by the sound of the horn, found them, they were gathered at the side of the road on a hill beyond the village while a black-and-tan terrier loudly boasted of the discovery he had made.

'Let me see, Aled.' Oblivious to bows and greetings, Gabriel dismounted from the sorrel mare he had taken from the stables. The huntsman's weather-beaten face was sorrowful as he handed over a soiled tendril of blue silk. Gabriel removed his leather glove and took the ribbon, smoothing it with his thumb. 'From her hat?'

'The young mistress was wearing it, Master, around the black hat with the high crown. I saw the flash of blue as she cantered away.'

Like a kingfisher, Gabriel thought, beautiful, fragile and gone for ever in a moment. 'Is this where they snatched her?'

The huntsman cast about. Gabriel saw nothing but criss-crossing hoof prints and water-logged ruts from cartwheels. Suddenly, Aled dropped to one knee. 'Here, look.'

Once shown, Gabriel could not think how he had missed the trail of broken hazel twigs and trampled stems of meadowsweet, their white, frothy flowers scattered by some disturbance. He picked up one of the bruised flowers. Its sweet, damp odour lingered; and he knew the smell of crushed meadowsweet would join his other memories of that dreadful day.

'They did not take her without a struggle,' he said.

Sounds of a galloping horse interrupted them. Ieuan skidded to a halt. 'A letter has come.'

Gabriel's parents awaited him in the parlour. Lady Alice's face was pinched with worry. Although she held herself erect as ever, Gabriel realised with a shock that his mother was no longer young. Sir Thomas was smiling bravely, but Gabriel could hear his quickened breathing as they embraced.

'My son.' Lady Alice clung to his hand when he raised hers to his lips.

'A poor homecoming for you,' his father said, 'We had a letter.'

Gabriel turned it over. The paper was poor quality, made from rags, such as was sold by pedlars. Its message was brief.

'Call off your dogs and your hunters. If we see men scouring the valley tomorrow, our bargain is void.'

'It was brought an hour ago by a gypsy child. There is a troop of them camping on the common. They are fleeing westwards from the fighting, I think.'

'What is this bargain?' Gabriel flared.

'There was an earlier letter. It is locked in my desk.'

'Show me.'

'Merfyn would have questioned the child, but he ran off directly,' Sir Thomas said as he led the way towards his study, Gabriel at his heels.

'Fetch the child.'

'It is not they who have her. Besides, they neither read nor write.'

'He may know where these men are to be found.'

The first letter was longer. Sir Thomas rubbed his hand across his brow. 'Read it aloud. The words are seared into my soul, but I keep hoping they are not as bad as I remember.'

Gabriel read,

'Your honour, you must know that we have your son's wife in safe keeping. If you wish her release from captivity, you will do what we bid you. You are a gentleman and man of honour. If your son, Gabriel Vaughan, will give his word to personally carry a letter we will give him, to Sir Henry Lucie at Oxford, delivering himself into his hands, we will free his wife when he has departed. That is all we ask.

Hang a bed sheet from the castle's round tower as a sign of your agreement. We are reasonable men and will wait while you fetch him back from the field of battle and his valiant endeavours. When he is returned, and ready to leave for Oxford, hang it out again, this time from the gatehouse, and we will deliver the letter he must carry.'

Remembering the sheet billowing from the tower, Gabriel was filled with a sudden calm. 'And so, you hung out the sign as they asked. You did right, Father.'

'Did I?' Sir Thomas moaned. 'We did it to gain us time for our search, time, as we hoped, to find Bess.'

'It was a good plan, had these men not been watching. I believe we may have drawn near to where they hold her. Aled found this in the road.' He pulled the ribbon from his pocket. 'It is hers, is it not?'

Sir Thomas shrugged his shoulders, utter hopelessness in the gesture.

'Let me see.' Lady Alice was standing in the doorway. She held the ribbon up to the light from the window. 'It is,' A tear trickled down her cheek.

'The gypsy child may be able to lead us to her,' Gabriel insisted. 'Find him.'

But the searchers returned without the boy. Their camp was gone. 'Nothing but a circle of stones and charred, smoking logs to show where they had been,' Ieuan said.

'We might pursue them?' Sir Thomas faltered.

Gabriel put a restraining hand on his arm. 'They have their secret ways and will have climbed into the Black Mountains, Father. No, we must obey the instructions in the letter. Tomorrow morning, hang the sheet from the gatehouse, as a sign that I have returned; that I am ready to travel to Oxford. There is no other way.'

CHAPTER 64

Bess awoke to her hand throbbing. Throwing off the rough blanket she sat up. There was a flash of a long, furred tail and a dormouse scuttled away. The intensifying smell of smoke told her the man was awake and had rekindled the fire. He seemed to lead a hermit-like existence, spending most of his nights at the cottage. The journey to the cottage from where the spy snatched her had taken no more than an hour, so she was no more than a few miles from The Allt. Yet she and the man might have been the only living souls in the world.

Closing her eyes, Bess conjured up the feeling of the baby's tiny fist gripping her finger, the sight of her blowing milky bubbles. She felt even more alone. Now her only companion was a dormouse.

Searching for the diminutive rodent she discovered the hole where it had chewed through the decaying wall of the cottage. The roof was in no better case. Reaching up, Bess thrust a finger into the mouldering thatch not far above her head. It was soft and spongy.

At the sound of the bolt being pulled back, Bess dropped onto the straw.

'Pease pottage and biscuit to break your fast.' That was the smell that had wafted in every day, plain pease, no ham or butter. Hard and crusted at the edges, the yellow mess was flaked with soot. The biscuit was burnt on one side, pale on the other but at least it was fresh. Bess began to eat with her left hand, digging the biscuit into the cooked pease.

'*Pease pudding hot, pease pudding cold,*' she thought. A hysterical giggle escaped her; and the first mouthful ended back in the dish. He was watching her closely, as he often did. 'Might I have a spoon? I am having difficulty eating the pottage.'

'Why not? I am in high spirits today.' He retrieved a greasy horn spoon from his pouch and handed it over with a bow. 'I will leave you to enjoy this repast.' His manners and speech were once more those of a man aping the ways of a gentleman. 'Your husband has returned and will leave today for Oxford carrying a letter. He has given his word to act as my messenger and your father will richly reward me. Tomorrow, you will be free to go.'

Smirking he left, bolting the door behind him.

* * *

The Allt

Gabriel bathed and Ieuan shaved him. He would take his leave of The Allt clean, presentable, head held high before family and household.

He knew what to expect as a prisoner in Oxford Castle. The guards would rob him of any valuables and most of his garments on his arrival. Chained to the wall in one of the stinking, overcrowded cells, a royalist officer among a crowd of parliamentarians, his fellow prisoners would maul him. If he were brought before a court martial, his stay in the prison might be brief, but it was unlikely any of his possessions would be returned to his family after his probable execution.

Could Bess's abductors be trusted? He believed they could because they asked no ransom. It was Sir Henry Lucie who would reward them. Gabriel was hopeful that as he travelled to Oxford Bess would be freed.

Ieuan's face was puzzled as he fastened the mismatched buttons, four of them pewter, the rest faded velvet, on his master's old green velvet doublet. Gabriel pulled on a pair of patched breeches and a brown woollen Monmouth cap.

'Are we in disguise? Must I find my old leather jerkin?'

'I am going to free Mistress Bess, Ieuan, but I am going alone. Those who hold her have agreed to release her on certain conditions.'

'They made it a condition that you dress like a serving man?'

'No, but they may rob me.' Gabriel laid aside his sword. He traced the Vaughan serpent swirling its silver way across the basket hilt with his finger. 'Will you lend me your sword?'

Ieuan scowled. 'You gave it to me when I became your body servant, your lifeguard. I have carried it for two years and drawn it in your defence. It may be only common steel, but . . .'

Ieuan's loyalty was more than Gabriel could bear. 'But he who carries it is not a common man. I know every scrape on the scabbard's leather, the nicks on the blade when you used it for cutting wood so that I might have a fire when the army camped in the field. It has hung by your side through defeat and victory. Will you honour me by lending it to me? I ask you as a friend.'

'I will.'

Gabriel grasped Ieuan's hand. 'Then I will leave this in your care.' Gabriel handed over his own sword and sword belt. Grabbing a rag, Ieuan began polishing the silver lace on the embroidered baldric with exaggerated care.

'This I must keep, for I may need to prove who I am to gain access to Sir Henry.' Gabriel replaced the signet ring on his finger but placed Michael's silver crucifix and chain in a box of polished walnut inlaid with mother of pearl and locked it away in a press. His favourite lute lay there. Gabriel ran his fingers over the strings. It was sadly out of tune, but it must wait for another day, or another lutenist, to remedy that.

'Master, why is that when you face the greatest dangers, you do it alone?'

'God willing, you will have other occasions risking your life for mine. You would have made a fine squire in times gone by.'

Ieuan gave a reluctant grin.

'Cease your cleaning before the silver lace is worn away. Ready me Llangenny, and food for my journey. I may be gone some days.' Gabriel glanced up at the miniature of his twin. 'Be with me, Michael.'

The signal was hanging from the gatehouse. Soon, very soon, the letter would arrive, setting him upon his way to Oxford. He would spend an hour praying for Bess's safety; and for strength and courage for what he must do.

CHAPTER 65

It all made sense now to Bess. If Gabriel was carrying a letter to her father, there could be only one reason. It was Gabriel himself who was the message. All these months her husband had evaded arrest. Now he was seeking it out to save her. Bess clutched the horn spoon in her undamaged left hand. It was blunt but sturdy; and the only tool she had.

Standing on tiptoe, she attacked the rotten patches in the roof. They yielded to the probing and prodding spoon, but the mouldering reeds were sharp. Within minutes her left hand was scored and lacerated, her nails torn and bleeding. Her grasp weakened and the spoon flew from her hand, disappearing into the straw. Like seeking a needle in a haystack, she sighed as she scrabbled. Recovering the spoon, her eyes fell on her leather gloves lying on the ground. She tugged them on, averting her eyes from the dried, bloody mess that was her right hand.

How much time did she have? For a horseman, The Allt was not far away. He might be back in little more than an hour, the letter delivered. And once he had that letter, Gabriel would leave for Oxford. Ignoring the pain in her hands, Bess attacked the hole with renewed vigour. Blood trickled out of her right glove and down her sleeve as the wounds bled afresh.

If she could reach higher, she could exert more pressure. In his haste, the man had forgotten to empty the pail. Tipping the contents into the straw Bess positioned the upturned pail under the growing hole. Within minutes she could see a fragment of sky. Elated, she thrust her head through the gap; but the hole proved too small for her shoulders.

Grunting and gasping like some strange kind of animal, Bess tore and butted at the thatch, her fears for Gabriel increasing with every passing minute.

It took a further half hour to create a sufficient aperture. Stepping down from the pail, she grabbed her cloak and threw it over the jagged edges before thrusting her arms through the hole. As she kicked with all her might the pail fell over, but Bess was at the point of no return. She heaved herself through the hole, but her petticoats caught on a sharp piece of thatch. Wrenching them free she slipped on the wet, sloping roof and fell, hitting the ground hard.

When she stumbled to her feet, pain shot through an ankle. Gritting her teeth, Bess hobbled from the thicket and down the slope in what she hoped was the direction of The Allt.

* * *

The signal flew from the gatehouse. Jones fingered the folded paper with the plain wafer sealing it. He had no signet ring, he brooded. When he received his reward from Sir Henry, he would have money for a dozen.

Vaughan would be waiting, racked with fear, for the letter he was to carry. The young lieutenant colonel had evaded him for too long and Jones relished the thought of his torment. Sidling up to the gate unobserved, he dropped the letter when the old fool of a porter's back was turned.

Returning to the hill, Jones munched a raw apple, dreaming of eating them with cinnamon, honey, cloves, baked by his own servants. He pressed the glass to his eye. A dun mare was being saddled while a groom checked the horse's shoes, tapping them with a hammer. Next came a small sack and a rolled blanket for a man leaving on a journey. They were for Vaughan, going to meet his fate.

Satisfied, Jones left his post. The next day he would keep to his bargain and release the girl. Musing on the reward, he saw nothing wrong as he approached the cottage. He tethered the nag, pissed in the garden and went inside. All was quiet. Unbolting the door, he was met by the sight of the overturned bucket. Careless wench, he thought before wondering why the room was so light. A moment later he realised with horror that she was nowhere to be seen. Above his head a strip of blue silk fluttered like a pennant at the edge of a gaping hole.

Jones was nothing if not a survivor. The instincts which had served him in war and in a lifetime of crime, served him now. He wasted no time in useless anger. Moments later, he was whipping the old horse into a canter. There was no knowing how long she had been gone, but she must be heading for The Allt and she was on foot. He must find her before she reached it.

* * *

Bess cowered behind a hedge at the sound of hoofbeats. A single horseman, travelling fast. He sped past, a yeoman farmer unknown to her. She breathed a sigh of relief, realising too late the man might have been of help.

'Wait,' she cried, but he was already out of sight. Her boot was unbearably tight. Unlacing it she discovered the damaged ankle had swelled to twice its size. There was nothing for it but to remove the boot. Sweat broke out on her forehead as she wrenched it off, but when she stood up again the pain was a little easier. Teeth clenched, Bess limped on.

* * *

Near the top of the hill where Jones had lain in wait for Bess days earlier, he stopped. Would she come this way? It was a direct path to The Allt, but what if she had anticipated his move and had gone a different way? Tethering the horse to a tree, he squatted behind the hedge and waited. Long minutes passed. Was he wrong?

No, for here she came, shuffling along with uneven steps, one foot bare. The battered girl in the soiled blue silk gown with one sleeve torn away, tangled hair straggling from beneath a filthy coif and jaw one great purple bruise was unrecognisable as the haughty young lady he had captured. Subduing her this time would be child's play.

Winding a scarf about his wrists in readiness to silence her, Jones straightened up and took a step forward. Then came the clip clop of trotting hooves and the rumble of a wagon. The girl called out, waving her arms. Had it been driven by a woman or a boy, Jones might have waylaid wagon, driver and girl. But fortune had decreed it was a ruddy-faced farmer, a hulking brute of a farmhand beside him. Moments later they had drawn the wagon to a halt and lifted her onto the seat between them.

Dismayed, Jones watched his hopes of becoming a gentleman disappearing around a bend. His only safety lay in flight. Turning his gaze away from The Allt, he headed north. Two miles further, he came upon an inn. Dismounting, he told the ostler to rub his horse down and feed him.

'Travelling north, Sir?' the man asked, dipping his head in thanks for the tuppence.

'Aye.' He waited until the man had led the nag away. By the time the ostler returned, Jones was galloping up the road on a well-muscled bay mare, leaving a broken halter lying in pieces on the ground. Once out of sight, he turned off the road and headed west. He knew the Black Mountains well. He would spend the night at Llangorse by the lake and see what tomorrow brought. Sir Henry Lucie was not the only powerful man with a grudge. It might be prudent to seek another patron until fortune's wheel turned again in his favour.

CHAPTER 66

Sitting between the two men, Bess fixed her eyes on the road, beyond the pricked ears of the trotting horse, willing it to go faster. The farmer flicked his whip at the horse's back, but the stolid beast continued at its own unhurried pace; and every yard seemed a mile. The pain from her lacerated hands and swollen foot blurred into the background, submerged beneath her fear and impatience. She could think of nothing else but the one question – would she arrive too late?

They were coming down the hill now towards the village. Here was the smithy, here the alehouse, now the horse was splashing through the ford. Reaching the other side, the farmer was forced to slow by a boy plodding behind a herd of cows, swishing a stick. Bess could scarcely draw breath by the time they reached the lane to The Allt. Ahead was the gatehouse. The wicket gate opened and Ieuan emerged, his face set and grim. He trudged towards the stables, feet dragging and eyes on his shoes.

'Ieuan!'

The manservant froze and turned his eyes towards her in disbelief.

'Where is he?' Bess locked her eyes on Ieuan's praying that the hopelessness in their depth did not mean that Gabriel was gone.

There was a quiet step outside Bess's bedchamber. The tread was uneven, that of a man who would always have a hesitation in his gait. Gabriel stood there dressed for riding, a woollen cloak over his arm; and a look of longing on his face.

'Oh Gabriel, I was so very afraid that I would arrive too late.' Bess launched herself at him while Gwyneth, arms full of torn and soiled stays and petticoats, opened the door to more maidservants bearing towels, bandages, pails of steaming water.

'I will care for her. Leave us.' Gabriel jerked his head towards the door.

'You are safe.' He kissed her tangled hair, her bruised jaw, shoulders, arms.

'What is this?' Removing the filthy bandage from her right hand, he saw the fingers sliced almost to the bone. 'What manner of men did this to you?' The colour had drained from his face.

'There was but one man. He came asking for you at the start of summer.'

'And knowing of him, I left you here unprotected. This is as much my doing as if I had held the knife myself. But we shall not be parted again. I will take you with me.'

It was what Bess had wished for. War held no fears for her when she was with Gabriel; and there would be no long absences for her to fill with absurd imaginings that he loved another woman.

'You must rest, yet I cannot leave your side, for I am afraid this is only a dream,' he said.

'I will rest if you lie beside me.'

Later, Bess woke to find Gabriel drowsing next to her, one hard, muscular arm thrown across her. He looked so young as he slept but he would turn twenty seven on Michaelmas Day, the feast day of the archangels Michael and Gabriel. He had grown thin; and there was a half-healed scar on his neck.

From the nursery came a faint cry. Gabriel stirred. 'The baby!'

'I thought you had forgotten you are a father,' Bess reproached him. 'The baby is healthy but,'

'But what?'

'You do not yet have an heir. The baby is a girl.' It was a challenge, not an apology and Bess lifted her chin.

'Foolish girl. I have already met our daughter. I wish to get to know her better, but first . . .' Twitching his shirt over his head, Gabriel bent and kissed the gentle curve of her belly where their child had grown, then covered it with his hungry body.

EPILOGUE

For a week the hunt continued for Bess's abductor before it was abandoned. Gabriel sat beside her playing a melancholy air on his lute. There were other matters to discuss, but he was not ready.

'Gabriel, we must talk. Harry writes when he can from Ireland, but I have not heard from Will for months and every time I mention him you say we will talk about him later.'

Reluctantly, Gabriel laid down the lute. 'What do you wish to hear?' His heart thumped. He had promised himself there would be no more secrets from his wife. He found it far easier to talk of Basing House. There, it was only himself who was at fault. But instead, he must talk of Will Lucie.

'You know something about him that you are not telling me. Is he dead?'

'No, Bess, but there is a reason why you have had no letters. When our armies marched into the west country, we rendezvoused at Exeter. Northampton's regiment was there. When I sought Will I was told that he had disappeared at Cropredy Bridge, but after the battle ended and had not been seen since. When he did not return and nothing was heard of in many weeks, they marked him as 'Run' in the muster rolls, as a deserter. I now know that he went straight to Lord Essex. He joined the enemy.'

Bess did not weep, but she clutched his sleeve, her pink fingernails turning white. He pressed his lips to her palm, crisscrossed with dark red scratches from escaping her prison. The other hand remained bandaged. She was strong and brave, but he longed to spare her pain.

'If his regiment has not heard from him, then how do you know where he went? Who told you? Ieuan said nothing of Will.'

'Ieuan was not present at our meetings.'

'Then you have seen him?' Bess's tone was half hope, half fear.

'I met him, in Cornwall. He – told me – he was with the forces of Parliament.'

'But how did you meet him?' Her eyes were drawn to his neck. 'Oh no.'

He brushed the scar with his fingertip. 'Will did not harm me, nor I him.' He waited for the next question.

'Where is he now?' He breathed an inward sigh of relief. She had abandoned her questions about the meeting, for the present.

'Was he well?'

'Weary, unkempt and underfed, but he was quite well. As to his present whereabouts, he escaped Cornwall with the rest of the rebel Horse. They fled as a body. We captured a handful of stragglers. Will was not among them.'

Bess's eyes brimmed with tears. 'But how can you be certain that he escaped?'

He pulled her close. 'I saw him through my perspective glass. He was helping one of his men. I saw him ride on with the rest.'

'So, all the Horse got away?'

'As I have said. Now you must excuse me. I will return in an hour or so.' Gabriel bolted from the room. He could bear no more half-truths. Facing Will in that tower room, the terrible jarring scrape as their swords clashed. *I will do whatever is necessary to secure my withdrawal, for my duty is to Parliament.*

Outside the sun was emerging from between banks of white cloud. Climbing halfway up the round tower, the wind ruffled Gabriel's hair as he gazed towards the Black Mountains. He filled his lungs, as if by doing so, the moisture-laden air could purge painful memories of that summer from his memory.

It would bring Bess no consolation to know of her brother's suicidal bravery and bid to recapture his troop standard; for it was the final proof that Will had embraced the rebel cause he fought for. He was proud to wear the tawny sash.

THE END

HISTORICAL NOTES (AND OLIVER CROMWELL)

This is a work of fiction. All the members of the Vaughan and Lucie families in this book are fictitious. I have, however, included quite a few historical figures. I have made every attempt to get the details of the historical background right, but all mistakes are my own. I have also taken a few liberties.

Captain Seymour Pyle of Pye's Regiment of Horse did not die at Lostwithiel, but I needed him to make way for Will. Colonel Gage's relief of Basing House happened a few days earlier than in the story. It was delayed so that Gabriel had time to get there from Cornwall. Sir George Vaughan's Regiment of Horse was present at all the battles mentioned but, being a fairly small regiment, there is not an awful lot of information about their actions. There are conflicting accounts of which cavalry regiment protected the retreating infantry after the battle of Cheriton, but it was not Vaughan's. At the battle of Cropredy Bridge, it was the King's Lifeguard who were sent back to help Cleveland's brigade, and the rescue of Lord Wilmot (he was actually captured and rescued twice), was not carried out by my fictitious hero. It is true, however, that the officer commanding Vaughan's Horse during the Lostwithiel campaign (a Major James Smith) was wounded in the neck leading a victorious charge at Restormel Castle.

The defeat of Essex's army at Lostwithiel might have changed the outcome of the war, but Balfour's daring night time breakout with the cavalry saved the loss of an entire army. They were pursued by no more than a handful of royalists. The embarrassment to the King's cause was huge; and the true story was swiftly buried. Accounts and excuses of how they managed it vary, but the official royalist 'spin' that the cavalry escaped by being very quiet is plainly not true. Between 2000 and 3000 horses make a lot of noise, so I have invented my own version.

On a lighter note, the lack of standardised uniform colours (and the absence of uniforms for officers) meant that soldiers were forever getting captured by the other side in the general confusion of battle. Different coloured sashes (or ribbons) did help – but a popular ruse was wearing sashes of a different colour to pass safely through enemy territory. The incident at Aldermaston where a royalist soldier forgot he was in disguise and charged at a parliamentarian patrol sounds like something out of *Blackadder* but is true.

A note on 17th century conventions- and religion.

A person's place in society was clear from how they dressed. In a rigidly stratified society, a person from the lower ranks (a servant or villager) would automatically defer to someone they recognised as being of a higher rank, showing respect by bowing, removing their hat etc. When gentry left their house they were usually accompanied by at least one servant. Respectable girls and women (including servants) covered their hair and wore an apron most of the day.

The offering of a 'safe conduct' pass for travelling through enemy territory (or to leave the country – origin of passports) was an everyday occurrence which had to be applied for by civilians as well as soldiers on both sides of the conflict. The unusual feature of the one given to Gabriel after escorting the defeated enemy army of the Earl of Essex, was that it was signed by all Skippon's senior officers as a tribute to the real royalist escort (under the command of Lieutenant Colonel Adrian Scrope). Lieutenant Colonel was (and is) an army rank just below Colonel, however officers holding the lower rank were addressed as 'Colonel' as a courtesy.

The English Civil Wars were fought partly over religion – which form of Protestantism should be adopted in England, Wales and Scotland. The official religion approved by King Charles I was the Church of England. Very few people believed in the principle of freedom of religion for everyone at the time, but nearly everyone, rich or poor, had religious beliefs. Vows sworn on the bible (such as those sworn by Will Lucie in part 2) were a serious matter.

The practice of the Roman Catholic faith had been illegal in England since the time of Queen Elizabeth. 'Papist' was an insult applied not only to Catholics but to Anglicans who were considered too 'high church'. King Charles I was seen as the lesser of two evils by Catholics and therefore those who fought in the Civil Wars fought on his side. In general, they kept their faith secret as there were instances of rank-and-file soldiers attacking officers they suspected of being 'papists'.

And Oliver Cromwell? There is only one passing reference to him in this story. By January 1644 (the start of the events in this book), he was lieutenant-general of Horse. He played a major role in Parliament's victory at Marston Moor, outside York that year. However, my characters are currently participating in fighting only in the south and west of England. Only Hugh Lucie has heard of the rising cavalry commander in the Eastern Association of East Anglia.

Locations

For those who like to know if locations are real, Boconnoc House, Restormel Castle and Basing House 'appear as themselves'. Tretower Court and Castle near Crickhowell, ancestral home of a part of the Vaughan family, bears a close resemblance to The Allt. although I have made some changes to the local topography.

In the case of Basing House, distressingly little remains of either Old House or New House and the internal layout is uncertain. The Great Barn stands, however, despite damage from cannon balls, and you can walk through Garrison Gate.

The main battlefields mentioned in the book, Cheriton and Cropredy Bridge, can still be visited. The Battlefields Trust has sign boards at both sites and walks across them are organised occasionally.

Thanks to

Rachel Miller Johnson, who patiently read and commented on the early drafts; Alan Turton, historian and former curator Basing House and his wife Nicola, 'Lord and Lady Basing' for advice on the Basing House sections, ongoing support, friendship and assistance, including an explanation of how to light a beacon on the roof of the Great Gatehouse without burning it down! Professor Stephen Rutherford, Cardiff University for further insights into 17th century battlefield surgery; Mrs Elizabeth Fortescue owner of Boconnoc House and her staff for kindly allowing me to tour it and answering my questions; Janet Colman my guide to Chester; Cadw, particularly the staff of Tretower Court and Castle; The English Civil War Society (especially Colonel Nicholas Devereux's Regiment); BCW Project; Battle of Worcester Society and the Battlefields Trust.

Also Elana, Ros, and the members of my writing groups (especially Greg and Rachel who read complete drafts). Last but not least, my longsuffering husband (who read every draft), children and dog.